MW00463246

IANTHE JERROLD
DEAD MAN'S QUARRY

Ianthe Jerrold was born in 1898, the daughter of the well-known author and journalist Walter Jerrold, and granddaughter of the Victorian playwright Douglas Jerrold. She was the eldest of five sisters.

She published her first book, a work of verse, at the age of fifteen. This was the start of a long and prolific writing career characterized by numerous stylistic shifts. In 1929 she published the first of two classic and influential whodunits. *The Studio Crime* gained her immediate acceptance into the recently formed but highly prestigious Detection Club, and was followed a year later by *Dead Man's Quarry*.

Ianthe Jerrold subsequently moved on from pure whodunits to write novels ranging from romantic fiction to psychological thrillers. She continued writing and publishing her fiction into the 1970's. She died in 1977, twelve years after her husband George Menges. Their Elizabethan farmhouse Cwmmau was left to the National Trust.

Also by Ianthe Jerrold

The Studio Crime

IANTHE JERROLD

DEAD MAN'S QUARRY

With an introduction
by Curtis Evans

DEAN STREET PRESS

Published by Dean Street Press 2015

Copyright © 1930 Ianthe Jerrold

All Rights Reserved

The right of Ianthe Jerrold to be identified as the Author of
the Work has been asserted by her estate in accordance with
the Copyright, Designs and Patents Act 1988.

Cover by DSP

First published in 1930 by Chapman and Hall

ISBN 978 1 911095 44 6

www.deanstreetpress.co.uk

To PHYLLIS

who, in her enthusiasm for wild strawberries,
kept us waiting at the foot of Hergest Ridge
long enough to give rise to the most lurid
surmises and to the plot of this story.

INTRODUCTION

On the strength of *The Studio Crime* (1929), the first of Ianthe Jerrold's pair of exceptional Golden Age detective novels, the author, an accomplished member of the literary Jerrold family (see the introduction to *The Studio Crime*), was invited to join the newly-launched Detection Club, a social organization of some of Britain's best crime writers, all of whom had pledged in their genre writing to respect both the King's English and the principle of "fair play" with one's readers. Jerrold accepted the invitation, thereby becoming one of the Club's original members, along with such mystery fiction luminaries as Agatha Christie, Dorothy L. Sayers, G.K. Chesterton, A.E.W. Mason, the Baroness Orczy, E.C. Bentley, H.C. Bailey, Helen Simpson, Clemence Dane, Anthony Berkeley, Henry Wade, John Rhode, R. Austin Freeman and Freeman Wills Crofts. Near the end of her first year as a member of the Club, Jerrold published a second detective novel, *Dead Man's Quarry* (1930), a work reflective of her recent acceptance into the ranks of the *crème de la crème* of British detective novelists.

Where *The Studio Crime* is a city tale, taking place in London's St. John's Wood and its environs, *Dead Man's Quarry* is a country novel, set in the beautiful Wye Valley, in the borderland known as the Welsh Marches. In this wild region Ianthe had traversed Hergest Ridge with her sister Phyllis, to whom she dedicated *Dead Man's Quarry* ("To PHYLLIS who, in her enthusiasm for wild strawberries, kept us waiting at the foot of Hergest Ridge long enough to give rise to the most lurid surmises and to the plot of this story.") The novel presents to readers some of the most characteristic features of classic English mystery: quaint villages, rustic cottages and inns, an ancestral manor, and a frontispiece map. The latter feature is no mere furbelow, for the opening chapters of the novel detail the rural ambles of a cycling party composed of the middle-aged Dr. Browning and his two children, precocious adolescent Lion and his art student sister, Nora; Isabel Donne, an enigmatic classmate of Nora's; Felix Price, a moody young photographer; and Charles Price, Felix's boorish cousin, recently returned from Canada, where he had been packed off years ago, to claim the local baronetcy after the death of the old squire, Sir Evan Price.

Abruptly a cloud looms over the cycling tour when one of its members mysteriously vanishes; and this cloud darkens menacingly after a brutally slain body is found in a local disused quarry. On hand to investigate these goings-on is amateur detective John Christmas, Jerrold's sleuth from *The Studio Crime*, providentially vacationing in the area with his bracingly unimaginative scientific researcher cousin, Sydenham Rampson ("I need a wet blanket," Christmas explains, "and the scientific mind is the wet blanket *par excellence*.") The circle of suspicion is large, encompassing members of the cycling party itself, various village locals and country visitors and certain individuals within the household of Rhyllan Hall, the ancestral home of the Price baronets, including Felix Price's haughty father, Morris, the longtime manager of the Price estate; Felix's calm and capable sister, Blodwen; and the Rhyllan Hall librarian, Mr. Clino, a distant relative of the Price family and closet mystery fiction addict.

Fans of Golden Age mystery will note amusing passages in *Dead Man's Quarry* where the characters talk what to Ianthe Jerrold at this time would have been Detection Club "shop"— i.e., detective fiction itself. "All great detectives have simple, rural tastes," Christmas pronounces at one point to Nora Browning, who for a time acts as the sleuth's official Watson (Miss Watson, he dubs her). "Sherlock Holmes kept bees. Sergeant Cuff grew roses. I, when I retire, shall cultivate the simple aster." On another occasion young Lion Browning, a confirmed materialist, opines that R. Austin Freeman is far superior to Arthur Conan Doyle as a writer of crime fiction ("More scientific," he pronounces.) Elderly Mr. Clino ashamedly admits that detective stories have "become quite a vice with me," after he has been caught with copies of *The Purple Ray Murders* and *Murder in the Purple Attic* (one surmises these novels are part of some "purple" series.) "In fact, as time goes on I read more and more of them and less and less of anything else. It's rather regrettable, really, for they're mostly bad….I try to cure myself of the habit, sometimes, by reading Scott and Thackeray, who used to be my favorites. But I find that my taste is so vitiated that I can no longer read good authors with enjoyment." He reflects that "there is always Wilkie Collins. But one can't go on reading 'The Woman in White' forever."

In her mystery criticism Dorothy L. Sayers ballyhooed Wilkie Collins's Victorian-era sensation novels, contrasting what she deemed the genuine literary art in those works with the mere craft of 1920s/30s detective fiction, which in her view tended to engage only the problem-solving part of the brain, leaving the human emotions untouched. Such criticism cannot be directed justly at a detective novel like *Dead Man's Quarry*, which boasts not only a clever puzzle, but also has, like Jerrold's "mainstream" novels from this time, an interesting setting, engaging characters, charming writing and a poignant depiction of complicated human relationships. In *Dead Man's Quarry* Jerrold anticipated the so-called "manners mystery" most strongly associated today with the Thirties detective novels of Sayers, Margery Allingham and Ngaio Marsh, in which authors strove to more compellingly portray characters and their social interactions. In my view Jerrold's novel is a worthy companion to such Crime Queen classics as Sayers's *Strong Poison* (1930), Allingham's *Death of a Ghost* (1934) and Marsh's *Artists in Crime* (1938). It is, as one contemporary review pronounced, "well-written and well-contrived."

After the publication of *Dead Man's Quarry*, Ianthe Jerrold, who later married George Menges (a brother of the celebrated concert violinist Isolde Menges) and with him acquired a rambling Tudor farmhouse in the Wye Valley, produced no other detective novels during the rest of the decade. The five additional novels that Jerrold published in the 1930s are all mainstream works (in 1940, however, there appeared another detective novel, *Let Him Lie*, followed eight years later by a spy thriller, *There May Be Danger*; both were credited to an Ianthe Jerrold pseudonym, "Geraldine Bridgman"). Perhaps Mr. Clino's words in *Dead Man's Quarry* had signaled an intended abandonment of the genre by one of its most distinguished, if least prolific, Golden Age adepts. Between 1945 and 1966 Jerrold would publish eight more mainstream novels under her own name, yet she was not entirely finished with crime fiction. Aside from penning the two Geraldine Bridgman books, Jerrold contributed a gripping inverted mystery tale, "Blue Lias," to *Detection Medley*, a massive Detection Club anthology edited by John Rhode, and she published four short stories in 1951/52 in *The London Mystery Magazine*: "Brother in the Barrow," "Cranford Revisited," "The Deadlier Twin" and "Off the Tiles" ("Cranford Revisited" sounds especially intriguing.) Additional Ianthe Jerrold mystery fiction may yet await rediscovery and republication. For now, classic mystery fans should derive considerable satisfaction from the reappearance in print of *Dead Man's Quarry* and *The Studio Crime*, a pair of superlative English mysteries that embody the best qualities of Golden Age detective fiction.

Curtis Evans

actual guide

Important:　happy:　umm:
Quotes:　sad:　foreshadowing:
Char:　anger:

CONTENTS

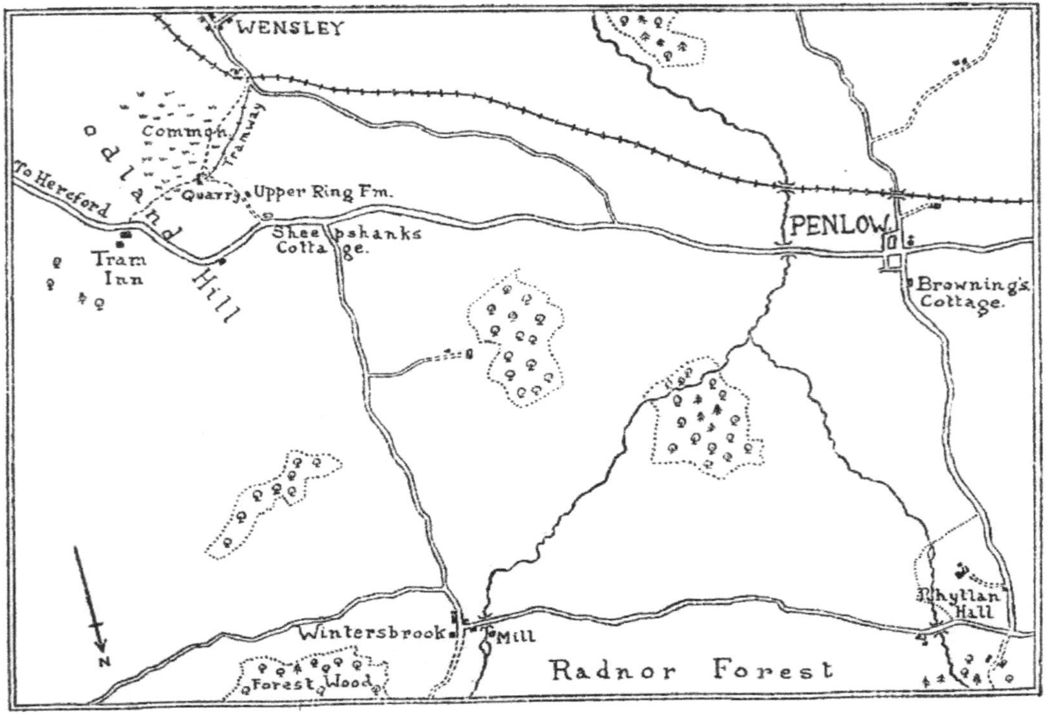

WENSLEY
Common
Tramway
Quarry
Upper Ring Fm.
To Hereford
odland Hill
Tram Inn
Sheepshanks Cottage.
PENLOW
Browning's Cottage.
Wintersbrook
Mill
Radnor Forest
Forest Wood
Hill
N

DEAD MAN'S QUARRY

CHAPTER ONE

TEA FOR SIX

NORA BROWNING, pausing uncertainly a moment in the dim, low-ceilinged passage of the inn, wondering behind which of its closed doors she would find the waitress, experienced a slight shock on seeing her own grave face looking at her from an unexpected mirror placed in a dark corner beside the back door. The mirror was dark and old and greenish, and the appearance in it of her own face against the background of the chocolate-coloured painted wainscoting peculiar to country inns pleased and surprised her, as if somebody had paid her a compliment on her looks. Forgetful of her mission, which was to order boiled eggs for tea, she went closer to the glass and looked critically at her own reflection.

Nora was not in the habit of noticing casual reflections of herself. She had grown up on good terms with her own face, which was indeed neither beautiful enough nor plain enough to trouble her, and until a few months ago she had paid it only sufficient attention to see that it was clean and not too unfashionably shiny. Lately, she had taken more interest in mirrors, and more time than had

I   A been her wont in pinning up her thick plaits of light brown hair, a process that often ended in a mental comparison between her own dissatisfied reflection looking back at her and another face, that of Isabel Donne. Isabel, with her fine pale skin and golden freckles, her elfish pointed chin and humorous narrow lips that made a teasing contrast with heavy-lidded dreaming hazel eyes, her fine reddish-golden hair cut straight and turning in softly like a child's around her small white neck, was a young woman to turn many a young man's head and to make many another young woman look with dissatisfaction at her own reflection. A committee of art professors nurtured on the Greek might have awarded the apple to Nora. But Felix Price was a modernist.

However, Nora, having the calm philosophical temperament that usually accompanies classic features, did not intend to allow her holiday to be spoilt either by her own love affairs or those of her companions. The county of Radnorshire was glorious after six months in London, the weather was only capricious enough to give variety to the landscape, and a bicycling tour with congenial companions was an excellent way of enjoying both. Moreover, Nora had recently sold two polychromatic and peremptory posters to the Underground Railway, and had received a commission to design two more. To a young artist, there is nothing like professional success for putting love in its proper place.

Having communed for a few seconds with her own pleasing features, Nora took leave of them with a childish and hideous grimace; but quickly composed them to their usual serenity as she saw from the reflection in the mirror that some patron of the Tram Inn was standing in its sunny front doorway, looking down the dim tunnel-like passage towards her. Turning quickly, in some embarrassment, she was in time to see the stranger, as if equally embarrassed, move away from the door and disappear.

At the same moment the waitress came out from one of the doors giving on the passage.

" Could we have some boiled eggs with our tea, please? "

The girl looked at her thoughtfully and replied in the soft sing-song voice peculiar to the county:

" I expect you could."

She paused a moment, as if considering the possibilities of her chicken-yard.

" How many eggs would you be wanting? "

" Well—twelve? " suggested Nora diffidently.

The girl looked faintly surprised, and having performed a simple division sum in her head, replied pensively:

" That'll be two each, I expect."

" One each would do," said Nora, not wishing to appear greedy, " if eggs are scarce."

" Oh, there's plenty eggs," replied mine host's daughter reassuringly. " I expect you could have twelve. And you'd like them soft-boiled, I expect? "

" Please. And plenty of bread and butter."

She sauntered back along the passage, sniffing the peculiar cool, pleasant odour of cider, stone floors and saw-dust that permeates small country inns, and entered the low-pitched square parlour with its windows full of geraniums and pot-ferns, and its hideous chairs of yellow wood and black horsehair ranged in prim rows against its panelled walls. Isabel, who was lying on the slippery hair sofa reading a volume of *The Girl's Friend* for 1885, looked up as she entered.

" Do listen to this, Nora. They had a short way with girlish aspirations in the days of Victoria the Good. ' Answers to Correspondents. *Anxious:* Certainly not; we make it a rule never to give young girls recipes for making themselves slimmer; be thankful, my dear Anxious, that you are not too *thin. Heliotrope*: Surely you are perfectly aware, without advice from us, of the impropriety of corresponding with a young man to whom you are not engaged.' Poor darlings! "

" At least," said Dr. Browning mildly, looking up from a book on the flora of South Wales, " your Victorian adviser wastes no words. She comes straight to the point in an admirable manner, and writes English. Very different from the illiterate compositions I sometimes notice in the domestic papers nowadays. I may add that, as a doctor, I heartily endorse her advice to Anxious."

Isabel smiled over her dog's-eared volume at Nora's father. - Dr. Browning

" What about the advice to poor romantic Heliotrope? "

Dr. Browning looked around him.

" Middle-age is in a minority in this gathering," he remarked. " As a middle-aged man and a coward, I beg to be excused."

Charles Price, sitting with an air of discipleship on a stool by Isabel's sofa, laughed, rather loudly and stridently. His laugh was in keeping with the rest of him. Just a little larger than life in every way, this new-found cousin of Felix's. Colonials in England often had an air, thought Nora, of being too large for their surroundings. She regarded the new baronet as no ornament to his title and estate, and privately thought it a pity he had ever returned from the prairie he was so fond of talking about.

Felix, standing by the window and putting a film-roll in his camera, laughed too, a little constrainedly. He was probably regretting now, thought Nora, the friendly impulse that had made him invite his cousin to join the party at Worcester. The carefree holiday spirit of the journey had been a little damped since the advent of Sir Charles. Perhaps it was as well that this was the last day of the holiday. It was natural that Isabel, who never lost her head or heart, should prefer a mutual flirtation with Charles to the devotion of Felix, who was a romantic and single-minded youth, incapable of flirting; but it was unfortunate for poor Felix and the rest of the party, although, to do Felix justice, his breeding rose superior to his misfortune.

Lion, Nora's young brother, looked up from the large and elaborate map of his own designing that was the dearest treasure of his heart. With youth's god-like indifference to emotional storms and stresses, its wise concentration on the essential things of life, he asked severely :

" Got the eggs? "

" I expect so," said Nora absently. " Yes, I've ordered them."

" Did you tell them to boil mine exactly three minutes and a quarter? "

" No, my son, I didn't waste my breath. I said soft-boiled and hoped for the best."

" There's no harm," murmured Lion reproachfully, " in telling people how to boil eggs properly, even if they don't generally listen. If these eggs really turn out soft-boiled I shall mark this inn on my map in green ink, with a label, ' Here We Had Soft-boiled Eggs for Tea.' Nearly all the other inns are marked in black, meaning Hard. Have you got my green ink, Felix? I may as well have it ready."

" Optimist," said Felix with a smile, feeling in his haversack and producing three or four little bottles of coloured ink. " How's the map getting on? Have you got as far as where we stopped last night? "

" Yes," said Lion gravely. " These little purple spots are the fleas."

" What's that long, eel-like thing a little lower down? "

" That's Charles meeting us at Worcester," replied Lion, looking complacently at his handiwork. " It's rather like him, I think."

" Living image of him," said Isabel who had left her

sofa to look over the boy's shoulder at this painstaking record of their holiday. "What are all these little figures?"

"Dates and times of arrival at the various villages and points of interest," explained Lion with studied nonchalance.

"I see, Mr. Bradshaw. When you've finished it we'll all subscribe to have it framed."

Charles, hoisting his long limbs up from the stool by the now deserted sofa, inquired:

"Did you remember to put in the banana you dropped and ran over this morning?"

The others laughed, but Lion answered with dignity:

"This is a small-scale map. There isn't room in it for unimportant matters like bananas."

"Hard luck on the banana," commented Isabel, "to be snubbed like that after being squashed as flat as a pancake."

"It didn't suffer," said Lion gently, removing his map from the table as the waitress came in with the tea. "It was a painless, instantaneous death."

With some ceremony the waitress placed an enormous cosy of Berlin woolwork over the teapot and withdrew. Nora, who was the kind of girl upon whom such duties naturally devolved, began to pour out the tea. The others drew up their chairs. Sir Charles hastened to seize Isabel's chair out of her hand and placed it at the table with a flourish, seating himself next to her rather hastily, as if he feared that Felix would forestall him. Idiot! thought Nora irritably, watching from under her eyelashes. She liked Charles less every time she looked at him. His elaborately gallant manner to herself and Isabel, the open court he paid to her pretty friend, offended Nora's fastidious taste. She did not consider such displays appropriate to the occasion of a country holiday, and missed the atmosphere of casual and kindly good-fellowship which had been suddenly dissipated at Worcester. Charles's good-fellowship was something to make one put cotton-wool in one's ears, so extremely noticeable it was.

" Old man," he was saying now to his cousin, " we must arrange plenty of bicycling expeditions before you go back to town. How long are you going to be with us? "

" Only a fortnight," said Felix regretfully.

" A fortnight! " echoed Charles. " I was hoping you were going to stay a month at least, and show me all the ins and outs of being an English squire."

" Wish I could," returned Felix amiably, opening his egg and looking with mild surprise at its firm and solid contents. " But I can't leave the studio so long. All the élite of London are waiting in a queue to be photographed. My dad'll show you all the ins and outs, he's used to them. And Blodwen'll back you up much better than I should."

Nora, still studying the bold, handsome, rather large-scale features of the new squire, thought she saw a slight, almost imperceptible change of expression on them as Felix mentioned his father; so slight a change and so swiftly over that it was impossible to guess what emotion had produced it, impossible to put a name to the change itself. One could not call it a sneer, but it approached a sneer.

" I'm looking forward no end to seeing Blodwen," he replied. " I haven't seen my sister for fifteen years. We were great pals as kids. I wonder what I'll think of her? "

" It would be more becoming," remarked Lion, carefully and hopefully chipping at his egg, " to wonder what she'll think of you."

" Lion," said Nora reprovingly, " don't be cheeky." But privately she agreed with him.

" Well, you'll soon see," said Felix. " She came back from France yesterday, I believe. She'll be waiting for your inspection when we get to Rhyllan, and will present you to her miscellaneous pack of hounds."

"I've seen some of them already," said Charles with his loud laugh. "In fact, the other day I shot one of them."

"Oh," said Felix, and did not seem to find this news amusing. He added rather distantly: "How was that?"

"Out in the corn-fields shooting rabbits. Little beggar went off its head with excitement and got between my gun and the rabbit." Charles glanced round the table, and perceiving a certain lack of sympathy in his audience, subdued his voice and manner. "Pure accident. Might have happened to anybody."

He looked at Isabel. She was looking meditatively at her plate.

"I tell you, old chap," he added feelingly, "I was terribly cut up about it. Afraid Blodwen'll never forgive me."

"It is certainly," said Dr. Browning mildly, "a rather unfortunate way of re-introducing yourself to your sister. Miss Price is devoted to her animals. But she'll certainly forgive you for an accident. She is a very reasonable girl."

"Hope you're right," said Charles genially. "But I don't know. Old maids are always perfectly cracked about their pets."

Felix winced, and Dr. Browning regarded Charles thoughtfully, as if he were an interesting specimen of a new genus of fern. There was a momentary, rather uncomfortable silence. It was broken by Lion. He put down his spoon and regarded his egg with an unfavourable eye.

"Nora," he remarked stoically, "ring for a hammer and chisel."

Nora laughed.

" I've just rung for some hot water. You can give your order to the waitress when she comes."

Charles, with an anxious sidelong glance at Isabel's pretty profile coldly averted from him, addressed her feelingly, trying to make up the ground which, as he was vaguely aware, his last remarks had lost him.

" I can't tell you how keen I am to see Blodwen again, and talk over old times when we were kids. I've got an old photo of her here I've been carrying about with me half over the world." He felt in his pockets and produced a little brown photograph for Isabel's inspection. " I want you to meet her, too. How long are you staying in Penlow? "

Isabel glanced with a smile at Nora, who replied for her :

" You're staying with us till we go back to London, of course, Isabel. Isn't she, Father? "

" I hope so," said Dr. Browning heartily. " You certainly can't do justice to our beautiful county in less than a month, Isabel."

" I wish I could stay till school opens," returned Isabel sweetly. " But I'm afraid I'll have to go after ten days. I promised my aunt to spend part of the holiday with her. You see, I'm all the family she's got, and she gets bored when I'm away."

" In that case," said Dr. Browning, looking approvingly at this exemplary niece, " we mustn't press you, I suppose, though we're sorry for our own sakes that your aunt has such a thoughtful niece."

Beaming approval at Isabel and pleasure in his own verbal felicity, he retired once more behind the " Flora of South Wales " propped against the sugar basin.

" Is your aunt staying in London? " asked Nora.

" Yes," replied Isabel. " She's enjoying the wild mountain scenery of our native Notting Hill. When I go back we shall probably go away together somewhere for a week. But don't let's talk about going back, yet. I've only just begun to realize what you give up, Nora, in the pursuit of Art with a capital A. If I had the choice between Radnorshire and the R.C.A. I should say give me Radnorshire."

" No, you wouldn't, my dear. Not if you wanted to earn your living decorating the hoardings," replied Nora, and privately wondered how long Isabel would really be able to endure the monotony of life in a small country town. Isabel's transparent little insincerities amused Nora, and were hardly even intended to deceive. They were a habit, like smoking or biting the nails.

Felix shot at Isabel a look of tender approval; he deeply loved his county, although his business kept him away from it for forty-eight weeks in the year. Glancing from his cousin Charles to the window, where the great hills stood far and golden on the horizon, he wondered what difference his cousin's advent would make to life at Rhyllan Hall, which had been so idyllic. Changes were inevitable, for the new baronet bore little resemblance to his late father, and a respect for tradition did not appear to be one of his outstanding qualities. A gentle, learned old man Sir Evan had been, a permanent invalid, and well content to leave the management of his estate in the capable hands of his brother Morris, Felix's father. Felix had received a letter from his father a few days before he started from London, a melancholy letter hinting at drastic changes.

" *If poor Evan could have seen what fifteen years in Canada have made of his son, I don't think he would have been so anxious to trace him before he died. I can only be thankful that the poor old chap was spared a sight of his heir. He was a bit of a young waster before he emigrated, as of course you know, but we all hoped that the colonial life would have made a man of him. So it*

*has, I suppose many people would think. My dear Felix,
your cousin is a coarse, ill-humoured lout, and fond as I
am of Rhyllan, I don't intend to endure his company very
much longer. This state of affairs cannot go on. In the
six weeks since he came here he has already shot his
sister's favourite dog, turned the head of one of the housemaids, and sacked old Letbe on the most puerile excuse.
He has also gone to the trouble of being exceedingly rude
to poor old Clino, practically telling him that the sooner
he takes himself off from Rhyllan the better. Poor Clino!
I don't know what he will do. He is too old to hope
to get fresh employment. I won't trust myself to write
any more. You will see for yourself. I understand that
you have invited him to join you and the Brownings at
Worcester, when you cycle up for the holidays. I shall
be glad of a few days to myself in which to think over
the future, but I am afraid you will regret your invitation."*

Recalling the phrases of this letter, which now lay in
his pocket-book, Felix smiled to himself, half ruefully,
half with amusement. His father had evidently written
in a white heat of anger, and was probably by now
regretting his strong language. A man of wrath, his
father, but too impulsive and generous to make a good
hater. Felix, who had been observing his new cousin
closely for three days, could not see cause for quite such
a bitter jeremiad. Charles was not the traditional young
English squire, but one could scarcely expect a Colonial
to take up such a position gracefully. He would learn
in time what he could and could not do in his new state
of life; probably his baronetcy had gone temporarily to
his head. Certainly he seemed a friendly, an almost
embarrassingly friendly, soul.

Thus Felix Price, trying conscientiously to be just to
the cousin he instinctively disliked; wincing at the close

proximity of that cousin's close-cropped head to Isabel's silky red-gold hair.

" Could we have some more hot water, please? "

The pale, colourless girl took the jug from the tray and asked anxiously :

" Was the eggs boiled all right? "

" Oh, yes, quite," said Nora with amiable mendacity. Meeting her brother's astounded and reproachful eye, she added sweetly : " A tiny bit hard, perhaps. But it didn't matter."

The girl looked relieved.

" I was so afraid they'd be hard as rocks, and after you asking for them soft-boiled, I didn't hardly like to bring them in. I'd just put them on to boil and taken a look at the clock, when I saw a man in the yard, going towards the orchard." She paused, caressing the warm jug and looking at Nora with large, worried eyes. " He had a look as if he didn't ought to be there. And we gets so many apples stolen, the orchard being a bit out of the way from the house, I thought I'd just run out and see as he was up to no harm. I couldn't see him in the yard, and when I went to the orchard gate and looked over, he weren't there, so I had just a look round, forgetting about the eggs, and then I thought : He'll have gone round the house to the front, I expect. So I goes round the house, but I couldn't see him nowhere, and then I remembers the eggs and runs in. And when I looks at the clock and sees the eggs've bin on nine minutes, I thinks : They'll be hard-boiled, I expect."

" You were right," said Lion solemnly. " An egg should be boiled three and a quarter minutes. But never mind. We'll say no more about it."

" Thank you, sir," murmured the girl, looking apprehensively at what she afterwards described to her father as " the most old-fashionedest young boy ever I saw." She was about to depart when Lion added :

" Could you tell me something? I do so want to know why this place is called the Tram Inn. Is Tram a Welsh word or something? "

" Welsh? " repeated the girl, staring at him. " Not as I know, sir. I expect it's called the Tram because it used to be called the Crown a long while ago, only the licence was took away, but that was long afore we come here. And then when old Mr. Lloyd, that was here before us and died in the place, took out a licence again, I expect it was called the Tram owing to there being a Crown at Rodland, a mile away on the main road."

" I see," said Lion, adopting the kind, brisk manner of an examiner with a well-meaning but rather backward pupil. " That's why it isn't called the Crown. Now could you tell me why it *is* called the Tram, instead of the Pig and Whistle, or the Fox and Geese, or the Rumtifoo Arms? "

" I never heard of an inn with a name like that last, sir," murmured the girl with a puzzled air. She added pensively : " I expect it's called the Tram because of the quarry."

There was a dazed pause.

" I see," said Lion after a moment, his face clearing. " There's a tramway somewhere about to fetch the slate from the quarry. Oh, yes! I see, thank you very much. I was thinking of those large, top-heavy things that go shrieking about the towns. Is the quarry near here? "

" Just across those fields," said the girl, pointing through the front window. " But it isn't used now, nor hasn't been since I dunno when. Some of the lines from the quarry to where the slate-house used to be is still there. . . ."

" How near is this quarry? I think I'll stroll over and have a look at it after tea. Then I can put it on my map to explain the inn."

" Not more than seven minutes' walk, sir. Just across

the field over the road and a bit of common ground. You can see the fence around the top as soon's you get into the field. They're talking of putting up a new one, for a great piece of the old was blown down in the storms last spring, and it isn't really safe, with children about on the common. But you'll be wanting your hot water, miss."

She vanished, and Lion rose from the table and strapped his pedometer on to his ankle.

"I think I'll just go across to the quarry while you people finish drinking and smoking," announced this enthusiast. "Anybody coming with me?"

"Oh, Lion!" protested Nora. "You aren't really going to look at this silly old quarry? You are the most restless kid. Do sit down and be peaceful for half an hour."

"No, thanks," said her young brother with a grin. "I'll leave that to you elderly creatures. I want to put the quarry and tram-lines on my map, to show how this inn got its ridiculous name."

"Can't you put them in the map without seeing them?"

"Certainly not," replied Lion, scandalized, and departed.

"That young man'll sure go far," remarked Sir Charles, producing a gold cigarette-case and offering it to Isabel. "He wastes neither words nor time."

"Could I have another cup of tea, my dear?" asked Dr. Browning. "The schoolboy in pursuit of his hobby is the most earnest and hard-working creature in existence, and an example to us all."

"At his age," said Charles, "there was nothing hard-working or earnest about me. My only hobby was to avoid anything that looked like work, and have a good time. What do you say, Felix?"

Filling his pipe, Felix answered thoughtfully:

"At fifteen? Oh, I think I took life fairly seriously. But I wasn't as practical as young Lion, nor as original. I was a bit of a day-dreamer, and saw myself as a second Michael Angelo. Now I'm a photographer, and haven't time for day-dreams. There's a moral, I'm sure. Have you any matches?"

"The moral," said Isabel, smiling at him, "is obvious. If you hadn't wasted your young years in idle dreams you might have been——"

"A second Michael Angelo?"

"A better photographer," said Isabel gravely.

"Bravo," remarked Dr. Browning. "Isabel, you're a girl of sense. No, thank you, Sir Charles. I prefer Egyptian."

learned about the family. they're in london, It's a special ocasson where there all together.

CHAPTER TWO

THE DOWNHILL ROAD

WHEN the six cyclists, refreshed and merry, left the
Tram Inn on the last stage of their homeward
journey, the sky was filled with the subdued golden light
of a fine, windless August evening. The long grey tree-
shadows lay perfectly still over the road, and the Welsh
hills on the far horizon lying in the sun had a look of
glassy fragility, as if they belonged to a distant fairy world.

The travellers all enjoyed that feeling of serenity and
well-being that only a large, satisfying tea after a day spent
in the open can give. Isabel declared herself ready to
cycle another thirty miles, and deplored the fact that
Penlow and the end of their journey were only nine miles
away.

"I suppose," said Dr. Browning to Felix, "that you
and Charles have a longer journey in front of you. Or
don't you intend to make Rhyllan to-night?"

"Not to-night," replied Felix, focussing his camera on
the picturesque, half-timbered little inn they had just left.
"We're staying at the Feathers in Penlow to-night and
going on to Rhyllan to-morrow. So we shall see you
to-morrow morning, and often again, I hope, before we
have to be back in London. . . . Hullo, Charles! Not
a puncture, I hope?"

"Back tyre seems beastly flat," said Charles, ruefully

16

pinching it. " It was perfectly all right when we arrived here. I think it'll hold, though, if I give it a good pump up. Lend me your pump, Lion, there's a good chap."

" Certainly," said Lion, detaching his immaculate pump from his immaculate bicycle; it was a new bicycle, and his own property, and he cleaned it carefully before every journey. " Those people in Worcester are absolute swindlers, hiring out a bike without a pump or mending outfit. I shouldn't pay them, if I were you."

" As long as I can borrow yours," replied Charles easily, " I don't mind."

" That doesn't alter the matter," said Lion severely, pursuing the ethics of the case. " They didn't know I had a pump. For all they knew, you might have been going to cycle a thousand miles all on your own."

" Come on, you two," called Isabel. " We're all going to coast down this hill, and see who goes the farthest along the flat at the bottom. Anybody using either pedals or brakes will be disqualified."

" I beg to be disqualified in advance," said Dr. Browning, eyeing the long, steep slope that stretched away in front of them. " My brake is my best friend. I suppose it's no use asking you children not to be fool-hardy. But for heaven's sake don't start racing down that hill all in a bunch. Go one at a time. Then only the first one will break his neck, and the others'll take warning."

Felix laughed.

" After that," he remarked, " I feel it's up to me to go first and save the lives of everybody else."

But Isabel had wheeled her bicycle out into the road and put her foot on the pedal.

" No," she said firmly, " I'm going first."

Half teasingly, half in earnest, Felix wheeled his bicycle alongside hers and prepared to start.

" Can't let you sacrifice your valuable life, Isabel," he

said jestingly. " Let me go first and flatten out the bumps."

Nora, watching the little contest, saw something like a flash of real temper pass over her friend's flushed, piquant face. It was gone in an instant, and she smiled at her devoted slave.

" No, really," she insisted. " I'm quite determined, Felix. Let everybody have about half a minute's start, and sit and wait for the others wherever their bicycle stops. Good-bye, Felix! You come next. What a gorgeous run it's going to be! "

Felix had no choice but to give way. Isabel mounted her bicycle and started, slowly at first, then gathering speed till her machine was whizzing down the long hill at a breakneck pace. Her hatless red head disappeared behind a clump of trees at the far corner of the downhill road.

" A reckless young woman," sighed Dr. Browning. " She seems to lose no opportunity of courting a broken neck. However, having come thus far without a disaster, I suppose she can be trusted to look after herself."

" Isabel will never break her neck," said Nora comfortably. " Don't you worry, Father. She has no end of presence of mind. As for me, I make no rash promises not to use my brakes. I don't like the look of this hill."

" Isabel is an idiot," observed Lion thoughtfully. " If she doesn't look out, she'll smash her bike to pieces. She won't care, because it's only a hired one. But I'm not going to take any risks with mine."

He looked fondly at his glittering machine.

Felix said nothing, but mounted his bicycle in grim silence. It was plain that he did not mean to descend basely to the use of his brakes. He whizzed down the hill after Isabel and reached the turning-point of the road, at least, in safety. Lion, calling to Sir Charles to be sure and not leave the pump behind, followed more cautiously, and Nora and her father, with a backward glance at

Charles, who was screwing the cap on his valve, mounted together and followed, gaining rapidly on the unadventurous Lion. Even with the judicious use of her brakes, Nora found the descent quite exciting enough. From the top of the hill, one could see a wide panorama of distant trees and fields lying below one like an enchanted country, protected by range after range of hills. The long, swirling lines of the nearer hills shone clear in the evening sun, and through their gaps the far Black Mountains showed like dim blue wraiths. One descended, and shot down-wards towards this enchantment, knowing all the while that one would never reach it, that as one approached, enchantment would retreat ever farther and farther away, calling one on. Trees and hedges closed in on one, shutting out the wide world.

For sheer delight in the sense of speed and the cool, delicious air flowing past her face, Nora released her brakes, and the bicycle leapt forward like a living thing. She turned the corner, and the road went on and on downhill, varying in steepness, but always taking her down into the valley. The blood flowed warmly through her veins, the air blew cool on her skin, and her brain seemed clear as crystal. She thought happily of the month ahead of her in her old home in Penlow, before the art school opened again; a month that would be spent in sketching, calling on old friends and expeditions with Lion and Isabel to the hills and Radnor Forest. Whizzing down towards the enchanted valley, she counted her blessings and enjoyed a sense of positive, conscious happiness. It was a pity that she had allowed herself to become so fond of old Felix, since he obviously cared more for Isabel's little finger than for a dozen Noras. But few people lived their lives without once suffering at least a faint intimation of unrequited love; and love was not the only spring of happiness in this lovely world.

She had left her father far behind, and just beyond the second turn of the road shot past Lion, with a derisive shout. Not to be outdone by his sister, Lion released his brakes and overtook her.

" Hullo! " he shouted breathlessly, as they sped along side by side.

" Hullo! " she shouted back, and had no breath for more conversation.

They turned another corner, past a small white-washed cottage where a woman stood watching them with the intent, rapturous expression of one who fore-sees an accident, and found that the wild descent was over. The road stretched tamely ahead of them, a flat, narrow ribbon between tangled hedges of hawthorn and briar. About a hundred yards farther on, Felix sat on the grass at the side of the road with his hands clasped round his knees, watching their approach. There was no sign of Isabel.

" Hullo! No Isabel," said Nora. " She probably got up enough speed to carry her all the way to Penlow without turning a pedal."

" Dead in a ditch, more likely," said Lion scornfully. " She'll come to a bad end, that girl."

" Oh come, Lion! If Isabel came to a bad end, nobody would be sorrier than you. So you needn't pretend to be hardened and cynical."

" Oh, she's not bad," admitted Lion grudgingly. " For a girl," he added, hoping thereby to arouse his sister's wrath. But she was looking along the road ahead of them with a worried expression, and did not hear.

" I do really wonder where she's got to. She said she'd sit and wait for us when her wheels refused to go round any more. And she can't surely have gone farther than we can see without pedalling. . . ."

" Oh, can't she," said Lion with a note of unwilling

admiration in his voice. " She can do anything, that girl. She's possessed of a devil. This is where I fall off."

He dismounted. But in her anxiety for Isabel, Nora cycled along the road to where Felix was now standing and waiting for her.

" Hullo, Felix! Where's Isabel? "

" I don't know! Her bike's a few yards farther on, the other side of that heap of stones. I walked on a bit to look for her, and came back. She must be all right, because her bike's quite intact."

" Oh, that's all right, then! " Nora was relieved. The reckless Isabel was a bit of a responsibility as a guest. " She'll turn up. Hullo, here's father. Wasn't it a lovely run? "

" I should have enjoyed it more if you children hadn't been so reckless. I was expecting every moment to have to jump off and set a broken limb, or worse. Where's Isabel? Oh, I see. Well, as long as you're sure she isn't lying somewhere along the road desperately in need of medical attention, I think I'll sit down and take a rest."

He mounted a stile giving on to a grassy meadow and contemplated the view about him, while Lion, who had sauntered up to join the party, spread out an ordinance survey map on the top bar of the gate and followed the road they had just travelled with a pin.

" Hullo," he remarked after a moment. " The quarry I went to look at isn't far away from here. There's a footpath a little farther down this road leading straight to it across some fields. I wonder whether one can see the face of it from the road."

" Probably," assented Dr. Browning absently. He did not share his son's passion for topography. Botany and architecture were his chief interests outside his profession, though the life of a popular country doctor left little room for them. " What a delightful old cottage that is! " he added, looking down the road to where a small half-timbered building stood back behind a long strip of garden. " A nd how pleasant to see that it hasn't been robbed of its old slates. I've no patience with the vandals who'll strip an old cottage of its roof to plaster the slates on to some millionaire's pseudo-Tudor country residence. A ll in the name of art, too. . . . I wish your young friend would put in an appearance, Nora."

Even as he spoke there was a flash of blue in the hedge about ten yards down the road, and Isabel jumped down from a stile and c ame sauntering placidly towards them, making a charming note of colour in the green landscape with her dress of faded blue cotton and hair of golden red.

" I take it I win," she greeted them. " I hope you didn't all think I was dead. I've been exploring the fields and hedges. Look what I've brought you."

She held out a large dock-leaf containing about half a pound of small ripe raspberries.

" Wild ones. I found lots of them, and they're delicious."

She offered the leaf to Dr. Browning, who helped himself to two or three and asked :

" Where did you find these? "

" Oh, just in the next field." She jerked her head vaguely over her shoulder. " Have some, Felix, and say you forgive me for having a better bicycle than you. I didn't cheat. I swear I didn't. A nd I never touched my brake. Did you? "

" Of course not," murmured Felix, oblivious of the raspberries she held out to him in his contemplation of her small shining head.

" Then you both deserve to be certified insane," declared Dr. Browning severely. " It's time we were pushing on if we're to get home before supper time."

There was a general movement towards recumbent bicycles. Lion folded his map and stowed it in his breast pocket, and was about to mount his machine when he stopped suddenly and hailed his father, who had made a few yards start.

" I say! Dad! Hi, everybody! What about the Baronite? "

" The what? " shouted Dr. Browning, wobbling perilously in the effort to look over his shoulder.

" The cousin, the Charles, the cow-puncher. . . ."

" Great Scot! " exclaimed Dr. Browning. " I'd forgotten all about him! "

The five looked at one another and then at the hill they had just descended, hoping to see the missing Charles turning the corner into view. But there was no sign of him.

" I'm so used to there being only five of us that I never missed him," said Felix with compunction. " I say! Do you think we ought——"

" You're not going to suggest cycling up that hill to look for him? " said Isabel in tones of horror. " Give him a bit longer, anyhow. Probably he found he had a puncture."

The others looked relieved at this simple and obvious explanation, but Lion remarked :

" He hasn't got a mending outfit. He'd have walked down the hill and borrowed mine."

" Has he had time to walk down the hill? " asked Nora. Her moment of groundless anxiety about Isabel made her quick to fear an accident.

Felix looked at his watch.

" Oh, heaps! I really think I'd better go and reconnoitre. We can't very well go on without him, and it's no use waiting here doing nothing."

" I don't think I'll come." Isabel sat down on the grass and smiled at the worried faces of her friends. " I

don't like the look of that hill.   Besides, I do really think
Charles can look after himself.   We lost him for half an
hour the other day, if you remember, and he turned up
with a bag of bulls' eyes he'd been a mile out of his way
to get, without telling anybody.   He's probably used to
doing things on his own, and it hasn't occurred to him to
think of our anxiety.   Not, personally, that I feel any.
Give me a cigarette, Felix, before you go."

" I think you're right, Isabel," said Dr. Browning
thoughtfully, " though we can't very well go on and leave
him to his fate, in case he is in trouble of some sort."
The doctor's private supposition was that Sir Charles, his
companions out of the way, had returned to the Tram to
refresh himself with something stronger than tea.   " Stop
this car," he added quickly, as a small two-seater came
down the hill towards them.   " They'll be able to tell us
whether they've passed a cyclist in distress."

The little grey car drew up in response to Lion's
energetic signalling, and the driver, a dark, thin-faced
young man with a look of merry intelligence on his lips
and eyebrows, leant over the side and said :

" Hullo! "

" I'm sorry to bother you," said the more formal Felix.
" But did you pass a cyclist on the hill? "

" I don't think we've passed a cyclist since we left the
last village," said the stranger thoughtfully, looking at
his companion for confirmation.   " Certainly not on this
hill."

" You might have passed him in a ditch and not
noticed him," observed Lion gloomily.

The young man laughed.

" We should certainly have seen traces of him.   No,
I can assure you we passed nobody.   There were one or
two bicycles standing outside the inn, and one or two
men sitting in the porch."

The driver paused and looked at his companion, a

rather older man with a square, wholesome, reddish face, spectacles and a thatch of fair bristling hair. Then he addressed Dr. Browning :

" Would you like us to scour the countryside for you? We're in no hurry."

" Oh, no, thanks! The young man's quite capable of looking after himself. He'll catch us up all right. We'll be pushing on."

" Well—*au revoir*," said the stranger with his pleasant smile, and the car slid forward.

" *Au revoir*," quoted Lion, mounting his bicycle and watching the retreating car. " Not very likely, I should say. That's a London number. As for the missing Baronite, I expect he's carousing merrily in the bar-parlour of the Tram."

Felix and Isabel laughed, and Nora, though she sternly shook her head at her young brother, exchanged a half-smile with Dr. Browning. None of them was particularly sorry to be deprived of Sir Charles's company for a mile or two.

fav chapter so far, loved the detail & character interactions.

CHAPTER THREE

THE FEATHERS in Penlow is an historic inn. It has, or so tradition says, for no one in these days knows where to look for it, a secret passage; and King Charles II hid in one of its small panelled rooms during his flight after the battle of Worcester. Few old houses in this part of the country lack a room hallowed by the uneasy sleep of a crowned head. Felix had calculated that of the forty-one nights occupied by his flight to Shoreham, the Merry Monarch had spent twenty-three in providing the inns and private dwellings of Penlow and its environs with interest for future antiquarians.

But even without these advantages the Feathers is a delightful inn, with its sombre brick and timber frontage, its narrow panelled passages and large, low-pitched bedrooms, its mahogany half-tester beds, its profusion of texts, its polished, uneven floors and scent of lavender and furniture polish. No period furniture by Messrs. Gilling & Staple undermines its atmosphere of true antiquity. No posters in unnatural spelling and evil print proclaim it "Ye Oldeste Radnor Inne." No hordes of motorists and cyclists arrive on Sundays to consume expensive teas and admire what the house-agents describe as period-features. It has no features, in that sense. The hand of the exploiter has not yet reached the Feathers. May it never do so.

26

Felix, having booked a room for himself and one for Charles, wandered restlessly to the doorway and looked up and down the road. Dusk was falling, and lamps were lit in the windows across the street. He felt distinctly hungry and tired, and yet unwilling to eat or rest until Charles had arrived and dispelled his slight sense of uneasiness. There was no sign of a cyclist coming up the narrow high street. Felix sighed, and silently anathematized his cousin as an inconsiderate, confounded, irresponsible idiot. Turning back from his fruitless inspection of the street, he encountered the friendly smile of a young man standing at the foot of the stairs. It was the motorist they had stopped on Rodland Hill.

"Good evening," said the young man, advancing towards Felix. "Hasn't your friend turned up yet?"

"No. I shan't wait dinner for him much longer. I can't understand where he can have got to, but I suppose he's all right."

"He couldn't have lost his way, I suppose?"

"Impossible. He saw us all start down Rodland Hill, and he knows we're staying the night here. He may turn up any minute. But——"

"But you don't feel quite easy about him. Is he the sort of person to go off on his own without warning?"

"Well," replied Felix, instinctively liking the stranger and glad to have somebody to talk the matter over with, now that the Brownings and Isabel had departed to the doctor's house, "I've only known him three days. But I should think he was, rather. It's frightfully thoughtless of him, if he has. I'm supposed to be going round to the Brownings after dinner, but I don't like to do anything till he turns up." Felix spoke gloomily, depressed at seeing the prospect of an evening in Isabel's company diminish before his eyes.

"Your other friends?"

"Yes. He's Dr. Browning, lives about a quarter of a

mile out of the town.   Charles and I live at Rhyllan Hall, four miles away, and are going on there to-morrow."

" If you care to go to your friends," suggested the stranger amiably, " we'll look out for the missing one, and send a message to you when he arrives. We're staying the night here."

" It's awfully good of you," said Felix gratefully. " But I think I'd rather stay on the spot." He sighed.

" Would you care to join us at dinner? " the stranger asked diffidently.   " We should be delighted if you would.   We're strangers in this part of the world, and you'll be able to tell us all the things a tourist should not miss, as they say in the guide-books. Do. It's much more sensible than waiting about for somebody who may have gone to Timbuctoo or somewhere by mistake.   I suppose your missing friend is of an age and character to look after himself? "

" Oh, quite," murmured Felix with a faint smile. " Well, thanks awfully. I should like to very much. My name's Felix Price."

" Mine's John Christmas. And here is my cousin, Sydenham Rampson. I vote we have dinner at once. If your friend hasn't turned up by the time we've finished, we'll take the car out and scour the countryside."

" It's awfully good of you. I do hope it won't come to that."

" *He* hopes it will," said the newcomer confidentially, nodding towards his friend.   " Anything for an unquiet life, is his motto. It comes of having no work to do and reading nothing but penny dreadfuls. ' The Vanished Cyclist,' or ' A Mystery of the Welsh Marches.' He just eats that sort of thing."

The fair, sturdy young man shook his head and sighed with an air of doleful pity, and they all proceeded into the large, dim, lamplit dining-room. But for two or three scattered diners at the small tables, they had the room to themselves, and took a comfortable table in a corner where they had a view of the window and the street.

"You mustn't take any notice of Rampson's libels," said Christmas cheerfully, as they seated themselves. "He's not human. He's by way of being a scientist, and has no interest in anything he can see with the naked eye."

"That," said Mr. Rampson equably, "is untrue. I feel a very keen interest in this soup, which is at present perfectly visible without a microscope."

"When I use the word 'interest,' Sydenham, I refer to intellectual curiosity, not to mere animal instincts, such as greed. Would you believe it, this is the first holiday Rampson's taken from his microscope for four years, and I had the greatest difficulty in disinterring him from his dingy lair in the Temple to bring him on it?"

"I hope you like my native country, as much as you've seen of it?"

"Wales? We've only just slipped over the edge of it. We've been wandering through Worcester, Shropshire and Hereford. I should love to go right through to the Welsh coast, but Rampson is getting fidgety about his amœbas and says it's time we started home."

"It's ten days since we left London," murmured Mr. Rampson reproachfully. "And the idea was only to be away a week altogether."

"It's just ten days since *we* left London," said Felix. "But we haven't covered so much of the country as you have. We came by a more or less direct route, and took our time over it."

"You live in London?"

"Yes. My native Radnorshire is only for holidays," said Felix with a sigh and a smile. "I'm a photographer by profession and a painter in my spare time. Sometimes I combine photography and art, and bring out a book of

photographs of Old English Cottages, or Country Occupa-
tions, or some such subject, with a little letter-press to
explain the photos. I got rather a good photograph of
the Tram Inn that'll probably go in a book I'm doing
on ' Old Inns and Taverns.' "

" You've had jolly weather for your tour."

" Rather. We're all sorry it's over. It was young
Lion's idea. He's just been given a new super-bicycle,
and naturally despises any other method of getting about."

" Lion? Is that the young windmill who stopped us
on Rodland Hill? "

" Yes. Lion Browning. He's at school near London,
you see, and has been staying the first part of his holidays
with Nora and some cousins in Sussex. Nora Browning's
an old friend of mine, we go to the same art school.
And as Dr. Browning had been staying in London, we
thought we'd all cycle up here together. It's been
gorgeous," added Felix regretfully, reflecting that hence-
forth a distance of four miles would separate him from
that delightful enigma, Isabel. " Miss Donne," he added,
" is staying with the Brownings for a week or so. She's
an art student friend of Nora's."

" And the vanished cyclist, as Rampson calls him? "

" Oh, he's my cousin Charles," said Felix in a worried
tone. " But I've only known him three days. He came
back from Canada about six weeks ago. You see, my
Uncle Evan died three months ago, and Charles inherited
Rhyllan, and naturally came back to live there. I wrote
to him when we started from London, inviting him to
hire a bike and join us at Worcester. I thought it'd be
a good opportunity of getting friendly with him."

" And was it? " asked Christmas with a smile.

" Oh, yes," answered Felix without enthusiasm. He
looked with a worried frown out of the window into the
darkness. " I do wish he'd turn up. I suppose you
think I'm an awful idiot to get nervy about an able-

bodied fellow older than myself, just because he doesn't
keep to the time-table. But it really is rather mysterious,
because he doesn't know anybody in the neighbourhood,
and doesn't know his way about yet, and he's just one
of those slap-dash sort of people that do come to grief. I
think I'll ring up Rhyllan as soon as we've finished
dinner, and see if he's taken it into his head to go
straight home."

"An excellent idea," agreed his new-found friend.
"Meanwhile, let's forget him and attend to this excellent
mutton. We've had mutton for dinner every night for
the last week, pretty nearly. And very nice, too.

> ' The mountain sheep were sweeter,
> But the valley sheep were fatter,
> And so we thought it meeter
> To bear away the latter.'

The mint sauce, please, Sydenham."

" ' Meat,' " objected Mr. Rampson, "is not an
adjective. I suppose you mean more meaty."

Christmas looked at him pityingly.

" ' Meet,' my dear Sydenham, is a word much used by
writers of verse to signify seemly, proper or expedient."

" Verse," said Rampson indifferently. " That accounts
for it. I don't read verse."

"Don't boast of your lack of culture, cousin."

" You," returned his cousin with composure, " can
quote a line or two of verse about these mountains and
valleys. But can you tell me what their geological formation is? Can you even tell me what mineral they
produce? No."

" Yes. I notice that most of the houses in this part
of the world are roofed with slate of a peculiarly charming
appearance. I imagine, therefore, that these hills produce
slate as well as mutton."

" Talking of slate," said Felix, " we had tea this afternoon at a small inn with the quaint sign of The Tram, called apparently after the tram-lines that used to run to a quarry nearby."

" I noticed it," replied Christmas, " at the top of Rodland Hill, and a very nice little brick-and-timber building it is. The name puzzled me for a moment, but I managed to make the right deduction. Is the quarry still in use? We might go over and see them blasting, or whatever they do to slate. It would improve Sydenham's mind."

Felix smiled.

" No, I understand from the girl at the inn that the quarry hasn't been used since she dunno when. So I don't imagine that there's much to see, except some rusty truck-lines and the usual mass of brambles and fern."

" There's always something a little ghostly and depressing, I think, about a disused quarry," murmured John Christmas pensively. " It always looks a little like an old scar. The brambles that grow in the hollow and the rubbish that people throw into it have a sinister sort of look to me.

' I hate the dreadful hollow behind the little wood,
Its lips in the field above are dabbled with blood-red heath,
The——' "

Rampson paused in the act of cutting an apple tart and groaned.

" There you go again! In my opinion all this poetry's bad for the brain. It fills the head with preconceived ideas, and prevents the conception of an original thought. You don't really think disused quarries are sinister. Very likely you've never even seen one. Yet as soon as the word's mentioned, the wheels start going round in your head and out trots a remark that disused quarries are sinister. As for heath being blood-red, such a comparison would never occur to anybody who'd ever seen heath and blood, no, not if a dozen corpses had been hauled up out of the hollow."

" It's a bad comparison, I admit," said Christmas cheerfully. " In fact, for a long time I imagined that the poet's heath was literally drenched in gore. It wasn't till I grew up and began to realize the shifts poets may be put to that it occurred to me he was referring to the natural colour of the heather. . . . Yes, waiter? What is it? "

" A 'phone call for Mr. Price, sir. Would you like me to take a message? "

" I'll go," answered Felix, getting up. " I expect it's Charles," he added in a relieved tone. " I shan't be long."

He left the room. There was a short silence while Rampson helped himself to another slice of apple tart.

" Rather a nice young chap, that," he observed casually. " He reminds me of a hen who's lost her one duckling."

" I suppose he feels responsible for his Colonial cousin," said Christmas. " But I don't think he feels any of the hen's protective love for her duckling. I got the impression that his enthusiasm for his cousin is lukewarm, to say the most of it."

" I suppose you'll be suggesting he's murdered him next," said Rampson resignedly. " I don't believe murder's half so prevalent as you novel-reading people imagine. I warn you, if he's murdered a dozen cousins, I'm not going to get mixed up in it. As soon as I see you getting interested in a mystery, I go home."

" How you do run on," observed John lightly. " You'd better take the first train in the morning, because I'm interested already. Why should one member of a party of six cyclists suddenly vanish within a few miles of home? "

"Oh, Lord! A puncture, a heart attack, a meeting with a friend or a motor-lorry, any one of a hundred things! "

c

"Exactly. I shan't be happy till I know which. I've promised to go out in the car and look for the missing cousin after dinner. You can come, if you like."

"Oh, I shall come, but only for the sake of a breath of air. But I don't suppose it'll come to that. Our young friend's probably heard all about his duckling's adventures over the 'phone."

"Probably," agreed John. "By the way, the Prices are rather a well-known family in these parts. There's quite a lot about Rhyllan Hall in the guide-books. It was built by Morgan Ap-Rice in the fifteenth century, and extensively added to in the sixteenth and seventeenth centuries by various Evans and Morgans. The façade, which is in the Queen Anne style of architecture, is a magnificent example of early eighteenth century design, and the park—— Hullo! Is the mystery solved?"

With a worried frown Felix entered the room and came across to the table.

"That was Dr. Browning ringing up," he said in a depressed voice. "He wanted to know whether Charles had put in an appearance yet. Of course I said he hadn't. And he seemed to think something should be done about it. You see, nobody knows him in these parts yet. If he had an accident, we might not hear for some time." He sighed. "It is tiresome, because from what I've seen of Charles it's quite likely he's just taken it into his head to go off somewhere on his own, and there's no means of finding out where until he chooses to turn up, if that's the case."

"Did you ring up your home?"

"Yes," said Felix moodily, filling his pipe. "He's not been seen there. Blodwen—that's his sister, my cousin—says that my father's been out all day with his car and not come back yet. It's just possible they may have met and gone off somewhere together. But it's most unlikely, I should think. They'd have come here, if anywhere."

He looked despondently out of the window, as if still hoping to see the light of Charles's bicycle approaching down the winding street.

"Well," said John briskly, rising from the table, " the best thing we can do is to take out the car and run back to the Tram Inn. Possibly the people there can give us some information. And it's a lovely night for a run."

It was indeed a lovely night, perfectly windless and clear, with a starry sky and dim, pale mists lying over the low fields. But Felix did not take much pleasure in the nocturnal beauties of the landscape. John drove slowly, and Felix peered anxiously along the hedge-rows, still obsessed with a fear that his cousin had crashed and injured himself and was lying unconscious at the side of the lonely road. They passed nobody between Penlow and the Tram Inn, which they found closed. The door was opened to them by the pale girl who had served tea to Felix and his friends that afternoon.

" I'm afraid I can't serve you, sir," she said in a civil but decided tone before John could speak. " It's gone ten o'clock nearly a quarter of an hour ago." Recognizing Felix, she gave him a dubious smile, and added: " I'm very sorry, sir."

" That's all right," said Felix, and proceeded to ask whether one of the gentlemen who had been of the tea-party had returned to the inn later, and whether she had noticed in which direction he had started. But no information was to be got from her. She had been working in the kitchen at the back of the inn, she said, at the time, and could not say who might have entered the bar. On this she seemed disposed to shut the door, but Felix persisted.

" Who was serving in the bar? Can't we see someone else? "

" My father was in the bar, sir," said the girl dubiously.
" But he's gone up to bed, and I don't hardly like to call
him, sir. If you'd call again in the morning——"

" I can't do that. It's important. My cousin may
have had an accident. Please ask your father if he'd
kindly come down for a moment."

The girl looked rather frightened. Her natural reluctance to offend a customer seemed to strive with a wholesome awe of her parent. She hesitated, looking over her
shoulder up the stairs, and shook her head.

" I couldn't do that, sir. He wouldn't like to be
disturbed." Her voice took on a faintly injured tone.
" It *is* after closing-time, you know, sir."

" Don't be silly," said John in tones of fatherly reproof.
" It's an important matter. Come, run along, there's a
good girl. I'll make it all right with your father." He
faintly and suggestively clinked some coins in his trouser-
pocket. But the girl seemed deaf to the alluring sound.

" It *is* after closing-time," she repeated with an access
of obstinacy, and jumped with a little cry of alarm as a
protracted guttural screech split the still air, and was
repeated again and again. John smiled. The resource-
ful Rampson was serenading the inn with his motor-horn.

His efforts soon had the desired effect. There was a
heavy thump overhead, and the tramping of feet on the
stairs. Then a gruff but lusty voice shouted :

" What the —— hell's going on, Ada ? "

The owner of the voice and inn appeared on the lower
stairs, clinging to the hand-rail, a burly figure attired in
a night-shirt and mackintosh, with ruffled hair standing
on end behind a high bald forehead and an eye filmed
with sleep or beer.

" Oh, Father, these gentlemen——" began the girl
timidly, but John interrupted her and explained the
situation.

The innkeeper, drawing his mackintosh majestically

round his corpulent waist, heavily descended to the bottom stair but one. From this vantage-point he explained at picturesque length his view of the ultimate destination of such abandoned persons as couldn't wait till morning for their drinks.

"We don't want drink," said John patiently.

"Eh?"

"I say, we don't want drink. I keep saying it, but you won't listen. We never drink. We're total abstainers. We advocate strict temperance and the abolition of the public-house. Now!"

"Eh?" repeated mine host owlishly. "Wellim-damned."

Words failed him. He sat down suddenly and heavily on the stairs.

"Then," he said ponderously at last, with surprising moderation, "what you come knocking public-house up after closing-time for? That's what I wants to know. Everybody got a right to opinions, no doubt. But want to bolish public-house, keep way from it. See?"

"Oh, let's go," said Felix impatiently. "We'll never get any sense out of this fellow."

But a renewed explanation from the more patient John elicited the information that at about half-past five that afternoon mine host had served a young man answering to Charles's description with a double whisky, and that the same young man had stood drinks to him and to two or three loungers in the bar.

"Friend o' yours?" inquired the landlord, endeavouring to cover his bare ankles with the flaps of his mackintosh. "He bain't no total abstainer, not be a long way."

"I dare say not," said Felix dryly. "Can you tell us which way he went when he left the inn?"

The landlord looked at him dreamily, and as Felix was about to repeat the question, said with some asperity:

"Shut the door, young gentleman. My ankles be cold."

Felix rather irritably did as he was requested, and the innkeeper, pointedly addressing himself to the more sympathetic John, went on:

"In a manner of speaking I did see which way the young gentleman went. He went into the quarry field, just across the road."

"Into the field!" exclaimed Felix. "But surely he came back again?"

"I doesn't know, I'm sure, and that's why I said in a manner of speaking. I didn't see he come back."

"Had he his bicycle with him?"

"Ah!" assented their host. "He took his bicycle, and an elderly gentleman."

"An elderly gentleman! What elderly gentleman?"

"Ts, ts, ts! Please to take it easy, young man. How can I say what elderly gentleman? An elderly gentleman as happened to be outside with his car."

"What kind of car?"

"What kind o' car? A large car," replied the landlord, measuring a distance of about a yard and a half between his hands. "Yes, a large green car. And very nice too," he finished abruptly, on a penetrating hiccough.

"Did the other man, the old one, come back, do you know?" asked John.

"Not as I saw him. But in a manner of speaking I suppose he must a done. Because half an hour arterwards the car 'd gone."

The girl, who had been hovering anxiously in the passage during this conversation, here broke in timidly:

"I saw the gentleman with the car come back from the field, Father. He didn't have nobody with him. It looked like Mr. Morris Price of Rhyllan Hall, I thought. As soon as I saw the car I thought, that's Mr. Price's car, I expect." She turned to John. "My boy's sister works up at Rhyllan, you see, sir, and having been up there once or twice with him I've noticed Mr. Price's green car. And sure enough, when the gentleman come back from the quarry field, I saw it was Mr. Morris. Or so I thought."

" You girls thinks too much," remarked her father ponderously. " The supper's spoiled and the chickens starves while you stands about and thinks." He winked laboriously at John.

" It sounds like my father's car, certainly," said Felix in response to John's look of inquiry. " Well—in that case it's all right, I suppose. Probably my father gave him some business message that sent him out of his way. We'll find him at the Feathers when we get back, no doubt."

He looked and felt extremely relieved. The vision of Charles, deserted by his friends, lying injured by the side of some lonely lane, vanished from his mental horizon.

Before they turned to go, John inquired:

" Where does the footpath over the quarry field lead to? "

The old man laughed.

" Depends which way you takes, master. You might take the right to Upper Ring Farm, or you might go straight over the common on to the Wensley Road. Or you might fall over the quarry edge and get a broke neck. I should say your friend's took the Wensley Road. You can get to Penlow that way. In time."

" Do you remember what time it was when you saw them going across the fields? "

" Well, it might be half after six," said the innkeeper thoughtfully, getting heavily to his feet. " Half-past six to seven, I couldn't say. The young chap was in here drinking and talking a while, and then he went outside, p'r'aps to sit on the bench, p'r'aps for a spin on his bike, I couldn't say. And some time arterwards I sees him going across the field along of the elderly gentleman. Well, I be going to bed. Many a hearty chap's been cut off in his prime through having less night air than what I've had to-night. Good night, masters. Thank you, sir. Ada, see the gentlemen out and bolt the door."

He departed with unsteady dignity up the stairs. The girl followed John and Felix to the door with an anxious look on her plain, pale face.

" I hopes you won't think as Father's allus like this, sir," she said timidly. " It'd do us harm if it was to get about as he took too much of his own liquors, they're that strict with the licensing nowadays."

Reassuring her, they left the inn and went back to the car where Rampson was patiently awaiting them.

" Probably," said Felix, " Charles met my father on the road and came back with him. . . ." He paused. " No, he can't have done that, because we should have seen my father's car if it had come along this road. I wonder what the dickens Charles was doing hanging about here all that time? We left at half-past five."

" Your father might have overtaken him going down the hill," suggested John, " and he might have got off his bicycle and walked back. Though it's a nasty hill to turn a car on, I doubt if it could be done, in fact. Anyhow, we'll probably hear all about it when we get back to Penlow."

But there was no sign of Charles at the Feathers, and Felix, after ringing up Rhyllan Hall and learning that neither Charles nor Morris had returned there, spent, in spite of his endeavours to reason himself out of his anxiety, an uneasy night.

CHAPTER FOUR

T HE sun rose the next morning shrouded in those soft mists that at such a time of year are the presage of a bright, warm day. Christmas, Rampson, and Felix stood in the doorway of the Feathers Inn, smoking their after-breakfast cigarettes and discussing plans for the day.

" You don't really expect me to turn towards London on such a day as this, Sydenham? I am sure the laboratory won't miss you for another week or two. And it seems a pity not to explore Wales a bit further. Besides, you haven't had nearly enough fresh air yet."

" The air I get in London is quite fresh enough for me," answered Mr. Rampson composedly, and indeed with his plump, fresh-coloured face and well-built, sturdy body he did not look particularly in need of country air nor any other restorative. " But I don't mind staying a bit longer. I have seen less attractive counties than this."

" I must get my bike out and start for Rhyllan," said Felix, throwing his cigarette-end away, " and see if my troublesome cousin has put in an appearance yet." The bright morning sun had dispelled his vague anxiety of the night before, and made him feel a little ashamed of his alarms. He hesitated. " I suppose," he went on diffidently, " you wouldn't care to come over and see Rhyllan while you're in the district? It's only four miles

away, and it's supposed to be worth seeing.   Part of it—
a very little part—is fifteenth century.   Blodwen and my
father would be delighted if you came to lunch, I know.
And so," he added quickly, remembering that Rhyllan
Hall had now a new owner, " would Charles."

John   Christmas,   in   whom   the   circumstances   of
Charles's   disappearance   had   roused   a   mild   curiosity,
accepted the invitation heartily.

" That's very kind of you.   We shall be delighted, and
we'll follow you to Rhyllan in an hour or two.   Meanwhile we'll have a look round this old town, shall we,
Sydenham?   It's market day, judging by the number of
sheep I've seen going through the town.   And here's
a sergeant of police coming to regulate the traffic.   No,
he's coming here."

" Mr. Felix Price here, sir? "

Felix, on his way upstairs to fetch his haversack and
pay his bill, turned at the sound of his own name.

" Yes, Sergeant? "

" Could I have a word with you a moment, sir? "

" Certainly," said Felix cheerfully.   Sergeant Dew was
an old friend of his.   But at the stolid, unsmiling look
on the officer's face, his own expression changed.   His
anxiety of the night before returned.   " Come in here,"
he said, and opened the door of a small sitting-room
likely at that hour in the morning to be deserted.

It was not long before he came out, followed by the
sergeant.   He hesitated a moment in the hall, with a
vague startled look on his face, as if he did not know
where he was, nor what to do next.   Then, catching
sight of John leaning against the lintel and watching
him sympathetically, he stepped quickly over to him.
His   pleasant   young   face   looked   suddenly   white   and
lined.

" A terrible thing has happened," he said in a low
voice.   " My cousin's been found dead in the quarry.

I——" He stopped and passed his hand over his forehead. "He's at the Tram Inn. I—I must go there. But first I must ring up Rhyllan and let them know, I suppose. God! It's ghastly!"

"A messenger's been sent to Rhyllan Hall, sir," said Sergeant Dew sympathetically. "No need for you to telephone, if you'd rather spare yourself. No need for you to go to the Tram, either. The inspector can call and see you at Rhyllan later in the day. My orders were just to let you know what's happened."

"Thank you," said Felix mechanically. "No, I must go. I feel—poor Charles! We ought to have gone back for him yesterday! I knew we ought to go back. It's my fault this has happened."

"Oh, come," said John gently, recognizing in his new friend one of those ultra-conscientious souls who have an endless capacity for tormenting themselves, "that's nonsense. You couldn't possibly have foreseen such a thing." He glanced at the kind-faced sergeant, who was looking at Felix with a sad and embarrassed expression as if, being the bearer of ill news, he felt himself responsible for its nature. "You'd much better do as the sergeant suggests —go home and await developments."

"No, no! I must go and hear how it happened. I must. One of the family must be there."

"Mr. Morris is sure to be there, sir," pointed out Dew deferentially.

"Is he?" said Felix rather wildly. "No. He's away, I think. . . . I don't know! Anyhow, I must go! Get me Morgan's car, Sergeant."

"I'll take you over," said John quietly. "I'll get the car out at once."

He went round towards the garage, followed by Felix. Sergeant Dew looked after them and then glanced at Rampson, who had been a silent witness of this conversation.

" A dreadful thing to happen, sir. Poor Sir Charles had only been back from Canada six weeks."

" A very extraordinary thing," agreed Rampson. " One wouldn't imagine it was easy to fall over a quarry edge in daylight, or during such a clear night as last. And there seems to have been no reason why he should go near the quarry."

The sergeant shook his head non-committally, and was silent for a moment. Then his interest in the mystery got the better of his professional calm.

" Looks like murder," he said in a low voice near Rampson's ear.

" Indeed! "

" Yes, sir. All them injuries was never done by a fall. Shocking."

" Really."

" Yes, sir. It's a shocking business."

A little disappointed at this stolid young man's reception of his news and rather regretting that he had cast this pearl before so unappreciative an audience, he suddenly resumed his professional dignity, said briskly : " Well—good morning, sir! " and departed.

The little grey car backed into the road. In response to John's interrogative look Rampson shook his head.

" You'll find me hereabouts when you get back. I shall go and have a look round the town."

There was almost complete silence between John and Felix during the nine-mile drive to the Tram Inn. Glancing occasionally from the corner of his eye at his young companion's face, John found it always the same, white and troubled, with a gloomy frown on the brows and a set droop to the lips. John could not help being a little surprised at the boy's apparent depth of feeling. A nasty shock, of course, to hear suddenly of the death of a man who, only yesterday, had been the companion of a happy holiday. But the acquaintance, in spite of the cousinship, had lasted only three days. And John had gained the impression that Felix and his cousin had not been by any means twin souls.

As they approached Rodland Hill Felix said, looking across the fields to where, some distance away, a grey face of rock showed through a gap in the trees:

" That's the quarry."

His voice was strained and strange.   There was no lightening of the gloom on his face.   He became more animated as they approached the top of Rodland Hill, sitting upright in the car and looking eagerly ahead of him.   But when the Tram Inn, standing among its tall trees a little way back from the road, came into view, he sank back with a sigh.   There was a handful of people standing about outside the small timbered building, and three cars were drawn up outside its door.   A large green car, John noted, was not among them.

" That red car's Dr. Browning's," said Felix listlessly. " He does the police work in this district.   And the little blue one looks like Blodwen's."   His face cleared for a moment.   " My father may have driven over in that."

But as they drew up outside the Tram a tall woman in a rough tweed coat and hat left the porch of the inn and came quickly towards them.

" Hullo, Felix," she said quickly, with a glance at John.   " Have you seen anything of Uncle Morris? "

Felix shook his head.

" Hasn't he come home? "

" No.   So I thought I'd better come down.   I wanted them to move the body to Rhyllan, but they intend to hold the inquest here."

It was characteristic of Blodwen Price that she wasted no words in vain expressions of horror or regret; that her grey eyes were dry and clear and her low voice steady and matter-of-fact.   She was a woman of thirty-six or seven, with a shrewd weather-beaten face redeemed from extreme plainness by a pair of singularly clear, deep-set grey eyes with fine dark brows and lashes. John noticed that the moody Felix seemed to become steadier and cooler at the first contact with her self-contained personality.

" When do they propose to hold the inquest? " he asked in a voice as low and matter-of-fact as her own.

" I don't know. It depends on Uncle Morris. Apparently he met Charles here last night. Did you know that? "

" Yes. This is Mr. Christmas. My cousin, Miss Price."

Miss Price's bright eyes measured John in a rapid glance as they shook hands. Then they turned towards the inn. It was not the time for an exchange of amiable sociabilities.

Dr. Browning met them in the passage, and explaining that the Superintendent was at the moment in the bar-parlour interviewing the landlord, led the way into a tiny crowded room at the back of the house that was evidently a family sitting-room. He looked pale and distressed as he greeted Felix and Blodwen.

" I'm afraid this is a sad home-coming for you, Miss Price. Please accept my deep sympathy. And you too, Felix. Dear, dear! To think that the poor young fellow was joking over the tea-table with us yesterday! "

" When was the body found? " asked Blodwen unemotionally.

" This morning. Young Hufton of Upper Ring Farm works on the railway as a plate-layer, and found the poor fellow at the foot of the quarry on his way to work. Quite early, I believe. But of course it took some time to get in touch with the police. . . . A terrible thing. What can the motive have been? "

There was a pause. Felix looked slowly from the doctor to Blodwen, and then from her impassive face back at the doctor again.

"What's that?" he said in a low voice, and then on a sharper note: "Then it wasn't an accident?"

"Haven't they told you?" asked Dr. Browning pitifully. "I'm sorry! No, it wasn't an accident." He hesitated, looking kindly and sadly at the boy's white face. "Nor suicide," he finished quietly.

There was a silence.

"Murder," muttered Felix, gazing stonily before him. He turned almost fiercely the moment after on the doctor. "How can you tell it wasn't suicide?" he cried in a strained, shaking voice.

Dr. Browning made no reply. He gave the slightest shrug to his shoulders and glanced at Christmas.

"Oh, Lord!" cried Felix, as if the full realization of what such a thing would mean had only just come to him. "What a ghastly business! Blodwen!"

He looked wildly at his cousin, then sank into the window-seat and covered his face with his hands. John, who had taken a liking to this sensitive and excitable youth, found himself wondering again why the death of a scarcely-known and unsympathetic cousin should cause this acute distress. Felix was obviously a youth of high-strung sensibilities, but he did not seem to John to be a weak or hysterical character. Patting his shoulder, John knew an almost paternal feeling for his young friend, though he had the advantage of him by certainly not more than five years.

It was not many moments before Felix recovered himself. Raising his white face he looked at his cousin Blodwen, who was regarding him with more surprise than sympathy, with an apologetic smile.

"He—he wasn't really such a bad chap," he said to her, as if in extenuation of his own weakness, and bit his lip and seemed to make a strong effort to regain his poise.

"And now," he went on, turning to Dr. Browning,

" I suppose they're all trying to find out who did it. I suppose we shall have all Scotland Yard down here sooner or later. Is there any clue? "

" Not so far as I know," answered the doctor. " His wrist-watch and gold cigarette-case are untouched, and there's five pounds in his breast-pocket. So robbery wasn't the motive."

" How——? "

" The poor fellow was shot in the head," Dr. Browning replied to the unspoken question. " At the base of the skull, at very close range. And afterwards, apparently, thrown over the quarry edge. He was found lying face downwards upon the stones at the foot. He's "—the doctor hesitated—" dreadfully knocked about, poor chap. The only thing which can be regarded as a clue so far is that his gold signet-ring is missing. I noticed yesterday at tea that he was wearing a large gold ring with a blood-stone seal."

" Yes, I noticed it too. Missing, is it? "

" Yes. Though it's hard to imagine why anybody should take it, and leave the gold cigarette-case, which is certainly more valuable."

" It might have slipped off," said Felix without interest. " Good morning, Superintendent," he added, getting up, John noticed, with a sort of nervous alacrity as that officer entered the room. " This is a horrible affair."

" It is that, sir," agreed the officer gravely. " And a mysterious affair, too, so far as appears at present."

Superintendent Lovell was a thin, hatchet-faced man of fifty, with the sort of quiet, reserved and rather autocratic bearing that inspires confidence. John liked his looks, but thought he would be a man difficult to get on with. There was obstinacy as well as integrity in his long tranquil face, and he had the straight mouth and perfectly level eyebrows that usually imply a lack of the sense of humour.

"I'm afraid I must ask you to come and view the body, sir," added Lovell, "as Mr. Morris Price is away. I'm afraid there's no doubt as to the identity, though."

"None in my mind," murmured Dr. Browning, noticing a gleam of animation appear on Felix's face, as if the policeman's words had inspired him with the hope that the dead man might, after all, prove to be a stranger.

"But we should like you to identify him for certain," finished Superintendent Lovell, and opened the door.

Felix glanced at John as if he would be glad of his support, and John rose and accompanied him to the door.

"I think," said Blodwen Price in her crisp, matter-of-fact voice, "I had better come too."

The four men looked at her in surprise, and Dr. Browning with dismay as well.

"Oh, really, Miss Price," he objected, "there is no need for you to undergo such a horrible experience!" He glanced at the Superintendent for support. He was an old-fashioned man, and while in theory he believed in the equality of the sexes, in practice he was very far from such a standpoint. He was well aware that Blodwen was a stronger, stabler character than Felix; yet her cool proposal to share her cousin's misfortune outraged his deepest feelings. "I don't think you realize," he added earnestly, "what it will be like."

"Yes, I do," said Blodwen simply. "Is there any objection to my seeing my brother, Superintendent?"

"None whatever," answered Lovell with profound indifference, much to Dr. Browning's disgust. "If you can identify him also, so much the better."

"But you can't!" protested Dr. Browning. "Surely, my dear Miss Price, if you haven't seen your brother for fifteen years, it will be quite useless——"

"I shall be able to identify him," said Blodwen placidly.

To John's eye she had the air of keeping well in check a certain impatience with the doctor's well-meant dissuasions.

D

She liked Dr. Browning, that was evident. But she did not feel in any need of his protection.

"I shall know at once whether it is my brother or not," she repeated calmly, "although I haven't seen him for fifteen years. Don't worry, Doctor. You can feel my pulse, if you like, before and after." And she led the way out into the passage.

"This way," said the Superintendent, indicating the back door, and they passed out into the soft, beneficent sunlight of the summer morning, down a narrow, flagged path to a large shed that stood at the end of the small strip of garden. A young constable stood on guard outside the door, and saluted as Superintendent Lovell approached.

"Had any visitors, Davis?"

"No, sir. Only the young 'oman from the inn come down the garden to tell I her've had a matter of half a dozen eggs took from the hen-coops yesterday evening. Seemed to think as I'd ought to leave my post and go off looking for the thief, sir!" A broad grin overspread his good-humoured face. "Her's a caution, her is! 'I've got a theft to report,' her says. Eggs! 'A rat-trap'll catch the thief better nor what I should,' I says to she, and off her goes to the orchard to see whether there's any apples been taken. Her counts they apples every day, I've heard tell."

The loquacious young man gave a guffaw and then, remembering the solemn business he was employed upon, broke it off in the middle and looked unnaturally serious, and then rueful as the Superintendent said with grave reproof:

"That'll do, Davis. That's not the way to make a report."

They passed into the cool, dusty shed, with its earthen floor piled with potatoes, firewood and gardening tools. A mangle stood in one corner, and a bin of chicken-meal in another, and against the farther wall something lay on a long trestle table, covered with a clean, faded bedspread. John Christmas noted that of his three new acquaintances Felix looked by far the most concerned and Blodwen Price the least. Felix's hands were clenched and his lips tightly pressed together, and Dr. Browning's kindly, humorous face wore a distressed, almost fearful look. But Blodwen looked merely pensive. Could a lengthy separation make one so indifferent to one's closest kin? Or was it by some effort of self-control that the sister appeared so unconcerned at the brother's fate?

She did change colour slightly when Superintendent Lovell, with a warning to them to be prepared, drew the cloth gently from the trestle table. The dead man was not a pleasant sight. John, after a moment of quick recoil, thought that if Blodwen had not seen her brother for fifteen years she would be hard put to it to recognize him now, in spite of her confidence. Felix gave a loud gasp, and his long hands went fluttering up to his face as if to shut out the sight from his eyes. But he dropped them again, and schooled himself to stand still at the table side and look down at the still, mutilated figure.

" Yes," he said in a low, forced voice. " It is Charles."

John saw the body of a tall, large-boned man, dressed in a rough tweed suit and cricket shirt, still wet with the heavy dew and streaked with dust and blood. The close-range bullet had terribly disfigured the face, but the round, smooth chin, thick hair and smooth eyebrows proclaimed him a man still on the youthful side of forty. The hands, one of which was bruised and broken at the wrist, were large, rough-skinned and ill-cared-for, but shapely.

There was a silence, during which the shed seemed to be filled with the loud humming of a large bee, which was endeavouring to find a way out through the closed, cobwebby panes of the window.

" Yes," repeated Felix. " It's Charles right enough. I'd hoped——"

He broke off suddenly and turned away.

"Dr. Browning tells me," remarked Lovell, looking quietly down at all that was left of Sir Charles Price, "that a signet-ring is missing. Did you notice a ring on the finger yesterday, Mr. Felix?"

"Yes," answered Felix, watching the exasperated bee with vague, unseeing eyes. "He always wore one on the little finger of his right hand. It may have fallen off."

"Was it loose?" Lovel picked up the limp right hand and casually compared its size with his own.

"I don't know," replied Felix. "I didn't notice that it was. But it may have been."

"Large knuckles," remarked the Superintendent. "It would have to be a very loose ring that would slip off that finger." He turned to John. "You're wearing a ring, sir. Would you lend it me a moment? That is," he added, perceiving something gruesome in his request, "if you don't mind."

John, not quite sure whether he minded or not, obediently slipped off the ring he wore on his little finger and handed it to Lovell. But the demonstration came to nothing. The ring would not go over the joint. Lovell handed it back.

"You can take my word for it, though," he remarked. "A ring that would slip off that finger would have to be so loose its owner would never dream of wearing it there. The ground's been searched both at the top and bottom of the quarry, too. Well, it may turn up. I should be glad if you would look over the contents of the pockets, Mr. Felix, and tell me if anything is missing as far as you know. You'll find them all set out on the bench over there. I've made a list."

While Felix glanced over the array of small objects set out on the dusty bench, Superintendent Lovell read from the paper in his hand.

"A gold cigarette-case, two boxes of matches, a note-case containing five pounds in paper, seven and twopence in loose cash, a silk handkerchief, a bunch of keys, a silver pencil-case, a fountain-pen filled with red ink, a small photograph, a tube of cold cream, a few strands of wool, two cigarette cards and a handkerchief which has been used as a bandage."

Felix looked vaguely at the small collection, which had a look of pathos set out thus neatly and incongruously on the dusty bench.

" I don't know what he had in his pocket," he said. " As far as I know, nothing's missing. I recognize some of the things. The handkerchief, and the cigarette-case, and the photograph. And I remember he had a tube of cold cream, for sunburn. And a fountain-pen with red ink in it. Yes, all those things are Charles's, I think, and I don't remember seeing anything that isn't there now."

" Whose photograph is this? " asked Lovell, pointing to the little browned photo which represented a smiling girl of twenty in a frilled, old-fashioned dress.

" My cousin's," answered Felix, with a glance at Blodwen, in whose eyes for the first time showed a sudden look of horror and regret. She gave one glance at the little photograph and turned aside.

" Did he always write with red ink? " pursued Lovell.

" I don't think so. But his pen ran dry, and we were miles from a shop, and he borrowed some ink from Lion Browning. Lion's black ink was Indian, which would have corroded his pen, so he had red."

Lovell nodded, and went on:

" Do you know what he used the bandage for? "

" He was limping a little the day before yesterday. He'd twisted his ankle. But I didn't know he had it bandaged."

" Limping? " ejaculated Dr. Browning. " Was he? I never noticed that. Nobody told me he'd twisted his ankle. I'd have bound it up for him properly."

ι

"Oh, it wasn't anything much," said Felix listlessly. "He ricked it scrambling on the river-bank that day we all bathed. He said he had a weak ankle and often ricked it a bit, and didn't want to make a fuss about it."

"Which ankle was it?" asked Dr. Browning, drawing down one of the dead man's socks and examining the skin.

"The left," said Felix uncertainly. "No, the right. I can't remember. But it was only a little twist, not anything noticeable, because I looked at it myself when he mentioned it."

"Hullo!" exclaimed Dr. Browning. "What's this?" He pointed to a spot half-way up the front of the shin where a large monogram forming the letters C.P. stood out in dark crimson on the white waxy flesh.

Blodwen glanced at it and observed:

"Yes. He had that done when he was a boy. I was thinking of that when I said I knew I could identify him. An old sailor in Cornwall did it for him on one of our holidays. He was about fifteen at the time. Our father was very angry about it. But tattooing is easier done than undone. I knew I should recognize my brother again."

"There's one thing more," said Superintendent Lovell, who had been listening intently to this explanation. "Where is Sir Charles's luggage?"

"Luggage?" echoed Felix. "His pyjamas and toothbrush, do you mean? Oh, I've got them. I carried the haversack, because I'd got a carrier on my bicycle and Charles hadn't. His was a hired bicycle and a rotten one."

"Did he have an overcoat of any kind?"

"A rain-coat, yes. I haven't got that. He usually slung it over his handle-bars."

"Well, it's missing," said Lovell briefly, jotting a note down in the book he was carrying. "Now, about this bicycle, Mr. Felix. You say it had no carrier?"

"No. It had no pump, no carrier and no mending-outfit."

Superintendent Lovell looked at him intently, and then meditatively at the far corner of the shed. John Christmas saw an old, rather shabby bicycle, much crumpled and battered, lying upon a sack. A green enamelled pump was lying by its side. They all looked at it and there was a brief pause.

"That's not Charles's bicycle!" said Felix at length decidedly. "Or—wait a minute! Yes, he borrowed Lion's pump just before we saw the last of him. But Lion's pump wasn't a green one!" He approached the bicycle and stooped over it. "And this bicycle *has* a carrier! No, Superintendent, that's not the bicycle Charles was riding. This is a Rover. His was an old Humber."

He straightened himself, quite flushed with the excitement of his discovery.

"This is very interesting," observed Lovell in his quiet, unemotional voice. "I suppose you don't recognize this bicycle, sir, as anybody else's?"

"No," answered Felix regretfully. "I wish I did. For surely it must be a very important clue. It must mean—why, surely it must mean that the murderer was also riding a bicycle, and pushed his own bicycle over the quarry in mistake for Charles's! And that must mean that Charles's own bicycle is still about somewhere! Why, if we can trace it, and trace the owner of this machine, we shall have the murderer!"

He spoke freely and excitedly. John, watching him, noted that with this discovery his concern over his cousin's death seemed to have completely dropped from him. He was like a man suddenly relieved from a heavy load of care. Queer, thought John, and stored the impression in his mind for future use.

Lovell smiled grimly.

" Not quite so fast, sir. What you say's possible, but by no means certain. Murderers do make extraordinary mistakes, and of course once he'd pushed the wrong machine over it would be impossible to get it up again. But on the other hand, the mistake may have been Sir Charles's. He may have walked off with somebody else's bicycle when he left the inn. Anyhow, our first business is obviously to trace the owner of this machine. That green pump on a black machine ought to make it fairly easy. I beg your pardon, Miss Price? "

Blodwen had uttered a small sound, as if about to speak. She was looking thoughtfully at the battered machine and seemed to hesitate.

" I seem to think I've seen a green pump on a black bicycle somewhere," she murmured. " Now where? Whose? I think——"

There was a silence, while they all waited expectantly. Suddenly she drew in her breath with a tiny, sharp hiss.

" No," she said slowly. " I don't think I have seen it before. I was mistaken."

Lovell looked at her keenly, and seemed about to protest, but decided to let the matter pass. Blodwen returned his glance calmly, then turned indifferently aside, as if the matter had lost interest for her. John could have sworn that in that silence, when she gave that little start, she had remembered.

" This looks interesting," he said to himself. " More and more interesting. Rampson, my friend, we are not going back to London just yet awhile."

Lovell shut his notebook with a snap and led the way out of the gloomy shed, carefully closing and barring the door.

" You will let me know as soon as Mr. Morris returns, won't you, Miss Price? " he asked courteously. " We can't fix a day for the inquest until we hear from him.

He was apparently one of the last people to speak to Sir Charles."

The anxious-faced daughter of the Tram's proprietor was waiting for them in the garden, idly poking with a stick at a small smouldering bonfire. She intercepted the Superintendent as he went down the path.

"Oh, Mr. Lovell, there's been somebody at my eggs! Seven eggs I've had took from the hen-house in the orchard. I don't know how they gets in there, I don't! I thought as there was somebody in the backyard yester-day evening as didn't ought to be there! But I went and looked over the orchard gate and nobody did I see! You'll bear me out, Mr. Felix, sir, for if you'll remember the eggs was all hard-boiled at tea, owing to me thinking as I saw somebody! And I thought I'd report the theft to you while you was here, Mr. Lovell, for robbery is robbery, if it is only eggs, and we all has to live, and the robber did ought to be stopped, and——"

There was a suppressed snigger in the background, and turning John saw the young constable on guard looking portentously solemn.

Lovell allowed a faint smile to disturb the wintry severity of his features, but answered politely:

"You shall tell me about it afterwards, Miss Watt. I'm busy now." He went on towards the inn, followed by Blodwen and the doctor.

The girl turned her worried face towards John, and encouraged by his sympathetic look, said in an injured voice:

"Well, I know as a murder has to take precedence, as they say, sir, but still it is a bit hard on poor folks to keep losing their goods this way! Them fowls don't hardly lay up to what they eats, at the best!"

"Don't you shut your chicken-house at night?"

"Why, surely, sir! These eggs was took yesterday evening, while I was busy about the house! And there's

been apples took too!   One of the boughs is broke
through being dragged down rough.   And if the police
isn't here to catch robbers, sir, what is they here for?
It's a bit hard on poor folks——"

Perceiving that nothing but his departure would stem
the flood of the young woman's eloquence, John looked
around for Felix.   He had taken a paper from his pocket
and was folding it into a spill.

" I've got a match," said John.

" It's all right," said Felix, and lit his spill where small
flames flickered round some straw at the side of the slow-
burning heap.   The paper did not catch well, and he had
to stoop to the flame again before he could light his
cigarette.   Then he thrust the spill in among the twigs
and smouldering grasses and sauntered after John towards
the inn.

John looked back to see whether Miss Watt had transferred her complaints to the young constable, but she had
evidently given him up as hopeless.   She was going with
a dejected air towards the orchard, to count her apples
again.

" I say," said John thoughtfully, as he and Felix
drove at high speed back to Penlow, keeping in sight
of Blodwen's small blue car, " what was that paper you
put on the bonfire, Felix? "

Felix, who was in the act of lighting a fresh cigarette
with a match he had taken from his pocket, turned quickly
and stared at John.

" What? " he jerked out.   " Why?   What, the spill
I lighted my cigarette from, do you mean?   Why, just
a paper I found in my pocket!   Why?   Why do you
ask? "

" Nothing private, I hope."

There was a pause.

" N—no," faltered Felix, and added after a moment:
" Why? "

Foreshadowing

"Because," said John, looking fixedly at Blodwen's little cloud of dust fifty yards ahead of them, "when I looked back the young policeman on guard had just retrieved it from the bonfire. Like his impudence, of course. But in a case of this sort a young policeman hoping for promotion sees clues everywhere. Of course if it was only a bill or something, it won't matter. But one doesn't want one's private letters read, even by worthy young constables. Does one?"

"Oh, it doesn't matter!" replied Felix with an unnatural jauntiness of tone, and a slight shake in his voice. The ingenuous young man was obviously not a good liar. After a moment he added: "Wasn't it burnt, then?"

"There was a good deal of it left," said John. "A smouldering bonfire can't be depended on, you know."

"Oh, well, it doesn't matter," said Felix again, even more jauntily than before.

"Give me a light, would you?" asked John, whose cigarette had gone out.

Striking a match, Felix seemed to realize that some further explanation was necessary.

"You see," he said carefully, "I couldn't find the matches in my pocket, so I took the first piece of paper that came to hand. I had some matches all the time— here they are—but I couldn't find them at the moment."

"*I* see," said John soothingly, as to a child's laborious explanation, and to himself: "This gets more and more interesting. Felix, you are a babe. Miss Blodwen, you are a sphinx. But surely, surely neither of you is a murderer!"

CHAPTER FIVE

R HYLLAN HALL, with its air of withdrawn and dignified antiquity, proved to have all the beauty that the guide-books claimed for it. Cloistered behind its high brick wall and the great trees of its little park, it presented to the drive a long, three-storied frontage of warm red brick with the tall, gracious, many-paned windows of great Anna's spacious days, and a beautiful stone porch opening on to a low flagged terrace. Below the terrace lay the formal Dutch garden created at the whim of some eighteenth-century owner, and beyond that the peaceful small park.

John Christmas and Rampson sat over coffee with Felix and Miss Price in one of the rooms looking over the terrace. It was a small room at one end of the building, and had probably been designed as a boudoir or writing-room. The painted panelled walls with their look of discoloured ivory and the long, faded curtains of fringed damask looked as if they had stayed untouched since first the room was decorated. Miss Price, sitting on the low seat in one of the deep window-embrasures, with her cropped dark head leaning back against the folded shutter, blowing rings of cigarette smoke into the rose-coloured folds of the curtains, seemed an anachronism. A silence had fallen upon the little party. Felix, supported by Miss Price, had begged John to keep his promise and come to

60

Rhyllan, in spite of the altered circumstances. He had been so earnest that he had soon overborne John's refusal.

Lunch, in spite of Miss Blodwen's conversational gifts and the tacit determination of everybody not to discuss the murder, had been rather a dismal meal. Felix had been absent-minded and practically silent; he had the strained, unhappy air of a man listening with all his ears for some long anticipated sound. But no car purred up the drive, and the garage, except for Blodwen's little Morris-Oxford, stood empty. Rampson, who never spoke when he had nothing to say, ate with enjoyment and said nothing. John and Blodwen had the conversation to themselves. They talked of Bordighera, from which delightful town Blodwen had returned two days earlier, of Italy generally, of motoring, of architecture, and of Rhyllan Hall. Her home, it soon appeared, was Miss Price's chief passion. She loved it with that intimate, personal love which people deficient in human emotion often bestow upon bricks and mortar.

The silence which had fallen upon them with the coffee and cigarettes was broken by Miss Price. Watching a blue ring dissolve against the window, she asked in a meditative voice:

" Felix, what did you think of my brother? "

It was the first time Charles had been mentioned since they left the Tram Inn. Felix shot a quick glance at her, then frowned at his plate, carefully flicking against its edge a minute portion of ash from his cigarette. He replied:

" I don't know, Blodwen. He wasn't bad."

She looked long and keenly at him.

" I see," she said softly. " *De mortuis* and the conventions."

Felix stirred restlessly in his chair.

" He couldn't help it."

" Oh, none of us can help being ourselves! " agreed

Blodwen softly. " I know what he was like. You needn't tell me, if it hurts you. I heard from Uncle Morris and Mr. Clino."

" What did they tell you? " asked Felix.

" Very little. But quite enough."

There was a pause.

" Where is old Clino? " asked Felix listlessly, looking vaguely about, as if he had just missed him.

" He wouldn't come down to lunch. He's taken this affair rather badly. I thought he was going to faint when the telephone call came this morning. You know what a nervous old creature he is." She added with a cold meditativeness that John, not a squeamish person, found a little horrible : " He ought to be glad. Charles meant to turn him out."

Once again Felix stirred restlessly, as if he found her plain speaking not to his taste, and glanced at John.

" Mr. Clino," explained Blodwen to her visitors, " is a distant cousin of ours. He was my father's secretary and librarian—more or less a sinecure, of course. And I know it was my father's wish that he should be allowed to end his days at Rhyllan Hall. He's sixty-seven, too old to start again, and practically destitute. Charles, however, did not intend to respect our father's wish."

Once again at the mention of her dead brother her voice became hard and cold. Once again John had a sensation of being chilled and repelled. No one admired more than he a clear and truthful mind. But he was sufficently conventional to feel that this was not the time for an analysis of poor Charles's faults. Silence fell once more. At last Felix jumped up, as if seeking in movement some relief from an inner tension.

" Care to have a look round the place? " he asked, and hardly waiting for John to express his pleasure, led the way out through the hall on to the flagged terrace with its border of late summer flowers. A lad who was trimming the low box-hedge round the Dutch garden looked up and touched his cap as they passed. Felix greeted him as an old friend.

" Hullo, David. Letbe anywhere about? "

The boy went red, hesitated, and answered sheepishly :

" He've gone, master. He've bin gone a week."

Felix bit his lip.

" Oh, yes," John heard him mutter. " I remember."

" Sacked," said Blodwen briefly. She and Rampson had caught up with them and overheard this little conversation. " By the new master. After thirty years' service. Reason not stated. So I understand."

" There must have *been* a reason," said Felix moodily, as if he felt it his duty to defend the dead man, and they passed on round the corner of the house. Here the terrace widened and a flight of steps led down from it to a wide green lawn, with a glowing herbaceous border at the end of it. There were long French windows here, opening on to the flags, and one of them stood wide to the westering sun.

" This is the library," said Felix, with his hand on the open window, and suddenly paused, transfixed, looking in. The look of incredulity on his face faded into relief and pleasure. " Hullo, Dad! Nobody told us you were back! "

A very tall man in rough light tweeds rose from a great mahogany desk in the middle of the room and approached the window, blinking in a dazzled way at the bright sun and the four people on the terrace. John saw a man of about sixty, of magnificent height and physique, burly and upright, with a broad-jawed, aquiline face, iron-grey hair and a heavy grey moustache. By the side of his father the slim Felix became insignificant. Yet the resemblance between them was strong. They were of the same Gaelic type, high-coloured, dark-eyed, hook-nosed. Both, Christmas judged, impulsive, irritable and capable of behaving

with the utmost unreason. The elder Price frowned as
the sun struck him in the eyes, and looked an extremely
formidable figure. He came out on to the terrace and
responded to his son's introductions with a pleasant but,
John thought, rather forced smile.

" Thinks this isn't exactly the day for a luncheon-
party," was John's mental comment. " And no wonder.
Well, now he's relieved his son's anxiety by reappearing,
I suppose my moral support is no longer required."

But, glancing at Felix, he was not so sure of this.
Morris Price was greeting Rampson with a few temper-
ately hospitable words, and Felix was watching him with
a close and painful attention, as if disturbed or disappointed by something in his father's appearance.
Certainly the elder man did not look well. His sunburn and high reddish colour had a sickly look mottled
over the yellowish skin, and the pouches beneath his dark,
rather fierce-looking eyes told of sleeplessness or ill-health
or both.

" Been back long, Dad? " asked Felix with a pretence
at casualness.

" An hour or more," replied his father. " I heard you
were at lunch, and as I was badly in need of a bath and
change I didn't disturb you. I left the car down in the
village—slight engine trouble—and walked up."

" Well, Uncle Morris," observed Blodwen, sitting down
in one of the wicker chairs and selecting a cigarette from
her case, " you've caused your devoted niece a sleepless
night."

" Why? " asked the big man brusquely, sitting down
beside her and refusing the cigarette she offered him.

" Oh, mystery of missing uncle, and all that," said
Blodwen lightly. " I expected you back last night."

" I did intend to come back when I'd finished my
business in Hereford. But it was such a lovely night I
thought I'd like to take a run on the Forest. I had one

or two things to think about, and I thought the air up there might clear my brain. And—well, to tell the truth, I stayed there all night, thinking what asses we are to waste every beautiful night asleep. The moonlight was wonderful."

He seemed aware that his proceedings had been rather unusual, for he spoke in a deprecating tone, and glanced at Felix as if expecting to be laughed at. But Felix did not laugh. There was a silence, while the five of them sat and looked across the smooth lawn and listened to the humming of bees among the flowers and the distant whir of a mowing-machine, all their minds, John thought, occupied with the same unspoken theme. At last Morris spoke it.

"I must borrow your car, Blodwen, and go down to the police station. I didn't hear of—Charles's death until about an hour ago, in the village."

"Lovell said he was coming up here this afternoon," said Blodwen, "so you needn't go down. He may be here any minute."

There was a pause.

"I saw him last night, you know," said Morris, idly twisting a piece of bass in his large strong hands and frowning down on it. "Charles, I mean. Walked with him as far as the quarry."

His dead nephew's name seemed to be distasteful or embarrassing to him, for each time he spoke it with a slight pause and jerk, as if forcing his lips to utter it. Like his niece, he uttered no formal expressions of sorrow or surprise.

Poor Charles, thought John to himself, seems to have gone his way unwept, unhonoured and unsung, by his own family, anyhow. He looked at the three Prices, with their odd likeness to one another, their hard-cut aquiline faces, close-set lips and bright, fearless eyes, and felt suddenly sorry for the dead Charles. An

E

intolerant lot, they looked, capable of making the life of an interloper anything but a happy one. And now not one of them would commit the ordinary decent folly of pretending to be sorry the interloper was dead. For Felix's distress was occasioned by something other than sorrow, John was prepared to swear.

Mr. Price seemed to become suddenly aware of his duties as a host, and abandoned the subject of his nephew's death as though it were of small importance.

" Are you staying in this neighbourhood? "

" At the Feathers in Penlow, at present. But not for long. We're touring with a car and move on as the spirit moves us. We may go towards Radnor to-morrow."

Felix looked quickly at John, and opened his lips as if to speak, but decided to say nothing.

" Or towards London," murmured Rampson hopefully.

John laughed.

" My cousin is one of those unfortunate beings who are never really happy on holiday," explained John. " He seems to regard time spent away from work as wasted. Very curious and very rare."

Mr. Price smiled his agreeable, rather formal smile.

" There's nothing like work," he said, " to give one permanent satisfaction. It's the only thing worth while. And life's so short."

His deepset eyes roved over the prospect in front of them, the lawn, the park, the great well-grown trees. And it was plain to see where his work lay, and that his heart lay with it. Evidently he shared Blodwen's love and reverence for his family's old home. And quite suddenly, as though something in the elderly man's proprietary look had raised the question, John wondered who inherited Rhyllan Hall. The answer, with the question, seemed to lie in Morris's fond, arrogant gaze: Morris, and after him Felix. The interloper had been providentially removed. A queer little shiver passed over

John, in spite of the warmth of the August sun, and it was with a faint unreasonable foreboding that he heard heavy steps on the terrace round the corner of the house.

The sad-faced Superintendent Lovell appeared, followed by a younger man in plain clothes. He greeted Morris Price with quiet deference.

" I'm glad you're back, sir. Could I have a few words with you about this terrible affair? "

" Certainly, Superintendent."

The big man rose and without further words led the two police officers through the French windows into the library. Felix half rose, with an anxious look, as if to accompany them, but receiving no invitation to do so fell back into his chair. There was a silence.

" Felix," said Blodwen slowly at last, " did you recognize that green bicycle pump this morning at the Tram? "

" No."

" I did." She paused, looked at Christmas and Rampson as if wondering whether or not to take them into her confidence. Then, impulsively : " It was poor old Letbe's."

" Letbe ! " Felix turned, startled, and stared at her. " No ! Are you sure? "

" Quite. I wasn't going to give him away to Lovell, but of course they'll be on his track in no time, without my help. Lots of people must have noticed he carried a green pump on his bicycle." Her fine grey eyes sought John's. " Mr. Christmas, you told me that you were specially interested in these sort of cases, and so I'm taking you into my confidence. You don't mind, do you? We're so isolated here, we see so few people. It'll be a help to be able to talk matters over with someone outside the family. For though "—her clear voice sank lower and slower—" though, as I suppose you've noticed, none of us is broken-hearted by my brother's death, still it is a terrible thing to have happened. We shan't be able to think of much else for a while, I'm afraid."

Felix cut through John's expressions of willingness to give every possible help.

" But, good lord! Does that mean that Letbe——? "

" Sh! " said Blodwen, and then, with a wry smile: " Oh, dear! I've read detective novels and laughed at them. And now I feel as if there were an army of detectives lurking round the corner of the house! " Meeting John's observant eyes, she said gravely, in a lower tone: " Do you think me heartless, Mr. Christmas? Remember that I haven't seen my brother for fifteen years, and that he went to Canada because—well, frankly, because we couldn't endure him at home." She added still lower: " He shot my dog Pelleas while I was away. They told me he laughed when he came upon the poor thing wounded and dying."

" Letbe! " repeated Felix again. " But, I say, Blodwen, how awful! "

John noted, however, that the young man looked more relieved than shocked.

" Letbe," explained Blodwen, leaning across her cousin and talking to John, " is our old head gardener. He'd been here nearly thirty years, longer than we have. He was here in my great-uncle Almeric's time. Well, my brother sent him away about a week ago." A flush rose suddenly in her thin cheeks. " It was—a horrible thing to do! He was the best man we had! His heart was in the place! "

" What was the reason, I wonder? "

" Uncle Morris said he wouldn't give a reason, beyond saying that the old man was too big for his boots, as he put it. But Mrs. Maur—that's the housekeeper—tells me that—that the trouble had something to do with Letbe's daughter, who was housemaid here. Oh, it's horrible! Charles kissed her, or something, and Letbe made her give notice. I suppose," she spoke through clenched teeth, " it'll all come out at the inquest. Delightful it'll be! "

" But do you mean to say," Felix spoke in a hushed voice, " that they think Letbe did it? "

" My dear Felix, how can I possibly tell what they think? I only say, it was Letbe's pump——"

She broke off as the voice of Morris Price, raised in loud, arrogant tones, became audible through the closed French windows.

" I see no reason why I should enter into details, Superintendent! It was on private business that I went into Hereford, and business that has absolutely no connection with your case! "

The murmur of Superintendent Lovell's dry, melancholy voice followed.

Blodwen looked startled for a moment at her uncle's loud, angry tone, then said with a half-smile :

" What a shocking witness Uncle Morris would make in a law case! I can just hear him saying to counsel, or even to the judge : ' Sir, I decline to answer your impertinent questions! ' "

Felix stirred and glanced uneasily at his cousin.

" He does hate being interfered with or questioned," went on Blodwen with a sort of amused affection in her voice, " and never sees any reason why he should explain himself even to his family——"

She broke off as footsteps sounded once more on the terrace and the voice of Mr. Price could be heard saying stiffly :

" I wish you good afternoon! "

The next moment he came round the corner of the house, frowning.

" Confound these policemen! " he said, taking the chair next to John and offering him a cigarette. " They seem to think the fact that they're investigating a case gives them the right to ask all sorts of questions that have no bearing on the matter at all! "

" Ah! " said Blodwen lightly. " In all the detective stories I've read it's been the thing that has no bearing that turns out to be the important clue! "

" I suppose," said Rampson in his deep, tranquil voice, " that until they know the answer to a question they don't know whether it has a bearing or not."

Mr. Price turned on him as if about to damn his impertinence, but recollecting himself, replied merely :

" Oh, possibly! " and went on : " It seems they found poor old Letbe's bicycle smashed up in the quarry. And they found Charles's bicycle at Letbe's cottage."

" I was afraid so," said Blodwen gravely, and Felix asked impulsively :

" Then do they think——? "

" Oh, Lord knows what they think! " exclaimed his father brusquely. " They're ' investigating the matter.' Letbe's story is that when he came out of the inn last night he found his bicycle gone, and as there was another bicycle standing about unclaimed he went home on that, thinking somebody had taken his by mistake. I expect the old idiot's been threatening blue murder in all the pubs in the district ever since he was turned off. Unless he's got proof of his story things will go badly with him, no doubt."

" Are there any other clues? " asked John.

" Apparently not. Unless you call it a clue that a ring seems to be missing. A signet-ring with a bloodstone in it. The police seem to make a lot of that. Lovell wanted to know if there was any history attached to the ring, anything that might make it interesting apart from its intrinsic value, which evidently isn't much. Charles always wore a bloodstone ring, that's all I could tell him; he was wearing it when he first arrived. But I can't imagine that anybody'd commit murder for the sake of a bloodstone ring. It's probably lying among the grass and stuff in the quarry."

"Possibly," agreed John. "Although, of course, there's always the possibility that the ring, valueless in itself, had some intrinsic value for the dead man and for another person. One's heard of such cases. There's always the possibility, also, that the ring, being loose, slipped off during a struggle into one of the murderer's pockets. In either case I'm afraid it's gone for good. The murderer would be very careful that it never came to light again. May I ask if the date is fixed for the inquest? "

"The day after to-morrow at the Tram Inn, at ten o'clock. And a beastly business it'll be," said the elder man irritably. "I'm one of the principal witnesses, I understand. Apparently I was the last person—last person but one, that is—to see my nephew alive. What made all the rest of you go off like that and leave Charles behind, by the way? "

"He stopped to pump up a tyre, that was all," said Felix. "And we never saw him again. We waited a long time at the foot of Rodland Hill——"

"Rodland Hill? " Morris turned a sharp eye on his son. "Charles gave me to understand you'd gone over the common on to the Wensley Road."

"Did he? But no, of course not! We went straight on down the hill! Did he say we'd gone over the common? "

"Yes," replied Morris. "At least, I think he said so. That was what I understood, anyway. I met him not far from the Tram, and stopped the car to ask whether the rest of you were about. He said you'd gone on, and he'd stopped for a drink and was just following you. I suggested walking a few yards with him, as I'd got something to say to him. And we went across the common. I thought the rest of you had gone that way." He paused a moment, looking thoughtfully at his son. " Well, that's damned odd. I thought Lovell looked queerly at me when I said we'd followed you across the common. He might have had the good manners to tell me I˙was mistaken. But these damned policemen love secrecy."

Blodwen laughed.

" Perhaps he felt it would be as much as his life was worth to tell you you'd made a mistake, Uncle Morris. You're rather alarming, you know, when people start asking you questions. Hullo, Cousin Jim! Uncle Morris has returned, you see! "

She spoke to an elderly man who now appeared walking along the terrace in a rather diffident and hesitating way, with a book under his arm. A tall, slight man of between sixty and seventy, with a rather weak but handsome face and very thick grey hair parted at the side and worn rather long.

" This is Mr. Clino—Mr. Christmas. We were sorry not to see you at lunch, Cousin Jim."

Cousin Jim smiled a friendly but rather absent-minded smile, and stood looking vaguely at an empty chair as if undetermined whether to occupy it or not. He did not look like a poor relation. In fact, there was something slightly dandified about his excellent blue suit and broad black cravat and the eyeglasses that hung from a broad ribbon round his neck. His hands, with which he fidgeted nervously, were beautifully white and slender. After an exchange of greetings, he did not speak. He looked absent-minded, shy, listless, but not in the least humble or self-effacing.

" Sit down, Clino," said Morris, pushing forward a chair. " The inquest's to be the day after to-morrow, at the Tram."

" Oh, dear! Shall we all have to go? " asked Mr. Clino pensively.

" Of course."

" Oh, dear! " said Mr. Clino again. He looked away across the grass and wall-flowers, and added simply: " Poor Charles! Poor boy! "

The simple humanity of these words, uttered at Rhyllan Hall for the first time since Charles's death, touched John queerly. So the Hall contained one foolish simple heart which could forget injuries in the presence of death.

" Do sit down, Clino," repeated Morris after a pause.

But Mr. Clino, with a vague murmured remark about having something to see to somewhere, took his departure, walking away along the terrace as slowly as he had come. Morris looked after him with a half-impatient, half-affectionate smile.

" ' Shall we all have to go? ' " he echoed ironically. " Who would think that poor old Clino was trained as a solicitor? And still regards himself as a lawyer, I believe, in his inmost heart, though he hasn't been in practice for twenty years, and never had enough clients to pay for the rent of his offices. A lot of lawyering he'd have been able to do if Charles had lived to turn him out, as he intended to! I hope," he added, as Christmas rose to take his leave, " that we shall see you again. You're not going on straight away, are you? "

" Probably not for a day or two," replied John, oblivious of Rampson's look of silent protest. " We shall be at the Feathers for a couple of days anyhow, and if there is ever anything we can do for you you have only to let us know."

Felix and Morris Price walked with their guests to the car. Morris and Rampson strode ahead, and Felix, walking behind with John, slackened his pace slightly as if he wished to speak on some private matter. But he only asked at last in a diffident, hesitating way:

" Shall you go to the inquest? "

" Yes. I'm interested in the case."

" Then we shall see you again," said Felix, looking rather relieved. " You've been very kind—turning out

last night on my account, and everything.   A happening
like this makes one feel so—so topsy-turvy.   And we're
rather lonely here.   It's a great help to feel that one has
somebody to go to for advice—if one should want it.   I
hope everything'll turn out all right—I mean, I do hope
they won't be able to fix anything on poor old Letbe, or—
or anyone one knows.   One knows everybody round about
here, that's what makes it so dreadful.   I should think
it was just a passing tramp, wouldn't you? "

" Not very likely," said John gently.   " Practically
nothing was stolen, you see.   And tramps don't as a rule
carry revolvers."

" No," agreed Felix rather gloomily.

As John started his car, he heard the elder Price speak
to a young man in shirt-sleeves who was crossing the drive.

" Will you go down to the village, Halfnights, and
fetch the Daimler from Lloyd's?   It'll be ready by the
time you get there."

" Yes, Sir Morris," replied the young man promptly
and with an indescribable note of satisfaction in his voice.

" Hear that, Sydenham? " asked John as they purred
down the drive. " The king is dead, long live the king,
with a vengeance.   I wondered who would be the heir
to this delightful little kingdom.   Sydenham, what strikes
you most about the death of Sir Charles Price? "

" What strikes me most," responded Rampson sadly,
" is that you're a great deal too much interested in it,
John.   I see we shan't get back to London for weeks.
Apart from that, the thing that strikes me most is that all
the unfortunate Charles's relations regard his death as a
nuisance rather than as a tragedy.   They don't want all
this publicity.   They hope it wasn't the discharged
gardener who did it, because they like him.   But they're
all jolly glad Charles is dead."

John nodded.

" Not only his relations, Sydenham.   His dependents,

too. That young chauffeur, for instance. He said ' Sir Morris ' in a voice like a cheer. I'm afraid Charles can't have been a very endearing character. What do you think of Felix? "

" Rather intense. Not my style. But a nice chap."

" Just so. But at the moment he has cause to be intense, my dear Sydenham. Unless I'm very much mistaken, he's mortally afraid his father is a murderer."

" You don't say so! " exclaimed Rampson, and seemed to consider this notion for a while in silence, as they hummed along the peaceful road towards Penlow. " Well," he remarked judicially at length, " now you come to mention it, I shouldn't be at all surprised if he's right. I shouldn't care to get on the wrong side of Morris Price."

" Quite," said John rather absently, slowing down to allow a flock of sheep to pass. " And he's rude to the police. And he has a rooted objection to answering questions. If he doesn't look out, he'll find himself in trouble. But he's a fine figure of a man."

CHAPTER SIX

THE SCENE OF THE CRIME

" I WONDER," said John, pulling up at the foot of Rodland Hill, " whether there's a way across to the foot of the quarry here. This gate must lead somewhere, I should think. Let's go across and see."

He ran his car on to the wide, grassy stretch at the side of the road, much to the surprise of a goat tethered in the hedge, and got out. Rampson followed, remarking that in his opinion the top of the quarry would be a better place to look for clues.

" Clues! " echoed John. " Not much hope of finding any clues lying about now, I'm afraid. The police'll have combed every blade of grass out by now."

" Then why need we bother? "

" Because I want to get acquainted with the scene of the crime. And because it's a lovely day for a walk. Don't be lazy, Sydenham."

" It's all very well," complained that gentleman, " but the part of Watson doesn't suit me. I'm not in the least interested in crime. It's a very crude and silly kind of human activity. And I can't admire your cold and logical intellect, because I don't think you've got one. So you see you'd much better leave me at home on these occasions."

" But I like your company," replied John placidly.

" I don't require admiration. A little cold-water throwing now and then is much more stimulating. That's a nice old slated cottage, and a garden full of asters, too. I love asters, don't you? "

" No," said Rampson with simple finality, and followed his friend across the field, where great-horned red cattle lifted their heads and stared, and rabbits in the distance showed a flash of white scuts and vanished.

Passing through a small coppice, they came out upon a rutty track which led to a small farmhouse huddled down among stacks and sheds. A thin, wild collie-dog rushed out, vociferously barking, as they approached, and a rather slatternly looking woman standing in the narrow doorway watched them sombrely. The track skirted the buildings, but it seemed scarcely polite to pass on without a greeting to the owner of the property.

" Good morning," said John, shouting above the volley of barks. " Can you tell me where this track leads to? "

" Quiet, Rover! It goes through Lower Quarry Field to the level crossing." The collie slunk into the house, and heavenly peace descended on the yard. " Was you thinking of seeing where the murder was done, sir? It's straight along the track. There's been two-three people come along already this morning." She paused, a thin, black-eyed woman with floury hair and a sharp-nosed, weary face, and then, with the hesitation of the Welsh borderer, who does not readily part with information, added : " This is Upper Ring Farm."

" Upper Ring Farm? " repeated John. The name sounded familiar. " Oh, yes! Then——"

" It was our lodger found the body," said the woman with a sort of mournful pride, as though she wished to assert her claim to the celebrity without boasting. " Yesterday morning. Going to work, he was, when he seed a man lying on the stones."

"Dreadful experience for him," murmured John sympathetically, as she paused for comment. She looked at him with lack-lustre eyes.

"Ah!" she assented unemotionally. "He didn't think nothing of it at first, his uncle being an undertaker and used to dead folks. But he felt terrible queer when he turned him over. He'd fell on his face on them rocks, you see. Terrible queer young Hufton come over. But he ate his breakfast." She added meditatively: "Very hearty he ate his breakfast."

It was plain that in some dim way she felt that young Hufton had shown a lack of dramatic instinct in heartily eating his breakfast. She shook her head, and as the howling of an infant arose within the cottage, turned back into its smoky, warm recesses. John and Rampson went on down the track, with the slope of Rodland Hill on their left hand and the low wooded country stretching away to far blue hills on their right. A tumbledown shed and some truck-lines red with rust showed that they were approaching the quarry, and rounding a corner they came in full view of the high grey face of rock like a scar in the green hillside. Four or five sightseers were standing about on the track, and one of them watched John's approach intently.

"Hullo!" A schoolboy with bleached, ruffled hair and a pleasantly freckled face greeted John with a smile of recognition. "It's the motorists! So it was *au revoir* after all! Isabel, it's the motorists we met on Rodland Hill."

His companion, a slender girl in a blue cotton frock, smiled a self-possessed greeting.

"Good morning. Have you come to see the sights? There aren't any, I'm glad to say. Lion would drag me here. He's a horrid little ghoul."

"I like that!" protested the boy indignantly. "Upon my soul, I like that!" He seemed about to enter on a lengthy refutation of this remark, but John broke in to introduce himself and Rampson.

" I'm afraid this is a sad end to your cycling tour. You all looked such a jolly party on Rodland Hill the other day I quite wished I could join you.   It's a horrible thing to have happened."

" Beastly," said Isabel composedly.   " Though of course none of us knew Charles well.   He was quite a stranger.   Still, for three days he was one of us.   I don't feel I ever want to go on a cycling tour again."

" Rats! " said Lion heartlessly.   " I say, Mr. Christmas, have you heard that Charles's bicycle is missing?   It was the wrong one they found.   Charles had my pump on his bicycle.   I should know it again anywhere.   That ought to be a clue, don't you think? "

John smiled a little at the boy's enthusiastic tone, but Isabel, with a sudden little shiver, said distastefully :

" Oh, it's horrible!   Come on, Lion!   Let's go home."

Lion, however, was so obviously disposed to stay and attach himself to John and Rampson that she relented and sitting on a great boulder a short distance from the quarry, began to draw in a little sketch-book.

The rugged face of the rock rose some hundred feet above the tumbled litter of fallen boulders that lay about its base.   Its weathered and mellow look and the bracken and sprawling blackberry bushes that grew among the boulders showed that the quarry had long been disused. But for the rusty lines that ran past it to the railway, this sudden hollowing of the hillside seemed the work of nature rather than of man.

" Fancy falling over there," said Lion, voicing the common thought.   " Beastly.   Awfully easy, too.   The grass is awfully slippery up above and the edge part slopes down."

" How do you know? "

" Went there the other evening, while the rest of them

were at tea in the Tram. I wanted to put the quarry on my map, as the inn was called after it, and of course I couldn't put it on the map without seeing it. It wouldn't have been fair."

" Oh, that map! " exclaimed Isabel Donne, turning at these words with the ghost of a laugh. " Don't let the child start talking about his map, Mr. Christmas, or you'll never have any peace."

Lion looked a little hurt.

" I don't talk about my map to people who aren't interested in maps," he said with dignity. " I was just explaining why I went to the quarry, Isabel, not talking about my map at all. I don't know why it is," he added detachedly, " but girls always love to call one a child if one happens to be a year or two younger than themselves. They think it annoys one. But of course it doesn't."

" Of course not," agreed John, suppressing a smile. " And as it happens, I am interested in maps. What kind of a map is this? "

Lion looked at him a trifle doubtfully, as if suspecting his good faith. He had evidently had to endure a good deal of teasing on account of his hobby. But he replied amiably :

" Well, it's a map of our tour, that's all, that I made myself. I put in everything that happened, with drawings and things, in coloured inks." He added in a louder tone, looking inimically at Miss Donne's drooped red-gold head : " I put in things like Isabel falling off her bicycle in the middle of Hereford High Street, and Isabel running away from two cows because they looked at her, and things like that."

Miss Donne raised her head from her drawing, put out the tip of a delicate tongue, and resumed her sketching. Mollified, Lion admitted with a grin :

" I made that up, that about the cows. Isabel isn't

really frightened of cows. She isn't frightened of anything."

"I'm frightened of you, young Lion."

"Rot," said Lion briefly. "Pax. Well, now, Mr. Christmas, do you see any reason why I shouldn't put in my map that Charles got killed? Nora says it's a disgusting idea, and I'm not to. But if my map's a proper map of the tour, I must put it in because it happened at the end of the tour. And after all it's no use pretending he didn't get killed, because he did."

John smiled at the boy's earnestness, and the spectacle he made of the artist confronted with a problem as old as art.

"Well," he temporized, endeavouring to be tactful, "I should leave it for a bit until——"

"Until they've caught the murderer?"

"Yes, and until people have got more used to the poor chap's death and more or less forgotten it. Could you show me your map some time? I should awfully like to see it."

"Rather, of course I will. I say, is Mr. Rampson looking for the ring that's missing? Let's go and help him."

"Hopeless, I'm afraid, in all this welter of rocks and brambles. Besides, we don't know that the ring's there to be found."

"No," agreed Lion. "But it's a funny thing that ring has disappeared, Mr. Christmas. Because it was awfully tight on his finger. I don't think it could possibly have slipped off. Once when I wanted to borrow it to use as a seal I tried to pull it off and it wouldn't come. And Charles had quite a job to get it off himself. It's been stolen, I bet. Hullo, Mr. Rampson's found something!"

"Coming over!" called Rampson from among the boulders, and a small object whizzed through the air.

Lion caught it neatly and looked at it with an expression of disappointment.

"An apple! That's not much of a clue! "

He was about to throw it away when John stopped him.

"Don't do that, I want it! Where d'you find this, Sydenham? "

"Best I can do for you," said Rampson, approaching. "Here's another one. Picnic-party's refuse, I should say. There are one or two rusty tins among the brambles, too. Don't put them in your pocket, you ass. You don't know who may have been handling them."

"Exactly."

Rampson laughed good-humouredly.

"Oh, they're clues, are they, *faute de mieux*? Shall I go back and fetch the sardine-tins? "

"Not if they're rusty. They must have been there some time. But these apples are perfectly fresh, though a good deal bruised."

"Probably some picnic-party up above, gorged to the eyes with ham sandwiches and bananas, threw them at a rabbit or something. Very wasteful, of course. But picnic-parties are inclined that way."

"It's possible," agreed John. "I wonder whether the worried damsel at the Tram Inn sells apples to passing picnickers. Most of the trees in her orchard are Worcester pearmains, and so are these."

"I say! " Lion, round-eyed and flushed brightly with excitement, exclaimed. "Are you a detective, Mr. Christmas? "

"Not really. I'm just a humble admirer of the great Holmes, like yourself, Lion."

The young generation raised an eyebrow and remarked that it preferred Dr. Thorndyke.

"More scientific. Everything he finds he puts under the microscope. I wish I had a microscope of my own.

Dad's got one, but he doesn't much like me using it when he's not there. I do like the sort of people that understand microscopes, and science and things."

John laughed.

" Then you'll like Rampson. He soaks in science and keeps one eye at the microscope even in his sleep."

" I say! " Lion looked rather shyly at this embodiment of his ideal. " Do you really? I say! Are you staying long? Would you come over and have a look at Dad's microscope, and my slides? All the slides I make look kind of blurred. Do you think——"

" Dirt," said Rampson laconically. " Righto, of course I will."

He did not by word or look reproach John for having thus deflected the stream of Lion's young enthusiasm. He was happy in the company of schoolboys, and when they turned to go home walked contentedly off with his new satellite, who was assuring him earnestly that the possibility of foreign matter appearing in his slides had been carefully guarded against by an extensive use of soap and water. Isabel shut up her sketch-book and rose from her boulder and smiled at John, who waited to be her escort.

" We left our bicycles at Upper Ring Farm," she explained. " Lion wouldn't risk his priceless tyres along this track. Gorgeous day, isn't it? Have you been up on Radnor Forest yet? I went yesterday. You can't think how lovely it is. Just hills and hills and trees and trees, and a little waterfall that's one of the loveliest things in the world. You must go, if you can find time from your detecting. Or is Lion wrong in supposing that you detect? Do you detect, or don't you? "

They followed in the steps of the two earnest scientists. The track was only wide enough for two, and John was extremely glad that a happy thought of his had transferred Lion's budding devotion from himself to Rampson, since it left him Isabel as a companion. Her light, clear voice which when she spoke of waterfalls itself suggested the sound of splashing water, her precise enunciation, her self-possessed and tranquil manner—all suggested a brain admirably clear behind that pretty white forehead. Pretty she was, too, in an elvish, sharp-pointed manner, with thin, humorous lips and heavy white lids that hid her thoughts.

" I do detect," replied John airily, responding to her manner, " when circumstances allow me. Do you? "

" Not I. I accept, and make no attempt to pierce the veil, as the spiritualists put it. Poor Charles! All your detecting won't bring him to life again."

" No, it has another object."

She gave him a long glance from the bright, hazel eyes under those heavy lids.

" What is your object? Do tell me."

John hesitated.

" I might say, a passion for abstract justice," he replied. " But it wouldn't be true. My object is just the interest the problem has for me."

She nodded.

" Some like algebra, some like chess, and some like detecting crimes. I don't much like any of them."

" What is your favourite amusement? "

" Talking to intelligent young men," she replied calmly. " And drawing. But I'm better at the former than the latter. I'm too lazy to study properly, and fall back on lightning-sketches and caricatures. There's one of you in here. Like to see it? "

She handed him her sketch-book, open at a page which showed a lively caricature of himself and Rampson examining imaginary clues among the blackberry bushes. John laughed appreciatively, admired and turned a few more pages.

" That's Dr. Browning," said Isabel, looking over his

arm, " looking pleased at one of his own remarks. That's Felix raising an eyebrow at Charles. That's Charles slapping Felix on the back."

" Oh, that's Charles, is it? "

John looked attentively at the large-featured, genial face, portrayed wearing an exaggerated smile. A wide mouth, a long chin and numerous open-air wrinkles around the eyes seemed to be the chief features of a jovial, but not particularly pleasant, physiognomy.

" That's Nora, but it's not very good," said Isabel, as he turned another page. " She's too good-looking to caricature well. And that's the lot," she added rather hastily, as he turned over again, " except for some art-school ones, not interesting and all bad."

John handed back the sketch-book.

" You ought to see Nora's books, if you're interested in drawing," observed Isabel. " She's worth twenty of me as an artist. But then she works and I don't. And Felix draws very well, though he goes in for photography instead."

" You all go to the same art-school? "

" Nora and I do. Felix only works there occasionally, when he can get time off from photography. I don't know whether I shall go back next term. It's amusing, but I think I've had enough of it. Oh, that dog! What frightful animals these farmers keep! We're told that the dog is the friend of man. Who would have thought it? Do you think we ought to give this woman something for looking after our bicycles, or not? I don't quite understand the social distinctions in this part of the world."

" Not," said John decidedly. " This is her own farm, such as it is. And, anyway, these people aren't so easily tipped as our southerners. They have a dour sort of pride quite their own."

" ' Taffy was a Welshman, Taffy was a thief,' "

murmured Isabel, as John wheeled her bicycle away from the yard. " By the way, has it occurred to anyone that the signet-ring you're all so bothered about may have been pocketed by the gentleman who found poor Charles? Mr. Hufton, or whatever his name is, the proud lady's lodger? "

" Rather risky," commented John. " After all, this is a case of murder."

" Hufton didn't know that. He probably thought it was an accident. And he *is* a bit of a thief," added Isabel meditatively.

John looked at her in some surprise.

" It seems to me," he remarked, " that as a detective, Miss Donne, you leave me standing still. I understand this is your first visit to the district, and you haven't been here forty-eight hours. Yet already you have detected a thief nine miles or so from where you are staying. Very good work, in my opinion."

Miss Donne's thick golden eyelashes quivered slightly. There was the fraction of a minute's silence, while all sorts of strange, vague surmises rose in John's mind, and his interest in this pale, pretty, self-possessed young woman suddenly became intensified. Then :

" Wild strawberries! " she cried in a sort of childish glee, and stooping to the hedge-bank began to collect the little scarlet globes in the palm of her hand.

" Look! Have one! Have several! I adore wild strawberries, don't you? Garden ones quite lose in flavour what they gain in size. As for my detecting, it's not really very brilliant. Somebody told me that young Hufton was lacking in respect for other people's property. I forget who. One of the servants, it may have been. Possibly it's not true. And here we are at the high road."

" I say, Isabel! " There was a shout from Lion, who was sitting on the gate beside Rampson, awaiting their approach. " Where did you find those wild raspberries the day before yesterday?   There ought to be some more ripe."

" My dear boy, we haven't time to go raspberry-hunting. We shall be late for lunch."

" Rot!   It's only twelve o'clock.   I could just do with a raspberry or so.   Was it in this field?   I don't see any signs of them."

A queer flash of ill-temper passed over Isabel's intelligent little face.   She looked for a moment as if she would gladly have consigned Lion and his gluttony to perdition. Then she said teasingly :

" Shan't tell you.   They're my own private preserve. Have a wild strawberry instead, and don't be a pig. Isn't that a sweet little cottage, Mr. Christmas?   Whenever I see a cottage like that I long to live in it and keep chickens and bees and wear a sun-bonnet and grow asters, which, I see, they do."

" Yes, and they sell ginger-beer," said Lion dreamily, with his eyes on a small notice-board over the door. " Now what I should like is a bottle of stone ginger. Not the fizzy kind, but——"

" Oh, come on, child!   I can't have you spoiling your lunch," said Isabel, with a faint note of exasperation in her amused voice.   " Besides, that notice looks a hundred years old.   And if they do keep ginger-beer, it's sure to be fizzy.   It always is."

" Let's go and see, shall we? " suggested John.

Isabel, in whom he was becoming every moment more interested, threw him a flickering, not altogether friendly, glance, but offered no objection, and the four of them went in single file down the narrow brick path between the rows of purple and pink asters and the tall heads of phlox to the unobtrusive front door that stood open on the sitting-room.   It was a typical cottager's sitting-room, crowded with furniture and hung with prints, photographs and mirrors; but the woman who appeared in it in answer to John's knock was not at all a typical cottager. John's first impression was one of surprise at seeing her there, in her short cretonne frock, shingled grey hair and patent leather shoes; his second, that she was surprised to see them. Surprise, uncertainty, even, John thought, apprehension appeared for a moment in her face. Then she smiled a good morning, and waited for them to state their business.

" We saw the notice over the door, and thought we should like some ginger-beer," explained John a little diffidently.

She laughed.

" Oh, I'm so sorry! I'm afraid I haven't any! I ought to have taken the notice down. But I've only rented the cottage for a few weeks. If lemonade would do, I've heaps of that."

The intelligent grey eyes in her long, rather plain face moved from one to another of her callers with a lively interest, dwelling especially, John thought, on Isabel.

" Oh, no, we shouldn't dream of bothering you," he said politely, but at Lion's long, plaintive sigh the lady laughed and invited them in.

She sat in a high-backed chair and watched them as they drank the excellent lemonade she provided.

" You've been over to the quarry, haven't you? " she asked. " What a dreadful thing this murder is! Poor young man! Have they found who did it, do you know? "

Without waiting for an answer, she went on, motioning to Lion to refill his glass:

" Really, it's terribly depressing, such a thing happening so close to one! I feel quite inclined to pack up and go home to London. I came here to vegetate. But now one hears of nothing but this dreadful murder. It appears the poor young man was quite an important person hereabouts.   Sure you won't have any more?   Are you staying in these parts, or do you live here? "

Isabel, to whom this question seemed more especially addressed, replied merely:

" Staying for a little while."   Her nonchalant composure seemed unaccountably to have left her.   She fidgeted with her glass, looked out of the window and at the clock, and as soon as Lion had finished his drink, rose with almost discourteous abruptness.

The other woman rose too, came out with them into the sunny garden and bade them a friendly good-bye. She stood by the door among her asters and waved to them as they turned out of the gate.   The bright sunlight showed her exquisitely neat and fresh, with hands white as cream and not a waved hair out of place on her smooth grey head.   A very urban, elderly lady, charming and sophisticated, like many other urban, elderly ladies.   She looked as if she spent a good deal of time with her hairdresser and masseuse.   But there was a quite unusual amount of character in her creamed and powdered face, with its heavy, curved eyebrows and large, mobile mouth.

" Isabel," said Lion severely, " I believe you pinched those raspberries the other day out of this garden, and that's why you won't tell me where you got them.   I saw a lot of raspberry canes round the side of the house. And I thought those ones you had were too big for wild ones.   You'll come to a bad end, my girl, if you don't mend your ways."

" My dear Lion," said Isabel with surprising asperity, " don't be idiotic."   Then with a sudden change of mood she laughed and patted his tousled head.   " Come on. I'll race you into Penlow.   Good-bye, Mr. Christmas. May heaven shower fingerprints on you!   *Do* come on, young Lion!   I never knew a youth so slow!   What will you be at fifty, if Nature keeps you alive? "

" I shan't be alive at fifty if I do much cycling with you, Isabel," replied Lion sadly. " It would be too much to expect of Nature. Good-bye! Good-bye, Mr. Rampson, and don't forget about coming to see the microscope! "

He mounted and rode off after Isabel, who was already some way down the road.

" You're not very chatty, John," remarked Rampson, as they overtook the cyclists and sped along the road dappled with the blotchy shadows of trees. " What are you thinking about? "

" About the kind lady who gave us all that lemonade. And about Miss Isabel Donne."

" Are you falling in love again? " asked Rampson placidly.

" I think not. Not this time, my dear Sydenham. No, not this time."

At the Feathers they found awaiting them Felix Price, white and heavy-eyed, smoking a cigarette and reading a paper in the lounge. He greeted them under the eyes of the porter with elaborate casualness, but there was that in his face which made John quickly suggest repairing to a more private spot.

" I had to come," he said, when the three of them were upstairs in John's large, cool bedroom. " I didn't know who else to go to. I feel you can advise me. But, after all, what's the good of advice? Nothing, I suppose! "

Wandering about the room, looking with unseeing eyes at the texts and Landseer prints, he spoke in short, jerky sentences, like a man under some heavy strain. Turning suddenly on John, he said, stiff-lipped :

" Christmas, the police came to Rhyllan with a search-warrant last night. Does it mean——? What does it mean? "

" May mean anything or nothing," said John quietly. " Were there—any results? "

" An extraordinary thing!   A—a terrible thing! Lovell asked my father if he kept a revolver.   And of course he does, in a drawer under some book-shelves in the library.   They asked to see it.   He was—oh, you've seen my father, you can guess how he fired up!   But he took them to the library.   It wasn't there, Christmas, the revolver wasn't there!   The house was searched, it wasn't anywhere!   They found a revolver in Charles's room, and I thought: Thank God!   But my father said he'd never seen it before.   It belonged to Charles.   So you see—my father's revolver has disappeared—and—and what can we do? "

He broke off abruptly and, suddenly calm, sat down in a creaking wicker chair and looked stonily at John.

" Can't your father remember what he did with his revolver? "

" He just says it was in the drawer last time he saw it. He was amazed that it wasn't there.   He swears he hasn't had it out for ages.   And he won't tell Lovell what he went to Hereford for on the day—it happened.   It's just obstinacy, of course.   He resented being asked about his business at first, and he goes on refusing to talk about it just out of stubbornness.   But it's so—so damaging! "

" Can't you persuade him to tell you? "

Felix gave a wry, painful grin.

" I?   No.   You don't know my father.   He's— entirely unpersuadable."

He stared out on to the sunny street of the quiet little market town.

" But what can we *do*? " he cried suddenly, turning towards John with outflung hands.   He jumped to his feet, as if the inaction of sitting still for more than a few moments were intolerable.   " My God! " he cried. " My God!   What a fool I was to burn that letter! "

The "note" he burned when lighting a Bonfire in Chapter 4

CHAPTER SEVEN

TWELVE GOOD MEN AND TRUE

THE coroner's inquest, held next morning at the Tram Inn, presented, apart from the uniforms of the police, a queer aspect of homeliness and informality. A long table covered with an ink-stained red cloth had been placed in the centre of the large parlour, but otherwise the room with its pot-ferns, horsehair chairs, piano and crocheted mats was much the same as it had been at tea-time on the day of Charles's disappearance. The blinds had been half-drawn at one window to shut out the cheerful sunlight, and the cold, clear light thus produced gave a look of pallor to every face, even to the dark, high-complexioned countenance of Morris Price, who, with the rest of his household, had arrived early.

The coroner, a Hereford solicitor, took the head of the table with his back to the window, the jurymen sat down one side, and a row of chairs at the opposite side of the room were occupied by the witnesses. Two or three newspaper reporters sat at the table and a dozen or so members of the public, including John and Rampson, occupied chairs behind the jurymen. At a small pedestal table near the foot of the long one sat a short, elderly man in gold-rimmed glasses whom John rightly guessed to be the dead man's solicitor.

The jurymen filed solemnly out to view the body where it still lay in that melancholy out-house, and after the lapse of ten minutes or so filed back again and as solemnly took their seats.

The first witness to be sworn was James Hufton, a short and powerfully built but not very intelligent young labourer.   His statement, uttered in the quick, clipped speech of the Welsh borderer, was patiently elicited from him by questions from the coroner.   He deposed to having found the body of a young man lying on the rocks at the foot of Rodland Quarry at about half-past six on the morning of August the twenty-seventh.   A much crumpled bicycle had been lying nearby.   He had turned the body over and assured himself that life was extinct.   Then he had walked back to Upper Ring Farm, where he lodged, and informed his landlord, Mr. Dolphin. Dolphin had started off on his bicycle to fetch the Penlow police, and Hufton had set out for his work on the railway once more.   Passing the body a second time, he had seen it and the bicycle lying just as he had left them.

Felix Price, who was the next witness, came forward and took the oath with an extreme quietness and precision that suggested great nervous tension.   He looked very pale, and the muscles about his mouth and jaw were stiffly set, and he did not glance at John nor anywhere but at the coroner.

" You have identified the body, Mr. Price? "

" Yes.   It is that of my cousin, Charles Almeric Price."

" When did you last see your cousin alive? "

" At about half-past five, when we left the inn after having had tea.   He discovered that one of his tyres was flat, and stopped outside the inn to pump it up.   The rest of the party, including myself, went on down Rodland Hill."

" When did you first become anxious for your cousin's safety? "

" That evening, in Penlow. He was to have spent the night with me at the Feathers, and when he did not appear I became a little anxious."

" Were there any special grounds for your anxiety? "

Felix did not reply for a moment. His hands, lying on the table in front of him, whitened at the knuckles. The coroner amended his question.

" I mean, was he a reckless or an inexperienced cyclist? "

Felix's pose relaxed slightly. He answered quietly:

" No. Oh, no! He was perfectly capable of looking after himself." Then he in his turn amended his former statement: " Perhaps ' anxious ' is rather a strong word. I became a little uneasy."

" Naturally. Before you arrived at Penlow, were you not surprised that he did not catch you up? "

" Yes. We waited some time at the foot of Rodland Hill. We were about to go back and look for him, but a passing motorist informed us that he had seen no sign of a cyclist on the hill, so I imagined that he had stayed behind on purpose, and would catch us up later."

" How long did you wait for him? "

" About twenty minutes."

" Had you any idea of what might detain him for that length of time? "

" Yes. He might have gone back to the inn for a drink. Or he might have found a puncture in his tyre and stayed behind to mend it."

" Was there a mending outfit on his bicycle? "

" No, but no doubt he could have borrowed one from somebody in the inn."

The coroner nodded.

" Do you recognize the bicycle found with your cousin's body? "

" No. It is not the bicycle he was riding."

" What make was your cousin's bicycle? "

"It was an old Humber machine. He hired it in Worcester from a firm named Martin."

There was a pause. One of the constables on guard at the door brought into the room a shabby, dusty bicycle and placed it where Felix and the jury could have a clear view of it. John, watching closely, saw an indefinable flicker of emotion pass over the young man's face—glad surprise, relief, hope, passed in a moment.

"Do you recognize this bicycle, Mr. Price?"

"Yes. It is the machine my cousin had."

"Are you certain?"

"Quite. I recognize the dent in the back mudguard and the scrap of label stuck to the side of the saddle."

The coroner nodded, as if this answer were the expected one, and made a note in the book lying in front of him. He was about to dismiss the witness when the foreman of the jury rose.

"May I ask a question, sir?"

"Through me, you may."

"I should like to ask the young gentleman, Mr. Price, that is, whether he knows of any reason why the deceased should have gone across the quarry field instead of down Rodland Hill, sir."

The coroner turned his mild spectacles upon Felix.

"Do you know of any such reason? Had your cousin mentioned any intention of following a different route from the rest of you, or expressed a desire to see the quarry, or the view from the quarry?"

"No. The quarry was mentioned at tea-time, but my cousin showed no interest in it. So far as I know, his intention was to follow us down Rodland Hill."

"Thank you. Next witness, please."

A short, elderly man with a puckered, irascible face, bright blue eyes and a ragged grey moustache stepped forward and stood by the table fingering his cloth cap and looking with a sort of truculent embarrassment from one stolid member of the jury to another. There was a stir of interest in the court. Evidently the witness was well known to most of the people present.

" Your name? "

" James Letbe, sir."

" I understand that you have identified the bicycle found below the quarry as your own? "

" Yes, sir."

" And that the bicycle you see here in court was found in your possession? "

" Yes, sir, but——"

" Will you explain how it came into your possession? "

Letbe fixed the foreman of the jury with a challenging eye. Evidently he was more than a little aggrieved at the prominence which circumstances had thrust upon him.

" It was this way," he began heavily. " Two days before yesterday I came here—to the Tram Inn, that is—just afore six o'clock. I was riding my bike that I've had a dozen years or more. I left it standing agin the railings outside and went into the bar. There was one or two bicycles standing outside. I left mine standing near un. When I got into the bar I come out again and went round to the side door. I——"

The foreman of the jury, a stout and jovial-looking soul with a ruffled cock's comb of dark hair and a crooked pair of pince-nez, rose immediately.

" I should like to ask, sir, why the witness changed his mind and went to the side door."

Letbe scowled at the zealous juryman.

" I was just a-going to tell you," he remarked. " I seen Sir Charles Price in the bar. I couldn't take my drink while he was by. He turned me out of my job that I've had thirty years. I went round to the side door to wait till he'd gone. In two-three minutes I seed him go. So I went through the house to the bar. I stayed till about seven. There's many can bear me out."

He looked slowly around the court, and there was a faint murmur of assent.

" When I went out," pursued Letbe, still in the heavy, rather aggrieved tones of the injured man, " my bicycle had gone. There was only two bikes there. One belonged to old Tom Lloyd, as I knew well. The other was a stranger. I went round to the door and arst Miss Watt if she'd moved my bike. No, she hadn't seen it. I went into the bar and arst all round if anyone claimed the other bike—the one as didn't belong to Tom Lloyd. No, it didn't belong to no one. I thinks then as somebody's took my bike in error for his own. I didn't fancy losing of my machine, nor I didn't fancy walking home. So I took tother chap's bike, the stranger's, leaving word with Miss Watt in case tother chap should turn up."

Old Letbe looked slowly again from juryman to juryman as though challenging them all to say that he had done wrong. Then he addressed himself to the coroner again : " It isn't thought that I did do wrong, I hope, sir ? I can't do wi'out a bicycle, living as I does in such a lonely place. And I can't afford for to buy a new one, having lost my place as I've held thirty years wi'out complaint. And it weren't such a grand bargain I made. My bike were old, but I'd kept it well. But this one " —he looked unfavourably at the rusty machine—" this one hasn't seen oil or cleaning for years, I know."

On the coroner's assurance that no blame was attached to him for appropriating the strange machine, he went back to his seat and sat heavily down with his hands on his knees, looking fixedly at the foreman of the jury, challenging to the last.

Two or three witnesses were next called to corroborate Letbe's statement. At each answer the old man nodded gravely, and when his statement had been fully and finally corroborated his face relaxed into an almost agreeable expression and he sat back to enjoy the entertainment.

" Call Mr. Morris Price."

Now there was a movement and rustle in the warm, crowded room, a sudden awakening of interest on sleepy faces, as Morris Price rose, approached the table and took the oath. He looked more himself than when John had seen him at Rhyllan Hall two days before. There was a ruddier colour in his cheeks and his fierce dark eyes were clearer. He took the oath in clear, deep tones and quietly awaited the coroner's questions. But there was an indefinable atmosphere of antagonism about him as he stood there; and a very formidable antagonist he looked.

" Now, Mr. Price. Will you tell the jury when you last saw your nephew, and in what circumstances? "

" I last saw my nephew Charles at a quarter to seven on the evening of August the twenty-seventh, three days ago. I was returning from Hereford, where I had been in my car on private business. As I approached this inn I saw my nephew standing at the side of the road with a bicycle."

" Was he alone? "

" Yes. So far as I noticed, there was nobody in sight. I hailed him as I passed, and pulled up a little farther along to have a word with him. This was about half-past six. He——"

" One moment. When you first saw your nephew, what was he doing? "

" Doing? Nothing. He was standing by the road-side, holding his bicycle and looking up and down the road. My impression was that he was looking for some-body, for the other members of the party, probably."

" Thank you."

" Well, I stopped the car and he came up to me. I asked where the rest of the party was. He replied that they had just gone on, and that he was about to follow them. I suggested that I might walk a little way with him, as I had something to speak to him about."

" Have you any objection, Mr. Price, to telling the jury what it was you wished to speak about? "

There was a pause.

" Yes, I have," said the witness calmly but determinedly. " It was on a private matter, and quite irrelevant."

In the small silence that followed John heard a faint sigh from Felix. The coroner glanced at the sad-faced Superintendent Lovell and then at his refractory witness. There was a slight chill in his tone as he asked :

" When was your nephew expected home at Rhyllan Hall? "

" On the following day."

" Then I take it that the communication you wished to make to him was one of great importance, if it could not wait until the following day? "

Morris returned his look with an arrogant stare before replying :

" It was not of importance—or rather, it was important but not urgent. It could quite well have waited until the following day, but I preferred that it should not."

" I see. Did your nephew consent to your proposal that you should accompany him a short distance? "

" Certainly," replied Mr. Price in a tone that said : " Who was he to refuse? " He went on : " We went through the gate into the field that leads to the common."

" Did you know that the rest of the party had gone down Rodland Hill? "

" Certainly not."

" Did the deceased say that they had gone across the common? "

There was a pause.

" As far as I remember, he did not actually say so. I took it for granted."

" Who made the suggestion that you should go across the quarry fields, you or he? "

" Neither of us. I took it for granted that the others had gone that way, and opened the gate. He followed me without making any remark. Our conversation then——"

" One moment, please! " interrupted the coroner a little impatiently. " You say that your nephew did not mention the route taken by the other members of the party? "

" Yes."

" And that you took it for granted they had gone through the quarry fields? "

" Yes."

" Did you know they were going to Penlow? "

" Yes."

" The direct road to Penlow is down Rodland Hill, is it not? "

" Certainly."

" Why then did you take it for granted they had gone across the field-path? "

There was a murmur of assent among the jurymen. Morris Price looked at them contemptuously.

" I don't know," he said abruptly. " All I can say is, that I did gain the impression that they had gone across the fields. Perhaps my nephew looked in that direction as he spoke. Perhaps he indicated it with a gesture. I certainly don't remember his saying so. But it was from him I took the impression."

" Who opened the gate, you or he? "

" I did, I have said so already. He was wheeling a bicycle behind me. He made no objection to my taking that route. Our conversation continued until we reached the quarry field, where we parted. My nephew, I think, went on towards the Wensley Road, and I turned back to my car, which I had left standing outside this inn."

" You say you *think* your nephew went towards Wensley. Do you not know? "

" I do not."

" How is that? "

" I did not turn back to see where he went after I left him. All I know is, he did not come back with me."

An elderly juryman with a lined face and a stony, conscientious eye here rose to address the coroner.

" Sir, I think it would help a lot if Sir Morris would think better of it, and tell us what it was he and the deceased discussed when they walked over to the quarry."

Before he had time to sit down again the spruce, grey-haired lawyer had risen from his small table at the end of the room.

" My name," he said in a dry, brisk voice, " is Hector Penrose. I represent the firm of Penrose & Johnson, Solicitors, of 47 Chancery Row. The legal affairs of the deceased were in the hands of my firm, and I am also the legal representative of Sir Morris Price. I object strongly to the question just asked by this gentleman."

He sat down with a flick of his coat-tails, and there was a pause while the coroner balanced a pen-holder thoughtfully on his forefinger and considered the matter. He said reluctantly at last:

" Although the question was in the first place my own, I think I have no option but to withdraw it as irrelevant. The answer cannot materially affect our business, which is, you must remember, gentlemen, simply to discover the cause of the death of Sir Charles Almeric Price. I will ask another question more pertinent to the matter. Did your nephew, Sir Morris, say anything which might have led you to suppose that he stood in any fear of an attempt upon his life, that he had an enemy, or that he expected to meet with some person other than his cousin and the other members of the cycling party? "

" No," replied Morris, " he certainly didn't. He said

very little at all.   I did most of the talking."   There
was a pause while the witness, frowning, seemed to
hesitate.   Then he burst out: "Oh, very well!   I'll
tell you what we talked about, since you're so anxious
to know!"

Regardless of the coroner's head-shake and Mr.
Penrose's sharp: "There is no need!" he went on
impulsively:

"I had made up my mind to give up my post as agent
to the estates.   I had made up my mind to leave Rhyllan.
I had been considering the step for some time, ever since
my nephew's return, in fact.   And I had just definitely
made up my mind.   My mind was full of my decision,
and when I unexpectedly saw my nephew, alone, I determined to tell him of it there and then.   So I told him.
And now you know."

This declaration caused a certain quickening of interest
in the audience, and a few whispers, which were sternly
suppressed by the coroner.   Even Blodwen, John noticed,
looked as if she could hardly believe her ears.   It was
evident that Morris Price had not taken his family into
his confidence.

"Thank you, Sir Morris," said the coroner.   "I
propose now to call the medical evidence, and that of the
police."

Dr. Browning stepped forward and took Sir Morris's
place.   He gave his evidence quietly and concisely, testi-
fying to having been called to the Tram Inn early in the
morning on August the twenty-eighth to view the body of
a man which he had identified as that of Sir Charles Price.
He could not say with certainty how long the man had
been dead.   Probably twelve hours or more.   The cause
of death was cerebral hæmorrhage caused by a close-
range bullet through the brain.   In his opinion a revolver
had been held within two feet of the man's head, and the
bullet had passed in at an upward angle through the

occiput and had emerged through the bridge of the nose. Yes, suicide was quite out of the question. No, it was not possible that the man might have been shot after he had fallen or been thrown over the quarry edge. The wounds caused by the shot had bled freely, but the slight wounds caused by striking the rocks at the foot of the quarry had not bled at all. Yes, Dr. Browning was of opinion that all the injuries found on the body, except the injury to the head caused by the shot, had been caused by the fall from the quarry, after death had taken place. There were no bruises on the throat or arms such as might have been caused by a struggle.

~ The melancholy Superintendent Lovell then took his place opposite the jurors. In a quiet, level voice he told of the removal of the body to the Tram Inn, its identification by Felix and Blodwen, and his own identification of the crumpled bicycle as Letbe's.

"That matter has been settled, I think, to the satisfaction of the jury?" said the coroner, looking at his twelve good men and true, who answered with solemn nods and murmurs of assent.

"Now, Superintendent," went on the coroner, and to John his grave, quiet voice seemed suddenly to take on a portentous note, "I understand that the bullet with which deceased was killed passed through the head without lodging in the brain. Has your search for the bullet met with any success?"

"Yes, sir," replied Lovell, and produced a small folded envelope. "I found the ·32 bullet, enclosed in this envelope, in the quarry field, at a distance of about eight feet from the quarry edge, yesterday morning."

There was a subdued noise of rustling and creaking as every listener sat up and craned forward to try and get a view of the envelope which Lovell passed to the coroner. John, watching the three Prices, saw Felix flinch as Lovell spoke, glance quickly at his father, and then fold his arms and sit back in his chair, as if determined to imitate that gentleman's pose of haughty impassivity. The coroner shook out the bullet on to the palm of his hand, scrutinized it and passed it to the foreman of the jury, who, after examining it with an expert air for a moment or two, passed it along to his neighbour.

"Also," went on Lovell in his quiet, rather dreary voice, "I found this revolver in a rabbit hole in the quarry field. Sergeant Dew and Constable Beaver were present when I found it, yesterday morning at about eleven o'clock."

"Hullo!" murmured John to himself, and glanced again at the enigmatic family opposite. This time nothing was to be read in their four impassive faces but the determination that nothing should be read.

"A Smith and Wesson pocket pistol," remarked the coroner, examining the small revolver, which still showed traces of earth from its sojourn underground. "Engraved with the initials M. R. P. Have you formed any conclusion, Sergeant, as to the ownership of this revolver?"

"It has been identified as his own, sir, by Sir Morris Price."

There was a pause of sheer astonishment, and then a subdued whisper ran round the court, and every eye was turned upon Morris, who sat between Blodwen and Felix with folded arms, looking at the floor, as if immersed in his own thoughts. He had gone pale, though, with the unpleasant mottled pallor of a florid complexion.

"Silence!" said the coroner sharply, as the whispering went on, and addressed himself again to Lovell. "You say that Sir Morris Price has himself identified this revolver as his own?"

"Yes, sir."

"It will be necessary to recall Sir Morris Price, but first I will take the remainder of your evidence. You say this weapon was discovered in a rabbit-hole in the quarry field. Whereabouts in the quarry field? "

" Very close to the common gate and the footpath leading towards this inn."

" Are there any marks upon the weapon which might serve as clues? "

" None, sir, beyond the initials which helped us to discover its ownership."

" Call Sir Morris Price."

The tall man rose and took his place once more at the witness table. Once more his dark eyes swept the faces of the jurors with a sort of insolent indifference and came to rest with a look of inimical inquiry on the coroner's grave face. But this time, John noticed, he moistened his lips with his tongue before he spoke and his hand rested heavily on the red baize of the table-cloth.

" Do you recognize this revolver, Sir Morris? "

" Yes. It is my own."

" When did you last see it? "

" I don't know. I should think, months ago."

" Can you not make a more definite statement than that? "

" No. I can't remember when I last saw it. I didn't know I was going to be questioned about it. If I had known, I would have made a note of the date."

Two small spots of red appeared in the coroner's cheeks at this coldly ironical reply, and he seemed about to remonstrate, but thought better of it. John distinctly heard Mr. Penrose, the solicitor, utter to himself: " Ts! Ts! " and saw him half shake his grey head with a reproachful glance at his client. Evidently he did not approve of Sir Morris's high-handed manner. Sir Morris added :

" A revolver isn't a thing one is constantly using. One may have it in one's house for years without ever seeing it."

" I take it, then," said the coroner coldly, " that this revolver has been in your possession for some time, Sir Morris? "

" Two or three years."

" Can you remember when you last used it? "

" I have never used it. I have had no occasion to. I like to keep a revolver in the house, for emergencies. But I hope to be spared the necessity of ever using it."

" Where did you keep this revolver? "

" In a drawer in the library at Rhyllan Hall."

" Did you keep it loaded? "

" Certainly not! "

" There is no need to answer so indignantly. These questions are necessary, I assure you. Was the drawer usually locked? "

" No."

" Was anything else kept in this drawer besides this revolver? "

" My regimental badges and a few photographs and other relics."

" Anything that would justify a second person in going to the drawer? "

" No, there was nothing there that would interest anybody but myself."

" Did anybody but yourself know of the whereabouts of this revolver? "

" Really, how can I say? The drawer was unlocked. Any member of the household who had sufficient curiosity could have looked in. I don't remember ever speaking of the revolver, if that is what you mean."

" Would the drawer be likely to be emptied when the room was cleaned? "

Morris uttered a short laugh.

" I don't know. My housekeeper may."

" When did you first discover that the revolver was missing? "

" The evening of the day before yesterday, when Superintendent Lovell saw fit to search my house."

Once again John saw the old family lawyer shake his head and sigh. And certainly the witness's manner was having anything but a favourable effect on the jury, to judge by their cold, embarrassed glances at him, their furtive, expressive looks at one another. An interesting relic of the feudal ages, this little Welsh squire; one might have imagined from his manner that he really supposed himself to be above the law and exempt from social obligations.

" Now, Sir Morris, do you recognize the writing on this piece of paper? "

A small piece of crumpled blue paper, charred at the edges, was laid on the red table-cloth under Morris's eyes. John saw Superintendent Lovell move a little closer to the witness and fix his eyes on that scrap of paper, as if holding himself ready for an emergency. Sir Morris glanced at the paper, half turned round as if to address his son, and then turning back towards the jury, replied with indignant surprise :

" Certainly I do! It is my own writing. This paper is part of a private letter to my son, and I should be obliged if you would kindly explain how it came into your possession."

So saying he put out his hand to take the paper from the table. John fancied that in another moment it would have been torn indignantly to pieces, had not the Superintendent's hand proved the quicker of the two. Sir Morris turned on Lovell's imperturbable face a look of cold, outraged fury, drew his breath sharply, bit his lip, and then stood drumming his finger-nails on the table edge, as if trying to get control of his anger.

" I must point out," said the coroner coldly, " that it is not in my province to make explanations. Quite otherwise. I will ask you to explain, however, in what circumstances you wrote the letter of which this piece of paper is a part, and to whom you refer in these terms: '*Your cousin is a coarse, ill-mannered lout and, fond as I am of Rhyllan, I do not intend to endure his company very much longer.*' "

There was a moment of silence while these words, which the coroner read slowly out from the charred paper in front of him, sank delightfully into the scandalized consciousness of the few sensation-mongers present.   A local newspaper man feverishly licked his pencil and gazed expectantly at Sir Morris, hopeful of Sensational Disclosures.   He was disappointed.   *The Western Clarion* had to be content instead with Sensational Behaviour of Witness.

" I will not," said Morris Price loudly and clearly, " explain this letter, nor any part of this letter.   It is a private communication from myself to my son.   I consider it outrageous that I should be asked to explain it."

" Sir Morris!   Sir Morris! " remonstrated Mr. Penrose faintly, trying to catch his client's eye.   He seemed to have aged ten years in the last five minutes.

" It's no use, Penrose," said the big man obstinately. " I won't answer such questions."

" You must surely see," said the coroner with praiseworthy urbanity, " that it is better for your own sake that you should explain this letter, now that it has been produced.   It is calculated, as it stands, to raise invidious questions in the mind of the jury.   Will you not think better of your refusal?   Your own legal adviser would, I am sure, urge you not to withhold an answer to this question."

He glanced with a certain brotherly sympathy at his fellow-lawyer, who was sitting with his chin on his hand looking at his client with an air of profound despair.

" No," said Morris Price, and glanced contemptuously at the twelve good men and true, as if he doubted their possession of minds capable of raising questions, invidious or otherwise. " I have said all I am going to say about this letter, and about my private affairs generally."

There was a moment's silence again, broken by the excited scratching of the journalistic pencil. The coroner adjusted his spectacles, looked silently at Price, and then turned his attention to some papers lying in front of him.

" Then," he said evenly, " all the available evidence is before you, gentlemen. Now, in drawing your conclusion from the evidence you have heard, you must remember that it is your duty——"

On the whole, John thought, an admirably clear, well-balanced summing-up. The coroner was evidently determined not to allow himself to be influenced by the annoying idiosyncrasies of his chief witness. But the neatly marshalled facts made a formidable array.

" You must bear in mind the fact that it is impossible to fix the time of death with any accuracy. Deceased was, so far as we know, last seen alive at a quarter to seven. Dr. Browning examined the body at half-past eight on the following morning, and you have heard him say that death had taken place twelve hours or more previously. This fixes the time of death at between a quarter to seven and half-past eight on the evening of August the twenty-seventh. We have not been able to discover a witness who could testify to having seen the dead man after a quarter to seven, but you must remember that this is a lonely, thinly populated district, where a man might easily wander for more than an hour and three quarters without being seen by a soul."

The fact remained that Morris Price had seen the dead man at a quarter to seven, in the neighbourhood of the quarry, and that nobody had seen him since.

" Then, as to the revolver. You must bear in mind the fact that this revolver was accessible to a great many people—to anybody, in fact, who may have entered the library at Rhyllan Hall within the last two years or so. It is not without precedent that a murderer should seek to divert suspicion from himself by using another man's revolver. It is, in fact, a common and obvious attempt to hamper justice. And the fact that the weapon was found hidden in a field suggests that its user dared not remain in possession of it, and had no opportunity of restoring it to its place."

All the same, as Mr. Tredgold, the auctioneer, remarked afterwards to his fellow jurymen when they sat discussing the matter in the small parlour, the revolver was Sir Morris Price's revolver, and get over that who could.

" There remains the letter which you have seen, and which Sir Morris Price acknowledges as his own. It is not for me to offer possible explanations when the writer refuses to make them. But I would remind you that Sir Morris has said that he intended to leave Rhyllan Hall."

" Not likely," opined Mr. Tredgold later. Being an auctioner by profession, he was not slow to speech, and of all the voices in the small parlour, his was the most eloquent. What, leave Rhyllan Hall when he was so set on the place! Leave Rhyllan when it was, in a way, his own home, and he'd had the running of it for ten years! Old Sir Evan might have been Price of Rhyllan in name, but everyone knew it was Sir Morris as ruled the roost. Ah, a nasty thing it must have been for him, a sore thing, when this young man came back to take his place! He wouldn't have been human if he hadn't wished the young chap at the devil!

" Mr. Tredgold," gently remarked Lloyd of Linger-Hatch Farm, " please not to mention the evil one in the same breath as the dead. It ben't fitting."

" Your pardon, Mr. Lloyd," said Mr. Tredgold, handsomely making concession to the farmer's well-known methodist habit of mind.

" And," pursued Lloyd mildly, fingering his patriarchal beard, " a chap might well wish a chap out of the way, without taking steps. Mr. Morris is hoity and he's toity, and a hard man when his will is set, not a doubt. But he's not the man to lower his family by taking steps."

Here the foreman, a prosperous builder, a free-thinker, and much respected as an educated man, remarked that it became an intelligent jury to consider the facts as put before them and not to air their preconceived notions of what a chap might or might not do.

" It's the facts, gentlemen, it's the facts that matter."

Lloyd of Linger-Hatch, who was not noticeably an educated man, shook his head. In his view, the unlikelihood of Sir Morris ever taking steps was a fact. But lack of eloquence hampered him, and he found no words to say so.

The jury considered their verdict for a slow three-quarters of an hour, while the court sat and awaited their return. A hum of whispering voices rose, sightseers began to wonder if they would be late for lunch, and the room grew intolerably stuffy. At the request of the coroner, a constable opened one of the windows, and a humble-bee came heavily in, and immediately, as if disconcerted by the crowd, shot out again. Sir Morris Price sat in stern silence, his arms folded, his eyes on the ink-stained table-cloth, and his thoughts, apparently, far away. Old Mr. Penrose, the lawyer, occupied himself with the papers in his despatch-box, looking up with a lack-lustre eye when the jury returned to their places. To him, at least, their verdict gave no shock.

" We find that deceased met his death by shooting at the hands of Sir Morris Price."

There was a second's blank silence, and then a faint sigh, from Blodwen or from Felix, John thought. Morris Price remained as if petrified in his seat for a moment. Then a strange, half-scornful, half-incredulous look came into his face, even while the last vestige of colour went from it.   He rose to his feet, and interrupting the coroner's first words, addressed the foreman of the jury in a tone more scoffing than angry, yet with a queer undertone of fear, as though he had begun to realize that a high hand will not always carry the day :

" Don't be a fool! "

John, who until this moment had been unable to make up his mind, now apostrophized his cousin beneath his breath :

" Sydenham, we're not going back to London for ages. I would bet my last penny that our feudal friend is innocent.   But he badly needs somebody to say to him what he has just said to the foreman of the jury.   And unless I'm much mistaken our Mr. Penrose intends to be the man to say it."

CHAPTER EIGHT

ECCENTRIC BEHAVIOUR OF A LADY

"I SUPPOSE you've no idea, Miss Price, of what sort of life your brother led in Canada? I mean there's always the possibility that somebody followed him over here for the express purpose of murdering him. A remote possibility, perhaps, but there it is. Of course if it had been Russia he'd been living in, or Turkey, or some other hotbed of political crime, the possibility wouldn't be remote at all. But there's something so peculiarly blameless about Canada."

"I haven't the slightest idea. He was working in a shop in some small town, I believe, when they traced him."

"That sounds innocent enough. You didn't write to him, then?"

"We used to write regularly for about a year after he went out. We gave up writing when he gave up answering our letters. For years we didn't hear a word from him. It's extraordinarily difficult," said Blodwen meditatively, "to keep up a correspondence with a person who's at the other side of the world. Even if you're great friends, it's difficult."

They were pacing slowly up and down the terrace in front of Rhyllan Hall. It was that peaceful hour of a summer afternoon when shadows are beginning to lengthen, and the tinkling of tea-cups may be heard in the kitchen. Two red setters basked in the sun on the steps leading down into the Dutch garden, and the whir of a mowing-machine came from some near invisible distance. At the other side of the Dutch garden the gardener's boy David was picking off dead pansies. The serene frontage of Rhyllan Hall presided benignantly over these summer afternoon activities. Sir Charles was murdered, and Sir Morris was arrested for his murder; but the lawns must be mown, and the pansies tidied up, and Blodwen's dogs be given their due hours of freedom. Felix had retired for an hour or two from the unbearable usualness of things and the legal importunities of Mr. Penrose, and at Blodwen's command had gone to his room, ostensibly to sleep. Rampson had fallen in with Lion Browning in Penlow, and had been taken prisoner and led off to view an unsatisfactory microscope. Blodwen and John had the summer afternoon to themselves.

" How long have Felix and his father lived at Rhyllan Hall? "

" How long? Oh, ever since my father came into the title. That was—let me see, thirteen years ago."

" After Charles went to Canada? "

" Yes, two years after. At the time Charles went out, we had no idea that Rhyllan would ever come to our branch of the family. It would have seemed the remotest thing, if we had ever even thought of it. Sir Almeric Price, my great-uncle, had Rhyllan then, and he had two sons and a grandson. But the three of them were drowned in a yachting accident in the Mediterranean, and a few months afterwards Uncle Almeric died of a broken heart. And so, all in a moment, it seemed, the baronetcy came to my father. It was a great change for us. My father wrote over and over again to Charles, but he got no answer, and the lawyers failed to trace him. So Uncle Morris and Felix came here to live, and Uncle

Morris took over the management of the estates. My father was never very strong, and was glad to leave all the business matters to my uncle. Felix was quite a child then, about thirteen, I suppose. They've lived here ever since."

" Both widowers, I suppose—your father and uncle, I mean? "

" N—o," said Blodwen slowly. " My father was. My mother died when Charles was quite small. But Uncle Morris's wife is still alive, I believe."

" You believe? "

" I haven't seen her since I was a child, and haven't heard her spoken of for years. I don't know whether even Uncle Morris knows where she is. It was a most unhappy marriage, I believe, though at the time I was too young to know much about it."

" Then Felix——"

" Oh, this wasn't Felix's mother! Felix's mother was Uncle Morris's first wife. She died when Felix was a baby. And then Uncle Morris married again. This was ages ago, long before any of us came to live here, so I can't tell you much about her, Mr. Christmas. I have heard that she was the daughter of an hotel-keeper in Bristol. Uncle Morris was practising as an architect in those days. He lived in Bristol, I know, and I fancy that was where he met his second wife. They were only together two or three years, I believe. She ran away with another man."

" Was there a divorce? "

" No. I know that, because I used to hear my father talking about the folly of it—the folly of not having a divorce, I mean. But Uncle Morris—well, he wouldn't. Whether because he wanted her back, or just wanted to make himself disobliging, I don't know. It's such ancient history, you see. It must be—oh, twenty years or more ago! "

" I see," said John slowly. " Twenty years! It sounds like a lifetime. But still——"

Blodwen looked at him doubtfully.

" You can't be thinking there's any connection between that old affair and this."

" No. But it's as well to know all one can, even about things that happened twenty years ago. One never knows where an investigation like this will lead one. And the more past history one knows, the less likely one is to be led astray. You don't know, I suppose, whether your uncle still kept in touch with his wife? "

Blodwen laughed.

" No. I've never heard him mention her name. All I know is from my father, who didn't admire the lady and thought her departure a good riddance. I don't think even my father knew how Uncle Morris felt about it. Uncle Morris isn't a man to talk about his private affairs to anyone."

" How long ago was this? "

" Let me see. It was the year I went to school in Germany. I was sixteen that year. So it's just twenty years ago."

" You don't remember her name? "

" Yes, I do! That's the one thing I remember clearly, because it was a queer name, and appealed to my schoolgirl imagination. Clytie Meadows. Aunt Clytie. I only saw her once, and don't remember much about her. Except that she used a marvellous scent, and had a general air about her of not wanting to be bothered with schoolgirls."

" And the name of the man she ran away with? "

" I can't tell you. I suppose I heard it at the time, but it wouldn't have conveyed much to me. Why, Mr. Christmas, this was twenty years ago! Cousin Jim may know. Is there any other family scandal I can rake up for your benefit? No, I don't think so. My Aunt Clytie is the only blot on the family scutcheon within my memory. Until—oh, Mr. Christmas! What a nightmare this is! Is it true? I keep asking myself: is it true? And for quite minutes at a time I can think it isn't, and Uncle Morris is in the library, or out on the farm. Though all the time it's hanging there in the background, something threatening that one's half forgotten! And then it rushes forward, and one can't deceive oneself! It is true! it is! It——"

She bit her lip and turned aside, and suddenly sat down on the steps of the Dutch garden and fondled her setter's long silky ears. When she looked round again after a moment or two, her plain aquiline face wore its usual serene, slightly ironical expression.

" Give me a cigarette, and a match. By the way, that young cousin of mine made a nice mess of it, trying to burn Uncle Morris's letter in full view of the constabulary. Young idiot! As if he couldn't have waited till he got home! And as if there was anything in the letter to feel so guilty about! Really, I don't understand Felix! I thought he had more backbone."

" My own impression is——" began John, and stopped, wondering whether he had better not, after all, keep his impression to himself.

" Well? " asked Blodwen, and something cool and intelligent in her grey eyes constrained him to go on.

" Well," said John, sitting down on the top step, and stroking the silky brown muzzle which was laid in an investigatory fashion on his knee, " I think that young Felix is, or at any rate was, afraid that his father really had——"

He paused, absurdly at a loss for a delicate way of putting it.

Miss Price, to his relief, showed no sign of indignation or even astonishment.

" Murdered Charles? Yes, it had occurred to me that

Felix thought so. Young idiot, again. But of course he's been away a lot since he grew up. He doesn't really know Uncle Morris well, not so well as I know him. And they rather exasperate one another. They're so alike in some ways, and so different in others, that they don't see one another at all clearly. But if Felix thinks so, there's all the more reason for him to pull his socks up. That's just one of the differences between him and Uncle Morris. Just when it's most necessary for him to stiffen up—he collapses. I'm very fond of Felix. But sometimes I do wish he had a little more grit. It's tiresome when one likes a person and can't admire him. It exasperates one."

" I say, you are rather a—well, a Roman cousin, aren't you, Miss Price? "

"Hard on Felix, you mean? Hard altogether, perhaps? Yes, I am," agreed Blodwen tranquilly. She added in a low voice : " But not so hard that I'll be able to bear to live if—if——"

" Then you——"

" Don't share Felix's fears? No, of course not. Uncle Morris might have done it, in a temper. But he says he didn't."

" But——"

" Oh, yes, I know. But a thousand things in his manner and his voice tell me that he didn't, besides his words. People can't lie to those who know them, about such a matter. Not simple people like Uncle Morris, anyhow. I suppose a Machiavelli can. But then nobody can claim to know a Machiavelli."

" Oh, surely they may *claim*! A successful Machiavelli would never label himself with a big M."

Blodwen rose to her feet, tumbling one of her lazy dogs down the steps on to the grass, where he picked himself up leisurely and looked reproachful. She admitted and dismissed this subtlety with a perfunctory smile.

" Isn't there anything we can do? If only I could do something! But to go on like this, to try to live as if nothing had happened! It's impossible! Leave everything to me—that's what Mr. Penrose says. But I don't want to leave everything to him! And he's a lawyer, one can't really tell what he thinks! He's got caution on the brain. And while we waste time here, the real murderer is getting farther and farther away! "

She threw her cigarette down among the roses with a nervous gesture.

" Well," said John briskly, " to begin with, let's go and look at the drawer in the library where the revolver used to be. And while we're looking at it you can tell me : who had access to this revolver besides your uncle? "

" My dear Mr. Christmas! " said Blodwen with a despairing laugh, as she led the way into the large, cool hall, so shadowy and grateful after the heat of the sun. " I don't think that question will help us much! *Everybody* had access to the revolver! "

They entered the long library, rich and dark with its loaded shelves, and Blodwen closed the door.

" At least," she amended, " everybody in the house."

" That is to say? "

" Uncle Morris. Felix. Myself. Charles himself. Cousin Jim. Any of the servants. And any visitor who may have entered the library since the revolver was last seen."

John smiled.

" It would narrow the inquiry down a little if we could find out when the revolver was last seen safely in its drawer. Perhaps the servant who usually cleans the room would know."

" Mrs. Maur would know," said Blodwen, " if anybody would. She dusts this room herself, because my father used to be so fussy about having everything left in its usual place. But I don't suppose she's opened any of the drawers since spring-cleaning. . . . Oh, Waters, will you ask Mrs. Maur to come here, please? "

The man-servant who had appeared in answer to Blodwen's ring bowed and withdrew. John noticed that as he turned to go he cast a quick, curious glance at the end drawer of a row of drawers built in under the massive book-cases which lined one wall of the room. As the door closed John asked quickly:

" Which is the drawer? That end one? "

" Yes. How did you know? "

" That chap Waters knows," observed John thoughtfully. " Though there may be nothing in that. The affair's been pretty thoroughly discussed in the servants' hall, no doubt. Do you know anything about the man? Has he been here long? "

" About three months, I believe. He's quite a satisfactory servant, I think, though Mrs. Maur did mention to me some weeks ago that he was neglecting his work and making one of the housemaids neglect hers. Love's young dream, I suppose. But I've heard no complaints about him since. And after all, one must be reasonable. Oh, Mrs. Maur, Mr. Christmas wants to ask you some questions about this drawer."

A short, elderly woman with a rather stern but comely face had quietly entered the room and stood with her hands crossed over her black silk apron, awaiting orders. An excellent housekeeper, no doubt, thought John, noting her respectful yet steady glance, her submissive but dignified pose. Faithful, energetic, intelligent and conservative; something a little inhuman, perhaps, in the large, regular features and close-shut lips; a good but not an endearing face; not much toleration there for love's young dream. She waited for the questions. It was not for her to volunteer statements.

" Did you know, Mrs. Maur, that Sir Morris kept a revolver in one of these drawers? "

" Yes, sir."

" Which one? "

" That one, sir."

" Can you tell me when you last saw it there? "

" Yes, sir. It was on the eleventh of August, sir, nearly three weeks ago." As if she felt that this accuracy needed some explanation, the old woman added : " When I heard that the revolver had been mentioned at the inquest, I remembered I'd seen it in the drawer not long ago. And I've been able to call to mind, sir, just when it was."

" Good. Only three weeks ago. Did you move the revolver? "

- " No, sir. It was like this. Sir Charles wanted some cartridges for his sporting gun and asked me where they was, he having used what he had and wishing to obtain some more, sir. I knew as I had seen some revolver bullets in this drawer, sir, when I turned out the room, and thought there might possibly be some of the kind he wanted here too, sir. So I came down and had a look. The revolver was lying in the drawer then, sir, at about half-past eleven on the morning of August the eleventh, sir."

" Good. That certainly narrows things down a bit, doesn't it, Miss Price? Do you know, Mrs. Maur, whether any of the footmen or housemaids knew the revolver was here? "

" That I couldn't say, sir," responded the little woman primly. " I can only say as they would have no business to know. But leave drawers unlocked, and nobody can say they haven't been opened by curious folks as had no business to open them, sir."

" Quite. Now, Mrs. Maur, can you tell me whether any visitors from outside have been in this room since August the eleventh? Take your time and think it over."

There was a pause, while the old woman looked

thoughtfully about the room, as if expecting to see the wraiths of its visitors lined up against its walls.

" We haven't had many visitors in these last weeks, sir, owing to Miss Blodwen having been away. There was many come to call on Sir Charles when he first come, but mostly before the date we're speaking of. And they would all have been shown in the drawing-room. Not many visitors ever come to this room. Mr. Morris was like poor Sir Evan in not wanting anything disturbed. The doctor—Dr. Browning, that is, sir—was here one day about three weeks ago, just before he went to London, Mr. Morris being a bit poorly. He came in here to see Mr.—Sir Morris, for I showed him in here myself, but when it was exactly I couldn't say. I should say it was about then, perhaps the twelfth or thirteenth. Yes, it was the thirteenth, I remember, because it was the day before the fête at Penlow, and the doctor asked me was I going, and said he was going to look after the coco-nut shy. Apart from the doctor, I can only call to mind the policemen who came three days ago to see Sir Morris, and a lady who called last Saturday when Sir Morris was out."

" Ah! " said John, who had noted the tone of faint but definite disapproval which had crept into the housekeeper's voice. " A lady last Saturday, eh? "

" Yes. August the twenty-fifth, sir."

" Two days before the murder. Who was this lady? "

" I couldn't say, sir. She give no name. She came at about half-past three in the afternoon. The front door was open, and I happened to be passing through the hall as she come up the terrace, and she asked for Mr. Morris Price. I wasn't sure if Mr. Morris was in or not, but I asked her to come through to the little drawing-room. ' Oh, it's pleasant out here in the sun,' she says. ' I'll take this deck-chair, and wait here.' So I went to ascertain. When I come back, the lady's scarf is lying over the deck-chair, but no lady. So I walked round the terrace, thinking she might have stepped away to look at the roses, and I met her coming out through the windows of the library, sir."

" Ah! Go on."

" She came out smiling, and I could see when the sunlight fell on her face as she was an older lady than I had took her for. I kept my thoughts to myself and I said : ' Mr. Price is out, madam, and will not be at home till the evening.' ' Ah well! ' she said. ' It doesn't signify. I thought he might be out, and I've left him a note,' and she laughs. ' Will you tell him as there's a note on his desk? ' And she took up her scarf and went. But before she went, just as she was turning to go, she turned back again and she said : ' What's the new baronet like? ' "

The housekeeper's pause here was instinct with outraged propriety.

" I answered : ' Sir Charles is also out, madam.' And she laughed again, and she said : ' Well, this is a decent little place he's come into. It ought to have a mistress.' And off she went, leaving me wondering whether I oughtn't to go after her and ask what she'd been doing in the library. But although she was a strange lady, she *was* a lady, sir, by her looks and the way she spoke, though what she said was queer. So—— I told Mr. Morris when he come back. Not all she'd said, but just that she'd been in the library and written a note. He said nothing, but he didn't look pleased, and he asked no questions."

" Can you describe this lady? "

Mrs. Maur looked a little dubious.

" Well, I don't know that I can, sir, not to help much. She was a tallish lady that looked about thirty-five in the shadow and fifty in the sun. Dressed in black, with one of these small hats with a little lace veil over her eyes. Dark eyes, she had, grey, with black eyelashes, and long ear-rings and—and——" The old woman hesitated, at a loss for words to describe some peculiar quality of the visitor. She said slowly at last:

" She had a way with her as if she meant to have her way, and didn't care how things looked. And a clear, loud voice. That's all," added Mrs. Maur, after a pause to ransack the corners of her memory. She went on, anxious to leave no false impression: " When I say she looked thirty-five in the shadow, that's only to show the tall, well-set-up, smart lady that she was, sir. She'll never see forty again. Nor fifty, I shouldn't wonder."

" Did she come on foot, this lady? "

" No, sir. She came on a bicycle. I saw her walk a little way down the drive and then take to a bicycle she'd left standing against the railings. It give me quite a surprise, for by her shoes and dress and that she looked more as if she had come in a car. And she rode off as quick and easy as anything, as if she was a girl and used to exercise and that."

John smiled and glanced at Blodwen, who had been listening with a puzzled air to this recital.

" We ought to be able to find out who this person was," she now said eagerly. " Why, of course Uncle Morris must know who she was, if she left a note for him! "

" Your Uncle Morris isn't exactly a mine of information, though, is he? " murmured John. " However, we ought to be able to discover the lady's identity without troubling him. It isn't difficult to make a guess at it."

" Why! " exclaimed Blodwen. " But I haven't the slightest idea——" She broke off abruptly, with a sudden surmise. " Why, do you think——? Never mind now. Is there anything else we can ask Mrs. Maur? "

" I should like to ask, if I may, whether the housemaid, Letbe's daughter, is still working here? "

Mrs. Maur glanced at Blodwen, as if to seek her

approval before she touched on a subject so painful to the family. Blodwen gave a faint smile and nod, and the old woman answered immediately:

" No, sir. She left directly after the trouble between Sir Charles and Letbe. The trouble was about her, of course. You'll have heard that, sir."

" Yes. Has she taken a new situation, do you know? "

" No, sir. She's at home, with her father and mother. She's to be married to Waters, the second footman here, and they've got a situation in London to go to, where a married couple is wanted."

" Oh, then Waters is leaving, is he? "

" He gave in his notice at the time Ellie Letbe left, sir."

" Is he a good servant? "

" Fairly satisfactory, sir. But it isn't satisfactory when two of the servants gets engaged, sir. It doesn't answer, I find."

" Must happen fairly often, I should think."

" We usually try to engage men-servants with previous attachments, sir, preferably local ones. We find it answers better."

" I see," said John, smiling. " And your maids—do you prefer them with previous local attachments, too? "

" No, sir," answered Mrs. Maur with perfect gravity. " We prefer our maids unattached. We prefer our maids to be without matrimonial tendencies, sir! "

" Dear me, Mrs. Maur! Are there any such? "

" Oh, yes, sir. Some young women take naturally to a single life, though there aren't very many of them." Her tone added: " Unfortunately." She went on rather apologetically, as if to excuse an error of judgment: " I should never have engaged Ellie Letbe if it hadn't been for her father, sir. I could see at a glance as she was one of the marrying kind. They never answer for long."

" Cold-blooded old person, isn't she? " remarked

Blodwen with a faint smile when Mrs. Maur had left the room. " But the housekeeper par excellence."

" Devoted to the family, I suppose, and been here all her life? "

" No, oh no! Only three years. And as for devotion —well, I don't know. Her devotion is to her duty, not to us. Housekeeping is her life, and as you have just heard, anything that doesn't conduce to good housekeeping has her strong disapproval. A marvellous servant, but not devoted in the—the emotional sense. Oh, no! Poor old Letbe was devoted in that way to Uncle Morris and the place." She sighed. " He must come back, poor old man. But not just yet, I suppose, for the look of the thing. When Uncle Morris comes back will be time enough." She broke off abruptly, and asked slowly, after a pause during which John looked inside the drawer : " It isn't possible, is it, that an innocent man could be judged guilty? "

" Not if he behaves sensibly."

" But he won't! "

" Don't let's think about that," said John gently, closing the drawer, which, as he had expected, disclosed nothing which could be regarded as a clue. " We'll need all our energies to find the guilty person. We must leave Sir Morris's affairs to himself and his lawyers."

" If only there were something I could do—now, this moment."

" There is," said John cheerfully. " Go and interview Mr. Clino, and find out all you can about your Uncle Morris's wife. He's sure to know something about her, being a contemporary."

" You think this woman who called last Saturday was Uncle Morris's wife? "

" Why not? "

" It was twenty years ago, and we've heard nothing of her since."

"If your uncle had heard of her, would you have known of it?"

"No. That's true. But she's never been here before, I'm certain."

"Come, Miss Price. Last Saturday a strange woman called here, and had every opportunity of abstracting your uncle's revolver, and, what is rather significant, no opportunity of putting it back again. Isn't it obvious that we must find out who she was? She may have been anybody or nobody—a traveller in vacuum-cleaners, or an eccentric district visitor. But it is more probable that she was your Aunt Clytie—delightful name! Remember what she said to Mrs. Maur: 'Well, this is a decent little place. It ought to have a mistress.' Significant words, if you think them over."

"You mean," said Blodwen slowly, "that when my father died, and they were such a long time tracing Charles, she thought——"

"That a title would become her, and that Rhyllan Hall would be a delightful home. Yes. But remember this is the merest surmise."

"I'll go and find Cousin Jim at once," said Blodwen. "He's asleep in the arbour, I believe." She gave an impatient little laugh. "Nothing would keep Cousin Jim from his afternoon siesta. He doesn't seem to realize at all how terribly serious things are for us. I like the old silly, but I try to avoid him when there's anything the matter. His 'Dear, dear, how tiresome, well, it can't be helped, let's go to sleep' attitude gets on my nerves."

"Who *is* your cousin Jim, exactly?" asked John thoughtfully. "I want to get everybody clear in my mind."

"Oh, he's second cousin of my father's. They were great friends when they were young men, and Cousin Jim was supposed to be very clever. But his parents made him a solicitor, which he was no use at at all, and he was naturally as lazy, as could be, I imagine, and when my father came here he took him on as secretary and librarian, finding him at a loose end and practically without the means to live.   And he's been here ever since.   Of course his work was really a sinecure.   But my father liked him. And Uncle Morris likes him too, we all do, really, though we get rather impatient with him sometimes."

John nodded.

" Mr. Christmas," said Blodwen, after a moment's hesitation.   " Have you thought?   If it were Aunt Clytie —there's a motive, isn't there? "

John shook his head, but not in contradiction.

" Don't let's go too fast.   It's fatal, because it means one's always either elated or disappointed.   And one can't think clearly in either of those states."

" All very well for you," said Blodwen on a faint sigh. " You're not—involved.   But I'll try to keep my feelings out of it, or at least not to give tongue to them.   If you'll promise to tell me what you're doing, and not keep me in the dark."

She looked up at him appealingly, and John found himself thinking how attractive a plain face could be, when it was lit by a pair of fine, clear eyes.   He hesitated.

" I can't promise that," he said gently.   " But I'll be reasonable.   When I am keeping you in the dark, I'll tell you so, if you ask me.   And I'll never be mysterious just for the fun of the thing."

Blodwen looked a little disappointed and seemed about to protest, but agreed without enthusiasm and held out her hand.

" It's a bargain.   Shake hands on it.   Hullo, Felix! I told you you were to rest till tea-time."

" Couldn't," said Felix, who, coming around the corner of the terrace, had looked a little astonished at finding John and his cousin standing with clasped hands.   " I must *do* something."

" Oh, dear! " said Blodwen, with a comical lift of her eyebrows. " That's just what I've been telling Mr. Christmas. I'm afraid he's going to find us rather a nuisance. We must try not to hem him round at every turn with our efforts to help him. Now who on earth is this? " she went on, as a small, grey car came slowly up the drive. " Some kind friends, I suppose, come to express condolence and satisfy curiosity. Oh, it's only Mr. Rampson! Well, I'm going to wake up Cousin Jim."

She departed, and John and Felix went forward to greet Rampson.

CHAPTER NINE

" HULLO! " said John. " Who's Sydenham got with him? A beautiful young lady."

Felix's face lit up, and then, as a tall, well-built girl in tweeds got out of the car, became dull and weary again.

" Nora Browning," he said without enthusiasm. " I thought——"

He left the sentence unfinished. John, watching the approach of a hatless young woman, fair-haired, with a serene and serious face, thought of Arcadian Artemis in tweeds and brogues, and wondered at the boredom in his young friend's voice. It was soon explained.

" Oh, Felix," said the young lady, after greetings and introductions had passed, " I was to say good-bye to you from Isabel. She had a telegram this morning from her aunt to go home at once, poor darling! Her aunt's ill. I was to say good-bye to you, and to—to say how frightfully sorry she was about everything, and——"

John thought he could detect in the girl's low, charming voice the apologetic note of one who knows that his news is ill news, but is not quite sure how ill.

" Oh," said Felix lifelessly. " I see. Thank you, Nora."

Little enough in that, but enough in the boy's schooled expressionless face to explain his indifference to Arcadian Artemis.

" She was awfully sorry," said Nora hesitatingly.

" Thanks awfully," said Felix, and said no more.

" Is that the Miss Donne I met at the quarry the other day? "

" When my young brother Lion made himself such a nuisance to you? Yes. She was to have stayed with us ten days. But you see her aunt hasn't anybody else to look after her, so——! Mr. Christmas, did you really say that you wanted to see Lion's map? He thinks you did, and made me bring it with me to show you. Here it is. I was to say you could keep it as long as you liked, until you've digested all its subtleties, I suppose, but that it's absolutely unique and isn't insured! I suppose that's a delicate way of saying don't put it in the waste-paper basket by mistake. Just have a look at it to please the child, and give me some encouraging message for him, and I'll take it back. He's terribly proud of it."

" I really should like to keep it for a bit, though, if I may. I say! It really is rather a good bit of work, isn't it? " John spread the sheet over the wicker table, and the three of them leant over it, prepared to admire and be amused.

Felix turned aside, folded his arms on the stone balustrade and looked across the smooth lawns at some remote and mournful visions of his own.

" He certainly is thorough, young Lion," agreed Lion's sister, with a smile. " Look! This is the Tram Inn, with a note about having hard-boiled eggs for tea. And this is the bit of river that we bathed in, and the leech that Father saw, which made us all scramble out. Oh, dear! It seems years ago, already! "

She glanced at Felix's inattentive back with a sweet and wistful sympathy which gave rise in John's mind to vague thoughts about the exasperating and time-honoured blindness of love.

" Sheepshanks Cottage," remarked Rampson. " That's

where the asters are—where we had the lemonade the other day. Upper Ring Farm, that's where they keep that fiendish dog and the lodger's uncle is an undertaker."

Nora raised her eyebrows at this, and John smiled.

" Young Hufton," he said, and as Nora's face remained faintly interrogatory, went on, with a sudden quickening of interest: " Do you know anything about young Hufton? His character, interests and habits? "

" Hufton? " repeated Nora, wrinkling her broad forehead. " Oh! " She glanced at Felix and spoke in a lowered tone. " Is that the man who found poor Charles? No, I don't know anything about him. I didn't know he existed before this happened. Why? "

John wondered for a moment whether he should mention Isabel's name, but decided on caution. Nora and Isabel were apparently bosom friends, and he did not want to prejudice the former against himself. She was obviously a strong-minded and intelligent girl who might be a very useful ally.

" I heard somewhere that Taffy would be a good name for him, that's all, and wondered if he were a well-known character in these parts. You know, ' Taffy was a Welshman, Taffy was a——' "

" Thief. I don't know, I'm sure. He may be. I never heard of him till a day or two ago. But——" Her expression said: " What of it? "

" Oh, nothing," replied John casually. " Only, as you know, there's a signet-ring missing. And young Hufton is the man who found the poor chap's body. It's just possible that he may have seen no harm in—collecting the ring, so to speak."

" Yes. But wouldn't he have taken the money, too? "

" Might have felt squeamish about turning him over and rifling his pockets."

Nora nodded.

" Although," she said slowly, " there's something

funny about the money, Mr. Christmas, and it looks to me as if somebody had helped himself—either the murderer or young Hufton. Because——"

" Well? "

" There was five pounds in his note-case when he was found, wasn't there? "

" Yes? "

" Well," said the girl thoughtfully, " he had at least twenty pounds in his pocket on the day he died. What happened to the rest of it? "

John, who had been lounging on the arm of a garden chair, stiffened abruptly.

" What? " he exclaimed. " Are you sure? Because this is important, Miss Browning! "

" Yes," she said. " I'm quite sure. I would have mentioned it before, but I've only just thought of it. You see, he insisted on paying for our tea at the Tram. And I was with him when he went to settle up with the waitress; he didn't know where to find her and I did, so I showed him the way to the kitchen. The bill came to ten and six. And when he paid it I saw—I couldn't have helped seeing—that he had at least two five-pound notes in his case, as well as a thick wad of treasury notes. You see," she added, " he took them all out of his case to find a ten-shilling note among them, and—and rather flourished them about. He was rather inclined to do that," said Nora with the faintest note of distaste in her voice; and then, as if regretting that slight censure, added : " Poor man! It was only that he wasn't used to having a lot of money, and felt pleased about it, like a child."

" Then," said John, " either Hufton is a Taffy, or the murderer made away with quite a lot of money, at least fifteen pounds. I wonder why he left the five pounds."

" I suppose, so that robbery shouldn't be suspected. Though it's funny he should have taken the ring. It wasn't at all a valuable one."

" He was a fool to take the five-pound notes," remarked Rampson suddenly. " They can easily be traced."

" They can," agreed John enthusiastically, getting to his feet. " By Jove, Miss Browning, this is frightfully important, you know! If we can get the numbers of those notes we shall be in a fair way to clearing Sir Morris! And as they were pretty sure to have been paid out by a bank, there oughtn't to be any difficulty about getting the numbers."

" But we must remember," Nora reminded him, though her own cheeks were glowing with excitement, " that they may have been stolen by young Hufton. And in that case they don't help us."

" True. I must see this Hufton and try to wangle the truth out of him. I saw him at the inquest, a lout of a fellow. I think I shall go now," added John. " Why not? "

For a fraction of a moment his eyes and those of Miss Nora Browning met. Hers, wide and clear, care-fully veiled but did not hide from John the excited childish request: " Oh, let me come too! " Well, why not? Clear-headed, quick-witted and hardy, with enough personal interest in the case but not too much, she was the ideal ally.

" Come too," said John casually, " if you care to. You can tell me one or two things I want to know as we go along."

She nodded, but glanced at Felix, as if she thought he had the prior claim.

John shook his head emphatically.

" Can't do our detecting in a char-à-banc," he explained. " Besides, I've got another job for Felix, if he'll do it."

Felix turned at the sound of his own name and came rather lackadaisically forward.

" What can I do? "

" Cheer up," replied John rather unsympathetically.

Felix flushed, looked angry and then reproachful, and finally squared his shoulders and made an attempt to smile.

" I'm sorry," he said. " I know it's no use to feel like this, but——"

" It's worse than no use, it's definitely harmful. There are no end of things for you to do, and you can't do them properly if you don't pull your socks up. Look. Do you know what bank your cousin used? "

" Barclay's."

" Well, the first thing you have to do is to go to the branch he used, find out when he last cashed a cheque and for how much, whether he had any of it in five-pound notes, and if so, what were the numbers. Can you do that? "

" Yes," said Felix in a rather forced tone of alacrity. He added immediately : " How do I find out? "

" Any way you like," replied John cheerfully, making towards his car. " I leave that to your ingenuity."

He had started up the car and begun to move down the drive when a shout from Felix arrested him.

" I say! The bank'll be shut! "

" Then go and disturb the manager at his tea. Take Rampson with you. He knows no shame."

" Aren't you rather brutal to poor Felix? " murmured Nora as they passed out at the lodge gates. " After all, just think! It's his *father*! "

" Exactly. It's his father who requires our sympathy, not Felix. One mustn't let one's sympathies wander from the real sufferer. The sufferings of his family and friends are only incidental, and if one's going to be any practical use one can't waste time condoling with them. Felix and Miss Price are going to be a bit of a nuisance," added John thoughtfully. " I can't find jobs for them to do every hour of the day, and I can't take the whole world into my confidence. Besides, Felix really isn't trust-worthy."

" Mr. Christmas! " cried Nora indignantly, flushing carnation.

" I didn't mean that," said John gently. " He's the soul of honour, I know. But lacking in even the simplest form of cunning. Look at the way he tried to burn that letter under the nose of P.C. Thingumytite."

" Yes," agreed Nora, subsiding. " He's like his father, impulsive." She sighed. " Poor Felix! "

" Why poor Felix? "

" Well——"

" Yes, I know. But why poor Felix in just that tone of voice? "

" I dunno. Only—one might think that a little thing like Isabel having gone home simply wouldn't matter at a time like this. But it's those little things that are just the last straw really. Aren't they? "

" Yes," agreed John, noting with surprise the little, quickly-controlled quiver in the girl's pleasant voice.

" I thought she would have come up to say good-bye to him," went on Nora. " But she wouldn't. Though there was heaps of time."

" Oh! They were on good-bye-saying terms, then? "

" I thought so," murmured Nora in a puzzled tone. There was a memory in her mind of a little riverside overhung with willows where they had stopped for lunch one day, and dispersed to wander in search of ferns for Dr. Browning's collection; of a drooping willow which, till she heard low voices, screened from her wandering a black and a red-gold head, drooped together under the grey leaves; a low murmur : " Oh, Isabel! Oh, Isabel! " which had sent her softly back by the way she had come. She sighed.

" But one never knows," she said. No, certainly one never knew with Isabel. Delightful Isabel, gayest of companions, one never knew what went on in that shapely head.

"Has your friend Isabel stayed here before?" asked John, pursuing his own thoughts which led him far from Felix's hypothetical love affairs.

"No, never. I've only known her about ten weeks."

John looked his faint surprise. Nora turned and studied him in silence for a moment.

"Why, Mr. Christmas?" She went on before he could speak: "Was it Isabel, then, who told you that young Hufton was a thief?"

"Dear me, Miss Browning, you're not at all the traditional Watson! Far too intelligent! Yes, it was. What do you make of it?"

Nora wrinkled her level brows.

"I—don't know!" she said slowly. "I suppose—she'd heard it somewhere. Yes, of course, why not? She didn't hear it from me. But she may have heard it, casually, from anyone. She talks to everybody, and everybody loves talking to her."

"But it's such a rum subject of conversation for people who're just passing the time of day! 'Good morning. Nice day. Looks like rain. Do you know Mr. J. Hufton? He is in the habit of taking what isn't his'n.' I mean to say, Miss Browning, is it likely?"

Nora half laughed, half frowned.

"No. But—one never knows what people may talk about! Why didn't you ask Isabel where she heard it?"

"I did, practically. She started picking wild strawberries."

"Picking strawberries! Whatever for?"

"Partly, I thought, but that may be merely my low, suspicious mind, to give herself time to recover from a *faux pas*. And then she said it might have been one of the servants."

"Well, of course, so it might," said Nora slowly.

She looked uncertainly and rather coldly at John. " But Mr. Christmas, if———"

" I know just what you're going to say. You're going to say : ' Isabel is a great friend of mine, and if aspersions are cast on her good faith, I'm off.' Aren't you ? "

" Something of the kind."

" But we can't turn every line of investigation into a cul-de-sac as soon as we find one of our friends standing on it, can we ? Our business is to find out whether Mr. James Hufton purloined the notes and ring, and incidentally what grounds there are for supposing he might have done. We must verify the things we hear, even the things we hear from our friends. Remember, Miss Browning, we're trying to save a man from being brought to trial for a murder we firmly believe he's not guilty of. We can't afford to take anything on trust."

" All right," said Nora simply. " I understand. Oh, what asters ! I love asters, don't you ? "

" I do. All great detectives have simple, rural tastes. Sherlock Holmes kept bees. Sergeant Cuff grew roses. I, when I retire, shall cultivate the simple aster. Let's go and ask if we may pick some, for a consideration."

" Oh, no ! There's lots of them at home ! "

" Yes, really. One must start a conversation some-how. This," said John, shutting off the engine, " is where our investigations start."

They walked up the narrow brick path.

" ' Ginger-beer, Lemonade, Licensed to sell Tobacco,' " read Nora from a board painted above the door. " Let's have some ginger-beer instead. I feel thirsty. Besides, it gives one an excuse for lingering."

" Awfully sorry, but the cottage is let to a lady with a soul above ginger-beer. You'll see."

CHAPTER TEN

" NO, young gentleman, I doesn't allow nobody to help theirselves to my hasters. They be all I got left to show for the work my nephew put into the garden back in the spring. What with the raspberries all ate, and the beans all picked and the flowers all scratted about and the weeds a-growing as tall as houses, I bain't hardly sure if this be my garden I left so trim, or no. So, young gentleman, it bain't no use a-talking to I about picking flowers, and a-jingling of the money in your pockets. Your young lady must just make do with buttercups. And I must bid you good morning, for the place inside is in that state like you never saw, nor you, miss, and I can't rest till it's put to rights, no, not if my daughter-in-law has twenty times twins."

She did not, however, immediately shut the door, but lingered on the step, blinking ferociously in the strong sunlight, a hand grimed and shrivelled with floor-scrubbing held above her eyes. Her large bosom, draped with layers of aprons, heaved with the immense, eternal grievance of the landlord against his tenant.

" Port drunk in bed," she exclaimed tragically, heedless of John's murmured condolence, " and Prince Albert smashed in four pieces. That's what's been going on here, young master, while my daughter-in-law was a-giving of birth to twins."

139

John produced a guttural sound meant to indicate sympathy.

"*Yes*," said the old woman with enormous emphasis. " That's what I find, master, and that's why I say never, no, never shall London ladies set foot in my cottage again, not though I've a daughter in Walton and one in Hereford, and a daughter-in-law down Wensley, and two in Australia, and likely to be called away any time."

" Yes," agreed John faintly.

Nora came to his rescue.

" And how are the twins going on? "

The light of battle dimmed somewhat in the old woman's eye.

" Fine, thank you, miss, though both girls, making five in all. Drat these girls, that's what I say, they're that stubborn in coming where they're not wanted! There's my daughter in Walton has four fine boys and three girls, all nicely mixed. But with my daughter-in-law it's nothing but girls, poor woman! " The natural inferiority of daughters-in-law to daughters was nicely indicated in the patronizing pity of her voice. " But there! " she added. " If the Lord sends girls, He'll send husbands for them! "

John judged it time to re-awaken the landlord in the grandmother.

" I'm very sorry you had such bad luck with your tenant," he remarked sympathetically. " I've seen her about. She didn't look the sort of person to be a bad tenant."

" All persons is bad tenants," replied the landlord briefly. " Though some is worse."

" I knew her slightly," went on John. " In fact, we called here the other day. A Mrs. Sinclair, wasn't she, from Hampstead? "

" I dunno where she come from, but Field's the name she goes by."

"Yes, of course," said John with duplicity. "How stupid of me! I thought she was going to stay longer than this."

"So her was. Her took the cottage by the week, meaning to stay a month, her said. But thank the Lord in His goodness her niece were took ill in London, and her went home when a week was up. Went home yesterday, her did, and sent a note to I by postman that her was off. So I come to look over the place, and Prince Albert and port spilled on the sheets and the bed not so much as made up is what I finds. And wet stockings hung up over the chiny textses, and to crown all a note will I send them on when they be dry? I'm not one to keep another's stockings, not even to defray expenses, so send them on I will, though the address I don't know, only the agents in Hereford."

"She took the cottage through an agent?"

"Eade & Mainspring of Hereford, they took the cottage for she, her wanting one in these parts and not many to be had. And a good rent her paid, I will say that, but not enough to defray damages and all the raspberries and garden stuff pulled about like 'tis. Five pounds a week her paid. Five pounds when her come in, in advance like, and five pounds her left I for notice in the table drawer."

John, who did not think there was any more information to be had from this outraged house-owner, was about to make his adieux when she added in an aggrieved tone:

"But I'd ruther have had the money more ordinary-like. 'Taint easy to get change for these foreign-looking notes, though they say the post office'll change them." And inserting a grimy hand bearing two large wedding-rings into the bosom of her inmost apron she drew out a worn leather purse. Opening it cautiously, as if she thought its contents might jump out and bite, she picked from its recesses and held gingerly out to John a folded five-pound note.

It was all John could do not to seize it out of her hand. Glancing at Nora, he saw in her look the reflection of his own wild surmise.

" Ah! " he murmured nonchalantly, and nonchalantly took the note and spread it out. " A five-pound note. It's perfectly all right, you know. No reason why anybody shouldn't be perfectly willing to change it."

Its owner looked at it with mingled affection and distrust.

" I never had one before but once," she said, " and a rare job I had to get Mr. Miller up at shop to change it."

" Mrs. Field didn't pay her first week's rent with a bank-note, then? "

" No. I ent seen one of these but once, and that was when old master give I one for a silver-wedding present."

" Well, it's quite all right," said John reassuringly. He added in a careless tone: " I'll change it for you now, if you like."

She seemed to hesitate, and for a moment John feared that her pride in this rare possession might outweigh her dubiety. He took his note-case from his pocket, and counted out five clean one-pound notes. The old woman hesitated no longer, but plumped for safety.

" Well! " said Nora excitedly, as they left the landlord among the terra-cotta ruins of Prince Albert and returned to the car. She added immediately: " But of course it may not be one of *those* bank-notes. Shall we go back and see whether Felix has got the numbers? Or shall we go on and see Hufton while we're here? "

" I think we'll go to Hereford," replied John, getting into the car, " and interview Messrs. Eade & Mainspring. Mr. Hufton can wait, perhaps for ever. After all, we had nothing against him except the fact that Isabel said he was a thief. This may be a perfectly innocent five-pound note. But quite apart from the note, this Mrs. Field may prove, I think, to be an interesting person."

" Why? "

" Well," said John, starting the car up Rodland Hill, " wait a second while I get my thoughts clear about her. By the way, did that old lady's remark about raspberries convey any idea to you? "

" No."

" No, I suppose not. You weren't here the other day when your young brother Lion accused Isabel of having pinched raspberries out of the garden."

" What, when she disappeared, you mean, after coming down the hill? She said they were wild ones. And anyhow, Mr. Christmas, really, Isabel wouldn't do a thing like that. Lion was only joking."

" Yes," agreed John meekly. " I think he was."

" But," went on Nora sternly, " do you mean to say that you think Isabel——"

" No, oh, no! I don't think she pinched them. But never mind that, Miss Browning, it's only a side-issue at present. Now, about Mrs. Field: firstly, I've seen her, and she didn't look at all the sort of person who would enjoy pigging it by herself in a primitive cottage in a remote part of the country."

" That's nothing. You can't tell what a person will enjoy."

" Nothing by itself, of course. But all these little things mount up. Secondly, she was anxious to get a cottage in this part of the country and employed an agent to find her one."

" Well? It may have had associations for her, or she may have had friends living in the district, or anything."

" Quite. I like your commonsense comments, Miss Browning, they help to clear the air. Please continue them. Thirdly, she departed in a hurry three days after the murder, on the day of the inquest."

" Her niece was taken ill."

" So she said. But of course she would have to say something. Fourthly, Morris Price has a wife, who, although she hasn't been seen by his relatives for twenty years, is still, as it were, extant."

" I know," said Nora slowly. " She was a barmaid or something, and ran away. But you can't mean that this Mrs. Field is Mr. Price's wife! Or can you? Did she look like a barmaid? "

John laughed.

" Dear me, this barmaid legend! How it crops up! You'll notice, Miss Browning, that whenever a man makes a *mésalliance*, rumour has it that it's with a barmaid. Though heaven knows there aren't enough barmaids to go round. No, no. Miss Blodwen told me that she was an hotel-keeper's daughter. And after all, there are hotels and hotels. No need for her to have served in the bar. I gathered from Miss Blodwen that she was a very present-able and rather awe-inspiring lady. Fifthly, there was a visitor at Rhyllan Hall——"

John recounted the story which he had heard from Mrs. Maur.

" Oh! " said Nora when he had finished. " Well, I've got no commonsense comment to make on that! It does sound suspicious, doesn't it? And of course if she were Morris Price's wife and meant to make it up with her husband, there would be a motive, wouldn't there, for the murder? " She paused a moment, as the first houses of Hereford came in sight and John slowed down to pass a large flock of sheep which were moving in mass formation from the town under the command of a small collie and a man on horseback. " Oh, Mr. Christmas! I've just thought: mightn't Mr. Price's busi-ness in Hereford on the day of the murder, that he won't tell anybody about, have something to do with her? "

" Good for you, Miss Watson," said John approvingly.

" It might.   Oh, blow!   Can't this man control his
sheep?   He seems to want them run over!   It's a funny
thing, but whenever I motor through a town it's always
market day.   I vote we run the car into a garage and
venture on foot among these horned monsters and savage
drovers.   Don't you?   And we can inquire after Messrs.
Eade & Mainspring at the same time."

Eade & Mainspring, House-Agents, Valuers and
Surveyors, had their offices in a pleasant old stucco
house fronting on the main street of the town.   Its
interior had an agreeably deserted air after the jostle of
the market street.   A young clerk sat on the edge of a
large pedestal desk at the end of a long, dim room, looking contemplatively at the ceiling with the air of a ship-
wrecked mariner watching the sky for signs of storm.
As Nora appeared he engineered himself into his chair
with one supple, practised movement, and began to make
play among the numerous ledgers on the desk, frowning
the frown of the busy and humming the tune of the
slightly embarrassed.   He was a little disappointed to
find that these two promising clients did not require to
buy a mansion nor even to lease a cottage.

" Mrs. Field? " he murmured, examining the tip of
a pen-holder with minute care.   " Yes, I remember, sir.
The lady who took a cottage near Wensley.   Rather out
of our line, leasing cottages for short periods, but the
lady was so anxious to have one near Penlow that we
were glad to oblige.   Though the only cottage available
was a good deal farther from Penlow than she wanted.
About eight miles this side, wasn't it?   Sheepshanks
Cottage, yes.   Queer name."   And the young man
smoothed back his glossy hair and appeared to con-
template from his urban height the grotesque place-names
of rusticity.

" Her address?   Yes, of course, we *have* her address
—in our books."   His tone indicated that extracting the

address from their books would be a matter of great difficulty. He hesitated. " Pardon me, sir, we have found it wiser to make a rule not to give our clients' addresses, except to—except when—except in matters of great urgency."

" This is a matter of great urgency. She's been called home suddenly, owing to illness, and hasn't left me her address."

" Perhaps, sir, you had better see our Mr. Mainspring."

" Certainly. Where is he? "

" At the moment he is away. But if you care to call to-morrow morning——"

" Let me see your Mr. Eade."

The young man assumed the slightly hurt and sorrowful expression suitable to the occasion.

" Our Mr. Eade, sir, is not an active partner. He is, in fact—ah! dead."

" Then," said John firmly, " I'm afraid you'll have to take the responsibility of giving me that address. I must have it. Come now, do I look perfectly respectable or do I not? I'll stand with my face to the light, so that you can have a good look at me."

" Oh, yes! Oh, yes! " murmured the clerk in an agony of deprecation. " It isn't that at all, sir. But——"

" But a rule is a rule, eh? I know. I make it a rule always to have my own way. Come on! It's somewhere in Kensington, isn't it? "

With a subdued sigh, the young man turned over the leaves of a large book.

" 8a Featherstone Terrace, W.8," he uttered hopelessly, as one whose soul is lost. " Mrs. Margaret Field, 8a Featherstone Terrace, W.8." He gently closed the tome and looked sadly at his persecutor. " Shall I write it down? " he asked, completing his damnation.

" Please. Thank you. Well, good afternoon! When

I want to buy an estate in Herefordshire I'll certainly come to you."

The young man smoothed his shining locks, smiled a pensive, sceptical smile and opened the door.

" Ornamental creature, wasn't he? " said John, as he and Nora turned down the narrow pavement. " But too docile to rise high in his profession. He'll never be the Emperor of Estate-Agents. Hullo! What is it, Miss Browning? Aren't you glad we've got one step nearer to the elusive Mrs. Field? "

" I don't know," said Nora in a subdued manner. She had gone rather pale, and as they approached a crossing was about to step in front of a large motor-lorry when John grabbed her by the arm. Her eyes had a vague, stern look.

" I'm sorry," she murmured. " I didn't notice it." They crossed, arm in arm.

" I say! " murmured John, stopping a little way up the quiet side-street to look at her pale face. " Is it the heat? "

He had a sister who was, to put it euphemistically, not a good traveller, and he recognized that pensive, remote and other-worldly look as a familiar presage of disaster.

" No," said Nora with a pale smile. " It's all right. I'm not going to be sick. I'm just—rather surprised."

" Whatever at? "

Nora looked up at him solemnly.

" That address."

" Mrs. Field's? "

" Isabel's. I don't think I like being a detective."

CHAPTER ELEVEN

" SUPPOSE," said John, making a neat parcel of
three banana-skins and several paper bags and
handing it to Nora to put in the basket, " that Mrs.
Margaret Field, Clytie Meadows and Isabel's aunt are
one and the same person. Let's see where it leads us."

It was the morning of the day following the visit to
Hereford, and John, feeling a need to discuss his dis-
coveries with Rampson far from the dangers of doors,
walls and windows, had suggested a trip to Radnor
Forest. True to her compact, Blodwen did not offer to
come; but she would have come, John knew, had he
asked her. He did not do so. He felt a strong desire
to get away from the Prices and the Price point of view
for a time. Their close connection with the murder
introduced an emotional note that was fatal to impartial
discussion. Besides, to the impersonal investigator that
a detective should study to be, Blodwen herself was a
possible suspect. She had been out in her car on the
afternoon of the murder; and there was no witness to
confirm her statement that she had celebrated her return
to her native land by joyously touring the roads from one
beloved landmark to another. Yes, on the whole it was
better not to admit the Prices to these conclaves. Blodwen
was a possible suspect, and Felix, though he had stiffened
to a more cheerful frame of mind since his interview with
the bank manager, was a youth of that uncertain and

impulsive temperament that can never quite be trusted to be discreet.

They had made their expedition to the Forest in John's two-seater, calling for Nora on the way. And now, having eaten the bananas and buns they had bought for lunch at a village shop, they were sitting among the bracken on a high slope within sound of Water-Break-Its-Neck, in profound peace and loneliness, surrounded by great trees where pigeons cooed and ghostly owls slept on the branches.

"I had a letter from Isabel to-day," murmured Nora pensively. "Just a duty letter, you know, written as soon as she got home. She says her aunt isn't seriously ill, after all. She writes from the same address. Mr. Christmas——" She hesitated, puckering her fair brows. "Isn't it possible that they both have flats in the same house? Isabel and her aunt live in a flat, I know. I can't believe——"

"What?" asked John gently. "That Isabel is Mrs. Field's niece?"

"That Isabel could be so—so secretive. And yet, oh dear! I *can* believe it! I suppose it's just because I can believe it so easily that I feel ashamed to!" She half smiled, half sighed. "Isabel was always a little strange. She told one nothing, though she talked so much. She knows everything about me. But now I come to think of it, what do I know about her? Nothing!"

"How long have you known Isabel?" asked John musingly.

"Since the middle of June. She came to the art-school then."

"What art-school do you go to?"

"The South Kensington. She came in the middle of the term. She'd just come to England with her aunt, she said. She'd been living for two years in——" Nora caught her breath, suddenly realizing as she spoke that

there might be great significance in what she said.
" Canada," she finished in a low voice.

" Ah! " said John. " She'd been living for two years
in Canada. Canada is a large place, of course. Did she
say where in Canada? "

" No. She'd been living there with her aunt, and they
had both come over to England to live. She said she had
no father or mother."

Nora paused, frowning and pulling a bracken frond to
pieces.

" Really, that's all I know. She was very popular at
school, because she's so amusing, and we made friends.
But she never talked much about herself."

" She made friends with you, and she made friends with
Felix. Was she more friendly with you two than with
any of the others? "

" Yes. With me, at first. And then, of course, as I
know Felix awfully well, she was friends with Felix too.
We used to go about together a lot. Museums and
theatres and things. I live with my sister in Kensington
during term-time. And Isabel used to come and see me
a lot. So did Felix."

" Did she ever ask you to visit her and her aunt? "

" No. I never saw her aunt, nor heard her name. I
took it for granted her aunt's name was Donne."

" Now, Nora, what made you ask Isabel to come and
stay with you? "

Nora looked a little surprised.

" Well, we thought it would be fun. What generally
makes one invite people to stay with one? "

" She didn't—invite herself? "

" No. At least——"

" Ah! "

" No, but she *didn't* invite herself, John! Only, one
evening when Felix and I first got the idea of bicycling
home with Lion, and were talking it over, she said that

she loved cycling. And soon afterwards it came out that she had no plans for the holidays. So of course I said: ' Come with us.' "

" And she said? "

" She didn't know whether her aunt could spare her at first. But next time I saw her she said she would love to come for ten days. But there's nothing in that! I mean, you can't call that inviting herself! "

" No, perhaps not. Let's call it gentle encouragement of a potential hostess."

John rolled over and lay chin on hands looking across the deep, narrow gorge of Water-Break-Its-Neck to the great mossy boulders and forests of tall bracken on the other side.

" Now, what do we know about Mrs. Field? One: she lives at the same address in London as Isabel Donne. Two: she was anxious to rent a cottage near Penlow during the time that Isabel was staying with the Brownings. Three: she left in a hurry on the day of the inquest, alleging that her niece was ill in London. Four: she paid her rent with a five-pound note which had been in Charles's possession four days earlier. Yes, Nora, Felix got the numbers from the bank manager in Penlow. And the number on our note is one of them."

" But good heavens, nobody but a half-wit would abstract five-pound notes from the pockets of a person they'd just murdered! "

" Softly, my dear Miss Watson! We're not accusing anybody of the murder yet. We're just reciting the facts. Now for Clytie Meadows. Blodwen was quite successful in pumping old Penrose about her. One: she was the daughter of a successful hotel-keeper in Bristol. Two: she married Morris Price in 1905, and lived with him in Bristol. Three: she left Morris Price in 1908. There was no divorce. Mr. Penrose did his best at the time to persuade Morris to apply for a divorce, but he refused, on the grounds that he did not believe in divorce and would never think of marrying again. Four: her description, allowing for the passage of twenty years, would be a good description of Mrs. Field. And now we come to a third person, the mysterious lady who called at Rhyllan Hall on August twenty-fifth, two days before the murder, and left a note for Morris Price. We have only a slight and vague description of her, but such as it is, it would do both for Mrs. Field and for Clytie Meadows, or Clytie Price, as her name must be. And the fact that she came to Rhyllan Hall on a bicycle suggests that she did not come from far. From Sheepshanks Cottage to Rhyllan Hall is about twelve miles, quite a nice cycling expedition. Altogether, I am inclined to think that Clytie Meadows, Mrs. Field, Isabel's aunt and the mysterious visitor are one and the same lady. Can either of you think of a sound objection to this theory? "

Nora nibbled thoughtfully at a grass stalk, and Rampson lit his pipe.

" I can't," he replied. " All I can say is, that the lady who gave us lemonade didn't look to me at all like a person out of a crook play."

" What did she look like? " asked Nora thoughtfully.

Rampson took several puffs at his pipe and considered the question carefully.

" A bazaar-opener," he answered finally, with quiet conviction.

" Perhaps she's that too," said John cheerfully. " Bazaar-opening isn't a full-time career."

" My dear John, people with four aliases don't open bazaars."

" Nobody suggests that she's got four aliases. She's Clytie Meadows, Mrs. Field, Isabel's aunt and a visitor to Rhyllan. Surely one can be an aunt and a visitor without leading a double life. By the way, Nora, didn't Isabel ever mention her aunt's Christian name? "

" Puffy."

" Eh ? "

" Isabel always spoke of her as Puffy."

" Giving people nicknames," remarked John sadly, " is a detestable practice which ought, in the interests of the detective profession, to be abolished by law. We'll ask Mr. Penrose if he used to call Clytie Meadows Puffy."

" He didn't," said Nora with conviction. " He called her my dear young lady, like he does me and Blodwen." She added : " But I think you're probably right. And I can see that if you are right the whole thing hangs together, and there's a motive for the murder. It's the details that seem so crude and unlikely. If Clytie Meadows wanted to murder Charles, have a reconciliation with Morris and come and live at Rhyllan Hall, would she have done the murder quite so near home? Would she have taken a cottage next door to the murder, so to speak? And that five-pound note! I can't get over that! "

" Again, Miss Watson, you go too fast. Whether she did the murder or not will appear later, we hope. Meanwhile the facts are that a lady who may or may not be Clytie Meadows *did* rent Sheepshanks Cottage, and that one of Charles's notes *was* in her possession after the murder. Our business is to follow up those two facts. They may lead us to the murderer, or they may lead us up against a blank wall. It's wasting time to try to guess which. I think we may take it as certain that the lady who rented Sheepshanks Cottage is Isabel's aunt, and we ought to be able to get at her through Isabel and find out if she is also Clytie Meadows."

" I don't quite see how," said Nora pensively. " Of course I could write and ask Isabel. But she wouldn't answer."

" No, no. We'll have to be more subtle than that. But let's leave Mrs. Clytie alone now, and turn our attention to the other possible murderers."

" Are there any? " asked Rampson with an appearance of surprise.

" Great Scot, yes!   Now what are the two essential qualifications of the murderer, whoever he may have been? "

" One," said Nora, " is that he hasn't got an alibi for round about seven o'clock on August the twenty-seventh."

" Yes.   That's the most important point, of course. And the second?   That he must have had access to Morris's revolver between August the eleventh, when Mrs. Maur saw it in the drawer in the library, and August the twenty-seventh, when the murder was committed."

" He must have had a motive, too," observed Nora, " unless he was a lunatic.   And as he took the trouble to use another man's revolver, I suppose we can leave stray lunatics out of it."

" We'll certainly leave them out," said John decidedly. " Murders by wandering homicidal maniacs are rare enough to be ignored.   As for the question of motive, I think we'll leave it out too, until we've got our list of people who fulfil the other requirements.   Motives are sometimes obvious and sometimes not, and we don't know enough about Charles to be able to guess at the motive of his murderer.   After all, until a few weeks ago he was living in Canada.   We don't know what enemies he may have made there.   Well.   Let's try and clarify our ideas. Possible Murderers."

Nora looked through a gap in the trees across the valley to the high ridge opposite, where a shepherd was walking with two small collies on the sky-line.   As she watched, he took the sloping footpath and descended into the little valley.

" What do shepherds do all day? " asked Nora dreamily.   " Walk about counting their sheep, I suppose, and contemplating the hills.   I should like to be a shepherd."

"There's dipping and shearing and folding and lambing," said Rampson the realist. "And foot-rot and maggots and——"

Nora laughed.

"Oh, don't! My kind of shepherd just feeds his flocks on the mountain and in the fine weather he sits among the bracken and reads Chaucer, and in the wet weather he sits in his little hut and reads Spenser. There's a shepherd's hut on the ridge side a little farther along, and when I was a child I used to think it the most romantic place, and a shepherd's life the most peaceful in the world. Don't destroy my illusions. Well, John? Am I a possible murderer?"

"You don't comply with either of the two conditions. Morris Price is the first and most obvious one. He was almost too obviously on the scene of the murder about the time it was committed, and he has an almost too obvious motive. And of all people, he most obviously had access to his own revolver. But as he has been arrested, and our business is to prove him not guilty, we'll leave him out of it."

"Of course."

"Then there's Mrs. Field. She's obviously a woman of mystery. If, as we suppose, she was the woman who called at Rhyllan Hall last Saturday, she had access to the revolver in the library. She had one of Charles's five-pound notes after the murder. And she left in a hurry on the day of the inquest. We certainly haven't done with her yet. Then there's Waters, the footman. Do you know Waters, Nora?"

"The young one? I've seen him once or twice at the hall. He's new. I haven't noticed him particularly."

"He could have got hold of the revolver. He's engaged to marry Ellie Letbe, the gardener's daughter—you know, the one there was trouble about. And he looked capable of violent revenges—a cold, crafty face,

I thought. Whether he has an alibi or not remains to be seen. It's one of the first things we must look into."

" Of course, all sorts of people may have been able to get hold of that revolver if it hadn't been seen in the drawer since August the eleventh," said Nora slowly. " The murderer may be somebody whose existence we don't even know of."

" Also," said Rampson, chewing a contemplative harebell stalk, " it doesn't seem to have occurred to you, John, that your Mrs. Maur, the housekeeper, may have been lying when she said she saw the revolver on August the eleventh."

" Oh, it's occurred to me all right! She may have been the murderer herself, for all we know yet. Though from what Blodwen said, I gather that it is a matter of complete indifference to her who she housekeeps for, as long as she housekeeps for somebody."

" Funny old soul, Mrs. Maur," said Nora thoughtfully. " She's been at the hall three years and I've seen quite a lot of her, one way and another. But she always looks at me as if she'd never seen me before. She's not human. She's the perfect servant. And the perfect servant is not human. But Blodwen says she's a marvellous housekeeper."

John threw a little stone over the edge of the fall, and heard its faint tinkle on the rocks below.

" Does the perfect servant, I wonder, require the perfect master? Or is it part of her perfection that she can adapt herself to any master, even to the kind that dismisses lifelong gardeners and kisses housemaids? "

" My dear John! " Nora half laughed in surprise and opened her grey eyes wide. " You're not going to suggest that Mrs. Maur might have murdered poor Charles because he didn't come up to her standards as an employer? She'd have to be a lunatic to do such a thing! "

"I'm not suggesting anything," said John lazily. "Only wondering what the perfect servant does when she gets an imperfect employer. And you said yourself that the perfect servant wasn't human."

Rampson suddenly sat up.

"When you've finished talking nonsense about what a hypothetical creature might do in an imaginary set of circumstances, may I say something sensible?" he asked meekly.

"Say on."

"Well, listen. You and Nora have mentioned three or four people who, according to you, may have had access to Price's revolver. But it doesn't seem to have occurred to you that there are several million people in the world and that all of them had access to the revolver."

"No. No," said John soothingly. "I think not. If the entire population of the world had converged upon Rhyllan Hall any time during the last three weeks we should have heard about it, I feel sure."

"Any one of them, I mean, you ass. And not at Rhyllan Hall, either. It doesn't seem to have occurred to you that Charles may have been carrying the revolver himself, and that the person who murdered him may have got possession of it from him, and not from the drawer in the library at all."

There was a pause. John sighed.

"I'm awfully sorry to disappoint you, Sydenham, but it *had* occurred to me. But I think it's unlikely. Of course, ordinary people don't carry revolvers on peaceful bicycling tours through rural England. But Charles may not have been an ordinary person, so I won't press that point. But if one carries a revolver, one carries one's own revolver, not somebody else's. And Charles had a revolver of his own. It was found in the chest in his bedroom the day after the murder, and is still there, so far as I know. You may remember that Felix told us the police had found a revolver in Charles's room when they searched the house."

Rampson looked a trifle crestfallen.

" Yes, I do remember now.   But still," he added obstinately, " there is no *proof* that Charles wasn't carrying Morris's revolver."

" No proof," agreed John, " but a strong presumption. And we're at the stage where one has to work chiefly on presumptions.   Proof will come afterwards."

" That's all very well, as long as you don't let yourself forget that your presumptions, however plausible, aren't proof.   It's very easy for a person with a hopelessly unscientific mind like yours to overlook the difference between fact and conjecture."

" I know," said John humbly.   " But you'll never let me overlook it for long, Sydenham, so it's all right.   Still, you'll agree that at this stage of the investigation I'm justified in the conjecture that the revolver was abstracted from the library drawer and not from Charles's person? "

" Certainly," agreed Rampson gravely.   " But you must keep the other possibility always in your mind, until it is definitely disproved."

" I will endeavour to do so," responded John with equal gravity.   " Now you know, Nora, why I won't let Rampson go back to his microscope.   I need a wet blanket, and the scientific mind is the wet blanket par excellence."

" So I perceive.   He won't let even a shepherd be Arcadian."

" Well, look at your shepherd," remonstrated Rampson. " There he is, coming along the footpath, followed by his faithful and flea-ridden dogs.   Does he look as if he could read his A B C, let alone Spenser?   Do you think he ever contemplates the hills except as food for his sheep?   Not he!   Ask him."

" I will, if he comes near enough," replied Nora with

a laugh. " I suppose he *is* a shepherd," she added doubtfully, as the figure approached along the little footpath
below. " He's got a funny-looking sort of raincoat on,
miles too big for him. And, Sydenham, he's carrying a
book under his arm! "

" So he is. But I'll bet you a hundred pounds, if you
like, it's not Shakespeare or Spenser, or whoever your
selections were. It's probably ' Diseases of Sheep.' "

" No," said Nora firmly. " Absolutely not. It's
plain you've never met a shepherd, Sydenham. ' Diseases
of Sheep ' is the one book you'd never find a shepherd
reading. They know all that by the light of Nature. Or
think they do, which is the same thing, of course. Hi! "

The little man wavered somewhat in his slow, shambling
walk, looked dubiously and shyly up the slope at Nora,
and then, evidently mistrusting his ears, walked on, his
two dejected-looking collies following dreamily at his
ankles.

" It's no use," said Rampson cheerfully. " He's too
much absorbed in contemplating Nature to be bothered
with you. That *is* an outsize in raincoats he's got on. I
don't believe it is the shepherd, after all. I'm sure he
wasn't draped in those classic folds when we saw him on
the opposite ridge. After all, everybody who keeps a
mongrel collie as a pet isn't a shepherd. Great heavens,
John, what is the matter? "

John had jumped to his feet, and making a megaphone
of his hands had sent a long " Hi! " echoing down the
valley.

The little man on the path below stopped dead in his
tracks and looked carefully around him from slope to slope
and down the valley, finally examining the clouds with a
meek and hopeful air.

" Hi! " shouted John again, fortissimo, and as the man
turned with an air of unwillingness in his direction,
gesticulated wildly.

The shepherd hesitated, turned and began slowly to retrace his steps. As he approached nearer, they could see that he was a man of fifty or so, with a long, pale face and drooping, light moustache and that look of kinship with his own flock that is sometimes found in the later generation of a long line of shepherds. At a distance so respectful that conversation was practically impossible, he stopped and shouted interrogatively :

" Aye, master? "

" Have some sandwiches," shouted John, hoping to lure him up the bank.

" No, thank you kindly. I be full."

" Well—hi! "

" Oh, aye? "

" Hi! "

" Ah! " shouted the shepherd enigmatically, and remained where he was.

John began to walk down the hill towards him, and at this he unwillingly advanced until he was within speaking distance of the trio. His dogs advanced at the same pace, and stood one on each side of him, surveying John with distrustful looks.

" Nice day," said John affably.

" Oh, aye," agreed the stranger. " But moisty."

" Rain? Not it! "

" Bain't going to rain these three days. Body-moisty, it be."

" You shouldn't wear so many clothes," said John reasonably. " People are always writing to the papers about it. Why wear a raincoat? "

A look of slow suspicion clouded the shepherd's light and placid eyes.

" Writing to papers? " he repeated uncertainly. " About I? "

" About wearing too many clothes in the hot weather. Why wear a raincoat? "

The other man regarded him sideways and uncertainly. At last he inquired:

"Be this your coat, master? If he be, you shall have he, for I bain't the man to profit by another's loss. But how'll I know as he be yourn?"

"Where did you find it?"

The shepherd made a vague gesture along the footpath.

"Near hut. Th' ole bitch sniffed 'un out. He were buried under the bracken, and a bit dampish, as you can see, but good for wear, so I put 'un on. For I thinks, a chap as buries his coat means the world to know as he hasn't no more use for he."

"No, no," said John thoughtfully. "He buries it because he doesn't mean the world to know."

The shepherd looked doubtful.

"If you says as he's yourn, master, you shall have he. Only say the word, and off he comes. He's a bit on the large side for I, it's true, but I were never a man to let things go to waste, so I dug 'un out. Hey! Mind my dogs, miss! They be ticklish-tempered."

Nora, who had suddenly jumped to her feet and approached to examine the cloth of the raincoat, drew back.

"John!" she cried. "But it *is* Charles's coat! I remember the funny buttons and the little tear in the pocket! But however can it have got up here?"

"If he be a gentleman's coat," said the honest shepherd, proceeding to strip it off, "let the gentleman have he."

"The police must have it, I suppose," said John rather unwillingly.

"They'll be delighted," observed Rampson. "It'll be evidence for the Crown in the forthcoming trial."

"Oh, no!" cried Nora. "Need we? Don't you remember, John, Felix's father said he spent the night driving and walking about the Forest?"

"Police?" echoed the shepherd, arrested with one arm

out of the disputed coat. " Now, master, I bain't a-stealing of he! "

A slow flush of indignation rose in his cheeks.

" No, no," said John hurriedly. " But there's been a murder, you know."

" Oh, aye? "

" Yes. You must have heard about it. Sir Charles Price of Rhyllan was found dead in a quarry."

" Ah, I heerd."

" Well, this is his coat."

There was a pause. The shepherd looked gently from John to Nora, removed his hat, scratched his head, and replaced the hat at a more comfortable angle.

" The gentleman be dead, you says, master? "

" Yes."

" And this be his coat? "

" Yes."

" Then he don't need 'un," said the shepherd with sweet reasonableness, and shook himself back into its damp folds.

" No, but the police do," said John firmly. " And I'm afraid you'll have to take it to them and tell them where you found it."

The little man fixed John with a slowly calculating eye, and thought this over.

" They'll think as I did the murder."

" Not they. They'll be pleased with you."

" Oh, aye? But I be paid for shepherding. I bain't paid for traipsing to police and back."

" I'll take you in my car. But first will you show me where you found the coat? "

" I bain't paid for traipsing after coats."

" I'll pay you," John assured him, fingering his note-case.

" Nay, nay, master," said the little man reprovingly, divesting himself of the raincoat and hanging it over his arm. " A shilling'll be plenty." And having thus put matters on a business footing he led the way back along the footpath which wound down into the valley and up again on the opposite ridge towards a small, lonely, slate-built hut standing high among the bracken and great boulders of the hillside.

" Here's where th' ole bitch sniffed 'un out," said the shepherd, pointing to a patch of bracken a few yards distant from the hut. " And here's where I found 'un. But there bain't nothing else thereabouts, young master, for I looked."

There was a patch where the stout, springy bracken stems were bent and scattered as though something heavy had pressed upon them. It was obvious that the coat had been lying there some time.

" Was it rolled up tight and pushed down among the stems? " asked John, looking at the patch, realizing the hopelessness of attempting to search this sea of bracken for further clues. " Or did it look as if it had been carelessly thrown down? "

" Folded up neat, he were, and laid down among the stalks. The gentleman meant to lose he, master. There weren't no forgetting."

John nodded and looked inside the hut, which contained nothing but a roughly made bench, a billy-can and enamel cup and a close, fusty smell.

" Nothing unusual in here? "

" Naught, master. 'Twere just as I left 'un, though I leaves the door unfastened, owing to my son from over Black Hill way using the hut sometimes. But there's not many comes this way, and I'm not one to complain if a chap should shelter here from the rain now and then, so long as they doesn't make too free with my gear."

He picked up his enamel cup and lovingly wiped it over with a flap of his weather-hued coat. But Rampson, who had been examining the floor of the hut, asked suddenly :

" Do you smoke? "

" I doesn't, master," responded their host in tones of

courteous reproof. " For smoke be the first step to drink, and drink be the first step to ruin. And my son, he doesn't smoke nor drink, having seen the light at Rodd Fair two summers back."

" I'm afraid some child of darkness has been using your hut," observed Rampson gently, and he held out to John a half-inch stub of cigarette which he had picked from the earthen floor.

John examined it carefully, looked rather grave and put it away in his pocket-book.

" Hatton's Ripe Virginia," pursued Rampson. " Know the brand? "

" Yes," said John. " I've smoked several of them myself during the past week. Very good tobacco, but too strong for my taste. And now let's go back to the car and drive into Penlow."

Walking back along the valley, Nora remembered her little passage-at-arms with Rampson, and asked their friend the shepherd :

" Might I look at that book you're carrying? "

" Oh, aye, miss, though he bain't mine. He were in the pocket of the coat, and a silly, sinful book he be, full of folly and vanity, and the covers has run a bit on to the pages, owing to the damp. You're welcome to keep he, if the police doesn't want him." And mildly frowning over the pomps and follies of this wicked world he handed her a small book with a damp-swollen, scarlet cover, entitled " The Etiquette of English Social Life."

Nora glanced at it, half laughed and was silent. Glancing at her, John was surprised to see her eyes full of tears. She brushed them away, laughed uncertainly and quickly passed the book on to him.

" It's so pathetic," she mumbled, searching for a handkerchief. " Charles—none of us liked him, really. His manners were so awful—kind of showy, you know— and we were so beastly critical. And all the time he must have been trying to—to be what he thought he ought to be. It's so pathetic! Oh, I am an ass! Thanks awfully, John. I shall make it beastly damp."

They walked on in silence to the farm-track where they had left the car. John fingered the pages of the little red book. It and Nora's broken words seemed to place the dead Charles for the moment in a more appealing light. As once before, John found himself pitying the Colonial who had had to take up the stiff traditional mantle of the English squire. Evidently, he had tried.

A tiny pain in his finger made him withdraw his hand sharply from the leaves of the book. There was a large darning-needle sticking in the skin and as he pulled it away a little bead of blood appeared. Looking inside the book he found two more huge needles stuck in the mild and admonitory pages; one of them was threaded with a short strand of brown wool.

" Oh, yes," said Nora, handing back his handkerchief. " Poor Charles could darn his own socks and said he always carried a needle and wool with him in Canada. He was rather proud of it, poor dear." She dropped her voice; Rampson and the shepherd were walking on ahead, discussing the influence of beer and tobacco on man's prospect of eternal felicity. " John," she asked earnestly, " Felix smokes that brand, doesn't he? "

" Hatton's Ripe Virginia? Yes. So does Morris Price, and so does Blodwen. And it's an uncommon and rather expensive brand. I don't like the look of it, Nora. All the evidence we've collected so far is evidence against Morris Price. And yet—why should Morris Price have brought Charles's coat away with him? Surely he would have left it with the body? "

" Why should anybody bring Charles's coat away and hide it on the Forest? "

" Yes. The question applies to anybody, of course. Find me the answer, Nora, and I'll find you the murderer."

CHAPTER TWELVE

EGGS IS EGGS

" DEAR me! " said Mr. Clino, raising his head with a sudden jerk and opening his eyes as John's long shadow fell across him and his deck-chair. " Was I asleep? Dear me! I suppose I must have been."

He took off his glasses, polished them and replaced them, and picked up the book which had fallen from his knees to the ground. Observing John's eye fixed upon it in some surprise, he asked :

" Do you read detective stories, Mr. Christmas? "

" Occasionally."

" They're quite a vice with me," said the old man, ruefully marking his place in " The Purple Ray Murders " and putting the volume in his pocket. " In fact, as time goes on I read more and more of them and less and less of anything else. It's rather regrettable, really, for they're mostly bad, and when they touch on legal matters they're nearly always absurd, which irritates me. I try to cure myself of the habit, sometimes, by reading Scott and Thackeray, who used to be my favourites. But I find that my taste is so vitiated that I can no longer read good authors with enjoyment." He sighed. " Of course," he added, brightening up a little, " there is always Wilkie Collins. But one can't go on reading ' The Woman in White ' for ever."

166

" Is there a library of detective fiction here? "

" No," replied Mr. Clino, looking a little guilty. " My old friend Evan had no taste at all for light literature. I don't know what he would have said if he had seen me reading a book like this! In fact, I think it was the necessity of secret indulgence that gave the vice such a strong hold over me. Of course, there is a circulating library at Penlow." He hesitated. " But I hardly like to go there, where I am so well known."

" Oh, come! " said John, half-amused and half-irritated by the old man's scruples. " It's not surely such a desperate matter as that! Why shouldn't you read what you like? "

" But a librarian! " protested Cousin Jim, looking genuinely shocked. " With a reputation for scholarship! How could I? Besides, if it had come to poor Evan's ears——! "

" We've been up on the Forest," said John, a little tired of the subject, but Mr. Clino was not to be diverted. He rose slowly and stiffly and methodically folded up the plaid rug which had been lying across his knees.

" One would imagine, Mr. Christmas, that this dreadful affair of poor Charles's death would have put me off my—ah—hobby. But it hasn't. On the contrary, I find myself turning more eagerly towards these foolish novels. They seem to take the mind off reality. But I must admit I feel especially ashamed of my taste for them at the present time. I shouldn't care for Blodwen to know how I spend my leisure." He looked half furtively, half humorously at John, as if appealing to him to keep the matter secret. " So you've been spending the day on the Forest. Did you lose Mr. Rampson there? "

" He's gone back to tea with the Brownings to look at a microscope and be worshipped. I left him and Nora there and went on to the police station." And as they walked across the sunny lawn where the shadows of the cedars grew every moment longer, John told the old man of the discovery of the raincoat among the bracken by the shepherd's hut.

" Of course," he finished, " I had to advise the shepherd to take it to the police. I didn't want to get him into trouble with the law."

There was a silence. Glancing at his companion, John saw that the colour of the old man's cheeks had faded slightly, and his usual dreamy, urbane expression had left him.

" Surely," he said at length, with a sort of stiff good-humour, " there wasn't any need for Miss Nora to recognize the coat so promptly and so—er—publicly? Surely it's rather quixotic to present the other side with evidence? "

There was a pause.

" Somebody must have left the coat there," said John slowly at last.

" Of course."

" Then the discovery of the coat ought to lead to the discovery of the murderer, and to the acquittal of Morris Price."

" But, my dear sir, Morris admitted that he spent the night roaming about Radnor Forest! Surely you can see the use that will be made of this discovery of yours? He spent the night," repeated Mr. Clino, with indescribable despair in his tone, " roaming about Radnor Forest! Isn't that bad enough, without the discovery of the dead man's coat there? Do you think a jury will find it easy to believe that a sane, innocent man would choose to spend an entire night wandering about the Forest when he might have been comfortably in bed? Isn't that bad enough in itself, without the further evidence of poor Charles's coat? " The colour had come back to Mr. Clino's face. He threw out his hands with a quaint, stiff little gesture of despair. " Whatever induced him to do such a thing as spend the night on the Forest I can't imagine! He must have taken temporary leave of his senses! "

" Oh, surely not! It's really a very sensible thing to do on a lovely night, and not so often done as it ought to be."

" But in the circumstances! "

" But Morris didn't know the circumstances until afterwards," John reminded him swiftly.

There was a short, tense pause.

" Of course," said Mr. Clino with a sigh, " I'm perfectly convinced of Morris's innocence."

" Of course," murmured John. And they walked side by side across the lawn towards a bed of brilliant fuchsias, turned and walked back.

John changed the subject.

" Did you ever meet Sir Morris's wife, Mr. Clino—his second wife? "

Cousin Jim gave him a surprised, interrogatory glance, but answered readily :

" Several times. Why? "

" Do you remember whether she was ever called by a nickname? "

" A nickname? Clytie, her name was," replied the old man, frowning slightly, as if she were a subject only second in unpleasantness to the murder. " Morris always called her Clytie. But yes, I remember meeting a young brother of hers, a quite dreadful young man, who used to call her by some foolish, undignified name. Now what was it? Something very absurd and unsuitable."

" Puffy? "

Mr. Clino stopped abruptly his gentle pacing.

" That was it! " he exclaimed in mild surprise. " Puffy. Now how did you know? "

" I didn't know," said John gently. " I only hoped. Have you met Mrs. Price at all since her departure? "

" Since she left Morris? Certainly not. I haven't the slightest idea what became of her."

" Will you have a cigarette? You don't know, I suppose, whether she ever expressed any desire to come back? "

" Not so far as I know. No, thank you. I haven't smoked the one Blodwen gave me after lunch yet."

" You are not a heavy smoker, then? "

" Hardly! I very rarely smoke, except for a cigar after dinner, and an occasional cigarette when I feel the need to compose my nerves. May I offer you a pinch of snuff? "

" Thank you. You take your tobacco in the more old-fashioned form."

Mr. Clino looked doubtfully at his tiny gold snuff-box.

" As a matter of fact," he confided, " I don't take it much. It makes me sneeze like anything. But there's a sort of elegance about snuff that's lacking from cigarettes—especially if one doesn't take it. And the little snuff-boxes," he added pensively, looking at the charming specimen in his frail, white hand, " are so pretty, aren't they? "

The Tram Inn, when, half an hour later, John pulled up in front of its timbered gables, seemed to have forgotten its brief excitement of two days before and wore its usual look of sleepy peace. The bar was closed and a large sandy cat slept on the convivial benches inside the little wooden porch. As John tried the handle of the door it roused itself, yawned luxuriously and rubbed an ear against his leg. John opened the door on to the dim, narrow passage that smelt pleasantly of sawdust and stale cider, and walked in. He could hear the tea-time sound of tinkling crockery from somewhere in the back rooms, and walked towards it. An old mirror in a dark frame at the end of the passage reflected the sunny doorway and made his own face appear pale and unhealthy in its greenish glass. The pale and worried Miss Watt, in tea-time négligé of carpet slippers and curling-pins, appeared suddenly in the doorway and remarked that the place, by rights, was closed.

"I know," said John ingratiatingly. "I came on purpose to see you, if you can spare me a few moments. I've got one or two questions I must ask you."

"About the murder, I expect," said Miss Watt with a resigned sigh, manœuvring herself in front of the mirror and touching her curling-pins with a depressed, uncertain hand. "I'm sure I'm willing to tell all I can, though I've told it again and again. I'm just damping Father's tea, but if you'll please to step into the parlour I'll be with you in a moment."

She led him back along the passage and into the room in which the inquest had been held. Lowered green blinds still gave it a funereal and gloomy air.

"You won't mind waiting a moment, I expect," observed the girl, and still anxiously fingering her curling-pins she departed.

John sat gingerly down on the broken-springed horse-hair-covered sofa and had just opened a volume of *The Girls' Friend* for 1885 when the door, which Miss Watt had gently closed, burst open. Mine host appeared, in his shirt-sleeves and with fiercely ruffled hair. At the sight of John he appeared surprised but not discomfited.

"Oh, ah!" he remarked profoundly. "Where be that damned girl?"

"I understand she's making your tea."

"That her bain't. I've a-damped it myself. Out a-counting of her hens, I expect, that's where her be. Her thinks more o' they hens than her do of her father, be a long sight. Wring all their necks one day, I will."

He scratched his grey-stubbled chin and looked dreamily

at his visitor, lost for the moment in this delightful vision of wholesale slaughter.

"So I would," he said regretfully at last. "Only, cold bacon for me breakfast goes agin me stomach. Well, come on!"

"Where to?" asked John in amusement, laying *The Girls' Friend* back on the bamboo table.

Mr. Watt made a wide and jovial gesture.

"I be having of me tea in back kitchen, and could do with a bit o' company. You could do with a cup of tea, I expect, with a drop in it. Come on!"

And mine host led the way back along the passage and into the large, stone-flagged kitchen which, with its open window, long deal table, great rough dresser and litter of utensils, made a pleasing contrast with the room they had just left. Lowering himself heavily into a protesting wicker chair, he poured John out a cup of steaming black brew, and passing him the bottle adjured him to help himself without embarrassment.

"I seed you at the inquest, master," he observed genially, soaking a slice of saffron cake in his tea and eating it with difficulty but zest. "What'd ye think of un?" he added, as if the affair had been an entertainment staged by himself for the amusement of his patrons.

"What did you?" asked John diplomatically.

"Oh, ah! Ada her can't abide an inquest, but I don't mind one now an' agin. 'Tis good for business, d'ye see. They has drinks while they waits, and them as can't get in has drinks, and they has drinks afterwards and talks things over. Got the right man, has they, master?"

"No, I don't think so."

"Oh, ah! Mebbe not. But I likes an inquest now an' agin. Last one we had here were when old Borley o' Wintersbrook were drownded. He——"

"Oh, Father!"

Miss Watt, her curling-pins removed and her dark

locks arranged in incongruous waves around her per-
manently worried face, stood in the doorway and looked
reproachfully at her parent.

" It's me as should say ' Oh, Darter! ' " he responded
good-humouredly.   " But I've damped the tea and poured
it out, so draw up and cut the gentleman a bit o' cake.
They dratted chickens won't come to no harm."

" 'Tisn't the chickens," protested Miss Watt sadly, and
sitting down she cut the cake with an air of dissociating
herself entirely from it and from the rest of the meal.
" Tis the litter you've got here, Father, with the kettle
on the table-cloth and all!   The gentleman'll think as we
don't know no better."

" Nor we does," replied her father, with the utmost
placidity.   He added: " Show me the man as can eat
without making of a litter, my girl."

The young woman's anxious eyes sought John's with
a look of depressed apology for her parent.   John changed
the subject, accepting a piece of dry, yellow cake.

" Have you missed any more eggs, Miss Watt? "

" No, sir, not since them I told you about on Monday.
But I've had padlocks put on the runs.   Superintendent
Lovell, he haven't caught the thief yet."

" My soul! " ejaculated her father, putting down his
brimming saucer.   " Do ee think as the police hasn't
nothing better to think of but a two-three eggs as the
rats took off?   Hant you heard o' such a thing as a
murder in these parts? "

A look of weak obstinacy settled on the young
woman's face.

" There was seven eggs," she observed with a long-
suffering air.   " And the police is there to catch thieves
same as murderers, I expect.   And a thief's a thief,
whether he thieves eggs or dimongs."   A tearful note
crept into her voice.   " You've made this tea that strong,
Father, it pretty near skins my tongue.   And as for

thinking o' nothing but the chickens, I'd like to know where the Tram'd be if I didn't sell fowls and eggs reg'lar and keep the money coming in. And it weren't the rats."

Mr. Watt favoured John with a slow, comradely wink.

" Woman," he remarked indistinctly, savouring a mouthful of the criticized brew, " be never happy unless they be thinking they're a-saving of a man from ruin. Ne'er fret, Ada. Put a drop out o' the bottle in yer tea, and believe me, my girl, it were the rats."

Ada cast a glance of extreme disfavour at the proffered bottle and replied simply :

" It were not the rats."

" I tell you, my girl, it were."

" Will I put you another cup o' tea, sir, with a little water from the kettle ? " asked Miss Watt, turning to John with an ingratiating air that subtly rebuked her contentious papa. She was unable, however, to refrain from murmuring confidentially to John's cup as she put in the milk that whatever it was, it wasn't the rats.

Either the aspersion on his tea-making or the meek obstinacy of his daughter's tone suddenly aroused the landlord's ready wrath. A great fist hit the table with a bang that made cups rattle in their saucers. The sandy cat, which had been waiting under a chair for its saucer of milk, streaked suddenly out of the window, as if its conscience had smitten it. The terrier lying on the hearth-rug looked mildly up and wagged a pacific tail.

" It were the rats ! " cried Mr. Watt. " I *know*, my girl, and I has my reasons for knowing ! So let's have no more of this contradictiousness, and don't drown the gentleman's tea. His nerves'll stand more'n what yours will, I'll be bound ! "

Ada Watt looked aggrieved, but contented herself with remarking in a tone of tremulous acidity that she supposed it was also the rats who took her apples.

"Do you often get apples stolen from your orchard?" asked John, thinking of the two Worcester pearmains which Rampson had discovered in the quarry.

"The boys is perfect terrors," Miss Watt assured him earnestly. "Though not so bad as a rule as it was last Monday, with the boughs dragged down and broken and all. Father'd say it were the rats, I suppose, but it were more like a gorilla." She cast a tearful glance at her father, but he appeared to judge the challenge not worth the taking of the saucer from his lips.

"Does anybody else near here grow Worcester pearmains, do you know?"

"There isn't no other orchard, not what you could call an orchard, nearer nor eight miles. There's apple-trees in the gardens, but they're little sour cider apples mostly. I don't know of anyone nearer nor Farmer Withers as grows apples like we've got, and he's over to Hereford way. It's to be expected as we should lose a few apples to the school children, I suppose. But what I can't get over is losing seven eggs to once like that. I never had no eggs took before."

"There you go again!" exclaimed Mr. Watt in tones of deep disgust. "Bain't I telling you it were the rats? Now I'll tell you how I knows. I wouldn't tell you afore, you was so set and silly, telling of the police and all. I knows it were the rats, for I found the shells when I were clearing the orchard ditch on Thursday. All dragged close to a rat-hole, they was, hid in the grass. I put some poison in the hole and I cleared the shells out of the way. So now you know as it were the rats as took the precious eggs. And for the Lord's sake let's hear no more about it!"

Ada Watt's pale, sharp-featured face attempted to express scornful disbelief but succeeded only in looking disappointed. There was a brief, uncomfortable pause.

"You did ought to have told me, Father," she said

tearfully at last. "Letting me go telling everyone as we'd had a thief after our eggs!"

"Dear Lord of Heaven!" exclaimed Mr. Watt picturesquely. "Hain't I told ye, and told ye, and told ye, and TOLD YE it were the rats?" He rose, scraping chair-legs on the flags. "And did ye ever know me tell a thing as I hadn't good reason for?"

His daughter, clearing away the tea-things, met this question with silence. Mr. Watt scratched his chin and eyed her enigmatic back.

"I'll show ye where I finded they," he volunteered.

"No, thank you, Father," she responded distantly. "I believes you."

The landlord led the way out of the back door into the garden with its rows of vegetables and clumps of parsley and thyme and its gooseberry bushes festooned with drying kitchen cloths.

"Obstinate, be Ada," he remarked sadly, untying the complicated knots of string which fastened the gate into the orchard. "Her's a good girl for work, but more obstinate nor what a man have a right to expect in his only daughter. And that be the truth." And with a heavy sigh he led the way in among the old, low-growing apple-trees, heavy this year with a rich load of fruit.

"What with wopses and birds," remarked Mr. Watt, dispassionately squashing one of the former pests on his sleeve, "and chickens and rats, a chap can't call his orchard his own. Here be the ditch as I were clearing out, as you can see, and here be the hole where I finded the shells. Show me the boy as'll suck seven eggs and leave the shells behind, when he might take they home and boil they! Boys, her says! Be that a rat-hole, master, or bain't it?"

John went down on his knees to examine the large hole in the bank below the hedge.

Mr. Watt laughed.

"You won't find the rats at home, master."

"Looks like a rabbit-hole to me," remarked John diffidently, slipping his hand into it.

"Oh, ah? No, no, mister. He be a rat-hole right enough. For why? Rabbits, they doesn't eat eggs."

John, judging that an attempt to instruct his host in the first principles of logic would be ill-advised, contented himself with a nod, and feeling round in the damp, earthy hollow came across something light and brittle. A broken egg-shell.

"Oh, ah!" exclaimed the innkeeper with satisfaction. "Now that proves my words, mister. Here be an egg-shell and here be a rat-hole, and here be an egg-shell *in* a rat-hole. Boys, her says, and goes and tells police about it!"

John examined the egg-shell, which, though caved in at one side, was still entire.

"Will you let me keep this?"

The landlord's genial expression faded slowly off into a look of dubiety, as though he found himself disappointed in John.

"Oh, ah!" he assented rather unwillingly, scratching his head. "I reckon he won't be much use to ye, mister. But he be no manner of use at all to I, so you be welcome."

"Thank you," said John gravely, and wrapping the shell carefully in a handkerchief, put it in his pocket.

The innkeeper watched him with a saddened, disillusioned air. He had taken John for a man of common sense. He hesitated, in silence. He had intended to top off John's tea with a drop of something more interesting. But in his opinion a man so lost to sanity as to collect hen's egg-shells might as well go dry as not. However, he was, when sober, a courteous and obliging soul; he contented himself by asking with slightly impaired geniality:

M

" Be there aught else I can do for ye, master? "

" If you wouldn't mind telling me where Mr. Letbe lives? "

" Ole Jimmy Letbe? He bides up at Wintersbrook, near five mile away. You goes out on the main road and takes the first turn to the right at the foot of Rodland Hill, and then straight along. But I doubt you'll not find he at home, master. He be working up at nursery-man's, and they goes on late these summer months."

" Will his wife be at home? "

" Oh, ah! Unless her be out. And he've a daughter to home now, too. There'll ne summun about, I expect. Do ye collect birds' eggs, mister? "

" Only this one," answered John, patting his pocket with a smile.

Mr. Watt conducted him out on to the road through the orchard gate which, John noted, was like the garden gate tied up with string, and stood watching him go with a disillusioned air. He replied to John's waved farewell with a friendly but not effusive gesture and went thought-fully back to the inn to open up the bar.

Wintersbrook was a tiny hamlet in the valley grouped round an old stone bridge over a narrow stream. A mill, a farmhouse and a dozen cottages comprised the little place, and John had no difficulty in finding the square, slate-built self-respecting little cottage in which James Letbe lived. After a casual inspection, he knocked at the cottage which had the neatest and best-laid-out garden, and to his inquiries for Mr. Letbe the woman who opened the door replied that he weren't to home, but would be presently.

" Is Miss Letbe in? "

" Yes, she is." The elderly woman looked him over doubtfully, shading her placid eyes from the sun with a plump, floury hand.

" Did you want to see my daughter particular, sir? "

" I'm from Rhyllan Hall," explained John, feeling his way carefully. He noticed that at the mention of Rhyllan a faint frown came into Mrs. Letbe's eyes. " I understand that your daughter was housemaid there until lately, and I want, if I may, to ask her a few questions about——"

" My daughter'd still be housemaid at Rhyllan if it weren't for the behaviour of one as is best not spoken of, being dead, poor soul! 'Twere no fault of hers she had to leave, and no fault of my master's as he were turned off after thirty years! A man must look to his girl's character, sir, in whatever walk of life. And if it's about that you've come, I'd liefer you spoke to me and not to Ellie, for there's been too much talk already and the girl's shy of it."

" No, no," John assured her. " It isn't about that. A few questions about some other matters which she may know something of."

Mrs. Letbe still looked dubious.

" Are you from the police, sir? "

" No. I'm a friend of Sir Morris's, and I'm trying to clear him."

" Ah, sir, if you only could! But I fear for ye. I fear for Mr. Morris. A kind gentleman and a fine one, he were, but a haughty temper that'd never brook thwarting! I fear for him. Still, if that's your wish, I can't refuse you a talk with Ellie, for there's nobody that wouldn't be glad to see Mr. Morris back at Rhyllan Hall, whatever the way of it. Please to step in, sir, I won't keep ye long. Just to put my pies in the oven and then I'll be with ye, and Ellie too."

Stepping through the front door, John stepped straight into the living-room, a low-pitched, pleasant parlour kitchen with an oven grate, a linoleumed floor and pots of geraniums lining two small windows. His hostess went into the scullery or bakehouse to finish her work and left him to talk to the canary and to observe the family gallery of photographs which adorned the mantel-shelf.

In a few moments Ellie came in, following her stout, protective mother: a pretty young woman with infantile soft features, large blue eyes and a row of blue china beads around a white neck. The belle of a countryside which did not run to feminine beauty. She looked timidly at John, moistened her indeterminate lips and edged nearer to her mother.

" Now, Ellie," said that matron in kind, sharp tones, " the gentleman wants to ask you a question or two about Rhyllan Hall. And you must answer sensible and not be shy, because it's for Mr. Morris's sake. Please to take a chair, sir. And Ellie, you'd better sit down too and not fidget."

" Well," said John, casting around in his mind for a question that would assist and yet disguise his drift, " to begin with, Miss Letbe, did you know that there was a revolver in the drawer of the library at Rhyllan Hall? "

Ellie's china-blue eyes darkened and she looked help-lessly round at her mother.

" No, sir, I never—I never touched it! "

John smiled reassuringly.

" Of course you didn't. But did you ever see it there? "

She looked fearfully at him, and after a moment returned his smile, half coyly, half distrustfully.

" Yes, I seen it," she admitted. " When I was help-ing Mrs. Maur to clean out the libery. I seen it in the drawer, along of a box of bullets." Her plump red fingers fidgeted with the table-cloth, and she looked up at John from under her eyelashes. " It frit me, for I can't bear to think of killing, and that. And I gave a kind of a start, and Mrs. Maur, when she see what I was looking at, she said never to open drawers or cupboards in the libery. But I was cleaning the room out, I didn't think no harm."

"Of course not. When was this?"

Her round low brow puckered becomingly—rather more than was necessary, John thought. He could well believe that under Mrs. Maur's stern regime the fair Ellie "would not answer" as a housemaid.

"I can't just remember. About a month ago, sir. Joe might remember, because——"

"Joe?"

"Mr. Waters, sir, who I'm engaged to." The pucker gave place to an equally becoming dimple. "He might remember, for I told him about the turn I'd had, and he said he didn't like to think of they guns where us girls might get fooling with them, and he'd take an opportunity of seeing as it wasn't loaded, by mistake, like. Because he said there's been dreadful accidents happen through guns being left loaded by mistake, and he didn't like to think of me turning out the libery if there was a loaded gun, like, in a drawer."

"Very sensible of him. So you're going to be married soon, are you?"

"Yes, sir." Mrs. Letbe spoke up for her daughter, who contented herself with looking at the table-cloth and smiling. "Next month, if all goes well. That's why we haven't put her out to service again, sir. It didn't hardly seem worth it."

"You must have been sorry to leave Rhyllan, if your young man is working there," observed John casually.

"Oh, sir! But I couldn't stop there, not after Sir Charles——! My Joe wouldn't never have allowed it."

"It were your father as wouldn't allow it, my girl," put in Mrs. Letbe with not unkindly tartness. "And it were your father as lost his job owing to your foolishness, not your Joe. 'Twould have been more seemly, to my way of thinking, if your Joe had stood by you and given up his place without staying on for his month's wages. He hasn't had it thirty years, like your poor Dad had! There, there, my girl! Don't start oh-mothering me! I knows as 'tweren't your fault! But I wish as we'd never thought of sending you out to service at Rhyllan! See what come of it!"

The stout and pleasant Mrs. Letbe seemed for a moment near tears. It was plain that she was divided between sympathy for her daughter and a disposition to blame her for the trouble that had come upon the family. Ellie's round pink and white face took on a sulky expression.

"I couldn't help it," she muttered sullenly and gave her mother a look which said plainly that she could dispense with her chaperonage. "It wasn't my fault, sir," she added to John in a plaintive tone. "I never thought as a gentleman like Sir Charles would ever notice a girl like me, and——"

"That'll do, Ellie, for goodness' sake!" said her mother more sharply than before.

Ellie muttered something inaudible and became silent, with a fixed sullen look staring at the table-cloth. John suspected that she looked upon herself as a touching heroine of melodrama in real life, and that her mother did not quite see eye to eye with her. No doubt there had been many tears and recriminations in this pleasant little parlour since Charles Price's bored glance had fallen upon the china-blue eyes of the second housemaid.

"Of course," said John tentatively, "you had left Rhyllan before the day of the murder?"

"Oh, yes, sir," answered the girl's mother, seeing that Ellie was not yet sufficiently recovered from the sulks to answer agreeably. "The girl left more'n a week before."

"On the eighteenth of August," muttered Ellie broodingly, scowling at her heartless parent.

"Were you at home, here, at the time the murder was committed?"

Ellie stared at him with widened eyes.

"I didn't have nothing to do with it!" she uttered thinly.

John perceived that his question had been tactlessly put. "No, no, of course not," he assured her, thinking what a silly little creature the girl was. "Nobody for a moment imagines that you had. Don't be silly. I asked because I wondered whether you might have seen any strangers about here on that day." John wished for a moment that the mantle of Superintendent Lovell could fall on his shoulders, so that he could ask the question he desired to ask straight out, without all this circumlocution. Strangers, indeed! The sensation-loving chit would probably invent dozens of them and waste no end of time describing their suspicious characteristics.

But, fortunately, Miss Letbe's inventive talent fell short of her desires.

"Oh, strangers——" she faltered, and was for a moment lost in eager introspection. "There was a man —no, that was Wednesday. We don't get many strangers come through here, sir. 'Tisn't on the high road, you see. But, Mother, wasn't there a man——"

"No, my girl, I didn't see one you could call a stranger not on Monday nor any other day of the week. The gentleman don't mean folk from other villages, but foreigners, like, tramps and that. And there weren't none, not to my knowledge, nor to yours, I'll be bound."

Ellie tried to protest, but could not.

"No," she said at last in a disappointed tone. "I didn't see no one. And if there had been anyone, in the evening at least, I should have seen him, for I was in the front garden tidying up the dahlias and keeping a look out for Joe. He comes to see me Monday evening, when he has his night out." A simper restored good

humour to her face. " And I gen'lly looks out for him
or goes to meet him. He was a bit late on Monday,
owing to Mrs. Maur having been out and him waiting
for her to come in, so I was in the front garden from
about a quarter to seven till quarter to eight."

" Long way for him to come, isn't it? "

" Oh, he don't think nothing of that, sir! It's pretty
near seven miles, but he has his bicycle."

" Seven miles! I should have thought it was much
farther than that! Why, it's eight miles or so from
Penlow to the cross-roads, and Rhyllan is four miles from
Penlow! "

" Bless us, sir! " said Mrs. Letbe with a laugh. " You
doesn't go to Rhyllan by the main road! 'Twould be
pretty near twenty miles! No, no, go straight over the
bridge and you come to Rhyllan the first village. 'Tis a
poor road, but handy. My Lord, the pies is burning!
Ellie, go you quick and take them out! "

Ellie rose slowly, looking exceedingly unwilling, and
departed. There was a momentary silence.

" My Lord! " sighed Mrs. Letbe at last, rising heavily
to fetch a bottle of ginger wine from the corner cupboard.
" Daughters is a trouble, to be sure, when they're handsome and think themselves handsomer still! I'll be glad
when Ellie is wed, though I wishes I could like the chap
better nor what I do. Will you take a glass of wine, sir?
It's home-made."

" Thank you very much. He isn't a local man,
Waters, is he? "

" Dear knows where he comes from," said Mrs. Letbe,
with knitted brows, pouring out a glass of wine. " He's
been here, there and everywhere, it seems. But 'tisn't
that. 'Tis these stories of him going with other girls I
don't like. This is a terrible place for stories, we all
know. Seems like people has nothing to talk of but their
neighbours. But there's no smoke wi'out fire, and I

seen the chap myself leaning on Lloyd of Linger-hatch's gate, talking to his granddaughter more pleasant like nor I cared for. There's some chaps must make theirselves pleasant to all the girls they meets, we know, but I doubt a chap like that's not the sort for our Ellie." She broke off sharply as her daughter appeared in the doorway, flushed with the heat of the oven. " Must you be going now? I'm afraid we wasn't able to tell you much, sir. I only wishes we could do more." She hesitated, looking at John with kind, worried eyes. " Could you——? But no! 'Twouldn't do."

" What? I'll do anything I can for you," replied John, noting with amusement that the shy Ellie looked extremely disappointed to discover that the questions which had so perturbed her were at an end.

" Well—I was thinking, if you could slip in a word for poor James with Mr. Felix or Miss Blodwen? He's eating his heart out in they dratted nurseries. But there! 'Tis too soon, I know, and 'twouldn't be seemly to speak until——" She paused and finished uncertainly : " Until Sir Morris is about again. Ah, dear! First one thing, then another! Seems like the end of everything to James and me! "

" Oh, no, Mrs. Letbe, I hope not. Sir Morris will be back at Rhyllan in a month or two. And so will your husband, soon after, I expect."

John drove away, leaving her standing square and pensive in the doorway, and Ellie posed picturesquely over the rose-tree, a virgin making much of time. He took the short road to Rhyllan which Mrs. Letbe had pointed out to him, and pondered his afternoon's work as he went. He felt that he had not done so badly. He had as good as established the fact that Clytie Meadows and the mysterious Mrs. Field were one and the same person. He had discovered that Waters the footman knew of the whereabouts of the revolver long before the crime was committed; and that Waters's alibi was, to say the least of it, shaky. It remained to be seen whether he had been speaking the truth when he told Ellie that he had been kept late at Rhyllan Hall. Then there was the discovery of Charles's coat on the Forest. And there was the egg-shell he had found in an obvious rabbit-hole in the Tram Inn orchard. John drew up to the side of the road and cautiously withdrew his handkerchief with its fragile contents from his pocket. Yes, he had thought so. The shell was punctured at each end with a tiny hole such as might have been made by the point of a penknife; and though crumpled it was not actually broken apart. The inner skin, in fact, seemed to be almost untorn.

John put the shell carefully away and shook his head.

" Do rats understand the art of sucking eggs? I should say not. But, oh, me! What human being would suck seven eggs at a sitting? "

John, who disliked raw eggs, shuddered slightly and let in his clutch.

" Yes," he said to himself, as the little car took the rough road again, " we've found out quite a lot of interesting and curious facts to-day. But do any of them fit together to make anything like sense? Oh, Lord! They do not."

CHAPTER THIRTEEN

REFLECTIONS

" AND so," said John, balancing the cracked egg-shell on his forefinger, " we deduce that the man must have been starving."

" Or," amended Rampson the pedantic, " that he had an uncontrollable appetite for raw eggs."

" But I don't see," said Nora gently, voicing the common thought, " what all this has to do with the murder."

There was a pause in the cool summer-house.

" I mean," went on Nora, " there's no connection between the person who stole the eggs and the person who murdered Charles, that I can see. I don't see why we should bother ourselves about Miss Watt and her eggs. I really don't."

" No—o," agreed John, gazing pensively at the blanched shell. " Still the egg-shell, obviously emptied by human agency, does prove that there was a stranger about on the evening of the murder. Because none of the local cottagers would have been in such a state of starvation as to eat seven eggs right off. A local person might have stolen the eggs. But, as mine host pointed out, he would have taken them home and boiled them like a Christian. The eating of them raw seems to suggest a tramp. And the fact that nobody noticed a tramp at the inn or on the road nearby suggests that if there were such a person he didn't want to be noticed."

"But," exclaimed Nora, "there were so many people coming and going round the Tram that he might easily not have been noticed."

"And," said Rampson, "the fact that he had designs on the poultry-yard would be quite enough to explain his invisibility without bringing murder into it."

"You're both perfectly right and reasonable," said John with a gentle sigh. "I count myself fortunate in being surrounded by such keen and critical intellects. *But*, all the same—forgive my obstinacy—there was a stranger at the Tram Inn last Monday evening. And there was a *murder* near the Tram Inn last Monday evening."

"Surely, my dear John," said Rampson peacefully, "you've got enough to do following up more promising clues, without bringing this egg-sucking stranger into it."

"I don't propose to bring him into it. I only propose to keep him pigeon-holed, in case circumstances should bring him into it. What is it, Nora?"

Nora, who had suddenly uttered an exclamation, was gazing out through the arched and pillared doorway of the summer-house with introspective eyes. She turned them half-doubtfully, half-excitedly on John.

"Do you know——" she began abruptly, and stopped.

"I feel sure I don't. Do tell me."

"Well, I've just remembered. There was a reflection in the looking-glass——"

"That," observed Rampson, idly ironical, "is remarkable."

"No, but there was. On Monday, just before we had tea in the Tram. Did you notice that old green mirror at the end of the passage, and how it reflects the front door? I was looking at myself in it, and I could see the opening of the front door over my shoulder. And a man came and looked in and went away."

"Well?"

"That's all, I'm afraid. He was standing against the

light and some way off, and I didn't get a clear reflection of him."

" But, Nora, then he may have been anybody."

" Yes," admitted Nora.   She was silent a moment. " But there was something in the way he looked in— something queer and furtive.   And in the way he moved off when I looked round—so quickly and yet—furtively, as if he were used to moving like that.   I couldn't really see him.   I should never be able to describe him.   I couldn't even tell what age he seemed to be.   But I can see again quite plainly that furtive, embarrassed movement.   One gets impressions like that much more from people's attitudes and movements than from their faces, you know."

" My dear Nora, you quite make my flesh creep," said Felix, who so far had been a silent member of the council of four.   " Are you sure he didn't move off quickly just because he was embarrassed at seeing you there? "

" He may have been," replied Nora slowly.   " Especially——" She laughed a little and coloured.   " Especially as I was amusing myself by making a face at myself in the glass.   He may have seen my reflection and thought I was an escaped lunatic.   You'd better not make too much of him, John.   But there he was, and you can pigeon-hole him along with your stray starving tramp, if you think he's worth it."

" Thank you.   I certainly will.   Are you sure you can't describe him at all?   His height or build or——"

Nora shook her head.

" I think I'd better not.   I didn't see him full-length, except just for a second as he moved away.   And one's so easily led into imagining things.   I think he was fairly tall—at least he wasn't short.   That's all.   I'm afraid you'll have to do with that, John.   And don't attach too much importance to him."

Felix murmured thoughtfully :

" Didn't that queer girl at the inn say something about seeing a stranger in the yard? Surely she did. Don't you remember, Nora? When she apologized for the hard-boiled eggs? She said——"

" Yes, she did! She said she'd seen a man in the yard who looked as if he didn't ought to be there. And she went out to see who it was, and that was how our eggs were hard-boiled. I remember now! But——" She hesitated, looking rather disappointed. " Of course it doesn't help us much. It only goes to prove what we knew already, that there was a suspicious character at the Tram Inn that evening, helping himself to eggs and apples. It doesn't get us any nearer to the murderer."

" What should get us nearer to the murderer," observed Rampson, " is that coat we found on the Forest yesterday. I take it that it's absolutely known to be Charles's? "

" Absolutely," replied Nora.

Felix stirred his long limbs uneasily. He did not like to dwell upon that clue. Like Mr. Clino, he saw it as a weapon in the hands of his father's accusers.

" Well," went on Rampson, fondling one of Blodwen's spaniels which had entered the summer-house in search of its mistress, " that coat was obviously left on the Forest either by the murderer or by an accomplice. And if it was not actually left there on the night of the murder, it was left soon after. It had been lying in that patch of bracken for some days. That was plain from the distorted shapes and pale colour of the young shoots trying to grow under it. So its discovery should narrow down your field of inquiry. It adds a further necessary qualification to the list we were making yesterday : the murderer must either have had an accomplice, or he must have had the opportunity of visiting the Forest within a day or two of the murder."

" True," assented John dreamily, and suddenly in his mind's ear a light, gay voice chattered like a stream of clear water: "*Have you been up on the Forest yet? I went yesterday. You can't think how lovely it is.*"

"Heavens, John," said Nora, breaking the silence. "What a frown! What terrible idea has occurred to you?"

"I was only thinking," said John, coming to himself with a smile, "about murderers and accomplices. Especially accomplices."

Rampson suddenly laughed.

"What's the joke?" asked Felix, amiably enough, but with a faint undertone of resentment. Since John's appeal, he had not given way to gloom. But cheerfulness was beyond his powers. His was the tense and high-strung temper that can meet cruel circumstance with courage but not with confidence.

Nora shot a glance at him half-pitiful, half-amused. Well she knew her Felix and his capacity for suffering. She could imagine him vowing, like King Henry, never to smile again: and keeping his vow for an appreciable fraction of eternity. John, noting that tender, critical glance, apostrophized her silently: *Nora, my dear Nora, must you love this intense, preoccupied young man?* And they both asked with a liveliness intended to disguise their inward thoughts:

"Yes, Sydenham, what *is* the joke?"

"Nothing much," replied Rampson with a grin. "I was just thinking of young Lion yesterday and his excitement when we put that darning-needle under the microscope and found traces of blood on it. He'd make a marvellous detective's assistant. I left him quite convinced that somebody had been stabbed to the heart with a darning-needle and that the police should be told of this amazing discovery forthwith. It wasn't the slightest use pointing out that people have blood in their fingers as well as in their hearts."

Nora smiled.

" I know. He thinks he's found the one important clue. I told him that if he started darning his own socks he'd soon discover the reason for the blood on that needle. But he wouldn't have it. It's too tame an explanation."

" Was there blood on the needle? It was probably mine. I pricked my finger on it yesterday."

" Don't think so. The blood wasn't fresh enough to be yours. And this looked like the trace of quite a deep puncture, not a little prick."

" Oh, well! It isn't important. But I'll pigeon-hole it along with the egg-shell and the other small matters."

Felix turned an austere and thoughtful eye on his friend.

" If you're going to remember things like Charles pricking his finger when he darns his socks, won't your pigeon-hole, as you call it, get rather in a muddle? "

" Not a bit of it. One should try to remember everything one hears, however trifling, about a man who's been murdered. It's always possible that something may turn up which will make all the clues we think important become insignificant, and all the stray facts we've collected become important. You never know. By the way, I'm going to have a good look at that map of young Lion's and see if it suggests anything to me, before I pursue the elusive Mrs. Field to London."

" Are you going to? "

" Certainly. We must get at the truth of this five-pound-note business somehow."

" Sweet innocent Sherlock," remarked Rampson piti-fully, " do you imagine that you will be able to induce her to present you with the truth? "

" Not for a moment. But the lies people tell are so enlightening. Clear that rug off the table, Sydenham, will you? I want to spread the map out."

Rampson did as he was requested and a book which had been lying among the folds of the rug fell to the

floor.   He picked it up and gazed at it with mingled
amusement and aversion.

" ' The Murder in the Attic! ' Is this yours, John? "
John, unrolling Lion's parchment, glanced at the dust-
cover, which showed a hideous green and yellow face
peering from a purple attic window.   He grinned.

" No.   But give it to me.   I'll restore it to its rightful
owner.   You know, Nora, your young brother is really
quite an accomplished draughtsman.   Anybody got a pin
or two? "

He speared the map at each corner to the wooden table.

" Now then.   You met Charles at Worcester.   Lifelike
portrait of Charles by the celebrated miniaturist, Mr. Lion
Browning.   You had lunch at the Crown, and then started
along the road towards Leigh.   You took various field-
paths—these are the cows, of course, and—did your father
really run over a pig, Nora? "

Nora laughed.

" Not really over.   He just grazed it."

" It came on to rain, and you all took shelter in a barn
—and what's this?   Told Travellers' Tales? "

" Yes.   I suppose those balloons coming out of everybody's mouths represent talking."

" Charles has an extra large one."

" Yes.   He was telling us about Canada, and about how
it felt to be back in England.   And then he and Felix
started talking about their extreme youth, when Sir Almeric
was at Rhyllan Hall and they both came to stay here in
their holidays."

" What sort of things? "

" Oh, I dunno.   The usual sort of things.   About how
they used to dress and go out after they'd been sent to
bed.   And about what a rotten shot at a rabbit Felix used
to be, and is still, aren't you, Felix?   And about fishing
and bathing in the river, and so on."

" Well.   The rain soon left off, and you went on, and

had no more adventures until you arrived at Highbury Down, where you spent the night. The next day it was very hot. This is the sun, jeering at you. You had hard-boiled eggs for breakfast. Charles found he had a puncture, and Lion kindly mended it for him. You started out at ten o'clock along a narrow lane full of chickens and other farmyard animals, and soon came out on a better road. When you'd gone about four miles you found that Charles was missing. You all sat and waited for him, and after a time he turned up. What on earth are these stripy things intended to represent? "

" Bulls' eyes. Charles had seen a sign-post saying half a mile to some village or other, and had gone down a side-road to buy some sweets—we were all awfully thirsty and pining for something to suck. It was really rather kind of him, because he didn't like sweets himself. But of course we all rather wondered where he'd got to."

" Yes. You went on without any excitements except some formidable-looking hills to Fairway, where you had lunch at the Merry Month of May. After lunch it was hotter than ever—I see the sun has grown a good deal larger. You went on about five miles until you came to a small river, where you bathed."

" Yes. It was lovely. So cool and clear. And there were water-lilies and dragon-flies—millions of them."

" Does this unpleasant object represent a dragon-fly? "

" No, that's a leech. Father said he'd seen a leech, and got out. The rest of us laughed and said it must have been a water-beetle or something, but we didn't feel quite happy about it. And then Lion said he could feel something biting his leg, and that settled it. We all leapt out. But it was a lovely stream, and we had a lovely bathe."

" Who's this standing on the bank? "

" That's Charles. He didn't bathe, because bathing when he was hot always gave him a headache, he said."

"After the bathe you lay about in the sun and slept. Except your father and Lion, who went to look at the mill. Then you went slowly on to Galton, and had tea there, late, and stayed the night. There was a fair there, and you collected several coco-nuts."

"Charles did. He was really good at it. And then we went on the roundabouts and swings."

"The next day was Sunday. You went on towards Hereford. It was another hot day, and there were lots more hills. You bathed again in a river. Who are these on the bank this time?"

"Father and Charles. Father had leeches on the brain, and Charles said it was too hot for him, so they got lunch ready on the bank instead. We'd brought sandwiches from the inn, and they made a fire and stewed some awful tea in Lion's billy-can."

"That seems to have been rather an energetic day. You got to Hereford about seven o'clock and stayed there the night, and started early the next day towards Penlow. I see from the size of the sun that it was a fine day, but not so hot. Isabel fell off her bicycle in Hereford, and was picked up by at least eight good Samaritans."

"Yes, it was really quite funny the way all the people in the street rushed to pick her up. She wasn't a bit hurt; she was laughing so much she couldn't move."

Felix moved restlessly, got up and walked to the opening of the summer-house and stood looking out at the brilliant lawns. Nora became aware of him and broke off suddenly. The animation faded from her face.

"And nothing much happened after that," went on John, "until you got to the Tram Inn and had hard-boiled eggs for tea."

He slowly re-rolled the map and slipped an elastic band round it.

"I'm afraid it doesn't suggest anything much," said Nora.

" I don't know. Why did Charles go off and buy those bulls' eyes without telling anybody? "

Nora looked mildly surprised.

" I suppose he wanted to give us a nice surprise. Isabel had been wishing she had some bulls' eyes or acid drops to suck, and I suppose when he saw there was a village near he thought he'd slip off and get some."

" Wouldn't he have told Felix or your father where he was going? "

" Well—he didn't."

" Perhaps because he was afraid somebody would offer to go with him."

" Why should he have minded that? "

" Perhaps he had other business in the village, besides buying bulls' eyes. Some private business."

Felix turned and stood facing them in the entrance, dark against the brilliant sunny grass and flowers.

" You didn't know Charles," he observed dispassionately. " If you had known him, you wouldn't have seen anything remarkable about his going off down a side-road without telling anyone. I don't imagine for a minute he had any private business there. He just thought he'd go and get some sweets and so he went, without considering the rest of us at all. He was like that."

There was a pause.

" How do you know? " asked John slowly. " You only knew him for three days. Did he do other things of the same sort? "

Felix kicked moodily against the table-leg and frowned.

" I don't know. He seemed to be a pretty complete egoist. Don't you think so, Nora? "

" Perhaps."

Felix resumed his seat on the bench at Nora's side.

" For instance," he said slowly, " that first night, when we slept at Highbury Down. I don't know whether your father told you this, Nora—probably not, he took it beautifully at the time and pretended not to notice anything. You remember, you and Lion and Isabel found rooms at the cottage by the bridge, and your father and Charles and I went to the pub? "

" Yes."

" It was a small pub and they only had one double room and one single one. Of course we took the rooms, because one's bound to get pushed in with another person sometimes, when there's a party of six looking for beds in a small village, and I took it for granted Charles wouldn't mind sharing with me. Well, he didn't say anything, but he just took it for granted he was to have the single room. He just went there, saying good night in the friendliest way in the world, and left your father to push in with me. I thought perhaps he didn't realize there weren't three rooms, so I went after him and said hadn't we better give the single room to Dr. Browning? Not that the doctor minded where he slept, really, but naturally one must give the ancients first choice. But I couldn't get Charles to budge. He said he hated sleeping with other people, and Dr. Browning and I were used to one another, so we'd better do the sharing." Felix broke off. " That was all," he added. " He just wouldn't budge. I got rather annoyed, but he was perfectly good-humoured, didn't ruffle a feather."

" That's interesting," said John slowly. " And it was typical of him, was it? "

" Absolutely. A chap who'd behave like that wouldn't have much difficulty about going out of his way on the road without warning anyone, would he? "

" I suppose not. And of course if he was that kind of thick-skinned egoist, my theory that he had some special motive in not telling you where he was going is rather discounted. But all the same——"

Nora Browning interrupted gently:

" But, Felix——" She paused, wrinkling her broad forehead.

" M'm? "

" *Was* that typical of Charles, that bedroom episode? It rather surprises me. I shouldn't have expected him to behave like that."

" Wouldn't you? Didn't you think Charles was the complete egoist? "

" Y—es." Nora spoke hesitatingly, picking her words with care. Evidently, in her view, there were egoists and egoists. " He was. But—he always seemed to want to make a good impression. His manners—they were too flowery, rather than otherwise. As if he'd learnt his book on etiquette by heart, poor man! I could imagine him taking the best room for himself, without thinking. But I can't imagine him sticking to it, after he'd been told that it wasn't expected of him. See? All the things like that—opening doors for me and Isabel, fetching and carrying and so on—he made one feel quite uncomfortable, he was so punctilious. No! You surprise me, Felix. I think he was an egoist, surely. But he was very anxious not to be thought a boor."

Felix pondered this in silence for a moment, then shrugged his shoulders.

" I dare say you're right, Nora. You're more observant than I am. But still! There it is. He *did* behave on that occasion in just the way I've described."

" Well, thank you both," said John cheerfully. " You've both been very enlightening. And we must remember that if a person's behaviour is based on a book of etiquette and not on habit, he may conduct himself beautifully most of the time and then behave very badly in circumstances which the book hasn't provided for. I think I shall take an opportunity soon of satisfying myself that he had no motive except bulls' eyes when he turned off to Moseley, all the same. What is it, Rampson? "

" I said," replied his friend, who seemed to have become suddenly afflicted with alarming facial convulsions, " that the shadows are lengthening."

Nora and Felix turned and gazed at him in surprise.

" My poor, dear chap," said John sympathetically. " Is it the heat? "

His friend made a fierce grimace evidently intended to convey some information, and frowned out on to the lawn.

" I know," he replied, " that it is still early in the afternoon. But already, you will notice, the shadows are lengthening out."

John followed the direction of his glance.

" Oh! Dear me, yes, I see they are. Well, it's September, you know. We can't expect the long summer days to go on for ever."

Nora and Felix turned their astonished looks on John, and saw what he saw—the shadows of a man's head and shoulders falling on the grass at the side of the summer-house. It remained very still. John wondered how long it had been there. Somebody had been listening to their conversation—was still listening. They were all simultaneously afflicted with a complete inability to think of anything to say. The shadow moved.

" Hullo! " said John. " It's Mr. Clino! . . . Come inside! We saw your shadow. I'm glad it's you, and not one of the big five from Scotland Yard. Though I don't think we said anything very incriminating, did we, Nora? "

" I'm sorry if I alarmed you," said the old man amiably. " I was watching a remarkably beautiful butterfly on the creeper." He looked vaguely about the sparsely furnished summer-house. " I was just coming for—yes, my rug."

He carefully gathered up the rug, felt about on it and looked in a worried fashion about the floor.

" My rug," he repeated. " Yes. Even on these warm

afternoons I feel the need of some kind of covering while taking the air. I shall go and sit in the rose-garden for a while, I think. Now I wonder where I can have left—— Oh, no, don't trouble, please! I just came for my rug."

He cast a worried glance around the summer-house and departed, the empty rug trailing dejectedly from his arm.

" Mr. Clino," remarked Rampson, when the old man had crossed the lawn and disappeared behind the rose-pergola, " seems a little distrait."

" I think he's lost something," said Nora carelessly; and then, with a laugh: " Oh, John! Don't tell me the 'Murder in the Purple Attic' belongs to him! "

" Hush! " said John solemnly. " It does. But it's one of the darker secrets of his life. That's why I didn't hand it over just now. He's sensitive on the subject of his literary taste, and doesn't want Blodwen and Felix to know how low he's sunk."

Felix half smiled, rather impatiently.

" Heavens! I don't mind what he reads, the old silly. Nor does Blodwen, I'm sure. We've got something else to think about."

" Of course you don't. But you'll oblige the old thing, won't you, by keeping his awful secret locked in your bosom? And now I must leave you. No, I'm not taking the car, Syd. Just walking into the house."

As he passed around the summer-house John casually examined the creeper growing on it for signs of insect life. He found none. But butterflies are notoriously averse from staying long in one place.

He went into the small panelled parlour, and finding it empty rang the bell. Waters, the footman, appeared.

" Will you ask Mrs. Maur to come here, please? "

" Certainly, sir."

There was the slightest pause.

" Well? "

Turning quickly from his feigned interest in a Kang s'Hi vase, John surprised a queer expression on the footman's narrow face—a look, he could have sworn, of amusement.

"Certainly, sir," repeated Waters, and withdrew.

"Well, I'm dashed," murmured John to himself. No doubt Waters had discovered that the fair Ellie had been questioned. And no doubt, being a man of intelligence, he had seen where the questions trended. His look of amusement could only mean that the story he had told the girl had been true. Mrs. Maur had been out, as he had said, and he had left Rhyllan late; and now he was enjoying the thought of his approaching vindication through the severe lips of Mrs. Maur.

"You wished to see me, sir?"

The housekeeper par excellence, in her tight, black bodice and full cloth skirt, entered the room and stood looking at John with cold, placid eyes.

"Please. Shut the door. It's just this, Mrs. Maur: can you remember anything that happened last Monday evening? When Sir Charles was killed, you know?"

He framed his question thus vaguely to avoid startling or offending her; but she did not, it appeared, appreciate his thoughtfulness.

"I can remember everything that happened, sir, but there was nothing unusual, if that is what you require."

"Were you at the Hall the whole evening?"

"Yes, sir. I did not go outside the house all that day."

John paused. In the light of Waters's confident, slyly amused look, this answer was unexpected. He must have shown a slight surprise in his face, for the housekeeper went on immediately:

"Have I your permission, sir, to ring the bell?"

"Certainly," said John, a little mystified.

Waters, the footman, appeared with suspicious promptitude.

" May I ask Waters, sir, to send two of the maids here? "

" If you like," said John, who had not bargained for an interview with the entire staff.

" Kindly ask Jenny and Lilian to come here, Waters. You see, sir," went on Mrs. Maur when Waters had departed, " I think it would save you trouble if I brought witnesses to prove as I was here last Monday evening. I can't expect you to take my bare word for it, of course, and I know that at a time like this everybody must be ready to answer questions, and prove their answers if they can, sir." She smoothed the back of one soft, small hand with the palm of the other and looked at the floor.

" I hope you don't think that any suspicion attaches to you," said John gently, with visions of Blodwen bereft of her ideal housekeeper through his clumsy handling.

" Not at all, sir," replied Mrs. Maur with respectful dignity, and having smoothed her hands to her satisfaction, clasped them together and turned to the door as two young girls entered and dropped quick, awkward curtsies. Their combined ages would not have totalled forty, and with their flushed pink cheeks, round, frightened eyes and white caps and aprons they looked almost like twins.

" Shut the door, Lilian," said Mrs. Maur sternly. " Now, tell Mr. Christmas what you were doing last Monday evening."

The two children looked at one another, at Mrs. Maur and at John, and appeared to be struck dumb.

" Don't be frightened," said John, smiling. " You haven't been doing anything wrong. Just see if you can remember."

Lilian, the taller of the two, swallowed and finally brought out in a nervous squeak:

" Last Monday? "

She looked anxiously round the floor, as if hoping to find last Monday under one of the chairs, and murmured desperately again : " Last Monday? " and at the house-keeper's disapproving tongue-click looked ready to burst into tears.

" Yes," said John encouragingly, " last Monday, when Sir Charles was killed, you know. What did you do after tea? "

" Oh, yes, sir. I remember now. We had tea at five o'clock, and then we washed up, Jenny and me. And then—then we went to Mrs. Maur's room "—she cast a shy glance at the dragon, who evidently inspired her with more awe than did John—" and helped with mending the linen."

" Who was there? " asked the housekeeper.

" Why, there was me, and Jenny, and—and you, ma'am," faltered the girl. " Don't you recollect? There was a lot of mending, and we was all at it from six o'clock till near seven."

" *I* recollect, Lilian. Please to answer questions, not to ask them."

The unfortunate Lilian went crimson and looked helplessly at her companion, who took up the tale.

" And then we was picking over bilberries to make jelly till near eight," she said nervously. " We was in the kitchen, if you remember, ma'am, while you was looking over receipts and seeing to the jars. And then at eight we had our supper."

" Was I there? " asked Mrs. Maur expressionlessly.

The girl darted a frightened glance at her.

" Why—yes, ma'am," she faltered in amazement. " You was there, in course."

Mrs. Maur slowly inclined her head, and Jenny's voice died away.

" Thank you very much," said John cheerfully. " That'll do. You can run away now, Jenny and Lilian." Which they did, hastily and with little bobbed curtsies, and jostled each other in the doorway, so anxious were they to be off.

Mrs. Maur looked placidly at John.

" Thank you, Mrs. Maur. It's good of you to help me like this."

" Not at all, sir. Is there anything further, sir ? "

" Monday is Waters's evening out, isn't it ? "

" Yes, sir."

" Did he go out last Monday as usual ? "

" Quite as usual, sir, so far as I know. He left just before six o'clock, directly we'd done tea."

" Oh! Thank you. Don't fall over Waters as you go out."

The door closed gently behind her. John lit a cigarette and sat down on the window-seat. Evidently, then, Waters had not told the truth to Ellie Letbe. He had left Rhyllan Hall at the usual time, six o'clock, and arrived at Wintersbrook at a quarter to eight. One and three-quarter hours. Rhyllan to Wintersbrook—seven miles. Wintersbrook to the Tram Inn—five miles. Back to Wintersbrook—another five miles. Waters could hardly have cycled seventeen miles and committed a murder in the space of under two hours. Moreover, he could not have known that Charles was at the Tram Inn at that time; therefore the murder could not have been premeditated. But if the murder had not been premeditated, Waters would not have been carrying the revolver. Besides, there was the question of motive. Jealousy? Charles had certainly done his best to turn the head of Waters's foolish little betrothed. No doubt men had been murdered for less. But to judge from the good Mrs. Letbe's remarks Waters was not by any means a devout lover. No, John was inclined to think that Waters as a suspect was a bit of a washout. It would be as well, though, to hear his account of what had detained him on the way to Wintersbrook that Monday evening. Thoughtfully once again John rang the bell.

CHAPTER FOURTEEN

BEFORE the bell had fairly finished ringing Waters was standing in the doorway with a look of respectful interrogation on his narrow face.

- " You rang, sir? "

" I did.   I might almost say I am still ringing.   What a very efficient bell-answerer you are, Waters! "

" I happened to be passing through the hall, sir."

" Good.   Did you also happen to hear any of my conversation with Mrs. Maur? "

Not a flicker disturbed the bland serenity of Waters's face.

" In view of the fact that I am leaving in a fortnight, sir, I think I may say that I did."

" Good.   Shut the door, Waters.   Then I suppose I needn't explain why I rang for you?   What are you laughing at? "

The man's face took an expression of shocked gravity.

" Laughing, sir? " he echoed reproachfully.

" Laughing, I said.   What at? "

" Really, sir, I shouldn't dream—— "

" Oh, come!   In view of the fact that you are leaving in a fortnight, Waters, you may as well admit that something amuses you.   You have my permission to forget your professional pride for five minutes and answer me as one man to another.   What is it? "

" Sir," replied the intelligent Waters with a faint grin,

" if I were really to answer you as one man to another, so to speak, I shouldn't answer at all—not in the way of giving you any information, sir."

John laughed.

" Don't split hairs. Now then! "

The footman's faint grin grew more pronounced.

" Well, sir," he said deprecatingly, " I can't help laughing a bit to myself when I think to myself that you think I might have murdered Sir Charles, sir. That's all."

" And what makes you think I think you murdered Sir Charles? "

" Well, sir, it stands to reason. You see, it was my turn to go to church this morning, sir."

John shook his head.

" No, Waters, I can't see that it stands to reason at all."

" Why, yes, sir. After the service, I happened to meet the young woman I'm engaged to. The girl Letbe, sir. And she happened to mention——"

" Quite. I see that it does stand to reason, after all."

" So, putting two and two together, sir, I gathered that you wished to test my alibi, as they say, sir."

" Quite so. And as you appear to find the matter amusing, I suppose you have an alibi? I should like to hear about it."

Waters smiled.

" Well, I have and I haven't, sir. That's to say, I have an alibi, but I'd rather it didn't come to the ears of my young woman, sir."

" There's no reason why it should. But I should like it to come to my ears, if you please."

" Certainly, sir. I left here just before six last Monday."

" Half a minute. You told Ellie Letbe that you left late because Mrs. Maur was out and you had to wait for her to come in."

" Yes, I did, sir, but that wasn't strictly true. I took

my bicycle, as usual, and went down the lane towards Wintersbrook to see Ellie. But there's friends of mine lives on the lane, and as I was passing, one of them was in the garden a-picking of damsons, sir. So I stopped to pass the time of day, and I started to help pick, and then what with one thing, what with another, I was there an hour or more. And very pleasant it was, too, sir. But I didn't think it would be discreet to tell Ellie, sir. It doesn't answer, I find, to let one's young woman know one has been kept late enjoying oneself. So I pitched that tale about Mrs. Maur and being kept at work, sir."

John looked at him severely. This, after what Mrs. Letbe had said of her future son-in-law, sounded like the truth.

"Thank you, Waters. Do you mind giving me the name and address of your friends?"

Waters hesitated.

"If I may say so, I shouldn't like it to get to Ellie's ears."

"Never mind. I can guess. It's Mr. Lloyd of Linger-hatch, isn't it? And his granddaughter."

Waters looked a trifle surprised, and nodded.

"It saves a lot of trouble, Waters, to tell the truth—even to the young woman one's engaged to."

Waters pinched his thin lower lip and appeared to think this over.

"When she's of a jealous nature, sir?" he inquired mildly.

"Especially when she's of a jealous nature. She'll take all the more trouble to verify your statements. As a matter of fact, it was Mrs. Letbe who mentioned Lloyd of Linger-hatch to me."

Waters looked thoughtfully at John.

"Of course, sir," he observed philosophically, "the truth should prevail, I know. And in theory, sir, I always tell the truth, even to Ellie. But the flesh is weak.

And when it comes to causing tantrums and spoiling an evening with one's young woman, sir, one's liable to slip into falsehood, just to make things pleasant." He looked at the bowl of roses and sighed. " It isn't me that objects to telling the truth to Ellie, sir. It's her that objects to being told." And on this delightful piece of sophistry Waters contentedly closed his thin lips and gazed pensively out into the garden.

John looked at him with some amusement.

"Well, you know, Waters, you can get round that difficulty by not doing anything she would object to hearing about."

The footman's close-set eyes travelled back to John's face and stayed there, thoughtful, while he appeared to consider every aspect of this suggestion.

" No, sir," he said gravely at last. " That wouldn't do. Because, pardon me, sir, my way of looking at things is freer and better than hers, sir. She would object to so many innocent things. And if I was to take to her way of looking at things, I should be taking to a way I can't approve, sir. And that would be falsehood all the time, instead of just occasional."

" Dear me, you're very philosophical! "

" I always had a turn for thinking things out, sir. Of course I see that the right procedure would be for me to educate Ellie to my ways, sir. But, oh dear! What unpleasantness there would be in the process! And when one only has one evening a week with one's young woman, it does seem a pity one shouldn't spend it pleasantly, sir! "

" It certainly does. Well, thank you for being so frank with me. That's all, I think."

But Waters still stood there, his hands at his sides, looking thoughtfully at John.

" If I might make a suggestion, sir——" he murmured hesitatingly.

" Well? "

"There was a strange lady came a week ago yesterday, sir. Perhaps you have heard of her?"

"I have." John looked interrogatively at the servant, who seemed to be suddenly afflicted with diffidence. "Why?" he asked encouragingly. "Have you anything to tell me about her? Did you see her?"

"No, sir," said Waters uncertainly. "I didn't *see* her. That is, I didn't see *her*. But——"

"Well? Go on. What's the matter with you all of a sudden?"

Waters sighed, and so far forgot himself as to scratch his head.

"Servants always read their employers' letters, you know, sir," he remarked sadly at length. "That's what the employers say, isn't it, sir? As a matter of fact servants don't, not very often, employers and servants living and having their interests in different worlds, sir, and one world not particularly interested in the other. I never made a habit of reading Sir Morris's letters, not even when they was lying about asking to be read."

"Well?" asked John patiently, as Waters made another embarrassed pause. He could not see for a moment whither this apologetic preamble was tending. Then he remembered. Had not the strange lady gone into the library to write a note? If Waters was trying, with this unexpected delicacy, to convey that he had read it, there might be cause to be thankful for his impudence. John's face expressed nothing of this. He had learnt from experience that information was apt to be most enlightening when it did not come in the form of answers to leading questions. To his surprise, Waters's face went quite pink. He cleared his throat.

"Well, you see, sir, Mrs. Maur having told us in the pantry about what a queer lady had called, and how she'd taken herself into the library without being shown, and

o

that about Rhyllan Hall having a mistress—well, we was all a bit intrigued, as you might say."

" Naturally."

" So when I went into the library later to see if there was plenty of wood—the master liking a fire in the library of an evening—well, when I happened to glance at the desk, and saw the lady's note lying there, not gummed down nor anything, well——"

" I see." John looked at the man curiously. " But what I don't see is why you're so squeamish about it."

Waters's dark eyebrows rose in sincere astonishment.

" Surely, sir, it's wrong to read letters that aren't meant for one! "

" It certainly is. And I'm glad you realize it. But you didn't turn a hair when I accused you of listening at the door just now. You seemed rather proud of it, in fact. What's the subtle distinction? "

There was a pause.

" Well, sir," answered Waters slowly, " as I look at it, there's quite a difference. When I listened at the door, I knew it was my alibi you wanted to ask Mrs. Maur about. And I had to protect myself. I was listening, you might say, for a purpose. But when I happened to glance on the master's desk, and saw the lady's letter there, and opened and read it—then I hadn't any object, sir. It was just curiosity, quite unjustifiable, like."

" You are the prince of sophists, aren't you, Waters? "

" I have a very ticklish conscience, sir," replied he complacently. " And it's worried me quite a lot since I read that note. That's really why I'm telling you about it, sir—partly to be useful to you, and partly to relieve myself, sir."

" Strictly speaking," said John dryly, " I suppose that passing on information gained in such a way ought to aggravate that conscience of yours, not relieve it. How many people have you told already? "

Waters looked quite shocked.

"Nobody, sir! How could I let anybody know I'd demeaned myself to read someone else's letter? And that's another reason for treating one's employer's letters with respect, sir. There's no sense in filling oneself with information if one can't pass it on and get some pleasure out of it. There was I simply bursting, and yet, so to speak, unable to burst with honour, sir. It wasn't a pleasant situation, sir."

"You deserved it. But I think you'd better burst now. It may serve a good purpose, and I dare say that accommodating conscience of yours will even manage to extract a little honour from the situation, though you won't get any from me."

"There *is* them who believes that the end justifies the means, of course, sir," responded Waters with a wrinkled brow. "But I don't go so far as that." Perceiving that John was growing a little weary of these heart-searchings he hurried on: "Well, sir, it was quite a short note, in a big, dashing sort of hand. It said: '*Dear Morris,— Meet me on Monday afternoon at three o'clock at the Queen's Arms in Hereford. I've got a bargain to propose. Don't be alarmed, you'll get more out of it than I will. If you don't come I shall call at Rhyllan every day till I see you.*' And it was signed just with a C. There! I won't say the letter was exactly in those words, sir, but that's as near as I remember and pretty near it is. Sounds as if the lady was some relation or something of Sir Morris, doesn't it, sir? But Mrs. Maur, she never set eyes on her before that day, she said."

"Thank you, Waters," said John absently. He felt a little disappointed. Here was proof, or near it, that the mysterious visitor to Rhyllan had been, as he had supposed, the wife of Morris Price; proof of the theory he had formed to account for Morris's trip to Hereford on the day of the murder. But he had hoped that the letter would yield some new, unlooked-for information: rather absurdly, he realized, for Mrs. Price would not have been likely to give much information away in a letter left lying about for any inquisitive servant to read.

" Thank you, Waters," repeated John in a tone of dismissal.

Waters hesitated with his hand on the door-knob.

" I take it, sir, that you are quite satisfied with my explanation of my movements on the night of the murder? "

" Oh, quite, quite," said John dreamily, and the footman quietly left the room.

I have a bargain to propose. You will get more out of it than I will. It was easy to read a sinister meaning into these words, in the light of what had happened. And yet—surely Clytie could not have made this assignation with her husband to propose and discuss the murder of his nephew! John could imagine the way in which the redoubtable Morris would receive such a suggestion. It was impossible! And yet—at that interview in Hereford something had happened to close Morris's lips. It must be something more than mere obstinacy that had closed them so tightly that he would not disclose even to his lawyer the nature of his business in Hereford on that Monday afternoon. Suppose that Clytie *had* made a suggestion of murder. On that supposition Morris's queer silence became comprehensible. He was shielding his wife. John lit a cigarette, and for twenty minutes or so remained sunk in reverie, his eyes unseeingly on the Aubusson carpet. Then he glanced at his watch, and finding that there was still an hour before tea-time, went out into the garden to restore " The Murder in the Attic " to Mr. Clino.

CHAPTER FIFTEEN

" DO you mind driving, Sydenham? " asked John early that evening in the garage. " I want to talk to you."

" Certainly," replied Rampson obediently, climbing into the driver's seat. " But why this sudden caution? I've never noticed that driving cramped your conversational style in any way."

" This isn't going to be a conversation," said John ominously. " It's going to be a monologue."

Rampson ostentatiously stifled a premonitory yawn.

" It's no use yawning," said John, shutting the door and taking a map out of his pocket. " You've got to go about eighty miles before dinner."

" *What?* I thought you just wanted to nose about after clues."

" So I do. Half a sec while I study the map. Yes, we start off through Penlow and on past the Tram Inn. Then the cycling party's road lay through Hereford, but I think there's a quicker way than that. Yes, we turn off to the left—or stay! I think we will go through Hereford after all, and take the Queen's Arms on the way."

" If I've really got to drive you to Hereford, which must be at least thirty miles off, I'm all for taking the Queen's Arms on the way," said Rampson with a sigh. " Where exactly is this clue of yours, John? "

" In Moseley, a small village the other side of Hereford."

213

" How far the other side of Hereford? " asked Rampson sadly, turning out of the park gates.

" About twenty miles as the crow flies."

" And as the car crawls? "

" 'Bout twenty-five, if you don't mind a bad road."

" I do," said Rampson decidedly. " I mind very much. I mind the whole expedition extremely. I mind being lured out to the garage on the pretext of taking a little air before dinner, and then being told I'm to drive eighty miles. I mind very much indeed seeing eighty miles grow into a hundred and ten or so before I've had time to protest. I suppose you know," he added with desperate calm, " that we shan't be back to dinner? "

" I have made that simple calculation, yes," replied John meekly. " Blodwen is going to see that there's something cold for us, so you needn't worry."

" May I ask why we're going to this place? "

" Moseley? It's the place where Charles bought the bulls' eyes. And I'm not sure what I'm going to find out there, nor whether there's anything to find out, but I should like to go and make certain that he did buy bulls' eyes and nothing else."

" Suppose you found that he bought clove-balls, would that be a clue? "

" Don't be foolish, Sydenham. It isn't what he bought, it's what he did, if anything, that interests me. And now start listening, because I'm going to talk. I think we can remove Waters from our list of suspects. Also Mrs. Maur. Waters's alibi wants verifying, but it sounds perfectly all right."

John gave his friend an account of his interviews with the housekeeper and Waters, ending with Waters's version of the letter left by the strange woman.

" So I think we can take it that when Morris went on that mysterious business to Hereford on the day of the murder, he went to keep an appointment with his wife."

There was a pause while Rampson negotiated the sharp corner out of Penlow High Street.

" And the latest theory is? " he inquired thoughtfully, as they took the peaceful road again.

" Clytie Price is the obvious suspect at present, isn't she? "

" I don't know. Let's hear exactly why you think so."

" Well. To start with, we'll assume for the moment, though we haven't proved it yet, that Clytie Price and Mrs. Field of Sheepshanks Cottage are the same person. This is the theory I'm working on at present—mostly conjecture, of course, but it hangs together : Clytie Price, or Meadows, or Field learns of the death of Sir Evan Price, and knows that the heir, Charles Price, is lost in the wilds of Canada and can't be traced. (There was difficulty and delay in tracing him at first, you know.) She realizes that Morris Price has a good chance of inheriting the title and estates, and that if she can manage a reconciliation with him, she would be settled in honour and affluence for the rest of her life. She determines to try to patch things up with her husband. But her plans are spoiled when the lawyers in Montreal succeed in tracing the direct heir. From being the probable heir of Rhyllan Morris becomes again a mere steward, whose prosperity and continuance at Rhyllan will depend entirely on how he gets on with the new owner. There is nothing to be gained by Clytie in a reconciliation with him in these circumstances. But she has thought the matter over so much, and seen herself as Lady Price of Rhyllan so clearly that she cannot abandon the scheme. And gradually the idea of getting rid of the interloper presents itself. How? Well, there is only one way—murder. She takes a cottage as near to Rhyllan as she can get, so as to be on the spot. But now she is in a difficulty. It is no use murdering Charles unless she is sure of a reconciliation with Morris, and she knows Morris too well to imagine that he will be

easily reconciled. The simplest way out of the difficulty
seems to be to involve him, if possible, in her scheme for
getting rid of Charles. If she could make him a con-
federate or an accessory she would have a hold over him.
When she wrote that note asking him to meet her in
Hereford, she intended to propose a plan for murdering
Charles, and to induce him to consent to it. The murder
of Charles was her side of the bargain she mentioned.
The reinstatement of her as his wife was Morris's side.
As I see it, Morris indignantly refused to have anything
to do with such a scheme—eh? "

Rampson, who had seemed about to interrupt, altered
his mind and shook his head.

" Nothing. Go on."

" Morris," resumed John, " refused to have anything
to do with her precious bargain, and left her. She,
however, determined to carry the scheme through, hoping
to be able to put pressure on Morris afterwards. She had
abstracted Morris's revolver from the library drawer during
her visit on the Saturday. She followed Morris out from
Hereford in a hired car, saw his meeting with Charles, and
determined that her opportunity had come. After Morris
had departed, she followed Charles across the common,
shot him and pitched him over the edge of the quarry.
Before throwing him over, she took the ring off his finger
and the coat he was carrying and went off with them.
She buried Morris's revolver in a rabbit-hole, hoping it
would never be found. Later she hid the coat on the
Forest and the ring somewhere else, hoping that they
would be found and so confuse the issue. She must have
seen that things would look rather black for Morris, and
it was necessary to her plan that he should be proved
innocent. Unluckily for her, Morris chose to spend that
night on Radnor Forest, and the coat she had hidden there
had the reverse effect from what she had intended." John
paused, looking expectantly at his friend. " There!

What d'you think of that for a reconstruction of the crime? "

" Rotten," said Rampson succinctly.

" Why? " asked John, and could not help feeling a little chagrined.

Rampson, his eyes on the long, downhill road ahead of him, meditated a moment and then spoke with quiet conviction.

" Well. It sounds all right, superficially. But it's simply bulging with query marks."

" Of course, it's mostly conjecture, as I told you. But it makes a working theory."

" Does it? " asked Rampson placidly.

" Well, doesn't it? Come on, Sydenham! Pick holes in it. It's what I gave it you for. I know there are holes. But I didn't think they were unmendable ones."

" Here goes, then," said Rampson, cautiously slowing down as he began to speak. " Firstly, how did Clytie know there was a revolver in that drawer in the library? Secondly, and more important, what on earth did she want with Morris's revolver? Surely she would have used a more non-committal weapon for her murder. She had no desire to throw suspicion on Morris. On your theory, quite the reverse. Next to her own safety, Morris's safety was important to her."

" She might," answered John slowly, " have taken the revolver with some vague idea of having a hold over Morris, if he didn't fall in with her scheme."

" Possibly," agreed Rampson. " But according to your theory, she not only stole the revolver, she actually used it, and used it in circumstances which could not fail to throw suspicion on Morris. Thirdly, what about the five-pound note? You haven't mentioned the five-pound note. Can we really assume that the woman could have been such an idiot as to pick the pockets of a man she'd just murdered? And not only to pick his pockets, but to pay the note away within the next day or two? She must have known that five-pound notes can be traced fairly easily! We can't, I think, assume that she would risk so much for so little."

John sighed.

"The note is a difficulty, I know. And I didn't mention it because, as you say, one can't bring oneself to think she can have calmly pinched it after the murder. But there it is! Unless that old woman at Sheepshanks was making a mistake or telling a lie, which doesn't seem likely, Mrs. Field *did* have one of Charles's five-pound notes. And after all, that fact in itself is suspicious."

"Too suspicious," said Rampson promptly. "Because when one tries to follow up the suspicion, one's led to what you've just admitted is almost an absurdity. Fourthly, how do you account for Isabel?"

"I don't know," said John thoughtfully. "She may have been an accomplice, or an innocent accessory—the latter, I'm inclined to think. Perhaps she was a kind of second string to Clytie's bow."

"Oh! How?"

"Clytie can't have felt very sure that Morris would fall in with her pleasant little plan. And she may have thought that the next best thing to being Lady Price would be to be Lady Price's aunt. In fact, her first idea, before Charles turned up, may have been simply to marry Isabel off to Felix, who, on the presumption that Charles was dead, was the next heir after Morris. When Charles turned up, she may have altered her scheme and planned to marry Isabel to Charles. And then afterwards it may have occurred to her that a future depending on her niece's good graces might not be very pleasant. And then she would conceive the idea of doing away with Charles and trying for the position of Lady Price herself."

"Dear me," observed Rampson, and meditated profoundly.

"Well? Why dear me?"

"Only you seem to think Isabel is a very accommodating young lady. She didn't strike me like that."

"Perhaps it was Isabel's own idea. Perhaps she and her aunt invented the scheme between them. I don't say that Isabel was a mere cipher. But roughly speaking, I think my theory accounts for Isabel, and for the whole thing, don't you?"

Rampson was silent for so long that John had to repeat:

"Don't you?"

"It might," said Rampson guardedly.

"But it doesn't appeal to you?"

"No."

"But is there any other theory that will account for the facts?"

"I think so."

"What?" asked John, instantly hopeful. He knew Rampson, and knew that any theory he had formed would be worth the listening to. And his own reconstruction of the murder, which he had just sketched out for his friend's benefit, did not really satisfy him. It was, as Rampson had said, too full of query-marks.

To John's surprise, Rampson slowed down and drew up by the side of the lonely road before replying. Taking a cigarette-case from his pocket he offered it to John, and lit one himself, and then, turning to face his friend with one arm over the wheel, he said gently:

"You won't like it."

"What?"

"My theory."

"Why not?"

"It's not a new one. It's the theory of the police."

John was about to protest, but Rampson stopped him.

"Better let me finish what I've got to say now, old chap. But first answer me one question. What is there against the theory that Morris Price murdered his nephew? "

" Well——" John cast around for some clinching argument, and found none. " I'm sure he didn't, that's all."

" Exactly. You're sure he didn't, but you can't bring one reasonable argument against the view that he did. You're sure he didn't. Why? Because you took a liking to him, and because you've taken a liking to his relations and want to help them. But——! " Rampson made a gesture of despair. " My dear John! How can you set up, even in your own mind, such a flimsy defence against such an overwhelming attack? Have you ever stopped to consider what there is against Morris Price? You haven't, have you, because you've been prejudiced in his favour from the beginning. But consider now. He had motive. Have you been able to find sufficient motive in the case of any other person? No. You have this theory about Clytie Price, but you must admit that it's only the wildest surmise. He was on the spot at the time the murder was committed, and he had a strong motive for the murder, and the murder was committed with his revolver. He has the devil of a violent temper, that seems to be agreed on all hands. The night the murder was committed he spent roaming about on Radnor Forest. Well! There's no reason why a perfectly innocent person shouldn't spend a moonlight night admiring the Forest scenery. But in point of fact, it was a thing that Morris had never done before. His family were extremely surprised at his doing it. It seems, therefore, to point to some stress of mind, which may have been a perfectly innocent stress, of course. He may have gone there, as he says, to think about his future and his approaching departure from Rhyllan Hall. But there it is! You can't say it isn't a strong point against him. And then Charles's raincoat hidden in the bracken on the Forest!   And the stub of a Rhyllan Hall cigarette in the shepherd's hut!   And his behaviour to the police! Any one of these things may be explained away, no doubt. But the cumulative evidence is enormous.   Can you really shut your eyes to all this?   Especially when you realize, as you must, that there's no real evidence against my other person?"

There was a silence.   John looked through a gap in the trees over the sloping fields to the far blue hills.   For a moment he was daunted.   But then he saw Morris Price again as he had seen him at the inquest—arrogant, ill-tempered, baffled and at bay.

"Thank you, Syd," he said quietly at length.   "I think I have been rather shutting my eyes to what we're up against.   You've made me realize there's no time to lose."

Rampson threw away his cigarette and looked at his friend, half smiling, half frowning.

"No time to waste in what?"

"In finding the murderer."

Rampson sighed, laughed, shook his head and turned back to the wheel.

"You see," said John, "I just can't believe that Morris Price is the murderer, and that's all about it.   Until the inquest I was inclined to think he had done it.   Half-way through the inquest, I was uncertain.   But at the end, you remember, when he told the foreman of the jury not to be a fool, I was sure that he was innocent.   He wasn't acting.   And there was something in his face— stupefied and yet indignant—that seemed to me simply to shout his innocence.   I can't forget it."

"I'm sure I hope you're right," said Rampson, as the car slid forward.   As for me, I've got no choice but to think him guilty, and that's why I've decided to go back to London to-morrow.   I've been trying hard to see some solution of the case that wouldn't involve Morris Price, and I can't. And for me, that raincoat and cigarette-end we found on the Forest simply clinch matters. And I don't feel very comfortable, living under what I suppose is his roof and thinking him a murderer. So I'm off, John. It's high time I was back, anyhow."

"We'll see," replied John. " I'm going up to London myself to-morrow. But I rather wanted you to stay at Rhyllan and hold the fort for me. We'll talk it over later. That's Hereford, I suppose. We must be nearly there."

The Queen's Arms proved to be a fair-sized, rather florid-looking hotel facing on the market square. John left Rampson in the car and went up the steps into a small square lounge full of wicker chairs and tables. A Sabbath peace brooded over the place. A porter who had been standing with folded arms contemplating the baro-meter sprang to life as John approached, and the young woman in the booking-desk raised a dreamy eye from the novel she was reading. After a cursory glance at the two of them, John decided on the porter. He had a jovial, intelligent and essentially tippable face. John beckoned to him.

" Can you tell me where I can get some petrol? "

A look of faint surprise came into the porter's pink and healthy face. He glanced across the square.

" There, sir. At the petrol station."

" Oh, yes, so I can. Wait a minute. There's some-thing else I want to ask you. We may as well come straight to the point." John put his hand into his trouser-pocket and the man's natural expression of good-humour became accentuated.

" Willin' to tell ye anythink I can, sir. But I ain't the Encyclopædia Britannica."

His accent struck gratefully on John's ears. The cockney was a good observer.

" You're a Londoner, aren't you? "

" Wish I'd stayed there. This place gives me the 'oly blues. Not the 'otel, I don't mean," he hastened to add, scenting a possible visitor, " but the town. But a job's a job in these days, and it ain't so bad in the summer. What was it you wanted to arst me, sir? "

" Were you on duty here last Monday afternoon? " The other stared, then laughed.

" Funny thing! You're the second as 'as arst me that! "

" Oh? "

" A copper with a face as long as me arm came in 'ere yesterday, and arst me that very identical question. 'E didn't give me nothink for answerin' of it, though."

" Oh! " John thought rapidly. Was Superintendent Lovell also following up the movements of the mysterious Clytie Price? Or had Morris broken his silence and given an account of his doings in Hereford? The porter's next remark seemed to dispose of the second question.

" You ain't the tall, dark gent as the copper was looking for, are yer, sir? No, I see you ain't. You ain't old enough. Wanted to know, 'e did, if a tall, dark gent'd bin in 'ere on Monday afternoon. Well, we 'ad a good many people in on Monday afternoon, as it 'appened, and tall, dark gents as thick as fleas on a pillow. So 'e whips out a photograph and shows me. ' No,' I ses, ' I ain't ever seen a face like that, to my knowledge.' And Miss 'Arfitt she ses the same. So then 'e wants to know if there's bin a big green car, a Daimler, outside the 'otel. ' There may a bin, or there may not,' I ses, ' but if there was, I never seen it.' So 'e didn't get nothink out o' me."

The porter grinned and seemed rather to relish his inability to supply the police with information.

" Answerin' questions and answerin' questions," he remarked, " an' all you gets at the end is a nod. Is it the same tall, dark gent you're after, sir? "

" No.   I'm after a tall, middle-aged lady, probably dressed in black, with ear-rings and probably a veil over her eyes, who was here at three o'clock on Monday afternoon."

The porter pondered, scratching his chin.

" Now was it Monday?   It was a busy day, I know. Yes, you're right, it was Monday.   There was a lady like you've described sittin' 'ere in the lounge, smokin' and 'avin' coffee and liqueurs all the early part of Monday arternoon.   All by 'erself, she was, I remember noticin' 'er.   She arst me for a match.   She 'ad lunch 'ere, I fancy.   She was sittin' 'ere from two o'clock till about three.   And then suddenly, off she went, and dropped a lighted cigarette on the floor, she was in such an 'urry. Sittin' in that chair and looking out o' the door all the time she was, not readin' nor nothin'.   And then she seemed to see a friend or somethin' in the square, and up she gets and off she goes.   She'll be the lady you're after, depend on it.   A tall, 'ansome lady, with big eyes and ear-rings and a lot o' powder and scent.   No chicken."

" Thank you."   Two half-crowns passed from hand to hand.   " Did the policeman who came here ask you anything about a lady? "

" No, sir, thank you, sir.   A tall, dark gent was all 'e wanted, and 'e seemed to want 'im very bad.   But 'e didn't get 'im.   Not out o' me 'e didn't."

Clytie Price, it seemed then, had not yet appeared upon Superintendent Lovell's horizon.   His inquiries at the hotel for news of Morris were probably part of a routine investigation of the prisoner's movements.

" Just one thing more," said John, turning back as he was about to depart.   " You had a party of cyclists staying here last Sunday night, didn't you? "

" Lor bless yer, sir, we 'ad the gentleman who's bin murdered—Sir Charles Price an' 'is party!   Didn't know it at the time, we didn't, owing to the rooms bein' booked in the name o' Dr. Browning. But we seed it in the papers two days arterwards. Emma, Miss Harfitt, that is, you could a knocked 'er down with a feather. And I 'ad a bit of a turn, thinkin' o' them all 'ere so frisky an' jolly, and then that to 'appen. 'Ad breakfast early, they did, and I fetched their bikes round sharp at eight o'clock, and orf they went. And then to think of what was to come! Poor chap! There don't seem much doubt about who did it, do there, sir? Funny thing, when I read in the paper about the wrong bike bein' found in the quarry, I thought to meself, well, p'raps young Smiler's right after all."

-" Young Smiler? "

" Lad as works 'ere—runs messages and that. Funny thing, 'e 'ad 'is bike stolen the same morning, and in 'e comes, all red in the face an' near cryin', an' ses the nobs have gone off on 'is bike by mistake. But I knew they 'adn't, 'avin' wheeled their bikes round from the shed meself, and knowin' young Smiler's bike be sight. Obstinate, 'e was, and 'e would 'ave it 'e'd left 'is bike a-standin' alongside o' the others, and one of them 'ad took it by mistake. ' Well,' I ses, ' use yer eyes, me lad,' I ses, ' if one of them 'as took it by mistake, where's the bike they mistook it for? And use yer sense, me lad,' I ses, ' none of them didn't go off ridin' two bikes at once.' ' Did you see 'em? ' 'e ses, obstinate-like. And as it 'appened, I 'adn't actually seen 'em go, bein' called inside to fetch some luggage down. So I gives 'im a good cuff and tells 'im not to be a young fool. But 'e never got 'is bike back. Some tramp must 'a' pinched it. 'Ard luck on the lad, it was, 'im 'avin' bought the bike second-'and not long before. And 'e's a good lad, though saucy."

" Did he inform the police? " asked John.

" That 'e did, rushed off straight away. But Lor'

bless yer, sir, what can they do? One bike's like another bike, and once they're stole, they're stole."

John returned thoughtfully to Rampson and the car and was silent so long that Rampson was constrained to ask, as they left the town behind:

"Well? Our friend the porter seemed a chatty soul. Did you collect any clues?"

John sighed.

"Young Smiler had his bike stolen."

"Eh?"

"Oh, Lord!" exclaimed John. "I go here and I go there, and everywhere I go I seem to pick up a piece of the puzzle. But no two pieces fit together. It's like an enormous jigsaw puzzle with half the pieces lost! Blow young Smiler and his bike! Where can I fit him in?"

"Probably nowhere. Forgive me, John, but in my view you're much too optimistic about these stray pieces of information."

"Optimistic! Good Lord!"

"But you are. You're inclined to regard everything you hear and can't easily explain as a clue to this murder. I can't see any reason for attaching any importance to half the stray facts you insist on storing up as clues. You've got a hopelessly romantic, novel-reading way of looking at things. Think it over. Nora tells you she saw a man looking at her down the passage of the Tram Inn. And immediately you think: a clue. Why? A man stopping for a drink must look in at the door of the Tram Inn several times a day. Miss Whatsername at the Tram sees a man making for the orchard, and lets her eggs boil hard while she looks for him and doesn't find him. A clue? No, not really. For, on her own showing, she's always having apples stolen from her orchard. Then the egg-shells you found in the rabbit-hole. What do they prove except that somebody had stolen some eggs? What reason is there to see the remotest connection between them and Charles's death? I don't know the story of young Smiler and his bicycle, but I suspect it of being no more sound than the rest of these clues. Smiler had his bicycle stolen, did he? And Charles was found dead in the quarry with a bicycle beside him. A bicycle appears in both cases. But that's no reason for connecting them. The world's full of bicycles, and they're very frequently stolen. It's all so imaginary, so hopelessly unscientific! Imagination's an excellent thing, kept under control. It'll arrive at the same conclusion as scientific reasoning, and get there quicker. But really, John, you're letting your imagination run away with you over this murder case! So much so that you're blinding yourself to the obvious. And when you get a really good clue, like that cigarette-end in the shepherd's hut, you ignore it, because you don't like the way it leads. It's the beginning of intellectual ruin when a man starts picking and choosing his facts to suit his private sentiments. It—it shocks me."

There was a pause, as they moved evenly along under the streaking evening shadows of great trees. Then Rampson glanced round at John. They looked solemnly at one another and laughed.

" It's all very well to laugh," said Rampson ruefully. " I don't like to see a promising young mind like yours going to the dogs."

" I'm sure you don't," agreed John amicably. " It's a terrible sight—the once keen intellect tottering on the verge of lunacy. Seriously, though, Syd, you *are* the heavy parent this afternoon, aren't you? "

Rampson answered gently:

" I'm afraid you're going to be disappointed, John, and I want you to be prepared for it."

A chill descended on John's spirit for a moment with his friend's gentle and serious words. Suppose, after all, the obvious explanation of the mystery were the true one?

But once again he heard the voice of Morris Price, astounded, indignant, suddenly shaken by an unexpected fear: " *Don't be a fool!* " No. Morris Price was innocent, and the obvious explanation was not the true one.

" I see your point," said John. " And I admit the justice of your remarks. But, you see, I am convinced that Morris Price is not the murderer. Therefore, the obvious clues, which all point to him, are no use to me. And I have no choice but to follow up others, the best I can get."

" You admit, then, that the obvious clues all do point to Morris Price? How do you explain that, if he is innocent? "

" Either they point to him by pure chance, or else the murderer took care to plant the crime on him."

Rampson nodded.

" Either explanation is possible. But the second is by far the more probable of the two. If we accept it, it means that the murderer must be somebody who knew, not only that Charles would be at the Tram Inn on Monday evening, but also that Morris would be there at the same time. Considering that Morris apparently told no one where he was going, and that the cycling party cycled and stopped as the spirit moved them, I don't see that anybody can have known."

" The crime might have been committed, on the spur of the moment, by somebody who saw them both there, and saw an opportunity of getting away with the murder," replied John, and his thoughts swung back to Clytie Price.

Rampson shook his head, but said no more.

" Well," said John, " we can't be far off Moseley, and perhaps when we get there we shall find a clue that will pass the acid test of your scientific mind."

" I see no reason for hoping so," said Rampson sadly, as they turned off the main road.

CHAPTER SIXTEEN

THE village of Moseley seemed to sleep around its triangle of green. A little knot of dark-clothed men sat on the benches outside the Carpenter's Arms. A small girl in a red frock trundled a perambulator across the grass, using the handle-bar as book and elbow rest. Four or five lads stood around the pond which lay at the base of the green, throwing chestnuts at a family of ducks. The square-towered, hump-backed church behind its little churchyard kept a close watch upon its flock.

The one small shop and post office showed dark green blinds, close drawn over door and window, and a little front garden that displayed, among its dahlias, asters and late roses, the notice of a Grand Fête and another of Petrol for Sale.

" This," said Rampson, drawing up before the little white gate, " is the very archetype of rural peace and innocence. A church, a green, and ducks upon the pond! Moreover, it is small. If there are any clues here, you won't have far to look for them."

" I shall look in the shop first. Coming? "

" No. I'm going to pursue some investigations of my own at the Carpenter's Arms. You'll find me there when you come out. Buy me some bulls' eyes."

" Can't. It's Sunday."

After a moment's hesitation, John decided to go round to the side door. The shop door was obviously locked, and the front door of the little house, with its glittering brass handle and doorstep of pure snow, had such a formal and inviolable air. The springs of conversation would flow more easily, he thought, at the back, where straggling honeysuckle made a porch over a rough door set ajar on a small kitchen. He knocked, and a masculine voice requested him cheerily to come in. A young woman was engaged in clearing away tea-things, and a young man with shrewd blue eyes and a ruffled thatch of hair sat on the edge of the table with a child on his arm.

"Anything you want, mister? The shop's shut, by rights, being Sunday, but if there's anything you want pertickerlar, I can get it for you. Can't I, Sam?"

The two-year-old addressed as Sam made no answer, gazing round-eyed surprise from a countenance besmeared with jam and dust.

"Oh, wash his face, Eddy, for goodness' sake!" said the young woman, offering her husband a damp dish-cloth, and to John: "Shall I put you a cup o' tea, sir? This is a bit cold, but the kettle's boiling and I can easy make some fresh."

A talkative young woman. On John's refusal to partake of tea, she entered into a dissertation on the weather, the harvest, the Shops' Act, and the difficulty of teaching infants not to suck their thumbs. It was some time before John could communicate his errand.

Wrinkling her brows and plaiting her apron into little folds, she thought she did remember a young man on a bicycle coming about a week back. She was silent a moment, travelling back over seven days of supplying people with stamps, ginger-beer, bacon, cotton-reels and bananas. At last her face cleared.

"Yes!" she said animatedly. "Of course I remembers! And it were on a Saturday, as you says! For I remembers it were my busy day. A tall young gentleman with fairish hair and a bicycle. Said he were going to

Hereford, and wanted a pound of bulls' eyes. 'That'll be a tidy big bag,' I says, and he said they was for his young lady. 'Why don't you ask her in?' I says. 'We've got ginger-beer and lemonade, or could damp some tea, and cycling's thirsty work?' But it seemed he'd left her somewhere on the road waiting for him. I remembers well, for when I were weighing out the sweets, I were thinking: A pound of bulls' eyes, they'll get in a tidy sticky mess in his pockets afore they're all ate!"

"Can you remember anything else he said?" asked John hopefully.

She shook her head.

"Nothing, except what a fine day it were, and how far were it to Hereford, and this were hilly country for a bike. Oh, and he wanted to know had I any iodine, because he'd gived his ankle a bit of a twist and it were beginning to come up a bit. I hadn't none, not in stock, but as it happened, there were a bottle with some in that I got for Baby when he cut his foot. So I looked it out for him, and put him some in a little bottle, and off he went."

Iodine. Yes, Charles had sprained his ankle slightly. Felix had said so, that day in the Tram Inn shed, when they were all standing round the body. What more natural than that he should supply himself with iodine? There had been no brown stain on either of his ankles when Dr. Browning had examined them in the shed. But he might never have used it. Or he might have used it once or twice and washed it off.

"That was all, sir," the young woman assured John, as he did not reply at once. "He didn't ask for nothing else, nor say nothing else that I remembers."

"Thank you very much for remembering him at all," said John. "You didn't happen to notice which way he went when he left here, did you?"

" Yes, I did, for I went to the door with him. He got on his bike and went straight off to the main Hereford Road. I seed him turn the corner."

John took his leave and crossed the green to the Carpenter's Arms. He found Rampson discussing the weather with the rustics gathered around the inn's long trestles, and joined them in a glass of sour but refreshing cider.

As they walked back to the car Rampson remarked:

"" Your friend Charles didn't do anything in this village but buy bulls' eyes, John. I found a man in the pub who saw him come and go, and he says he wasn't in the place above ten minutes. He was cutting the grass on the green, my aged friend was, and he saw a young chap on a bicycle come in from the lane and go straight to the post office. And then he saw him come out of the post office and get on his bike and go straight back up the lane. So I'm afraid this village isn't exactly a hotbed of clues."

John nodded.

" It isn't. I've discovered the reason why he didn't invite anybody to come with him, and it's a perfectly innocent reason. He wanted to buy some iodine."

Rampson laughed.

" Iodine? Is that a reason for creeping off by stealth? I thought you were going to say cocaine or opium, at least, if not prussic acid. I shouldn't mind buying iodine with the whole population of England looking on, personally."

" Of course not. But when they said in the shop he'd been buying iodine, I remembered Felix telling us that he had spoken of spraining his ankle a little—not much of a sprain, you know, just a nasty twist. Of course he wanted the iodine for that."

" And still I don't see the need for secrecy. It isn't a crime to sprain one's ankle."

"No, but I also remembered Dr. Browning asking Felix why Charles hadn't mentioned it and had had free medical attention. And Felix said that Charles had asked him not to say anything about it, because he hated having any sort of fuss made, and didn't like people to know he was ass enough to have anything the matter with him, or words to that effect."

"That," said Rampson approvingly, driving off, "is the first good word I've heard said for Sir Charles Price. But it rather puts the lid on your theory of mystery at the cross-roads, doesn't it?"

"It does. I'm sorry I've dragged you all this way for nothing, Syd. But at any rate I can cross Charles's secret expedition to Moseley off the list of suspicious circumstances, and forget about it. And that's something, in such a welter of apparently disconnected facts."

"Apparently!" echoed Rampson, shaking his head. "My dear John, never forget that apparently disconnected facts are often actually disconnected. Far, far more often than Mr. Sherlock Holmes and Mr. John Christmas seem to imagine."

"Now, Sydenham," said John firmly, "don't start trying to depress me again. I need all my strength to think out a plan of campaign for to-morrow."

"To-morrow?"

"I'm going to London to-morrow to look for Clytie Meadows. I shall probably take Felix with me, and Nora's coming to fetch some canvases from her sister's. You're going to stay behind and keep an eye on things at Rhyllan."

"Things? What things?"

"Oh, things," answered John vaguely. "Nothing in particular, but I shall feel happier if I know you're there."

"But," protested Rampson as they flew along the road towards Hereford, "I've already told you that I don't feel I can stay at Rhyllan and eat the bread of Price any longer."

"You must just stun your tender conscience as best you can, Sydenham," said John firmly, "for staying you are. After all, you're doing the Prices a good turn by staying, whatever your private views may be. Anyhow, I'm not going to have my plans spoilt by any nonsensical squeamishness about eating bread, so if you can't stay with a clear conscience, you must just stay and suffer pangs."

"I wish you wouldn't talk about bread and pangs, John," said Rampson plaintively. "You've made me realize it's past dinner-time and I'm ghastly hungry. Oh, confound these geese! There ought to be a law against letting animals loose on the highways."

"There *is* a law against letting motorists loose on the highways," replied John gloomily. "Do moderate your hunger, Sydenham. I really can't afford a broken neck just now."

CHAPTER SEVENTEEN

THE INNOCENT LADY

" "GOOD-BYE," said Blodwen. "When will you be back?"

She spoke mechanically, as if she did not care when they came back, nor whether they came back at all.

"Late to-night, if we're lucky," replied John, opening the door of the car for Nora and her rugs. "But don't worry if we're not back till to-morow. I'll take care of Felix."

"What about you, Nora?"

"Oh, I'm not part of the flying squad. John's just giving me a lift to my sister's. I've got to fetch some canvases I left behind," explained Nora, tucking the rug carefully around her ankles.

John, who had a shrewd suspicion that Nora's wish to go to London was not prompted solely by a desire for canvas, smiled and said:

"I promised your father I'd leave you at your sister's, Nora, and leave you out of our search for Mrs. Field. And I'm afraid I'm a man of my word."

"All right," said Nora innocently. "Of course. I know."

"Well," said Blodwen, "I wish you success."

She spoke absently and did not smile, and then, as though suddenly herself aware of the omission, gave a hard artificial smile and waved her hand.

" Good-bye!   Good-bye! "

John hesitated, his hand on the clutch.

" We're leaving you Rampson to look after you."

A queer dark look came into Blodwen's fine bright eyes.

" Thank you."

Still John hesitated. He glanced up at the curtained windows of the room where Rampson was still sleeping. He glanced again at Blodwen Price. The clear morning light did not suit her. She looked old and tired standing there on the steps with the early sun on her. One of her red setters sidled up and rubbed his silky head against her knee, but she seemed oblivious of it. Oh, well! Rampson could be trusted to look after himself!

" Good-bye!   Good-bye! "

The car slid down the drive and into the dewy freshness of the September morning.

" What's the matter with Blodwen? " asked Nora in mild surprise, looking back towards the terrace where Miss Price was still standing, quiet as a waxwork, looking over the lawns.

John shook his head, but Felix, sitting in the dicky, replied in a low voice :

" The matter?   What's the matter with all of us? What should be the matter in these delightful circumstances? "

" I'm sorry, Felix. Felix, don't!   What's the use? But Blodwen does seem to have something extra the matter with her this morning. She was quite herself last night."

" Probably," said Felix coldly, " she hasn't slept much." He hesitated, and took the hand Nora held out to him across the back of the seat. " I'm sorry, Nora," he said in a low voice. " But it's all very well for you people to say what's the matter? and what's the use? For you, it's just—fun, all this. Isn't it? "

There was a pause.

" Partly," replied the truthful Nora at length. She seemed about to say more, but altered her mind, withdrew her hand and turned thoughtfully away.

It was nearly two o'clock when they entered the Brompton Road. John turned to Nora.

" You turn down opposite the Brompton Oratory," said Nora placidly. " Will you stay to lunch at Eveline's? Or can't you spare the time? "

Feeling a trifle baffled, John turned down as directed. Was it possible that Miss Watson had no ulterior motive in coming with them to London? She had not, apparently, any desire to accompany Mr. Holmes on his -adventures. John was exceedingly relieved, for he had anticipated some difficulty in carrying out his promise to Dr. Browning. Ridiculously enough, he was a little disappointed, too.

They left Nora at her sister's pleasant little house in a quiet Kensington street, promising to call there when their mission was completed, and refusing an invitation to stay to lunch.

" I wonder," murmured John to himself, as they drove off.

" What? "

" Whether Nora's got anything up her sleeve. She didn't mention anything to you, I suppose? "

Felix looked surprised.

" No. What sort of thing? What do you mean? "

" I thought at first that fetching canvases was just an excuse to join in the hunt for Clytie Meadows. But I suppose I was wrong."

" You promised her father you wouldn't take her, didn't you? "

" I know," said John pensively. " That's what makes me wonder, as I said before, whether she has anything up her sleeve. I didn't hear *her* make any rash promises to her anxious parent. I've kept my promise, but I feel a bit responsible for her. And she's rather a lively person to be responsible for."

" Is she? " murmured Felix absently.

John was moved to reply :

" Well, isn't she? You ought to know. You've known her for years, and I've only known her a week."

A certain sharpness in his voice caused Felix to turn and look at him in surprise. There was a pause.

" Yes," said Felix at length in a subdued voice. " I know she is. I don't know why I said is she? in that loutish way." He hesitated. " To tell you the truth, John, since this dreadful thing happened, everybody and everything has become strange and a little out of focus to me. I've kind of lost my hold on reality for the time being."

" It's a pity," said John, turning into the Kensington Road, " to lose your hold on your friends. You'll want them again some day."

" Nora? " said Felix vaguely. " Oh, but Nora and I are great friends, we always have been. Do you mean that Nora's getting fed up with me? "

John, noting half with approval, half with a queer disappointment, the genuine note of anxiety in the boy's voice, judged that he had said enough.

" I don't mean anything," he responded lightly, " except just what I said."

They passed the Albert Memorial. The trees in the park were changing colour, and the grass was thick with the brownish early-dropping London leaves. Felix, having recovered from his first surprise, spoke gloomily :

" I'm sorry if I've been behaving badly to my friends. But in the circumstances, isn't it a good deal to ask of a man to expect him to think of such things? "

" Why not ask a good deal of a man? " replied John gently, and there was silence until the shops of narrow crowded Kensington High Street came in view.   Then, with a rather chastened air, Felix asked :

" John, what are we going to do, exactly? "

" Now? "

" Yes."

" We're going to No. 8 Featherstone Terrace.   And we're going to ask if Mrs.—now, that is a bit of a problem! "

" What is? "

" I don't know what her name is when she's at Featherstone Terrace.   She was Miss Meadows before she married, and Mrs. Field at Sheepshanks Cottage, and I suppose she's really Lady Price.   But heaven knows what she is when she's at home!   Never mind.   I shall ask for Miss Isabel Donne."

There was silence.   Glancing round out of the corner of his eye, John saw Felix's profile pale and thoughtful.

" I think you'd better come with me, Felix," he said gently enough.   " You know Miss Donne better than I do.   Perhaps she'll tell you more than she will me."

There was another silence.   At last Felix said tonelessly :

" Isabel doesn't tell anybody much."

" So Nora said."

" One tells her everything, but she tells one nothing."

" Yes.   So Nora said."

A pause.

" Last Monday," said Felix, suddenly and impulsively, " seems a hundred years ago.   If you had asked me then to question Isabel as if she were a criminal, I'd have wrung your neck.   But now—does it matter?   Will anything ever matter again?   I'll go anywhere with you.   I'll do anything you say.   Because all the time there's only one horrible thing in my mind that crowds out everything else.   And you seem to be the only person in the world who really believes that it'll pass.   Isabel! "   He spoke the name softly and lingeringly, as if trying to wring the utmost music from it. "Isabel! It's become just a word in my thoughts, a word that ought to mean something, and does not." He broke off abruptly as if half regretting having said so much, and after a while went on: "What will you do then? Suppose they won't see you?"

John laughed.

"I don't suppose they will. In fact, I don't suppose we shall find them there. I expect we shall spend the entire day in trying to discover their whereabouts."

"Are you assuming, then, that Mrs. Field had a hand in the murder?"

"I am assuming what is obvious, that she wished to avoid her identity becoming known."

"Are you sure of her identity?"

"It's not proved. But personally I am quite sure. But whether my theory as to her being Lady Price is correct or not, we must find out how she got hold of that five-pound note. We have something definite to go on there. And this, I think, is Featherstone Terrace. And there is No. 8."

They drew up in front of a terrace of stucco houses that fronted on to a peaceful residential street. It was a pleasant enough looking row of houses, adorned with iron balconies, window-boxes and a variety of classic orders, painted in all shades from pristine white to a dark and peeling grey, with front doors that ranged in colour from the sombre green of the old regime to a lively scarlet.

Felix looked a trifle surprised as John drew boldly up at No. 8.

"Isn't it a pity to give them time to see you coming?" he asked hesitatingly. "They'll say they're not at home."

John laughed.

"I've left my false beard and blue spectacles behind,"

he said cheerfully. " So I'm afraid there's no disguising either of us. Pull up your coat collar and jam down your hat and walk with a stealthy, cat-like tread up the front door steps, and you'll attract no attention at all."

Felix looked for a moment a trifle hurt, and then decided to smile.

" What are we going to say, exactly? " he asked rather nervously as they got out of the car.

" If we see Mrs. Field we'll ask her straight out where she got that five-pound note. If we see Isabel we'll ask her to lead us to Mrs. Field. But probably we shan't see either of them. My only hope is that they haven't left the country."

" Left the country! " echoed Felix distastefully. " Why should they have done? There's nothing against them except that five-pound note, which may have quite an innocent explanation."

" It may," said John grimly. " And the fact that Isabel told none of you her aunt was staying near Penlow may have an innocent explanation too. So may the fact that they both left for London a day or two after the murder. I should like to hear all these innocent explanations. 8A is the address. That'll be the upper maisonette, I suppose."

They passed into the little lobby and John rang the bell of one of the twin front doors. There was a silence, while they both listened for footsteps on the stairs inside. Suddenly Felix turned restlessly towards John and asked :

" John, why did you bring me here? "

" To protect me, of course," replied John with a faint smile. " It's better to hunt in couples. There's always a slight element of risk in this business, you know. Do you mind? "

" Risk? " repeated Felix, shrugging his shoulders. " Lord, no, I don't mind that. But—I have wondered —why me, rather than Rampson, this time? "

" Thought I should like a change of Watson," said John lightly, and as the boy's face remained moody and thoughtful, added: " Rampson didn't want to come, and I thought you'd like to have something to do." He did not add that he had not cared to leave Rhyllan Hall for a whole day unwatched.

A very young, very neat servant-maid opened the door with an interrogatory smile.

" Is Miss Donne at home? " asked John, expecting the girl to disclaim all knowledge of such a person. But to his surprise she replied equably:

" She's out, sir. But Mrs. Field is in. Will you come in? "

They followed her up the narrow stairs on to a light and pretty landing hung with Japanese colour-prints. John, who had fully expected to find that his quarry had run to a new earth, had to make a quick readjustment of his ideas. Was it possible that, after all, Mrs. Field was a perfectly innocent lady? Was it possible that she had no connection at all with Morris Price and Rhyllan Hall, and that he must look elsewhere for the mysterious Clytie Meadows? He had time to murmur into Felix's ear, " Keep your eyes open, and keep your head whatever happens," before they were ushered into a small, pleasant drawing-room with long windows giving on to the balcony.

A lady rose from a pretty chintz-covered chair near the window, and exclaimed in accents of surprise and pleasure:

" Why, it's the young man who wanted ginger-beer! "

John saw the smiling, clever face of the late lessee of Sheepshanks Cottage. So far, so good.

" My name's Christmas," said John, taking the muscular hand she held out to him. " This is my friend, Felix Price."

The grey eyes made a quick survey of Felix's sombre young face.

" I've heard of you from my niece Isabel," said

Mrs. Field amiably. "I'm pleased to meet you. Poor Isabel, it was a shame she had to cut her holiday short! All for nothing, too, because my illness turned out to be just an ordinary tiresome cold! As a matter of fact—do sit down! That's a comfy chair—I had a dreadfully sore throat the day you called at the cottage, and by the evening I was feeling so bad I quite thought I was in for something serious, and my one idea was to get back to my comfortable home and have Isabel to nurse me. She's quite a good nurse, Mr. Price, though you mightn't think it from her heartless way of talking. So I flew home and went to bed and sent for Isabel. But by the time she arrived I was perfectly well. Isabel was very cross with me, and it really was a shame to interrupt her holiday. Though the dreadful death of that poor boy had rather cast a cloud over things, of course."

Her rich voice softened and dropped. She leant sympathetically towards Felix.

"He was a relation of yours, wasn't he, Mr. Price?"

"My cousin."

"Ah, I'm sorry! Poor boy! You're going through a dreadful time. We've seen reports in the papers. But it'll come right in the end. Don't lose heart."

Her kindly, maternal voice, her gentle phrases that yet had a certain conventional stamp as though she spoke of a matter that did not closely concern her, might almost have convinced John that he was stirring a mare's nest. Yet this same agreeable lady who now spoke so naturally of her niece Isabel had confronted that niece without a sign of recognition at Sheepshanks Cottage, less than a week ago. As if she had read his thoughts, Mrs. Field turned to him and said:

"It was funny that it happened to be my cottage that you came to for ginger-beer. And you must be thinking it very funny that Isabel and I didn't seem to know one another. The fact is—it sounds rather silly, I know—

but I'm not very strong. I suffer from occasional mild but very tiresome heart attacks, and I'm such an idiot that I hate Isabel going far away from me. She's the only person I've got in the world, you see, and—well, it sounds morbid, I know! "—she laughed in an embarrassed way—" but I hate the idea of being taken ill, and perhaps dying, with Isabel hundreds of miles away. Oh, I'll probably last for years! We chronic invalids always do, you know. But there it is! I've got an invalid's obsession. And I haven't been very well this summer, the attacks have been getting more frequent, and when Isabel was asked to go and stay with the Brownings, I almost implored her not to go! But it seemed selfish, so I compromised and took a cottage as near as I could get to where Isabel was staying, so that I could feel that she wasn't out of reach. And we decided not to let the Brownings know, because it would have seemed rather an imposition on them. I mean, they might have felt they had to offer me hospitality. It would have been rather awkward. You had the young Browning boy with you when you came for ginger-beer, and for all I knew you might have been one of the Brownings yourself. That was why Isabel and I met as strangers, as they say in the melodramas." She laughed pleasantly. "We both felt awful idiots."

John expressed polite interest and amusement, and condoled with his hostess on her ill-health. She did not look like a lady subject to heart-attacks, sore throats and obsessions. Her eyes were bright, her smooth, powdered face firm and clear-skinned, and there was a suggestion of strength and vitality in her figure that a younger woman might well have envied.

" Isabel has told me about you, Mr. Christmas," went on Mrs. Field, ringing the bell. " She says you're a detective. I suppose I mustn't ask whether you've made any progress towards finding the murderer of that poor young man in the quarry? In fact, now I come to think of it, your presence here is rather alarming! " She gave a little laugh, and told the maid who answered the bell to bring in an early tea. " Don't tell me," she went on with a humorous lift of her thick, dark brows, " that you've called in an official capacity! "

" Oh, but I have! " said John gently, and closely watched her face. It expressed nothing but merry surprise and disbelief. Once more he was shaken, once more inclined to think that Mrs. Field knew no more of the Price's affairs than did her little servant-maid. But whether she did or not, there was the matter of that five-pound note to be cleared up. " Really," John assured her, " we do want your help."

" Ah! " she said, smiling and arranging a becoming cushion of peacock-blue at the back of her shining grey head. " That's a sweet, pretty way of putting it! And of course I'll help you all I can, though I can't imagine how. Thank you, Amy. Is Miss Isabel in yet? "

" Not yet, madam," replied the little girl, and withdrew.

" I hope she won't be long," murmured Mrs. Field. " She's just gone out to buy Whatman paper. What do you think of her drawings, Mr. Price? I think they're really rather clever."

" Very," replied Felix, and seemed indisposed to say more. There was an air of constraint and uneasiness about him. Poor youth! He was not the perfect Watson. And John's thought swung back for a moment to Rampson, holding the fort at Rhyllan Hall. Mrs. Field evidently did not expect loquacity from him, for she looked at him with grave sympathy and turned to John.

" Now tell me how you want me to help you."

" Did you come across a man called Hufton while you were at Sheepshanks Cottage? " asked John.

" Yes," answered the lady promptly. " I caught him stealing beans out of the garden."

" Ah! " murmured John. " I thought so."

Mrs. Field raised her expressive eyebrows.

" Thought so? "

" The first time I met Isabel she informed me that Hufton was a thief, and at first I could not imagine how she knew. But I soon deduced that she had heard it from you."

There was the slightest pause, while Mrs. Field took the cosy off the teapot. Then :

" Did you know, then, who I was? Before you came here this afternoon, I mean? " she asked in a casual, expressionless tone.

" Of course." John spoke gravely, and his eyes met hers directly, hoping that they might betray her. Certainly she looked surprised. But she only said, absent-mindedly smoothing down the cosy's embroidered cover :

" Well, I think it's awfully clever of you. But I do hope you didn't let the Brownings know. They'd think it so curious, Isabel not letting them know that I was there. But really, we did it with the best intentions."

John evaded this question.

" I hope," he said gently, " you won't be offended when you discover how much I know about you, Mrs. Field. You see, when one's investigating a case like this one's bound, incidentally, to find out quite a lot about people who have no connection with the case at all."

She laughed and affected to consider her reply, looking thoughtfully at a pointed finger-nail.

" What awful revelations are you going to make, Mr. Christmas? No, of course I won't be offended. I don't think I've been doing anything very dreadful lately, so you can be quite frank. Fire away."

" Well," said John bluntly, judging that it would be politic to come quickly to the point and not give the lady time to exercise her invention : " You paid your rent to the old woman at Sheepshanks Cottage with a five-pound note."

" Yes? "

" That note had been in the possession of Charles Price only a day or two before.   We have reason to think that several notes were taken from his wallet after he was shot, and that your note was one of them."

He watched her closely as he spoke.   She flushed pink, then scarlet, and seemed for a moment at a loss for words. The consternation on her face was genuine, he could have sworn.

" But do you mean to say——" she began, and broke off, looking from John to Felix, from Felix to John.

" So of course," finished John more gently, and began to feel assured that the lady was innocent, " we're awfully anxious to know where you got that note."

She gazed at him with bright, troubled eyes.

" But——! " she said.   " You don't mean that you think I—— But no, of course you don't!   Oh, let me think! "

She bit her thumb-nail and looked out of the window. Suddenly her face cleared.

" But of course! " she cried.   " I got it from Upper Ring Farm in exchange for a cheque! "   She turned excitedly to John.   " Yes!   I didn't want to leave a cheque for the old lady because I knew she hadn't a banking account.   And I hadn't enough spare cash to pay her.   So I went up to the farm and got them to change a cheque. They gave me two five-pound notes.   I was a bit surprised at the time, but I thought they probably had a hoard under the bed or somewhere.   Of course!   I believe I've still got the second note somewhere.   Shall I go and see? "

She got up.   She was flushed, excited, glad to help. Genuinely excited, genuinely glad to help, John felt perfectly sure.   She left the room, and John heard another door on the landing and then a drawer being hastily opened.

" I say! " said Felix with the first sign of animation he

had shown since they had arrived. " If that's true—it's something definite, isn't it? Why, it means—why, that Hufton or somebody did it, for the sake of the money! Doesn't it, John? "

" Seems like it," agreed John for the benefit of the lady in the adjoining room. At heart he was troubled. Was it really possible that all the elaborate edifice he had constructed round Mrs. Field was without foundation in fact? He seemed to hear Rampson's kindly, warning voice : " It's hopelessly unscientific! I'm afraid you're going to be disappointed, John! "

" Yes, it certainly seems like it," he repeated with a cheerfulness he did not feel, as the lady re-entered the room.

" There! " she said triumphantly. " That's the other note! I say! I've just thought—could it have been Hufton? I'm not only thinking of the beans. According to my old lady, he had a bad reputation all round."

She hung excitedly over John as he took a notebook from his pocket and compared the number of the five-pound note with a string of numbers written there.

" Yes. This is one of them." He laid it down on a side table and looked thoughtfully at the carpet, then at Mrs. Field, who had resumed her place beside the tea-table. " Can you remember exactly when you got these notes, Mrs. Field? "

" It was the evening before I left for London," she replied promptly. " The evening of the twenty-ninth. I went up to the farm myself and saw the woman there. I didn't think she would really be willing to change my cheque, though you never know with those Welsh farmers. Often they've got no end of money and quite heavy banking accounts, for all they live so simply. But she was quite ready to change me one for ten pounds. She went off upstairs and came back with two five-pound notes. Oh, I am glad I've been able to help after all! " Suddenly her face fell a little. "But, Mr. Christmas—if the notes were stolen from Charles—surely she'd never risk putting them into circulation so soon?"

"Oh, I don't know! She seemed a fairly ignorant sort of woman. Perhaps she didn't realize they could be traced. We must go and interview her as soon as we get back. Thank you very much, Mrs. Field. This may be the beginning of the end of all our troubles."

But he did not really think so. What should Hufton have been doing with Morris Price's revolver? If the notes came from Hufton, how much more likely that he had stolen them from the dead Charles when he found him lying in the quarry! The five-pound notes, John feared, would prove to represent a blind alley in his investigations.

"And now," said Isabel's aunt gaily, "we'll have some tea, and you shall tell me all the other dreadful things you've discovered about me. Tell me honestly—now do, I shan't be offended—did you ever think that I had anything to do with the murder?"

John laughed.

"I kept an open mind."

"No, but really! You must have thought it very suspicious my having that five-pound note. Do tell me. Really I shan't mind. How could I mind? I was a perfect stranger to you, and for all you knew I might have been capable of anything."

John was about to make a tactful evasion, but suddenly altered his tactics. He determined to make one more attempt at shocking the lady into self-betrayal before he allowed his growing conviction of her innocence to have its way with him. He looked her straight in the eyes.

"I hadn't any clear theory as to what you'd done," he replied. "I had a very interesting theory as to who you were."

Did her grey eyes snap with a smothered alarm? Or

was it a very natural surprise at a turn of the conversation she had not looked for?

" But do tell me," she said, with the sugar-tongs poised over the basin, " who did you think I was? "

John replied gravely:

" I thought you were Felix's stepmother."

There was a pause. Mrs. Field looked at Felix and Felix, in some embarrassment, at her. Then she gave a little deprecating laugh.

" Oh, but I'm sorry I'm not! " she said, and added with half-humorous gravity: " I should like to have a stepson, and such a nice one. I've got nobody but Isabel, you see. But why ever did you think so, Mr. Christmas? Doesn't Felix know his stepmother, then? "

" No. He hasn't seen her for twenty years."

" Dear me! Then of course he wouldn't know her. Well, I wish I were she. It would make such an interesting story. Does Felix want to find his step-mother? "

She smiled in friendly, teasing fashion at the embarrassed Felix, who looked at John.

" I do," said John frankly.

" She may be dead."

" No. She was at Rhyllan Hall a week ago."

Mrs. Field looked up with vivid interest.

" And you mean to say she's vanished since? Sugar, Mr. Price? Oh, dear! Amy's brought the wrong milk! The worst thing about a flat, Mr. Christmas, is that there's no cellar. I do hate tired milk, don't you? "

She rose and departed with the little silver jug. John sat and looked round the room. A pleasant little room with its pink, chintz-covered chairs, light walls, and bowls of roses. It gave no clue at all to its owner's past. There was not a photograph, not a book beyond two or three novels lying on the work-box. The front-door bell rang.

" That's Isabel, I expect," said John.

Felix agreed indifferently.

"I expect so." But he turned his face with a sort of strained expectancy towards the door.

Mrs. Field came in with the jug of fresh milk and resumed her place at the table.

"And now," she said, "we'll really have some tea. That was Isabel, I expect. Do you take sugar, Mr. Christmas?"

"Please."

"Hullo! Hullo, Felix! What are you doing in London?"

Isabel, cool and pale like a mermaid in a dress of green flowered muslin, entered and threw her hat on to the piano. She took Felix's hand with an easy, unembarrassed friendliness, and stood thus a moment, smiling, before she let it go.

"Hullo, Mr. Christmas! Now don't say you've come here to look for clues, or I shall be so nervous, I shan't dare to speak a word! Tea, give me tea, Puffy darling! I'm simply exhausted with trying to explain to those idiots at the stores what kind of paper I want."

Puffy! One of the names by which Clytie Meadows had been known in her youth. Not such a very uncommon nickname, perhaps, in a world of idiotic nicknames. A coincidence? Perhaps, but a teasing one. John looked at Isabel and her aunt. How easy, how unembarrassed was their behaviour. How satisfactorily Mrs. Field had explained all the circumstances which had seemed so suspicious! A kindly, middle-aged lady and her pretty niece. And yet—Puffy!

"Has Aunty Margaret told you about the weak-minded way she first followed me to Penlow and then dragged me away from it? You must have thought that an awfully good clue." She stood at the table selecting a cake. "Oh, Margaret! You've got the wrong milk! Never mind. I'll change it."

She took the little silver jug which had already made one journey to the kitchen and back, and was at the door before her aunt could speak.

" No, darling, it's fresh! I've just fetched it myself! "

Isabel sniffed it daintily and made an expressive grimace.

" You must have gone to the wrong bowl. Shan't be a minute."

She vanished.

Extremely particular about the quality of their milk, these ladies. John noticed that Mrs. Field had flushed pink, and that her finger-nails were beating an impatient tattoo on the silver tray. She looked for a moment, in fact, extremely cross.

" I hope you're not taking all this trouble for our sakes," said John, as Isabel returned with the jug and set it on the tray with a queer, defiant smile at her aunt's still rather resentful face. " Neither Felix nor I take milk in our tea."

There was a pause.

" I do," protested Felix. " I hate tea without milk."

" My dear Felix," John reminded him firmly, " remember what the doctor said. No milk in either of our teas, please, Mrs. Field."

Felix submitted. Isabel gave a little laugh.

" Then I've fetched fresh milk for nothing! " she said merrily. " For Aunt Margaret and I both take lemon."

She handed their cups and offered slices of lemon, which Felix, with a regretful glance at the milk-jug, refused. They talked of this and that. A queer constraint had settled upon the little party. Was it the advent of charming Isabel, waking numb wounds in Felix's heart, that caused it? Mrs. Field became almost silent, and Felix spoke only in monosyllables when Isabel addressed him, stirring his milkless tea and looking out of the window. Only John and Isabel chattered through the little meal.

Isabel saw them to the door when they rose to go. A little comedy of cross-purposes took place on the landing. Felix made an attempt to detain Isabel for a few private words, and Isabel seemed determined to hurry after John for the same purpose. John, going downstairs, heard her impatient:

" Oh, bother, Felix! I want to speak to John! "

She had her way. Felix passed them in the hall, and with a stiff " Good-bye, Isabel! " stalked past them to the car.

" John," said Isabel, " what did you come here for? "

" To ask your aunt some questions," replied John frankly. " She'll tell you about it."

The girl hesitated. She looked at Felix, standing with the haughty immobility of a Pharaoh beside the car, and looked up the stairs, and then back at John.

" Don't come again," she said earnestly, in a low voice. " Please, John. Don't come again. Or if you must come, don't bring that silly infant, Felix, with you. It isn't fair to him."

She turned abruptly and went upstairs again without a backward glance, leaving John pensive. Was it Felix's wounded heart she wished to spare, or something even more important to him, perhaps his life?

John and Felix drove in silence back to the Brompton Road. Poor Felix! He had over-estimated his imperviousness. Isabel at a distance might have become a shade, but the lady's near presence still had power to wound.

At the neat, pretty house of Nora's sister they were informed that Nora was out.

" She didn't expect you to come for her so soon," explained Nora's sister, an older, smaller, prettier copy of Nora's delightful self. " In fact, we didn't think you'd be going back to Penlow till to-morrow. You'd better leave

Nora here, I think. She can go home by train to-morrow or the day after."

" Where's she gone? " asked John, vaguely uneasy.

" What, now? Only to buy some paints. You'll stay to dinner, won't you, and go back really late, if you must go? "

" No, I think we'd better get back," answered John. He added, still not quite at ease : " Had Nora anybody with her? "

Eveline looked a trifle surprised.

" Yes. A cousin of mine who's staying here went with her. Why? "

" Oh, that's all right," said John, with immense relief. " Then I think we'll start for Penlow, Felix. We can get a bite of food on the way, if there's time. I should like to get back in time to see the people at Upper Ring Farm before they go to bed. If we start now we ought just to do it."

" Have some tea before you go, anyhow."

" No, thank you, we've had some. We'll be off."

" Why," asked Felix, as they sped out of London, " did you make me drink my tea raw at Mrs. Field's? It was beastly. And I still can't see what the object was. I'm afraid I'm quite as dense as the real Watson. What did the doctor say? "

John laughed.

" The doctor? Oh, he said : ' When in Rome, drink what the Romans drink.' "

CHAPTER EIGHTEEN

I T was after ten o'clock when John drew up at the foot
of Rodland Hill. Dusk had fallen and a large warm
moon hung low in the sky. He left the car upon the
grass by the road where he had left it once before, and
passed with Felix through the gate. A lamp still burned
through the red blinds of Sheepshanks Cottage, and the
asters showed wan and colourless in the moonlight. They
trudged along in silence over the field where spectral cattle
lifted great horns and watched them, up the cart track
and through the coppice to Upper Ring Farm. The
watchful collie, tied to his kennel for the night, broke
into wild barking long before they were in sight of the
square, small house and its long, low buildings.

" Oh, shut up! " cried Felix irritably, which had the
effect of spurring the creature to louder, fiercer efforts to
alarm the household.

Both John and Felix were tired, depressed and hungry.
Standing on the narrow brick path that ran around the
farmhouse, looking over the low fields from which the trees
rose swathed in damp whitish mist, John had a sudden
revulsion of feeling. Almost he could believe that
Rampson was right, and that Morris Price had murdered
his nephew. Almost he was inclined to abandon the
whole affair. What were the Prices to him that he should
lose sleep and go without food chasing wild geese for them

255

all over the country?   Why couldn't that arrogant, obstinate idiot, Morris Price, speak out for himself and tell his lawyer about his meeting with his wife and what happened at it?   It was as Rampson had said; all the clues that did not lead to Morris Price led up a blind alley. Lord!   Couldn't these confounded people open the door and tell their dog to stop barking?   Standing stiff and weary, with that insane barking in his ears, John felt heartily sick of the Prices and their affairs.

"Poor old John, you look fagged out," said Felix.   He added in a low voice : "What should we have done without you this last week?   Gone mad, I think."

And so nicely adjusted are human emotions, and especially the emotions of tired and hungry humans, that on the instant at Felix's words and his serious humble look, John's conviction of Price's innocence came back to him.   It became the major object of his life to set Morris free.   He heartily resumed his attack on the door of Upper Ring Farm.

"I am feeling a bit depressed," he admitted cheerfully.   "It's the way all my best clues seem to lead nowhere that exasperates me.   And I bet this one'll prove no better than the others.   Hufton stole those notes from poor Charles's wallet when he found him dead, you can bet your boots.   In fact, at the moment, there's only one thing sustaining me in hope."

"What's that?"

"The milk we didn't drink at tea-time.   Lord!   I should have liked to have taken samples from those three lots of milk and had them analysed!"

Felix's face in the moonlight was a study in horror.

"John!   You don't mean—I've been wondering what you meant by that remark about the Romans.   You don't —you can't——"

"Can't I?   You must admit the ladies were strangely particular about the milk destined for our tea—not for their own, mind you. I wouldn't mind betting there was more than milk in the second lot. I'm not sure about the third. I'm inclined to think that was a return to the *status quo*. Oh! Good evening. Is Mr. Hufton in? "

The dark, thin-featured mistress of the farm stood in the doorway with a candle in her hand and looked at them suspiciously.

" Quiet, Rover! " she cried shrilly, with magical effect. Silence settled upon the landscape like a benediction. " Hufton, he's in bed. What is it you wants? "

" I want to speak to you and Mr. Hufton," replied John. " May we come in? "

She hesitated, then grudgingly opened the door and led them through into a comfortable kitchen dimly lit by a large but ill-burning table lamp. A heavily built man of middle age who had been warming his feet by the fire turned as they came in and bade them a gruff good evening. The woman made an attempt to turn up the lamp which immediately emitted thin streamers of black smoke.

" Drat! " she remarked perfunctorily and turned it down again and relit the candle she had blown out. She did not ask her visitors to be seated, but stood at the table looking at them from under black brows with an ill-humoured expression, as though she found them a nuisance : as, no doubt, she did.

" The matter is this," said John, addressing the woman, who appeared on the whole a more lively and intelligent person than the man. " Last Wednesday a Mrs. Field, who was staying at Sheepshanks Cottage, came to you and asked you to change a cheque for her."

The woman's black eyes sought her husband's. She seemed about to deny John's statement but thought better of it and nodded.

" She gave you a cheque for ten pounds, and you gave her two five-pound notes. Now, Mrs.——"

R

"Dolphin, our name is. But I don't——"

"Mrs. Dolphin, I want you to tell me where those two five-pound notes came from."

"We didn't steal them, if that's what you means," said the woman shrilly, flushing dark red. "And if you're going to say as we did, I'll ask you to step outside, master. We're honest people here, besides having no need to steal, and can have five-pound notes in our purses as well as anybody else, I suppose!"

John waited a moment and then said calmly, noting that in spite of her indignation the woman looked confused and nervous:

"Hufton gave them you, didn't he?"

"I'm sure I don't remember," replied Mrs. Dolphin, with the air of one to whom a five-pound note is a bagatelle. "Where did you get them notes from, Henry?"

She looked meaningly across the table at her peaceful husband. But he failed her.

"What you be talking about," he remarked, scratching the stubble on his cheek. "I doesn't know no more'n this chair."

"Oh, Henry! You've forgot!"

"No, I hasn't. I knows as you said tother day you'd give a lady change for a cheque, because didn't I say more fool you without making sure it were a good 'un? But I thoughts as you'd took the money from the box in the wardrobe. I never heard naught of a fi'-pun note."

"Oh, Henry! You forgets everything!"

"No, I doesn't," said Mr. Dolphin with placid obstinacy. "I ha'n't never seed a fi'-pun note but twice, and one o' them were a bad 'un."

John cut into the conversation before the farmer's disappointed wife could tell him what she thought of him.

"Perhaps you don't know, Mrs. Dolphin, that all five-pound notes are numbered and can be easily traced?"

She had not known, that was obvious.

"I've seen the two notes you gave Mrs. Field," went on John, "and I know where they came from. They came from the pocket-book of Sir Charles Price who was found dead in Rodland Quarry a week ago."

The woman's thin lips fell apart and she gazed at him in silence. She went pale, then flushed.

"What?" she asked stupidly, and then, as the import of his words came home to her, broke out: "I never knew that, I swear I never knew! Hufton, he told me he found them in a field, and I thought no harm for him to keep them, not knowing the owner, for why should the police have them more than the chap as found them? Oh, you're not going to say, sir, as Jim Hufton stole them! He's a good lad, if he is a bit sly in some ways, and he pays his lodgings regular and doesn't drink!"

"I'm not going to say anything till I've heard where he got these notes," said John patiently, and taking the hint the woman went to the foot of the little enclosed staircase and called shrilly:

"Jim! Jim! Come down! You're wanted!"

The lodger was heard to reply that he was asleep, but a bellowed summons from the master of the house brought him down in a few moments. He stood at the foot of the stairs, blinking and scratching his head, a pair of trousers hastily slipped on over his night-shirt. He was a heavy-faced, sunburned youth of twenty or so, with rather prominent teeth and a pair of sleepy, good-natured little eyes.

"What?" he said simply with the curtness of one aroused from a comfortable bed.

"Them notes, Jim—them five-pound notes you asked me to change—where did you get them?"

" Found 'em," replied Jim laconically and gave a cavernous yawn.

" Oh, Jim! You ha'n't been doing anything as you shouldn't? " asked his landlady with sorrowful solicitude.

" Findin's keepin's." If Jim Hufton had indeed stolen the notes his conscience did not appear to be unduly disturbed thereby. He yawned again, sighed deeply, supported himself against the door-post and with his big toe manœuvred the door-mat under his bare feet.

" Make a clean breast of it, Jim," urged Mrs. Dolphin, who seemed suddenly to have decided that guilt would be more interesting than innocence. She watched the possible criminal with an entranced eye, evidently hoping for the worst.

Mr. Dolphin, finding the strain of simultaneously keeping his feet on the fender and his eye on the lodger too much for him, reluctantly moved his feet to an adjacent chair and turned a solemn, disinterested gaze on the little scene. Mr. Hufton slowly woke to a sense of something wrong. He turned a filmy eye from John to Felix.

" I found 'em in the field," he repeated in a slightly aggrieved tone. " What of it? Whoever left 'em there didn't want 'em or he wouldn't 'a' left 'em there." He contemplated his big toe-nail in silence for a moment. " That's sense," he added more cheerfully, struck by the rare wisdom of his own words.

" What field did you find them in? " asked John, convinced that this lethargic person was speaking the truth. Only an innocent man or an experienced actor could have shown such indifferent obtuseness.

" Eh? In the field near the common just afore the railway."

" What, just lying about in the field? "

" Ah. Pushed under a gorse-bush, they was. I happened to stoop to tie me boot-lace and I seed a bit o' white paper poking out from under the furze. And that's what it were, sir. Two bank-notes. Well, it stands to reason the chap as put 'em there didn't want 'em, and——"

" When was this? "

" Eh? Oh, it were the day I found the chap in the quarry, same morning. I'd come back for me breakfus' and I were going to work again. And it stands to reason, findin's keepin's and the chap as put——"

" Thank you," said John, a bit weary of this piece of deduction, sense though it might be. He took up his hat. " That's all I wanted to know."

" Well, the chap as put 'em there," said the man of sense again, " can't have 'em back. 'Cos they're spended on a sideboard and a wedding-ring and a clock. And it stands to reason——"

John got himself and Felix hastily outside the front door. The farmer's wife seemed as loath to let them go as she had been to let them in.

" Will he be arrested? " she asked with bated breath and enraptured eyes.

" Lord, no. I don't see any reason to doubt what he says."

She looked disappointed.

" He oughtn't never to have kept them notes, did he? He ought to have took them to the police," she pronounced severely, determined not to be baulked of her lodger's guilt.

John foresaw endless trouble for the luckless Hufton and determined to avert it.

" You're just as bad, aren't you? " he pointed out gently. " You actually changed the notes."

And having thus silenced Mrs. Dolphin's tongue and put a premium on her lodger's perfect innocence, John took his leave.

CHAPTER NINETEEN

THEY arrived at Rhyllan after eleven. Blodwen had retired to bed, but Rampson and Mr. Clino conducted them to the small parlour and watched them ravenously devouring cold meat and salads. Both Rampson and Cousin Jim seemed exceedingly pleased to see the wanderers return. There was about both these gentlemen a slight air of tedium, as if they had spent a long while in one another's company without much entertainment.

" Dear me! " observed Mr. Clino, as Felix once more attacked the ham. " The detection of crime seems to induce hunger. I hope you *did* detect something, after all your journeyings? "

" Yes, oh, yes! " said John cheerfully, though he was a little surprised at a certain note of unfriendly irony in Mr. Clino's tone. " We detected a lady and her charming niece having tea in a drawing-room."

" You found Mrs. Field, then? " said Rampson.

" Oh, yes, we found her all right and she gave us a very nice tea."

" That all? "

" And lots of explanations," added John.

" Reasonable ones? "

" Oh, quite reasonable, if you accept the fact that she's a valetudinarian, which she certainly doesn't look."

" She does not," agreed Rampson emphatically. " She appeared to me exceptionally spry and lively. What's the disease? "

" Bad heart, sore throat and weak nerves."

" And she chose to stay by herself in a cottage miles away from anywhere! " murmured Rampson sceptically. " Don't you believe her, John. She is fooling thee."

" Ah, but that was just why. She wanted to be within call of her loving niece."

" Within call! Is Sheepshanks Cottage on the telephone? "

" Shouldn't think so. But that's what she said. And of course there's no accounting for the caprices of a *malade imaginaire*. In fact, I should probably have believed her if she hadn't tried to poison my tea. Very inartistic touch, that. Puts one on one's guard at once. Well, I'm going to bed," said John, much refreshed in spirits. " Good night, Felix. Good night, Mr. Clino."

" Good night," responded the elderly gentleman without warmth. " I think I shall take a turn on the terrace before going up. What about you, Felix? "

" I'm off to bed, Cousin Jim," responded that young man uncompromisingly, and followed Rampson and Christmas up the broad, shallow stairs. He paused with them outside Rampson's room.

" I say, have you told Rampson about that bank-note? If what Hufton says is true, it's valuable evidence on our side, isn't it? Because no one could imagine that my father would have taken the notes. And they were found in a field at the other side of the quarry. My father came straight back to the Rodland Road."

" Hufton's evidence is certainly valuable," replied John guardedly. " And I don't see any reason to doubt the truth of it. Won't you come in for a moment or two and have a talk? "

Felix refused, somewhat to the relief of John, who wanted a private word with Rampson, and with friendly good nights went along the passage to his own room.

" What was all that about Hufton and evidence? " asked Rampson, closing the door of his room. " Didn't sound very convincing to me. If Morris could do the murder, I don't see who's going to imagine he'd stick at pinching a bank-note or two and planting them in a field."

" No, of course not. But I wasn't going to discourage Felix's new-born optimism. Hufton's evidence wouldn't be in the least convincing to a jury. But I think it's convinced Felix. Hence his sudden cheerfulness."

" Oh, well! " said Rampson, shrugging his shoulders. " I don't understand these Prices. They're altogether too temperamental for me. Old Clino seems to be the most rational one of the bunch, and he's an unspeakable old bore, goodness knows! "

Rampson spoke feelingly and sighed.

" We've been fatiguing one another to death all day," he explained, " except for an hour in the afternoon when he providentially fell asleep in a deck-chair. I was sorely tempted to go off by myself for a ten-mile walk, but I remembered what you said about staying on the premises, so I stayed. But nothing happened, except a few more hours of boredom. Funny thing," added Rampson pensively, " I believe he found my society quite as tedious as I found his."

" Remarkable."

" Ass! No, but seriously. After tea he just sat on the terrace with me and yawned at nearly everything I said. Yet when I got up for a stroll, up he got too and trailed along by my side, obviously racking his brains to think of something to say to me that he hadn't said before. He even asked me who were my favourite

authors, and said he never read any novels but Scott and
Thackeray. Oh, Lord! I've had a hell of a day! I
feel a wreck! "

"Didn't you see anything of Blodwen? " asked John,
lighting a cigarette.

"At lunch-time. I don't know where she was all the
rest of the day. Lying down, perhaps. I must say she
didn't look at all well at lunch. Quite white, and she'd
put rouge on her cheeks, and looked ghastly. I suppose
she didn't want to harrow our feelings by looking ill.
But her conversation wasn't equal to her cosmetics. She
hardly said a word all lunch-time, but just stared out of
the window like a—like a sick little owl. After lunch,
I ventured to be sympathetic and said that she must be
feeling the strain of this business awfully; and she gave
a kind of ghastly smile and said : ' Strain? What strain?
I don't know of any. If you mean this absurd business
of my uncle's arrest, I can assure you it doesn't disturb
me unduly. *I* am quite confident of the outcome. But
then, *I* know my uncle.' And she turned her back on
me and went away. Did you ever? ' This absurd
business! ' And I used to think Blodwen was a sensible
woman, though as hard as nails. Really, John, I'm
awfully sorry for the Prices, especially as you seem to
like them, but they're enough to drive an ordinary person
crazy."

John looked thoughtfully at the tip of his cigarette.

"Didn't you see Blodwen again all day? "

"Oh, yes, at dinner. Same white face, same ghastly
rouge, same silence. I wonder," said Rampson thoughtfully, " whether this business has unhinged her mind.
Or do you think she believes at the bottom of her heart
that Morris is guilty, and can't keep up the pretence of
courage any longer? "

"Her emphatic remarks to you certainly sound like
it," murmured John. " But it's a very sudden loss of

courage, if so.   She seemed perfectly cheerful yesterday.
So you've had a quite peaceful day? "

" Peaceful! " echoed Rampson scornfully.   " Oh, yes,
awfully peaceful, with old Clino chirping in my ear all day.
Tell me, John, why were you so keen on leaving me to
hold the fort here?   Did you expect anything to happen? "

" No.   But, you see, Rampson, we haven't found the
murderer yet, and so long as we haven't found the
murderer, anybody may be the murderer."

Rampson thoughtfully drew back the chintz curtains
and let up the blind on to the moonlit garden scene.

" I see.   Even Blodwen."

" Yes."

" Well," said Rampson with a sigh, leaning on the sill.
" I hope she didn't.   Not that I like her much, but I felt
sorry for her to-day.   When she made that idiotic speech
about not feeling any strain there was real blank fear in
her eyes, I could swear.   I was sorry for her.   Well.   It's
a lovely night.   The moon's almost at the full."

John stood by his side and looked out over the grey,
mysterious lawn to the black shrubbery and trees beyond
the roses that showed pale in the moon.

" Lord, what fools we mortals be! " he murmured
softly.   " Why can't we leave one another alone? "

" We can't do that," said Rampson, " for obvious
reasons.   But we can, and should, leave one another
alive.   Well, good night, John.   See you in the morning
sometime.   At present I feel it will take me a week to
sleep off the tedium of the day."

It was about an hour before John finally dropped into
an uneasy, dream-haunted sleep.   He woke abruptly,
every nerve taut, to hear his name whispered urgently.

" John! John! "

The room was in darkness, but the door stood ajar
and somebody stood in the opening.

" John!   John! "

" What? "

" Wake up!   There's something going on."

It was Rampson.   Wide awake on the instant John sprang out of bed and had stretched out his hand for the switch when his friend, a dim shape in the darkness, caught his sleeve.

" No, don't show a light.   It's in the garden."

" What? "

" I don't know."   Rampson padded to the window and looked out.   " I couldn't sleep after all, and I thought I heard somebody moving about the house and a door opening.   It sounded like the front door.   So I went to the window, and there was somebody in the garden. The moon's gone down.   I saw an electric torch go on among the bushes."

He spoke in whispers.

John, slipping on his tennis shoes and dressing-gown, felt a queer thrill of excitement go through him, mingled with apprehension and—yes, fear.   In the darkness, listening to Rampson's fluttering whisper, he knew a strong foreboding of disaster.

" Are we going out to see who it is? "

" Of course."

" Have you any idea who it is—out there? "

" No," whispered John, getting to his feet and pocketing his own electric torch.   " I'm a rotten failure as a detective.   I've collected dozens of clues, but none to account for this.   Come on."

At the door Rampson paused.

" What about a weapon?   Have you got one? "

" Lord, no!   I suppose we ought to have something. Half a jiffy."

He disappeared into the room on the opposite side of the passage and came out in a moment with something gleaming in his hand.

"The revolver out of Charles's room," he whispered as they crept cautiously downstairs. "Luckily for us it was still there, and the cartridges with it."

In the wide, ghostly hall he paused a moment to load the weapon. The front door stood ajar. Silently, keeping under cover of the house, they crept along the terrace and across the lawn in the shadow of the rose-pergola. The shrubbery was before them, pitch-black and faintly rustling, as if small, secretive creatures were moving stealthily among the stems. John stood still a moment, trying to pierce that darkness. And suddenly a faint gleam of light showed among the rhododendron bushes and went out again.

He took a few paces forward, his eyes fixed on the leaves where the light had shown through. He dared not use his own torch as yet. To his strained ears his own quiet footsteps sounded loud, alarming. A dry twig cracked and he stopped, listening for a repetition of the sound.

Suddenly Rampson at his side closed his fingers gently and firmly over John's forearm. John turned. Had Rampson touched him suddenly he would have been hard put to it not to utter an exclamation. But the hand closing gently over his arm seemed more urgent in its message than any sudden clasp.

"Look!" murmured Rampson in his ear, and turning his head John saw a dark figure moving stealthily over the lawn by the herbaceous border towards the shrubbery.

"Another!" he breathed, and strained his eyes to identify the figure that crept along so quietly; hunch-shouldered, draped in some loose, dark garment, oblivious of John's and Rampson's eyes. John could dimly make out that the person, whoever it might be, was carrying a stick.

About six yards away from the two friends, in the shadow of a tree, the figure came to a sudden halt. Too late John realized that Rampson and himself were standing unprotected from such light as there was in the sky. Too late he realized that they had been seen.

" He's seen us," he murmured to Rampson. " Don't make a sound. Stand still. Leave the first move to him."

For what seemed an age they stood quiet, watching the figure which, dimly made out under the tree-shadow, stood equally quiet, as if watching them. John gripped his revolver tightly, and perhaps the slight gleam of the barrel caught the eye that was watching from the darkness. For without warning there came a sudden explosion that sounded deafening in the stillness of the night, and the stranger stepped away from the shadow of the tree, levelling his gun for another shot.

" Good God! " said John. " He's got a gun! What lunatic is this? Take cover, quickly! Behind the cedar! "

From behind the great cedar that stood near the edge of the shrubbery, John peered out across the lawn. The dark figure was plainer now, standing out in the open. Muffled in a long garment that fell almost to the ground, with the gun still pointing from the shoulder. John was somewhat relieved to observe that it was pointing several degrees to one side of him. The nocturnal rambler, whoever he might be, was obviously not a crack shot. He took aim with his own revolver at a spot a foot or so to one side of where the stranger stood.

" Fire, John! " said Rampson urgently. " Don't hit him, but fire, fire! Frighten him off and then we can go for him."

John perceived the soundness of this advice. A revolver in a capable hand was a more effective weapon than a sporting gun in incompetent ones. He pulled the trigger, expecting to see their adversary take to his heels. Nothing happened. No report broke the stillness of the night.

He quickly examined the hammer, and taking aim, pulled again, with the same result.

"Fire, John, fire!" whispered Rampson urgently.

"There's something wrong!"

"Is it loaded properly?"

"Yes. Did it myself. Oh, damn! It's no use, Syd. The spring's gone. This revolver's a dud. We must just chance a rush at him. He'll never hit us with that great awkward thing."

"I'm game," whispered Rampson. "Both at once. Now!"

The figure on the lawn, as they emerged simultaneously from behind the tree and rushed towards him, seemed to make a tremulous, ineffective effort to fire his gun, hesitated, dropped the weapon and fled. The flapping draperies flew around the corner of the herbaceous border, but as John broke through the tall flowers in the same direction, doubled and came back straight into Rampson's grasp. There was a squeal, a gasp and the sound of curses and blows.

"Good God!" said Rampson blankly, as John came up. "It's old Clino!"

Flashing on his torch John saw the old man struggling in Rampson's hands. A grotesque, queer figure in a long Inverness cape over pyjamas of purple silk, and a black Homburg hat crammed down on his thick grey hair. His eyes were wild with terror and a sort of exaltation, and he was resisting Rampson's hold to the utmost of his powers.

"Villains! Crooks!" he was gasping as he struggled. "Lay a finger on me if you dare! You daren't! You daren't!" he cried, oblivious, apparently, of the fact that Rampson had all ten fingers on him. "Crooks! Villains! How do I know you're not even murderers?"

"We're not yet, and we don't want to be," said Rampson patiently. "Do stop struggling. I don't want to hurt you. It's no use, you know. We're two to one."

But one was quite enough to hold the old man, towering with his wrists imprisoned over his stocky captor. A queer group in the light of the little torch. John was irresistibly reminded of a healthy terrier with his teeth firmly fixed in the throat of an effete greyhound.

" I'll leave him to you, Syd," said John hastily. " I must go after that light we saw in the shrubbery. Let him go, but not out of your sight. Get him to explain what he's up to, if you can."

" Explain! " cried Cousin Jim violently, as John hurried off. " It's you, sir, who should explain! Ruffians! Yes, murder me if you like, you scoundrel! Put another nail in your coffin! "

Rampson's patient voice floated to John's ears as he picked up Mr. Clino's abandoned gun and hurried towards the shrubbery :

" Well, let's both explain, then. But you start. After all, you *did* try to shoot us, you know! I do think you owe us——"

John switched on his torch, for after the uproar caused by the capture of Cousin Jim he could scarcely hope to take the other wanderer by surprise, and flashed it around from tree to tree. He could still hear his friend remonstrating with his captive, who was more peaceful now, though an occasional objurgation broke through the even tenor of Rampson's voice. Even while all his senses were on the alert for sign or sound of the walker in the shrubbery, John's mind was puzzling over Mr. Clino and his part in this night's work. Was he an accomplice of that other who a few moments ago had shown the light of a torch among the rhododendron bushes? And if so, what in heaven's name were they doing? Then a more plausible explanation struck John, and he almost laughed aloud. Possibly Cousin Jim, like themselves, had become aware of movements in the house and garden and had bravely ventured forth with a gun to defend his cousin's home; and had taken John and Rampson for burglars.   But this hardly explained his terror at the sight of Rampson nor the maledictions which he was even now calling down on that peaceable person's head.

John gave the problem up, and the next moment the light of his torch fell on something which put Mr. Clino and his aberrations entirely out of his head.   A piece of pale drapery billowing in the soft, light breeze from the other side of the cedar trunk where he himself had lately taken cover.   He approached cautiously over the close-cut grass, and stopped, waiting for a movement from whomever stood there hidden from him by the stout bole. The light of his torch fell on the glitter of sequins and beads: the long sash of a woman's evening gown.   And still there was no movement, except that the piece of silk still fluttered limply, caught around the rough bark of the great tree.

Suddenly John became afraid.   Had some second dreadful tragedy taken place in this dark graden?   In a moment he moved round the tree, holding his torch at the level of his eyes, and though he experienced a shock of surprise, he did not see what he had dreaded.

Blodwen Price was standing with her back against the tree, her head leaning supported on the rough bark.   Her hands hung limply at her sides and her eyes were open, looking straight into John's with a queer pensive stare. She was fully dressed in evening clothes, hatless and cloak-less, and her hair, caught on the scarred surface of the trunk, strayed out in filaments like spiders' webs.

" Blodwen."

She said remotely : " Oh, it's you, John," and took his arm, swayed and leant heavily on him as though tired out or faint.   But something wary and calculating in her bright eyes belied her action.

" Whatever's been going on? I heard a gun go off. I was—I was frightened and hid."

John caught the hesitation and reluctance of her tone, and intuitively knew that this last statement was a lie, and a lie she hated to tell. A woman of Blodwen's strength of character does not care to write herself down a coward.

" It was Mr. Clino. He thought we were burglars or something."

" Cousin Jim! Whatever is he doing out at this time of night? "

" What are you, Blodwen? " asked John seriously, resisting her attempt to draw him away from the trees out on to the lawn.

She looked at him with wide, feverish eyes.

" Do turn off that beastly torch, now you know I'm not a ghost. It blinds me."

John lowered it from her face, but did not turn it off.

" You've stained your dress," he remarked.

She glanced down at the green moss-stain on her light draperies.

" I know," she said indifferently. She began to speak very fast: " The fact is, John, I thought I heard a rabbit squealing in a trap—I know that wretched little David sets traps about the place, though he's been told not to— and I couldn't bear to think of the poor creature suffering out here, so I came down to look for it and put it out of its misery. I'm a fool about animals, I know."

" Find it? " asked John laconically.

" No. I must have been mistaken."

" I'll go and have a look for it now I'm here."

She pulled impatiently at his arm.

" No, no! I've looked everywhere. Take me indoors."

He caught up the hand she had laid on his sleeve and looked at it in the torchlight. It was grimed with soil, stained with moss, and the nails were full of brown earth. He looked up from it and met her eyes, wide, desperate, full of an appeal he could not understand.

" Blodwen, what have you been doing in the shrubbery? "

" I've told you."

" The truth? "

" Of course." Morris Price himself could not have looked at a questioner with a haughtier stare.

John detached himself from her grasp and taking his torch and Clino's gun went on into the shrubbery among the rhododendrons where he had seen the light. The rhododendron bushes formed a little screen to a small hollow where pale heather, some harebells, moss and ferns grew in confusion. He flashed his torch over the ground and it lit at once upon a small wooden stake with a broken end of string attached, such as gardeners use to mark out borders. He picked it up and found that it was covered for eight inches from the point with traces of damp and brown soil.

" John."

Looking up he saw that Blodwen had followed him. She stood a little way off like a ghost in her light gown and addressed him with sudden tremulousness.

" Don't bother any more, John. Go back to London and forget about us. You've been kind—so kind. It isn't fair to take up your time. Leave us alone now to manage as best we may. Don't bother any more. I ask you not to."

One thing was plain—there was a secret she wished to keep. What that secret might be John had for the moment no idea. But her bright eyes clung to his, her pale lips smiled with a ghastly attempt at cajolery, her hand fluttered caressingly up and down his sleeve. And suddenly John felt sick and weary. Could Morris Price only be vindicated at the expense of Blodwen? Was this woman he had liked and admired really a monster willing to let her uncle go to the gallows for her own crime? In a flash John's thoughts travelled back over all that he knew of Blodwen and found no certainty anywhere. He asked aloud:

"Blodwen, was it you, then, who murdered your cousin?"

In the light of the torch he directed on her, he saw the strangest expression of surprise, uncertainty, even something like relief, pass over her face. She hung on the verge of a denial. Then, after a pause in which she seemed to collect and marshal her wits:

"Should I tell you if I had?" she asked very low.

Her eyes wandered to the earthy stake lying on the moss, and John, looking downwards, thought he could detect a small patch of moss around which the tiny filaments were flattened and earthy—a patch which had been removed and relaid.

"No, no!" cried Blodwen as he stooped, and would have caught up the gun, but he was too quick for her. And even as he put his finger under the little patch of moss and found that it came loosely away, he thought: Is this the behaviour of a guilty woman? To give herself away so utterly?

The earth was disturbed below the moss, loose and crumbling. He pressed it with his forefinger and it gave way, like a hole which has been lightly filled in. He looked around for some instrument to clear the hole, but had perforce to use his fingers. Whatever lay buried there was small and, to judge by the earth on the gardener's stake, lay not more than eight inches below the surface. But it is not easy to clear with one's fingers a vertical hole made by a pointed stake, especially when one has a loaded gun at one side of one and a desperate woman at the other. Luckily the ground, covered by moss and protected by the bushes from the heat of the sun, was fairly soft.

Blodwen, after watching him in still despair for a moment, suddenly dropped on her knees at his side.

" John, John! " she said brokenly. " Don't! Don't! For your own sake as well as ours! It can do no good. You're under no compulsion to go on with this case! Give it up! It wasn't I who killed Charles! If it had been, I'd find a better way out than this! "

Cautiously widening the hole with the stake and thrusting his hand down, John felt some small, hard thing like a pebble. He drew it up, and brushing the earth from it held it in the torchlight. It was a man's heavy signet-ring of gold, set with a large oval blood-stone.

Blodwen became silent as suddenly as she had begun to speak. They crouched together over the torch, gazing in silence at the dead man's ring. Then John rose to his feet and offering his hand to Blodwen helped her to hers.

" Blodwen," he said in a matter-of-fact voice, " I know what's the matter with you. You've made up your mind that your uncle's guilty after all. Just when we've brought Felix to think him innocent, too. Do you know what Rampson says? He says you Prices are enough to drive a sane man crazy. And so you are, you know. All these dreadful doings at dead of night, with Mr. Clino firing guns at one, and Miss Price burying things in shrubberies, are enough to upset the nerves of Sherlock Holmes himself——"

John let his light, matter-of-fact voice run on, hoping to bring back the overstrung woman at his side to a sense of normality. But the darkness, the night wind, the rustling, ghostly rhododendrons, were not conducive to common sense.

" I did think," he ended sadly, " that you were a sensible person, anyhow."

The sensible person gave a dim, pathetic smile and suddenly burst into hysterical tears in his arms. For a moment John wondered whether she had final, fatal proof of her uncle's guilt. Murmuring the commonplaces of comfort he looked at the little trinket in his hand—a commonplace little ornament enough, with its plain, solid hoop of gold and unengraved seal of red-flecked green stone. Looking through the bushes, he saw that the lights were on in the library. There was peace in the garden, but for Blodwen's smothered sobbing. Rampson had managed to lure his captive withindoors.

In a moment or two Blodwen had regained her self-control.

" I'm sorry," she said, drawing stiffly away from him. " I didn't think I could be such a fool. There seems to be a limit to what one can bear, after all. And now this —this horrible ring! I'd better tell you, I suppose——"

There was a questioning note in her voice as if she were still half-minded to leave him in the dark to think what he would.

" You certainly had," said John emphatically. " And whatever the truth is, it can't be so dreadful after all. You wouldn't have thought it so dreadful yourself if it hadn't been for the strain you've been living under this past week. Come, Blodwen. I am certain that your uncle is innocent."

" But why? But how? " she faltered. " Oh, so was I at first! But everything points to him and I can't be certain any longer! I feel a traitor, but I can't, I can't! "

She seemed disposed to weep again, but mastering herself said quietly :

" I found that ring pushed down at the side of the seat in my uncle's car. That's all. The car he was driving when he—when he met Charles. I was out in the car last night, and I dropped a shilling in the dark. And I felt about and pushed my hand down at the side of the cushion, and found—that."

" And you think he put it there? "

" Who else? It was the last straw, John! I've been

fighting and fighting not to think him guilty. But that coat found on the Forest! And now this! Oh, it's so like Uncle Morris! To be so careless, I mean, to be so thoughtless—to underestimate so the forces that would come to work against him! "

" There's one obvious thing to be said, my dear. What did he want with the ring at all? Why didn't he leave it on Charles's finger? "

" Oh, I don't know! You said yourself, long ago, it might have slipped off in a struggle."

" A ring must be loose to slip off accidentally, very loose. But be comforted, Blodwen, this ring was tight on Charles's finger. Lion Browning told me so, and young Lion's an intelligent observer."

" But who——? "

" Who took it off and planted it in your uncle's car? Ah, who? The murderer. And who is he? I don't know yet. Obviously not a friend of your uncle's, that's all we can say at present. But I'm feeling rather optimistic to-night."

Blodwen, a little cheered by his calm and talkative manner, took his arm, and they went together across the lawn towards the house.

" Optimistic! " she echoed with a faint sigh. " Oh, John, why? Has anything happened that I don't know about? "

" A lady tried to poison me this afternoon," said John with enjoyment. " Perhaps two ladies, but I think only one. Nothing makes a detective so happy, my dear, as an attempt on his life. It shows that somebody is finding him a nuisance."

CHAPTER TWENTY

R AMPSON and Mr. Clino were occupying chairs opposite one another in the library. As John came in from outside the latter rose hastily. He was still wearing his Inverness but had laid aside the Homburg hat. His thick grey hair stood up like the crest of a tropical bird. He was obviously puzzled, offended and very much on his dignity. So much so that even the sight of Blodwen, dishevelled in her evening dress, did not cause him more than a momentary surprise.

" Blodwen, my dear! " he exclaimed. " Were you also disturbed by our guests' curious behaviour? " He glanced balefully at Rampson. " Perhaps, sir, you will now be so good as to allow me to return to my room."

" Really, Cousin Jim," said Blodwen with a faint smile. " I do think you owe our guests an explanation, if it's true that you've been trying to shoot them."

" Oh, that's all right," said Rampson in some amusement. " We've been having a heart-to-heart talk about it. Mr. Clino thought we were burglars, and very natural too. All forgiven and forgotten."

But Mr. Clino was not to be thus pacified.

" Not at all, not at all," he declared peevishly. " All is not forgotten. And I never for a moment took you for anybody but yourselves."

" And yet you tried to shoot them, Cousin Jim? "

" I had no intention of killing them," said the old man with dignity. " I merely intended to—ah! wound one of

279

them a little.   And I did not fire at all until I had plainly seen a revolver in the hands of this—ah! gentleman."

" It was awfully kind of you not to kill us," murmured Rampson, who appeared to be enjoying himself.   " Do you often have midnight shooting-parties here with harmless humans for targets? "

" Harmless! " echoed Mr. Clino, quivering with indignation.   " I don't regard you as harmless, sir! Neither you nor your so-called detective friend!   Harmless people don't prowl about people's gardens in the small hours of the morning flourishing revolvers———"

" Nor sporting-guns," put in Rampson mildly.

" I've had my suspicions of you two for some time," continued Cousin Jim.   " No, Blodwen, I will have my say.   The time has come to speak plainly.   Who are these two people living under our roof?   Nobody knows. What are they doing here?   Investigating the crime! Ha!   Their own conduct needs a little investigating, I think.   We're not the first household to be taken in by a pair of presentable crooks.   Investigating the crime, indeed!   *Quis custodiet ipsos custodes?*   *You* may take it as a matter of course, Blodwen, when slippery-tongued young men descend from nowhere and plant themselves under your roof as amateur detectives.   *You* may even take it as a matter of course when they go downstairs in the middle of night and flourish revolvers about the garden, but———"

" It's not a scrap more extraordinary than one's cousin flourishing a gun.   Do stop it, Cousin Jim!   If you want to know, John and Mr. Rampson were looking for me with a revolver just as you were looking for them with a gun, and with the same worthy motives.   I'd no idea "— she gave a pale smile—" that I should disturb the entire household.   Now do apologize to them, Cousin Jim, for calling them crooks, and then we'll all go to bed."

Mr. Clino, however, stood firm.

" I'll apologize," he said coldly, " when I learn that I have reason to."

Blodwen flushed angrily and seemed about to make a stinging retort, but John interposed.

" Mr. Clino," he remarked pensively, " has been reading his favourite authors again, I imagine. I mean, of course," he added, meeting with a placid eye Cousin Jim's look of swift suspicion and reproach, " Scott and Thackeray."

There was a pause, while Mr. Clino seemed to advance to the very verge of a furious tirade and then, cautiously, with an eye on John's tranquil face, to retreat from it. And suddenly John was sorry and wished he had not taken this advantage. Poor dilettante Cousin Jim, with his purple pyjamas and his Holmes-like Inverness and his sporting-gun and his sense of dignity! He was not lacking in courage, when all was said. For the old man to venture alone into the garden at dead of night in search of two desperadoes was no mean feat of bravery, even allowing for the spiritual exaltation natural to one whose mental diet is stories of detection and crime. And it is never agreeable to discover that the marauding wolf one has strung oneself up to capture is only a poor sheep after all.

" I'm sorry," said John sincerely. " Don't let's be rude to one another. We've all been horribly excited and——"

" I," put in Mr. Clino, with *sotto voce*, cautious indignation, " am never excited."

" ——and now we're all suffering from reaction. We'd better all try and get a few hours' sleep."

" Sleep! " echoed Blodwen softly, as if the sweet word had almost ceased to have a meaning for her. " I'll go to bed, because there's nothing else to do. But I don't think I shall sleep."

" Neither shall I," said John, " until I've discovered what it is that's worrying me."

" Worrying you? "

"Yes. Do you know that feeling when you're trying to work out a problem and you feel you're nearly there—so nearly, and yet not there at all? I've got it now. You've got all the facts in your mind, and you feel that it only needs a touch, a thought, to make them all slip together into a solved problem. But the touch won't come, though you think and think. It's like when you forget a word you know as well as your own name. You've used it hundreds of times, but the more you try to call it up the more it hovers just out of reach, teasing you with ghosts of its shape and sound. That's how I feel. Until this evening I've had just a collection of stray facts in my head, with one or two carefully worked out possibilities, but I've had none of that sense of conviction, of utter certainty, that comes with the right word. It came for a moment, or rather it nearly came, this evening —when was it? I don't even remember now when it came."

John looked thoughtfully from Blodwen to Mr. Clino and around the room. His wandering eye fell on the log-piled hearth.

"Yes! Yes!" he cried. "Sydenham, it was when we were standing behind the cedar and you whispered: Fire! Fire! and I found the pistol was broken. It seemed in a moment a terribly important thing that the pistol was broken; it was like the key to a puzzle, and I had a sense that if only I could keep my mind blank for a moment the puzzle would be solved. But "—he glanced humorously at Mr. Clino—" there was a pressing reason why I couldn't keep my mind a blank. And the thing never happened. The flash passed over. But that sense of being on the verge of the truth and yet not being able to reach it—I've got that dimly still."

Blodwen, who had listened with eyes half sceptical, half hopeful, said quickly:

"Can't we help? If we talk it over together?"

" No, no. Leave it alone, as one leaves alone the word one can't remember, and it may come of itself. I'll go to my room and read some not too exciting book, and perhaps it'll come to me through the print. Or, if not, in my dreams."

But John was not destined either to read or dream that night. Suddenly, with an eerie urgency, the telephone bell began to ring. Dulled beyond the thick library door, yet penetrating and insistent, so startling at that hour of the night that the four people in the library looked blankly at one another without moving, its hard, mechanical purr suggested the vague alarm of some far-off, unforeseen disaster. Without a word from anyone Blodwen left the room.

The three remaining in the library said nothing, each mind occupied with its own surmises. She was a long time away. Felix, awakened by the ringing of the bell, put his head into the room, said blankly : " Hullo! What the deuce? " and without appearing to need an answer lit a cigarette and joined the group round the mahogany desk, waiting for Blodwen to return.

When she came back it was hurriedly, but with eyes more puzzled than alarmed.

" It's Dr. Browning," she said. " Ringing up about Nora."

John's heart stood still for a moment.

" It seems she's disappeared or something."

" What? "

Felix's cigarette dropped and he glanced quickly at John.

" What do you mean? What did he say? " Slowly John grew cold all over with the premonitions of disaster.

" Well," said Blodwen, " he wanted first to know whether she'd come here. It seems her sister rang up to tell him the silly girl had started to drive home by herself."

" What, at this hour? "

" Well, of course she started hours ago, but she hasn't turned up, and Dr. Browning's naturally getting worried. Apparently she went out in the afternoon with a friend to do some shopping, saw the friend into a cinema and went off somewhere by herself. Then about seven o'clock she came home and said she must drive back to her father's straight away. Her sister tried to stop her, but she would have her way, borrowed her sister's car and set out in it. And she hasn't arrived yet. The doctor's half off his head with anxiety. I must say I don't quite see why. Nora's quite capable of driving herself home, though it's a silly thing to do when she might just as well have waited till to-morrow and let her father sleep in peace. After all, it's only half-past two now, and one can't drive fast at night. Besides, she may have had a puncture. But of course the doctor's afraid of an accident."

John and Felix looked at one another.

" Did Nora's sister know the name of the friend Nora went to see? " asked John quietly.

Blodwen looked at him in surprise.

" Friend? Nobody said anything about her going to see a friend! "

" No, of course not. But that's what she did, I'm sure." John looked stonily at the desk. " I ought never to have taken Nora to London. I ought to have insisted on her coming back with me. I ought to have made her promise —oh, what's the use of all this? We must drive back to London and look for her, that's all. What else can we do? But a five-hour journey, and at the end of it— what? "

Felix said swiftly:

" But think, John! Even if it's true what you fear, they'll never dare hurt Nora. For they know that you suspect them. They'll never dare."

" That's true," said John slowly. " It ought to be

true. But one never knows what desperation will drive a person to. Suppose Nora did go there. Suppose she found out something—something that we don't even guess at. Oh, if only I could see the meaning of all this! For one minute when I pulled the trigger and that revolver wouldn't fire, I thought I was on the verge of knowing everything. But it's gone, gone, gone and won't come back. Yes, Felix, we'd better fling some clothes on and drive to London. We daren't take any risks. There's too much at stake."

He was about to follow Felix out of the room when Blodwen said in a low voice:

" You'd better take care of—this, John."

She held out to him the blood-stone ring which, in the stress of this new fear, he had put down upon the desk and forgotten. He took it and slipped it hastily on to his little finger, and was about to go when his mind, below the stress of his fears for Nora, seemed to become suddenly, deeply aware of some vague anomaly. The ring? He looked at it. Yes, a blood-stone ring. That was a blood-stone, wasn't it, that dark green, red-flecked stone? He used force, he pushed, he pulled, he tried it on the little finger of his other hand above his own signet-ring. He stood quite still, frozen, looking down at the ugly blood-stone ring which, try as he might, would not pass the middle joint of his little finger.

" But of course," he said to himself very quietly. " Of course. Of course. Of course. And now we know."

Felix, hovering in the doorway, looked at him with impatient surprise, and Blodwen asked with a wild hope that she tried to disguise as scepticism:

" What do we know? "

" Everything," said John. " Everything. Who murdered Charles, for instance, we know that now. Oh, it all fits in so beautifully now. All the stray facts, one after another, up they come and fall into place. Yes, the apples in the quarry, and the egg-shells in the orchard, and the red ink in the fountain-pen and the blood on the darning-needle, and the iodine at Moseley, and the rain-coat on the Forest and the broken revolver in the bedroom. Even young Smiler's bicycle. I wonder where it is now, young Smiler's bicycle? At the bottom of what pond? And Charles took the single room that ought to have been Dr. Browning's, didn't he? That fits in, too. And he didn't care for bathing—yes, that, too. Oh, yes," finished John quietly, " we know now. Everything. Everything except what's happened to Nora. And you don't tell me that, do you, ugly little blood-stone ring? But you let me guess! You let me guess! "

That nightmare drive was a thing John never forgot. Almost in silence the three of them drove towards Penlow, on a clear road, with the queer grotesque tree-shapes of night all round, and an absurd cock at some distant farm proclaiming morning. Rampson drove the car, while John occupied himself with fruitless guesses at Nora's actions. Why had she suddenly decided to drive home, alone, at such an hour? How had her sister, who had appeared to be a sensible young woman, come to consent to such a thing? John smiled grimly in spite of his anxiety. He could imagine that Nora Browning was not the person to wait for anybody's consent when she had made up her mind to a course of action. If she had determined to drive home through the night, her sister's commonsense objections would be less than the dust beneath her borrowed wheels. But what could have brought her to such a determination? John could think of only one thing. She had taken the law into her own hands, and sought out Isabel and her aunt; and she had discovered something which seemed to her so important that she had set out immediately to bring the news to John.

" I shall never forgive myself," said John between his teeth, " if Nora's come to harm."

" Nor I," said Felix.

" You! " said John, and for a second there was the queerest little flash of enmity between the two of them. " You're not to blame. You didn't know what Nora intended to do. I did. I guessed, I spoke of it, I made a joke of it, and at the slightest, vaguest reassurance I dropped my responsibility."

" Neither of you," said Rampson, reaching sixty miles an hour, " can be held to blame for what a grown-up person like Nora chooses to do." But neither of them thanked him for his comfort.

They passed Dr. Browning's house, and noted a light burning in one of the upper rooms—the doctor anxiously sitting up for his missing daughter. There was no travel-stained car standing outside the garden gate.

In Penlow High Street a solitary policeman was conversing with a thin and anxious-looking black and white kitten. He answered John's beckoning hand with alacrity, and the kitten trotted after him, tail erect and all the troubles of the world reflected in her anxious eyes.

Yes, a car had passed through the town about an hour ago. Driving faster than it had any business to, even on a clear street. He'd taken its number, a London number. A lady driving? No! This was a large coupé, with two or three people in it and a man driving. No, he hadn't noticed any car driven by a lady pass through the town, and he'd been on his beat since midnight. He was prepared to swear there hadn't been a car with a lady driving, not through the town since midnight. Oh, yes, he was quite sure it was a man driving the coupé. Driving faster than he'd any right to, too. There might have been a lady inside, he couldn't say. A party coming back from a dance, he opined, and a bit above theirselves.

They'd feel different if they got summonsed. Nearly run over the kitten, they had.

" But we'll let them off this time," went on the good-natured constable, " seein' as the road were clear. They were a bit above theirselves, not a doubt. Had the sauce to wave to me as they went by and I stood looking at their number, one of them did. Waved a swell handkerchief, and dropped it, and serve them right, I say, for their sauce. They didn't come back for it, and if they had I'd have asked 'em what they meant, driving at that pace. Fifty miles an hour, if it was ten. Cost a bit o' money, a handkerchief like that, I shouldn't wonder."

He took from his pocket and with a grin delicately shook out a large striped silk handkerchief. With a gasp Felix snatched it from his hand.

" It's Nora's! "

John also had recognized it as one Nora had been wearing that morning around her neck.

" But what does it mean? " cried Felix, white-faced and puzzled.

" I'm afraid it means that she wanted help," said John unemotionally. " We must turn quickly and follow. An hour ago, did you say, officer? Which way did they take? Did you see? "

" Road to the right," answered the constable, looking somewhat surprised. " The Forest road. But they'll be fifty miles away by now, or else tucked up in bed and asleep! "

John thanked him briefly and the little car leapt forward and took the Forest road at a speed that must, after his recent remarks, have struck the policeman as asking for trouble.

He stood in the roadway, mechanically noting the number.

" Well, I'm goshed," he muttered emotionally, and returned after a minute to his conversation with the kitten.

CHAPTER TWENTY-ONE

THEY passed not a soul along the road until they came to the tiny village of Rodd lying under the Forest hills. It was too much to hope that there would be a friendly policeman here, but John and Felix kept their eyes open for a sign of human life. And just outside the village, lying uncomfortably on the grassy edge of the road by the hedge, near the burnt-out remains of a little fire, were two young men under a rug. One of them raised a weary head from his rucksack pillow as the car approached. Rampson drew up with a jerk.

" Seen a car go by? "

" Pardon? " said the young man, raising his head a little higher and blinking politely in the headlight's glare.

" Have you seen a car go by lately? "

" A car? Well, not very lately. Have we, Bertram? "

Bertram, raising his head from somewhere in the vicinity of the first speaker's feet, shook it gently.

" We've been asleep," he declared, with the pride of the hardy camper who can sleep through anything, even a night in the open air.

" How lately? " asked John.

The two heads considered the question at exasperating length.

" Hours ago," said the first speaker at last, and added as an afterthought: " What's the time now? "

T

" Twenty-past three."

" Oh, Lord! Is that all? Well, a car went by at ten-past two. It seems hours ago. There hasn't been one since."

" How do you know? " inquired the head called Bertram curiously.

" Because," said its twin with the bitterness that comes to campers in the early hours of the morning, " I've been bally well awake all night."

" Oh! *I've* been asleep," responded Bertram of the superior hardihood, and once more composed himself to slumber.

Rampson drove on. The Forest hills stood all around them now, dark against the paler sky, the long ridges like walls shutting in the road and the long valleys opening and stretching dimly away between wall and wall. There was the gurgle of water running under the road.

" But what can we do? " cried Felix in despair. " Go on? But where? Go up on to the Forest? But what part? It's hopeless to look for Nora here! John! We can't afford to lose a moment! Yet searching the Forest we'll lose hours! Hours! "

" Stop here," said John to Rampson, and getting out of the car where a track ran up a wild valley he flashed his torch upon the road. There were distinct tyre-marks in the dust where a heavy car had turned off the road on to the rutty track that led, possibly, to some farm sheltering under the hillside in the valley.

" Why," said Rampson, looking around him. " This is the valley we came to the other day. The waterfall must be up this valley."

" Yes," said John, returning to the car. " Follow up this track as far as you can go, Syd, and we'll try the shepherd's hut. It's a chance—our only one. We shan't be able to take the car far. It's an awful road."

" We can go as far as the other car went, I suppose,"

said Rampson, bumping over the ruts and tussocks; and about fifty yards up the track they passed a closed car standing in darkness under a group of trees in the damp field that edged the road. Rampson was about to venture over the uneven field towards it, but John stopped him.

"Leave our car here. We may want it for getting away," he said, and jumped out.

Rampson stopped the engine and turned off the lights while John and Felix went across the grass to investigate the apparently deserted coupé. It was empty, and there was nothing in it to give a hint of its owner. But returning to where Rampson awaited them on the track, holding the torch to light their feet, John saw and picked up something from among the tufts of coarse grass—a cigarette-card. It had not been there long. It was almost dry, and the grass was wet with the heavy September dew. Somebody had passed this way not long before.

They joined Rampson, and in silence the three of them followed the track to where it turned aside towards a small farmhouse lying under the ridge. A foot-track ran on up the valley beside the shallow, pebble-strewn brook that wanly reflected the sky. They crossed the stream by the plank bridge, leaving the high tinkling of the waterfall and the dark woods on their left, and followed the path where it wound up the opposite ridge among waist-high bracken and scattered boulders. A sheep-bell tinkled near at hand and ghostly, and there was the soft scurry of some disturbed stoat or rabbit running through the bracken in alarm. They came in sight of the shepherd's hut standing against the sky. A blundering moth struck John in the eyes, and he had to bite his lip to repress an exclamation.

A softly spoken word from Rampson brought him to a halt.

"I don't know what you expect to find, John,

but I suppose—something dangerous. Don't be rash. Remember we've got no weapons."

" We ought to have brought old Clino's gun," said John with a pale grin, and then stood transfixed as Felix gripped his arm and whispered:

" Look! "

A flickering light shone in the little square window of the hut, shone like a warning beacon for a second and went out. The three men looked at one another.

" There's only one thing to be done," said Felix, white to the lips, but more alert and forceful than John had seen him yet. " It's no good worrying about having no weapons. We're three, after all. We must go straight in and rush the situation—whatever it is. Whatever it is," he added in a low, brooding voice as they pushed on among the brushing bracken leaves.

But when they approached close to the hut a voice spoke from within and brought them all to a standstill, looking at one another's faces which they could dimly, wanly see now in the cold, grey dawn breaking over the eastern ridges. It was a woman's voice, and to one at least of the men standing there in that cold autumnal dawn it carried on its light, reedy notes broken thoughts of comradeship and gaiety and sunshine.

" Do you think," asked the clear little scornful voice that floated out through the open doorway of the hut, " that nobody noticed you driving at about a thousand miles an hour through all the towns between here and London? Do you think no obliging policeman took our number? And you think you'll be able to get away with this! You silly ass! I tell you you'll be in handcuffs within a week—within a day! "

A man's deep voice vibrating with anger answered thickly:

" You'll see to that, I suppose! "

" I'm not sure that I shan't, if you don't leave Nora

alone," replied the light voice calmly. " You needn't look at me like that. I'm not in the least afraid of you."

" Is this what you call loyalty? "

" Yes," said the calm voice, and there was the scrape and flicker of a match and a pause as though a cigarette were being lit; and then a candle, for the wavering light remained. " I rather like Nora."

" Pretty! " sneered the masculine voice. " A pretty touch of sentiment! "

" Yes, it is rather touching. You ought to be grateful to me. If I didn't like her I'd have let you do as you liked and go your own way——" There was a pause, and then, very deliberately and thoughtfully : " To the gallows."

" Stop it, you little devil! I've a good mind to——"

" Wring my neck," finished the girl's voice. " I know. You've said it so often."

There was a silence, and then a sound as if somebody were moving restlessly in the cramped space of the hut's interior. When the man spoke again it was in a queer, half threatening, half whining tone that grated horribly on the ears of the three men listening outside.

" I believe you'd give me away for twopence. I don't believe you care a hoot about me."

" Upon my Sam," said the girl with a sort of quiet pity in her voice more scornful than laughter, " that's pretty, if you like. Care for you! You'll be asking me next if you're the only man I've ever loved. I care for you as little as you care for me. No! Less! Because I'm not afraid of you, and you are a little afraid of me. I said I wouldn't give you away, and I haven't, but——"

" Very kind of you, wasn't it? Weren't thinking of your own part in that affair, were you? "

" What affair? Oh, that! Pooh! That wouldn't have hurt me much. I was going to say : but I draw the line at murder, really. Really, I do. You'll leave Nora alone."

" So that she can rush off to the police, eh? "

In the pause that followed John could well imagine the graceful shrug of Isabel's thin shoulders.

" You've had your chance. You should have cleared out while there was time."

" And died of blood-poisoning."

" It might have saved you trouble in the end. In any case, I'm not going to give you more than another week to clear out in. Then I shall go to the police myself."

" I don't think! They'll have an account to settle with you, my dear, as well as me. You'll hold your tongue all right."

The girl began to speak suddenly with a concentrated passion which took her hearers aback, so different was it from the light, cool manner in which she had spoken before.

" Do you really think I'm going to protect you for ever? Do you really think I'll let that silly old man be brought for trial? Ah, you're a fool! You're a fool! You sicken me, you silly, conceited fool that doesn't know the difference between one person and another and thinks every woman'll lend you her shoulder to whimper on and her brains to save you from what you deserve! Do you think I care *that* what happens to you? Do you think it's for your beauty that I've done all this? "

Suddenly the passionate voice dropped, stopped. When the girl spoke again it was quietly, lightly, as if she were conducting a formal conversation at a tea-party.

" No. It was honour. Thieves' honour, you know. Well, I've warned you. But you're stupid, stupid! Lord! How I hate stupidity! "

There was a silence, as if, in spite of himself, the man had been momentarily cowed by this outburst. Then the woman's voice came again :

"Listen. I'm going to take Nora down to the car. And I'm going to take her home."

"Home?" echoed the man thickly. "What? To London?"

"No. To her own home near here. Why not? I can tell them some yarn to put them off for the moment. and——"

"And what about me?"

"You can do whatever you bally well choose. I'm sick of nursing you. I told you to leave Nora alone. You wouldn't, and you can take the consequences. Clear out, if you can. I won't give you away for a week."

"You infernal little——!"

There was danger in the low, thick voice, danger in the pause that followed.

"Good God! It'll be daylight in five minutes! And you think you're going to leave me here, do you, you vixen? I know a better game than that! You're not afraid of me, aren't you? More fool you, if you're not afraid of a desperate man! What does it matter to me how many I swing for, if I've got to swing? But I'll make a good run for it, you bet your bottom dollar, and I shan't leave you and your precious baby-friend to run and tell tales!"

There was the sound of a movement inside the hut. John switched on his torch and prepared for a rush, but Felix was before him. There was a wild, throaty cry, a sharp gasp from Isabel. John, following Felix close, had an instant's vision of Isabel's little white face set as a mask of astonishment, and that of a tall, large-featured man with murder in his eyes. Then the candle which had been standing on the earthen floor was kicked over and John saw the barrel of a revolver gleaming in the man's hand. He switched off his torch and tried to drag Felix from the entrance, where he stood outlined as a target. But Felix seemed to have been turned to stone,

as though he had seen Medusa's head. Oblivious of his
danger, oblivious of the revolver that pointed at his chest,
he stood frozen there in the doorway and kept saying
blankly, in a voice from which all expression had been
wiped away:

" It's Charles. It's Charles. It's Charles."

Unable to move him, John pushed swiftly past him and
sprang at the hand holding the revolver in the dark of the
hut. There was a report, and a bullet hit the ceiling.
Rampson followed his friend and the confined space of
the hut became filled in a moment with plunging,
struggling human bodies. John fought for possession of
the revolver, but could not reach it. God! The man
was strong, and slippery as an eel! Even in the stress
of the fight John was conscious of Isabel dragging something heavy out of the way of the trampling feet, a human
form wrapped in a rug, dragging and tugging it out
through the doorway into the air.

Suddenly John felt himself hurled back against the wall,
and a dark form rushed past him to the entrance of the
hut, out into the open, out among the bracken, where it
turned and stood still. There was a terrifying moment
when John was conscious of nothing but a revolver taking
slow, deliberate aim, and Felix standing like a fool, like
a stone, outside the hut, not attempting to move.

There was a sharp report, and involuntarily John closed
his eyes. He opened them at once to see that threatening
weapon drooping, falling, the man behind it standing very
still, then, with the queerest, quietest movement, spinning
round a little on his heel and dropping quietly among the
waist-high fern.

Isabel stood not far from the hut with a little pistol
smoking in her hand.

CHAPTER TWENTY-TWO

FOR a long, long minute nobody moved or spoke. The silence that settled on that damp hillside in the grey mirk of dawn after the struggle and stress of a moment ago was like a miracle, holding everybody from speech. All eyes were turned on that spot among the bracken where lately had stood a living, cursing man. It seemed miraculous that he did not rise again.

" Well," said Isabel unemotionally at last, breaking a silence that had something unearthly in it, " you can all bear witness that I didn't shoot him until I had to."

She looked with wide, faintly curious eyes at the little weapon in her hand, then laid it down near where Nora, white and dishevelled, lay extended on the grass.

" She's all right," said Isabel, still in that cold, far-away little voice. " She'll come to in a minute. She's had several little whiffs of chloroform. I didn't want her to hear what we were talking about in the hut."

She dropped on to her knees and with the calm precision of a nurse at a blameless bedside, proceeded to feel the pulse of the unconscious girl, to prop her head up on the rug and to rub her hands.

" Are you sure she's all right? " asked Felix huskily, looking down at Nora's ashen, sleeping face.

" Quite," replied Isabel placidly, and it was not more than a moment or two before the girl lying on the ground moved her head a little to one side, half raised her eyelids and uttered a sigh.

Rampson, who had walked away across the bracken, returned now and joined the little group round the drugged girl.

" He's dead," he said quietly.   " Shot through the head."

Isabel looked up.

" Good," she said, and paused, and added : " Good, for him.   And for everybody.   Better now, Nora ? "

Nora's eyes opened, heavy and expressionless at first. Then slowly, gazing into the heavy-lidded hazel ones that looked down on them, they filled with an expression of intense fear and supplication that wrung John's heart.

" It's all right," said Isabel in a business-like tone.   " I said I wouldn't let him hurt you.   And I haven't.   Like to sit up ? "

Nora looked with wide, solemn eyes from Isabel to Felix, to Felix and John.   She looked faintly interested to see them there, and after a moment raised her head, struggled to sit up, and was sick.

" Oh, poor angel! " murmured Isabel.   " That's the way.   You'll be all right now."

And indeed it was not many minutes before Nora, pale and shaky and clinging with damp, cold hands to John's arm, was on her feet and declaring through chattering teeth that she felt perfectly all right.

She was not that, but she was alive and in no danger. And now that anxiety on her account had passed, a queer, strained silence descended upon the little group standing there under the slowly lightening sky.   Felix's glance was drawn again and again in horror to that patch of bracken where a dead man lay hidden, and John mechanically chafed Nora's cold hands and looked at Isabel, and Isabel stood with her hands folded before her, looking meditatively at the ground.   But Rampson, the practical, who had been busying himself in the hut, stood in the doorway and called them in.

" I don't know what the water's like," he remarked. " I found it here, but it'll be all right boiled. And there's only two cups. And no milk. But there's still a spot of brandy in my flask, and a hot drink's an excellent thing after a dust-up."

A dust-up! John could not but smile faintly at the inadequacy of his friend's description. A tin kettle was already steaming gently on the little oil-stove inside the hut, and a large brown teapot and two white mugs awaited the brew.

John installed Nora on a rug on the floor with her back against the bench, and himself sat on the bench to keep it steady; and Rampson, with the serious air of a house-wife performing a domestic rite, heated the teapot, counted out six spoonfuls of the shepherd's tea and poured on the boiling water.

Isabel still stood like a wraith in the doorway. She looked fey, witch-like, with the lamp's illumination on her pointed, thin-lipped face and the light, monotonous sky behind her.

" Do you want me to come in? " she asked in a low voice.

There was a meaning in her tone that made Felix at least look once again with a vague horror towards that patch of bracken and then quickly avert his eyes.

" You saved my life," he said huskily.

" Ah, well! " she said. " I owed you that. You haven't cause to thank me for anything else, Felix. But I'll come in, and share your tea, if I may. It'll be for the last time. And I think "—she stepped into the hut and carefully folded up her coat into a cushion, sat down on it with her small hands clasped round her knees and looked at John—" I think a touch of candour would be a good thing. Don't you, John? "

" I suppose," said John gravely, " it's time."

" You know," said Isabel pensively, looking at the yellow flame of the oil-stove, " I thought as soon as I met you that you'd be too clever for us. I told Charles so and warned him to get out of the country while he had a chance, but he wouldn't. That first day I met you, when you jumped on me so quickly for saying that Hufton was a thief—silly slip!—I knew he'd have to look out for you. How long have you——"

Nora interrupted, putting down her cup and staring at Isabel as if she were a ghost.

" Charles," she said, " Charles is dead, in the quarry. But I saw him. I saw him yesterday, looking out of the window of your house as I went down the steps. And —afterwards——"

Isabel answered her gently as one might speak to a child.

" You've never seen Charles Price, Nora. Charles Price is dead, he was found dead in the quarry. You've only seen Gavin Marshall—I've got into the habit of calling him Charles. And now he's dead too. Never mind," she added, as the look of distress deepened on Nora's face. " You'll understand soon. I was going to say, John, how long have you known that the man they'd all known as Charles Price was the murderer, not the victim? "

" I never guessed for a moment until to-night," answered John. " And then I knew. I knew absolutely when I tried to put the blood-stone ring on my little finger. It wouldn't go on."

" Well? "

" But my own signet-ring had been too small for the dead man's little finger. So I knew that the blood-stone ring had never belonged to the dead man. The rest followed."

" Where did the ring turn up? "

" It was pushed down beside the cushion in Morris Price's car."

The girl nodded.

" It was silly of him to try to plant the murder on the old man. He'd have done better to have left things alone. But he seemed to hate the old man. I believe that was why he would stay in England, partly : to read the papers and gloat over the thought of Morris Price in prison. Oh, he was a horrible creature," said Isabel in a low voice. " A stupid creature. Stupid and malicious. Yet once I thought him a man."

There was a pause, while the girl, with her pointed chin on her fist, stared bleakly at the fire. Suddenly she said slowly :

" It's funny to be sitting here talking to you as if there were nothing between me and the rest of you. There is, really, you know. There are bars between us—prison bars."

She looked slowly up and about her as if she could really see a network of iron separating the hut into two compartments, with herself alone upon one side. She shivered a little.

" You first, John. Tell us what you know. I'll fill in the blanks afterwards. I don't much feel like talking, after all. But let's get it over and said."

" It won't take me long," said John, " to tell you all I know or guess. Gavin Marshall, I take it, met the real Charles Price at some time, out in Canada. He also, at some time in Canada, met Mrs. Clytie Price, and—and you, Isabel. Is she really your aunt, by the way ? "

Isabel nodded.

" Well—cousin. Near enough."

" Marshall must have resembled Charles fairly closely, I suppose."

" He said so," answered Isabel. " And of course he must have done, or nobody would have taken the dead man in the quarry for the Charles they knew. But I never saw the real Charles."

" And when he heard—perhaps he saw advertisements —that Charles's family wanted to trace him and that he'd been missing for thirteen years, he conceived the idea of impersonating Charles and coming into his inheritance."

" It was Clytie who conceived the idea," put in Isabel. " But go on."

" It was a risky thing to attempt, but I suppose Marshall thought Charles was dead or otherwise safely out of the way."

Isabel nodded.

" He had the best of reasons for thinking so."

" You all came to England, Charles having managed to pass the Canadian lawyers. Of course Mrs. Price could have supplied him with a certain amount of information."

" And he had some papers and photographs and things he'd stolen from Charles Price."

" Well. I think you and your aunt came over first, I suppose, to find out how the land lay. You started work at the school of art in Kensington, having found out that Felix took lessons there."

Isabel nodded, and returned Felix's sombre glance with a faint ironic smile.

" You made friends with Nora, and through her with Felix." John paused. " I don't know quite what you and your aunt were to get out of all this. Unless— forgive me for speaking plainly, but of course you didn't help Marshall out of pure friendship for him—unless you were to——"

" Marry him. Yes. I was. All right. Go on."

Felix got up abruptly and stood at the window with his back to them, watching the sun streaking the sky with pale yellow in the east.

" Well," went on John, " then something went wrong. I think Clytie must have decided at the last moment, when she saw Rhyllan Hall, that she was a fool to help to cheat her husband of his inheritance. For I suppose she also believed that Charles Price was dead. I think then she realized that living on Marshall's bounty, even with a strong hold over him, might be rather precarious. I think then she conceived the idea of a reconciliation with her husband."

Isabel nodded briefly.

" I couldn't understand it at first," went on John. " I thought perhaps she meant to murder Charles with Morris's co-operation, though I couldn't imagine that she would really hope to get her husband to consent to that. But I see now. If she could get a promise of reconciliation from Morris, she intended to—well, blow the gaff. So she asked her husband to meet her in Hereford, and he did so. But he wouldn't consent to a reunion, and the gaff wasn't blown. Meanwhile the real Charles had followed the impostor to England. He was more or less destitute, I take it—perhaps he was walking or lorry-jumping to Rhyllan from whatever port he landed at. Anyhow, I think it was at Hereford that he first came face to face with Marshall and realized who it was that had supplanted him."

" Yes," said Isabel. " The evening we arrived at Hereford I noticed that something was wrong with Gavin. But he wouldn't tell me what it was. I still thought then that the real Charles was dead."

" You started early the next morning. And soon after Charles Price found an opportunity of borrowing a boy's bicycle and followed you. He didn't, of course, know what road you'd taken. But he'd guess that you were going towards Rhyllan. He caught you up at the Tram Inn, where you stopped for tea."

" Then——" began Nora.

" Yes, Nora. I think he was the man you saw looking in at the doorway of the Tram, waiting for an opportunity of having it out with Marshall. And he was the man Ada Watt saw going to the orchard. He was pretty well down and out, I think, or he wouldn't have waited to see Marshall before going to Rhyllan and claiming his own. He was afraid he'd be too thoroughly disbelieved, perhaps turned out. He helped himself to Miss Watt's eggs and apples and lay in wait for Marshall. Marshall must have seen him, I think. I think he stayed behind on purpose, perhaps intending to bribe him, perhaps to threaten him—I don't know.

" After you'd all coasted down the hill, Marshall went back into the inn for some Dutch courage, and then took his bicycle—he took Letbe's bicycle, as it happened, but that, I imagine, was a mistake—and walked slowly into the quarry field, knowing that Charles would follow. I don't imagine that he contemplated murder, yet. He chose the quarry field for the sake of privacy and loneliness. Charles followed, with the bicycle he had stolen from young Smiler in Hereford. They walked together towards the quarry. I don't know what happened then. Perhaps they quarrelled. Marshall, I take it, was always fairly ready with his gun. Anyhow, it wasn't long before Marshall, either in a rage, or with some wild hope of keeping what he had stolen, shot Charles in the head and killed him. It was a foolish thing to do. And I think he realized, when he stood there with the man lying dead at his feet, that he had not only made himself a murderer, but lost the very thing he had murdered to keep. He dared not return to Rhyllan as Sir Charles Price."

" Why not? " asked Felix in a muffled voice.

" For one thing the dead man was tattooed on the leg with Charles Price's initials. Marshall might, of course, have shot him in the leg or otherwise obliterated those tell-tale initials. But there were bound to be pretty close investigations. No doubt Charles had talked of his wrongs pretty freely during his journey. There would be awkward witnesses to a tale of imposture, and awkward questions asked. And Marshall's own credentials and his own tattoo-marks would not have born too close a scrutiny. Oh, yes, he also was tattooed with the initials of Charles Price. He did it himself, with Lion's red ink and a darning needle, that night you stopped at Highbury Down and he insisted on taking the single room. The tattoo-mark was a thing Clytie Price hadn't known about. He heard of it for the first time when you sat in that shed on the first day after he joined you at Worcester and exchanged reminiscences. He must have thanked his lucky stars at the time that you were led to mention it. Otherwise he might have joined your river-bathing parties and shown a tell-tale undecorated leg."

Isabel gave the faint shadow of a smile.

"He made an awful mess of it," she said pensively. "It was horribly inflamed for a day or two. Clytie thought we'd have to call in a doctor, which would indeed have been awkward. But it got better."

"I think," went on John, "the murderer must have had a dreadful moment when he stood there with Charles's body at his feet, and realized that he had all to lose and nothing to gain; realized that Charles Price was dead for ever, and that Gavin Marshall must come to life again, as a hunted murderer. There was only one thing to be done. To make it as sure as possible that no question of identity should be raised. So he crouched under the hedge and dressed the dead man in his tweeds, and himself put on poor Charles's clothes. He felt in the pockets, I think, and found little there except a couple of apples stolen from the Tram Inn orchard, which he pitched over the quarry edge. There was no money. So he took about fifteen pounds from the wallet that had been his own a moment ago—enough for emergencies. He was a Canadian, and it did not perhaps occur to him at first that five-pound notes are dangerous things. He took two five-pound notes."

Isabel nodded.

" Yes. And then afterwards he remembered some yarn he'd read in a magazine about tracing criminals through the numbers on notes. And he hid them in a field. We didn't know this until yesterday. And meanwhile Clytie had been in possession of the notes, all unknowing. She was furious," said Isabel meditatively, " and they had the very devil of a row yesterday evening."

" The other contents of the pockets," went on John, " he left undisturbed. He even remembered to take off his blood-stone ring. But that defeated him. It wouldn't go on the dead man's finger."

" I wonder," said Rampson thoughtfully, " why he didn't leave the raincoat with the body."

" I think," said John, " that he feared that before he got clean away he might meet with somebody who knew him as Sir Charles Price. And the clothes he had changed into were dirty and disreputable and quite different from the tweed suit he had been wearing. He thought it best to stick to the raincoat for a while. So long as he wore it his appearance was hardly changed, and he could, if necessary, be Sir Charles Price. Well, having made sure that he had missed nothing, he pushed the dead Charles over the quarry edge and after him he pushed the bicycle he thought was his own, but which happened to be Letbe's. Lord, it must have been nerve-wracking to do all that in daylight! But, as the coroner remarked at the inquest, this is wild, thinly populated country. Nobody saw him. He picked up young Smiler's bicycle and the revolver and walked back towards the road. He must have been startled when Morris Price appeared on the scene. But then it appeared providential. Had not the murder been committed with Morris Price's initialled revolver? For Marshall, being one of those men who never feel safe unless they are carrying weapons, had borrowed the revolver out of the library to take on this peaceful cycling tour.   His own, as I discovered to-night, was out of action.   In a moment the scheme had formed itself in his mind of planting the murder on Morris Price. Motive, opportunity, publicity—all were ready-made for such a course.   He slipped the superfluous ring unobserved among the cushions in Morris's car.   He conveyed the impression to Morris that you had all gone through the quarry fields; he led him through; he walked with him as far as the quarry; he let him return alone.

"When he had seen him depart in his car, he buried the revolver in a fairly obvious place, disguised his appearance as much as he could, walked over on to the Wensley road and cycled off.   I don't know what he did then.   I fancy he hid on the Forest that night.   I fancy he hid in this very hut, and left the incriminating rain-coat here among the bracken.   I imagine that young Smiler's bicycle is waiting here in some bracken patch to be discovered.   It's a strange thought.   Morris Price and he may have passed close to one another that night on the loneliness of the Forest.   Suppose they had met."

There was a silence.   Nora, Rampson and John sat looking at the light of the oil-stove, white and feeble now in the strengthening daylight.   Felix at the window gave a long sigh.   Suddenly Isabel began to speak in a cold, unemotional voice :

"My father was a portrait-painter.   He was very successful—for a time.   When I was a schoolgirl he was making five thousand a year and spending seven thousand."

Perceiving a faint surprise in her listeners' faces, she smiled a little and said :

"You're wondering what that's got to do with it.   It hasn't anything.   It's—perhaps—an attempt to excuse my part in this.   But why excuse it?"   She sat with her chin on her hands and looked sombrely at the ground. " One is—what one is."

" No, Isabel, that's a counsel of despair! "

It was Nora who spoke and stretched out an uncertain hand. Isabel looked at her gravely from under her heavy lids and ignored her gesture.

" No, it's not that," she said. " Despair . . . I've never known despair, but only discontent. He was a jolly soul, my father, and a fairish painter, and a marvellous spender. How he enjoyed, how he adored, his success! He thought it was going on for ever, I suppose, but of course it didn't. Great artists can go on for ever, perhaps, but not the clever ones exploiting an amusing trick. There are too many of them waiting in the wings. He lost his vogue and he lost his money. He put down the first to the machinations of fellow-painters and critics "—Isabel smiled a faint, ironic smile —" and the second to my mother's extravagance. As for me, he had brought me up to think myself a genius and to despise work. I wasn't much use to him. Do you know "—she paused and stared out through the doorway into the cold light of the morning—" still, at the bottom of my heart, there lives that childish me that nothing'll teach, that childish phantom of superior gifts and cleverness. Still, at the bottom of my heart, I despise the industrious journeymen of art, like you, Nora. Despise you, envy you, and—fear you. So ordinary, so slow, so—yes, even stupid you seem to me, but you take everything I ought to have. Success, money, everything you get in the end, with your maddening patience and your stupid good-temper. You get it, and you don't know what to do with it. And if you don't get it, you're just as good-tempered, just as placidly happy, being some-body's wife or teaching in a school. The itch for success, for recognition, for a proud place in the world—you don't know what it is! All the same," said Isabel, with a sudden change to a lighter, cooler tone, "I like you, Nora. Well, that's all about me. I deserted the sinking ship—I was only helping it to go down faster, anyhow, and went with my cousin Clytie to America. America didn't want us particularly. I got one or two jobs fashion designing, rotten jobs, and I was a mannequin for a little while, and then I joined a touring company, which failed. And then another touring company, which chucked me out. And all the time we hadn't enough money.

"When I first met Gavin Marshall, Clytie was keeping a boarding-house in Montreal. I was staying there in the intervals of finding loathsome jobs and losing them again. Oh, it was beastly! Gavin had had rather the same sort of life as mine—he'd been an actor, and a tram-conductor, and a farmer. It was when he was farming that he fell in with Charles Price. They bought a bit of land between them, on borrowed money, and went into partnership trying to farm it. But Gavin couldn't stick to anything long, and I should think Charles was a pretty hopeless sort of person. And they came a cropper. And then Charles got pneumonia, and Gavin cleared out and left him."

"Left him alone?"

"Yes. I didn't know that at the time. This is what I've heard during the last few days. Yes, we've been extremely frank with one another during the last week, Gavin and Clytie and I. Lord, I'm glad it's over! Gavin just told us at first that he knew Charles had been living under another name and was dead. But apparently he wasn't dead when Gavin scooted with their joint possessions, only nearly. Unfortunately for everybody he recovered. You know the rest. Oh, Lord!"

Isabel suddenly sprang to her feet and stretched her arms above her head with a laugh.

"Oh, Lord! If Clytie could hear me sitting here and

telling you all this! Well, she'll know soon enough, I suppose."

She yawned ostentatiously, dropped her arms and picking up her coat shook it carefully and began to put it on.

Nora said huskily:

" When you and—and he caught me up beyond Hereford, I was frightened of you as well as of him, Isabel. But you saved my life, didn't you? "

" Yes," said Isabel pensively. " I suppose so. I can't help liking you, Nora. But it wasn't only because of that. I really do draw the line at murder. Besides! What good could it have done? When the game's up, it's no use making a fuss and doing unnecessary damage. And anybody but a fool could see that the game was up then. The game's up, now."

Nora rose to her feet with cheeks that slowly paled again and a sudden foreboding in her eyes.

" Isabel," she murmured, going hesitatingly closer to the other girl, " you won't—you don't intend——"

The two looked at one another. Isabel laughed then, and put out her hand with a maternal gesture as though to touch Nora's pale cheek, and dropped her hand and laughed again.

" No, child. Nothing would induce me to. I've told you—I don't know the meaning of the word despair. Besides "—she glanced at John—" I'm not as handy with poisons as my delightful Cousin Clytie. Oh, but I'm almost glad the game is up! It was never worth the candle! Clytie and Gavin! Whatever happens to me now, I'm free of them for ever. When I go to—wherever they put conspirators and accessories after the act of murder, I shall be free—free of everything except myself. And I shall never be free of that. But don't worry about me, Nora. Sometimes I hate, I hate, I hate myself. But most of the time, oh, how my self amuses me! "

CHAPTER TWENTY-THREE

LET'S GO BACK TO LONDON

"AND now," said Rampson, "do, John, let's go back to London. It's been a nice holiday, a peaceful, refreshing change of scene, but I seem to remember that I've got work to do."

They were sitting in the pleasant dining-room of the Feathers in Penlow, looking out on the narrow High Street and smoking after-lunch cigarettes.

"I *did* want to get through to the Welsh coast," said John regretfully, with an amused eye on his friend's anxious face. "I say, is this a specially comfortable and peaceful inn, Sydenham, or is it only the change from the electrical atmosphere at Rhyllan Hall? I'm beginning to recuperate nicely."

"Oh, it's a very decent pub," said Rampson firmly, "but we're not going to recuperate here. London's the place to recuperate in after a holiday. You know," he went on pensively, "I'm awfully glad you were right over that affair, but you had no business to be. I still maintain that your methods were hopelessly unscientific. I wonder what'll happen to Isabel. Think she'll get off lightly?"

John sighed.

"Depends what you call lightly. She'll get a stretch, no doubt, though her counsel will probably manage to persuade the judge that she was under Clytie's thumb."

"She ought to have informed the police at once," said Rampson, shaking his head, "instead of making herself an accessory in that idiotic fashion."

John stirred restlessly and sighed again.

"Of course she ought to," he agreed. "And yet—to give a man away when he comes to you for shelter—a man you know—a fellow-conspirator—there's something horrible to the feelings in such behaviour, however much it may appeal to reason. One can only go back to the beginning and say she ought never to have got herself in such a position. She ought never to have touched the scheme at all. Which is only to say that there's something in her too good for such dingy, silly things. I can think of Clytie and the wretched Marshall with equanimity. But—I'm a sentimentalist, I suppose—the thought of Isabel hurts and depresses me. I hate to see a fine character stultified. She has brains. She has what's rarer, courage. Need she have made such a mess of things as this? We shall probably have to give evidence at the trial, you know, when it comes off. I hope she'll get off lightly, and do something sensible with the rest of her life. But don't let's talk of it now."

"I suppose," said Rampson, in contemplative after-luncheon mood, "Felix and Nora will make a match of it, eh?"

"Sure to," said John, carefully dropping his cigarette-end in his coffee-dregs and watching it sizzle.

"Do you know——" began Rampson, and stopped, looking curiously at his friend.

"I don't. Enlighten me."

"I thought for a moment—nothing."

With deep interest John watched his cigarette-end swelling and beginning to disintegrate.

"I know what you've so discreetly decided not to say, you old ass. You thought I was a bit hit myself. Well, so I might have been, if I'd had time. But when one's so busy keeping one's head one hasn't time to lose one's heart.   Besides—match, please—girls like Nora always marry men like Felix.   I've noticed it again and again. It's fate.   It's part of the mysterious workings of the universe.   And it's no good struggling against things like that."

John lit his cigarette, threw the blown match gently on to his friend's expanded waistcoat and grinned.

" Don't look so sentimental, Sydenham, you'll make me weep.   Some day I'll meet a Nora who hasn't got a Felix, and then there'll be a rush to the altar that will leave you gasping.   Dear Nora!   She'll be so surprised when her Felix brings his broken heart to her to be mended.   Yet it's been written in the skies from the first day they met.   You know "—John absently took up his spoon and stirred the loathsome mess in his cup with the concentration of a professor of chemistry engaged in a scientific experiment—" there's some truth in what Isabel said.   People like Nora get what they want in the end. They get it just because they are so ready to do without it.   They get it because they are stronger than their desires.   They are the salt of the earth.   They are—— But if I go on in this strain you'll think I'm really leaving a broken heart among the Radnor marshes.   And I'm not, truly.   Only a deep admiration and a hope—a hope that's perhaps got in it a thousandth part of envy, not more—that she won't be disappointed in her Felix when she gets him.   And now, let's go back to London.   We'll go through to the Welsh coast some other, more peaceful time when policemen cease from puzzling and revolvers are at rest.   Yes, now I come to consider it, the thought of London is quite refreshing.   Let's go back to London. Waiter, the bill."

.

Lightning Source UK Ltd.
Milton Keynes UK
UKOW06f2110110116

266202UK00001B/55/P